A CLOSED MOUTH

A CLOSED MOUTH

LAURYN POUSSAINT

Cover design by Ivica Jandrijevic
Interior layout and design by www.writingnights.org
Book preparation by Chad Robertson
Author Photo by Nick Marek Photography
Edited by Taryn Wieland

ISBN: 978-1-7377567-0-5
LIBRARY OF CONGRESS CATALOGING-IN-PUBLICATION DATA:
NAMES: Poussaint, Lauryn., author
TITLE: A Closed Mouth – A Novel / Lauryn Poussaint
IDENTIFIERS: ISBN 978-1-7377567-0-5 (Perfect bound) |
ISBN 978-1-7377567-1-2 (eBook)
SUBJECTS: | Fiction | Erotica | Interracial Romance | Romantic Comedy
CLASSIFICATION: Pending
LC record pending

Published by Tilted View Press, Oklahoma City, 2021
Printed in the United States of America.
Printed on acid-free paper.

24   23   22   21   20   19   18   17   8   7   6   5   4   3   2   1

For those who have taught me how to recognize, nurture, and express love.

"You get in life what you have the courage to ask for."
—Oprah Winfrey

CONTENTS

ACKNOWLEDGEMENTS

To my husband, thank you for giving me the time, space, and opportunity to pursue this dream and every other dream I've had. Throughout our life together, your love, encouragement, and support have been unwavering and mean everything to me. I love and appreciate the man you are today, tomorrow, and always.

To my children, I don't always get it right as a mom, but the most significant thing I've ever done was be the vessel God chose to bring you into this world. I encouraged you to continue to be good and honest people. My desire for you both is that you live and love authentically. I hope, in some way, my life encourages you to dream big and achieve your goals. I love you.

Mom and Dad, thank you for loving me, constantly being my guides, my inspirations, my source of laughter, creativity, sensitivity, and for giving me my sense of adventure. It's because of you that I'm able to be unapologetically me.

To my late Grandparents, you took in three little ones and raised them the best you knew how. Life wasn't peaches and roses, but it taught me how to persevere. I hope I've made you proud. Rest peacefully.

The Sibs, thank you for hours of playing, fighting, creating, coloring, and fun. It's because of our playtime that I developed such an expansive imagination. Life was so simple when we watched PBS and pretended to be explorers and chefs! I love you, and I hope I make you proud.

Penguins, you are the original squad, always and forever! We had some adventures, haven't we? I hope you can see your attributes in the bond shared by the phenomenal women in this book. I love and miss y'all more than you know.

NeKisha Peoples, thank you for over 20 years of friendship. This page can't contain all you are to me, sister, confidant, giggle partner, etc. You have been a listening ear when I needed one the most. We're like Celie and Nettie...we never part. P.S. I'm still waiting on you to read the chapters I sent you. Yes, I'm side-eyeing you right now.

To Shannise Johnson-Waters, thank you for being my friend. You allowed me to be my authentic self when doing so was frowned upon by you know who. You were there when I needed to bounce ideas off you and, you challenged me not to be ordinary by following the status quo. I genuinely love and appreciate your brilliance.

To Hashim Brown (Hash), you've been rocking with a bird since junior high. I know I am a handful, especially with my ALSE. I want you to know that our conversations are everything and then some to me. I genuinely love you, Bro.

Tyrell J. Wolfe, since the day we were introduced to one another and told to take care of each other, we've done just that. Thank you for being honest, trusting me, and being protective. I truly appreciate you always giving me your perspective.

Thank you both for being gentlemen in a world full of idiots. I know, mushy. Yuck!

To my Beta Readers (Jennifer Pankhurst, Jessica Hill, Tasha Miles, and L. H.), I entrusted you with my manuscript, and you didn't let me down. Your notes were honest, unbiased, and straightforward. I love, love, loved your notes! You believed in and encouraged my work. For that, you have my sincere gratitude.

Taryn Weiland, you're truly unique. I'm still in awe of the way you tapped into the voice of this book, the characters and helped take this novel to the next level. You are a very gifted editor. Thank you again for your quick and diligent work editing this book. I look forward to working with you on my next book.

Chad Robertson, you don't know this, but I searched the world for someone to finish this project. Funny how I found you in my backyard. I was afraid to publish this book, and you gave me the nudge I needed to proceed. Thank you for your meticulous work formatting. Thank you to Ivica for creating the cover. I look forward to working with you again.

To the readers,

Thank you for your recent purchase/download of my debut novel, *A Closed Mouth*. This endeavor was indeed a labor of love for me, with emphasis on the word "labor." I began writing this book in 2018, as I battled a severe bout of pneumonia. My physician wanted to hospitalize me, but I promised to stay in bed, do breathing treatments, and rest. In the beginning, I wrote in between the treatments and naps. I even had to rewrite an entire page because I fell asleep with my hand on the keyboard. Nevertheless, I triumphed over pneumonia and writing while drowsy.

Additionally, writing this book was cathartic for me. I had been severely ill earlier that year. Having pneumonia brought on a bout of depression because it reminded me of the independence I had lost after being forced to medically retire. There were times when I took extended breaks from writing, as well. However, through the encouragement of my family and friends, counseling, and writing, I began to find my way back to the light of my former self to finish this novel.

The joy of finally finishing this book was akin to the thrill a mother feels when her newborn is placed in her arms for the first time. I absolutely adore this novel, the characters, and the story. I hope you have as much fun reading this novel as I did while writing it.

Sincerely,

Lauryn

Prologue

"So, what happened last night?" Stacy asked as she kicked the door open to my bedroom. She was balancing a tray of tea, fruit, and some other baked confections when she entered my room. She set the tray gingerly on the bed, as she had done so many times throughout our friendship. She slid it slowly to the middle of my bed, careful not to spill any of the tea on my all-white linens, then sat down.

"Hey, Stace," I said drearily. "I don't even know. Girl, all I remember is how Shea looked at me and the color of his eyes." Every time I thought about his eyes, I got sick to my stomach.

"The what? Whatchu had said?" Stacy asked quizzically. I could tell she was confused.

"Shea's eyes change depending on his mood. When he's angry, sad, happy…they change from hazel to green to bluish-grey. Last night, they were the oddest color I've ever seen. I've never seen him look so angry," I said sadly.

"Green-eyed devil," she said jokingly under her breath, then continued. "Maev-ie, I'm sure he's pissed. Girl, you ruined their rehearsal dinner. After what you did, can you blame him?" she asked sympathetically.

Chapter One
THE GOOD OL' DAYS

I had been up for about thirty minutes reminiscing about the previous night's adventure. You see, I was with my best friend, Seamus "Shea" McGhee for game night at the Guerilla Bar. Imagine, if you will, a bar made of old shipping containers strategically placed together (three to be exact) laid out in "U" formation with a patio in the center. With the landscaping, you felt like you had been transported, *Star Trek* style, to a tropical command center other than downtown Chicago, where it was located. On occasion, officers stationed at Navy Pier frequented the establishment, since it wasn't too far from Great Lakes Naval Station. Seamus and I loved the atmosphere from the moment we found it.

We considered ourselves to be expert-level trivia buffs. So, we hit up Trivia Wars as many Fridays as we could. Last night had been brutal, and we got our asses handed to us by fucking college kids! Of course they knew the answers—little fuckers. Hell, the information was still fresh in their minds. Fuck those kids! I couldn't even be salty that we lost. One of us, namely me, should have been able to identify Ida B. Wells. After all, she helped found the National Association for the Advancement of Colored People. NAACP, hello! Did I mention I was tired? The look on Shea's face when I missed that one—priceless!

"Becky knew the answer and you didn't, Maeve! Really," Shea joked. Yup, I got beat by a little white girl.

"Shut up, Shea. You didn't know it either!" I laughed so hard I had tears streaming down my cheeks.

"Nah, man! You said, with confidence I might add, 'Madame. C. J. Walker, for the win!' I wish you could've seen the look on your face." He was cracking up at the image of me, and my overinflated ego, incorrectly answering a Black History question. Man, I just knew I had the right answer too. I couldn't even play like I was drunk. I stopped drinking months ago.

We settled our tabs and made our way out of the tiny hole in the wall we'd been frequenting since our college days. He hugged me around the neck, pulling me close to him as we walked toward the exit.

"I'm entitled to a brain lapse, Shea. Shoot! I'm tired!" I said, plugging my ears to the rest of his taunts. You'd think I was tired because I was out drinking, but we'd been on this clean eating kick, and liquor was not on the menu. I'm old, so I definitely can't kick it like I used to in college. No one tells you, at thirty, the body begins to break down, creak, and pop. Shit! I could barely keep my eyes open after 9:00 pm. We headed to our respective cars, hugged it out, then headed home. I texted him when I got home.

Me: Home 💩
Bing!
Shea: Me too. Good night!

The next morning, I woke up to a text notification.

"Really?" I snarled at the early notification.

Bing!
Shea: Good morning my beautiful 🦋
Me: Morning... ⚠️
Shea: You still in bed?
Me: I slept in my clothes.
Shea: WE need to work on your sleep schedule. ☺

Me: This is YOUR fault. You know I can't hang yet you insist on keeping me out late.

Shea: Who me?? 😬

Me: 😩😩😩

Shea: Sorry ● LOL

Me: Yeah. That would be funny if I didn't feel like crap.

Shea: Only 💀 can keep you from this evening!

I absolutely love it when he quotes *The Color Purple*.

Me: I'll keep you posted!

Shea: Ay... so what's the craic?

One of the things I loved about Shea was his use of Irish slang. I found it admirable that he didn't feel the need to be fully Americanized. It took a while to learn it, but our friends wanted him to be his authentic self.

Me: No, craic, buddy.

Shea: Ok. Let me be more specific. Are you seeing someone?

Me: What? Where's this coming from?

Shea: Well, last night, when you were in the jacks, you got a notification from Stacy that said, "Love?? You sure."

Me: I was in the restroom for two seconds. Dang, Snoopy!! Spy much! 🕵️

Shea: It popped up. I read it. 😅😬

Me: You should've found some business, Nosey Nelson. LOL

Shea: It's like that, BESTIE??

Me: It's nothing serious. We were talking about DW...from college.

Shea: 😐😐😐

I lied salaciously. Stacy and I had been discussing how I felt about Shea. I wasn't quite sure if I was in love with him, but it sure felt like it. I made a mental note to change my phone setting to deliver my text messages without the review. *Fuck*!

> Me: We were talking about "first loves." Nothing serious.
> Shea: You think you were in love with DW? That dope!
> Me: We're all at different levels, Shea.
> Shea: Oook! If you say so! See you tonight?

Shea took the hint to drop the subject.

> Shea: ✌
> Me: ✌

I set my phone back down on my nightstand and rolled over to look out of the window for a moment. The steady rhythm of rain soothed me as I thought about the texts from Shea. Storms had a way of making the colors outside my window look more vivid, even though the water skewed the view. I laid back on my pillow, thankful my friend hadn't accidentally spilled the beans. Had Stacy worded her text improperly, Shea and I might have had a completely different conversation. He and I had been friends for years. Don't ask me when or how I fell for him. It had happened, and I couldn't shake it. Shea, on the other hand, had a never-ending stream of booty calls. I practiced abstinence because my mother had scared me into keeping my legs closed. Was I jealous of the women he fucked? Hell, yeah! But what could I do? I wasn't going to profess my undying love or put out. In this situation, I found it was best to let this sleeping dog lie.

I thought about the last phone conversation I had with Shea. He had recently begun filling me in on his sexual conquests. His stories amused and stimulated me, mainly because they were funny, intimate, and overtly explicit. His voice, dripping with sensuality, captivated me when he spoke of the graphic deeds he'd performed. When I asked him why he shared such private details, he simply responded, "Best friends share those types of things." His stories were so arousing that some nights I masturbated as he shared them. I wondered if he heard me. Did he want me to please myself as he shared the intimate details? Did he want to do those things to me? Did I want him to do them to me? The thought of us together aroused me intensely. I reached for my phone, unlocking it, to search for a video Shea had sent me.

Yes, he shared pictures and videos of his sexual encounters. I had them saved in a private folder like a pervert.

I scrolled until I found what I was looking for. It was a video of Shea pounding a woman from behind. I wasn't able to see his cock, or her face, but from her moans, I'd wager he was huge. Shea was very discreet and exclusive with the women he chose to get involved with sexually. I always wondered what made women consent to the various elements of the non-disclosure agreements he presented them. He was into some kinky shit. He said the NDA was protection for everyone involved. *Everyone?* I didn't ask what that meant. Why had he never made me sign one, since he took the liberty to share his sex life with me?

I guess when you're a part of a particular world, certain things are to be expected. Within our group of friends, we had an unspoken NDA, as well. We knew to keep the shit we knew, were told, texted, shown, and involved in private. It wasn't the first video of a friend I'd seen engrossed in coitus. It was, however, the only one I'd pleasured myself while watching. I hated myself for it, too. *Don't,* I told myself, hesitating with my finger hovering over the video's thumbnail. I should've deleted it, but I wasn't ready yet.

"Dammit," I whispered as I closed the folder and set my phone back down.

I allowed my mind to think of safer things, like working out tonight.

I was definitely on the fence about it. I was tired as hell from being out with Shea last night. Come hell or high water, he was going to drag my ass to the gym, so I resigned myself to a tiresome fate. Honestly, working out with him did have some perks. Did I mention Seamus was FOINE as hell? Whew!

Shea and I worked out together because I complained about being pudgy. He made it his life's mission to whip me into shape. He was rough and a bit over the top, but I liked it. This evening, we were going for a run. I didn't know what I was getting myself into by asking for his help, but it allowed me to be around him more often. He had changed my diet, forced me to buy activewear, running gear, and shoes. We were on a strict regime of workout, eat, sleep...repeat. No liquor, no junk food, no sweets! I did reasonably well on most days. Living with a gourmet chef who loved to whip up, and crank out, delicacies didn't help either. It's incredibly hard to have sweets and treats in the house and not eat them. Ever since Stacy found out I was trying to tone up, she'd been undermining my progress. Her baking frenzy was no help.

"You need to put on weight, not lose it," she said, as she sucked air through her teeth.

"Stacy, I'm thin, but I have no muscle tone," I whined.

"You'll be a stick if you keep taking that fool's advice! You know, brothas like a little cushion," she said as she swayed her hips.

"I have some! See?" I said as I tried to imitate her movements. She rolled her eyes as she sucked air through her teeth again.

"What?" I said, laughing.

"Chile!" she said, joining me in laughter.

Did I want to be fit like Shea? Truthfully, no. But the time we spent working out together allowed me to spend more one on one time with him. I had been crushing on him for years. Hell, his Adonis belt made my nipples tighten on sight. I fantasized about him sharing my feelings. Classic story. Boy meets girl then puts her in the friend zone, while girl pines for boy. You know, typical. Therefore, telling him just wasn't an option. It's not worth the risk because I don't want to lose him. Period.

I'm sure this never works either, but a girl can hope, right? At least I'd get a well-toned body out of it!

Seamus was charming. My Grams said he could charm the fangs off of a rattlesnake ready to strike. All he had to do was flash that thousand-watt smile and look at you with those devilish green eyes. Putty, that's what you'd be...putty. I remembered our last conversation about him. I was at her house, helping her prepare one of our family dinners.

"Maeve, do you ever plan on telling Seamus how you feel about him?" Grams asked over a colander full of green beans she was snapping for Sunday dinner.

"Wait! What?" I asked, taken aback and laughing nervously.

"Chile, he has your nose open wider than Maezella's hips," she said, cackling.

"Grams, it's not like that! He's like—like a brother to me! He's my best friend, and I've known him for like ever. He's so not my type. At all!" I sputtered in my best attempt at lying.

"You know, your Aunt Maez's hips are wide as all outdoors," she said, chuckling at how wide her sister's hips were and my vain attempt to deceive her. "I see how you look at him. I know you, Maevie. I know you know that I know when you lyin' too. Like now..."

She never looked up from that colander. She just kept on snapping beans. I had spent so much time with her that I knew she was adept at discerning my true feelings.

"Grams, I—I..." I stammered dejectedly. Caught! Plus, I couldn't lie to her again.

"Baby, you playing with a fire that's gon' singe your very soul if you don't tell that boy how you feel about him."

"Grams, I don't want to ruin our friendship," I said.

"That's the lie you keep tellin' yourself, huh? Baby, some of the greatest relationships are based on friendship. How did you think your Pop-Pop and I stayed married all these years? That man drives me crazy but at the end of the day...he's my bes' friend!"

"Grams," I exhaled deeply, "you always said don't chase a man. Let him come to you. I'm trying to do that but Shea's just—"

"Not pickin' up whatchu puttin' down? Baby, if men ain't nothin' else, they slow. Slow as molasses, I tell you what. You jus' gotta throw the right bait. Toss out that 'more than friends' bait, he'll come around. I'm sho he will."

What the hell was "more than friends" bait? The woman was a wealth of information, full of conversational gems and pearls of wisdom. Nosey as fuck, at times, too. Was it that obvious? How come everyone saw it except Shea? Grams was seventy-eight years old, slim, and very petite. She walked every day and occasionally attended yoga with me. I know her and Pop-Pop still got it in too. Well, that was because I found Viagra on his nightstand. The thought of those two older people, in love, made me think maybe there's still hope for me. My mind wandered from the conversation I had with my grandmother back to Shea.

Seamus McGhee was the definition of sexy to me. I was the only one who called him by a nickname. He had the body of a highly-trained athlete. There wasn't an ounce of fat on him. He was six feet two inches of pure muscle, long and lean with broad shoulders, beefy pecs and abs you could see through his clothing. I knew because I peeped them as often as I could without getting caught. God broke the mold after forming his body. He kept a shadow of scruff on his face most of the time. His hair was a reddish-brown with hints of gold flecks, which made it look sun kissed. He wore it combed over to one side, like Cristiano Ronaldo, during the workweek and wildly tousled and spiked on the weekends. He had a bevy of tailored business suits, but he was unrecognizable on the weekends. He lived in Adidas gear or something casual yet designer. His physique made everything look great on him. Well, there was that one time at a 90s party. Let's just say he looked like Vanilla Ice in Hammer pants. It was not a good look.

Shea was born in Northern Ireland. His parents migrated to the United States when he was in elementary school and settled on the Northside of Chicago. When Seamus spoke about the area, he did so as though it had been gentrified by the influx of non-Irish people. *Can white people gentrify an area that is already predominantly white, though?* After Shea's father retired, he purchased the family home for them so they could afford to live there. With homes creeping into the six hundred thousand range, they weren't able to pay their property taxes. I argued that he could easily fit his parents into his mini mansion.

"The Irish folk are, uh, proud...yeah, proud people," he reasoned. "They want to stay where their friends are, where their church is. That sort of thing, you know." He was rubbing his head, so I knew he was lying. That was his tell. No poker face either. I let him have it, though.

"Ok, Big Fella," I laughed. "If you say so!" I topped off my comment with a wink to let him know I picked up what he was putting down.

"I hate you!" Shea joined in with my laughter.

The McGhees were always so welcoming. Growing up, I believed Irish people didn't like Blacks. They dispelled that stereotype by allowing our troops of friends to crash at their house. Mama McGhee took such good care of us. Shea's brogue was always thickest when he was with his parents or *bleedin' gargled*, meaning drunk. They occasionally spoke the Ulster dialect of Irish. I laughed unconsciously the first time I heard it, because it sounded like the language spoken by The Sims. I loved listening to him on the phone with his mom. He spoke so softly and sweetly to her. He told me he raised his voice to her once. We had been drinking that night, I remembered.

"Once?" I questioned. We had been watching a movie. We chatted as the credits rolled. Shea stretched out, languidly, on the other side of the couch.

"Do ye know what 'e ded?" he asked, sitting up to grab his drink off the table. His movement caused the blanket we shared to fall off me.

"I haven't a bleedin' clue," I said in my best Irish brogue, pulling the blanket back up over me.

"'E bahxed me ears," he said. I knew he was drunk because his brogue was more exaggerated.

"So...he spanked you," I interpreted.

"I had never seen him so *buck daft*. You 'da thought I 'ad 'it her," he said. It was funny to hear his full accent. It was just as bad as my Chicago accent. We both struggled with consonants when we were drunk. The accent was so pretty at times it seemed like he wasn't speaking English.

"Well, Shea, you have been over six feet tall since you were thirteen. I'm sure he didn't want you to forget yourself," I hypothesized.

"*Féileacán*, you know I'd never hit a woman," he paused to finish his drink. "Unless she asked me to." He set the empty glass down then winked at me.

"*Feckin' eejit*," I said, laughing at him. He loved it when I used Irish slang correctly.

"I'm *bleedin' gargled*," he said, slurring his words. "Let's go to bed."

Oh, how I wished he had meant the same bed and not separate rooms!

What red-blooded American woman doesn't like a man with a foreign accent, right? Sometimes, he sounded as American as me. Then, there were days it seemed like he masticated his words—chewed every single syllable. As I lay in bed, I pondered my Seamus situation for a while longer before my mind wandered to work. I knew I had to go over some second-quarter financial reports, but I was exhausted. I was swaddled snugly under the super high thread count sheets I had paid good money for, and I intended to enjoy it. I heard my roommate moving around, but I just wasn't ready to drag my lethargic carcass from the cocoon of warmth I was enveloped in.

"Maeve!"

I heard Stacy calling me, but I ignored her, hoping she'd think I was still asleep. I wanted to be alone with my thoughts for a little longer.

"Wakey, wakey, eggs and bakey, Maevy Wavy!" she sang out from the kitchen.

I stared at the rain droplets as they cascaded down my window. I adjusted my satin-covered pillow so I could look outside without straining my neck, then went back to gazing thoughtlessly out the window. The soothing sounds of rain and the steady rhythm rinsed all thoughts of work right out of my mind. I loved how it made everything look so new and fresh. It distracted me for a moment. Shea's text had already awakened me, but I chuckled to myself at Stacy's predictability. Whenever I ignored her, she sweetly sang my name in a charmingly accented lilt. I pulled my arm out from under the comforter and sheets like a skilled choir director poised to direct the church choir on Friends and Family day.

"Maaa-aaa-evie," she sang, right on cue with my direction.

Amused, I continued to ignore her. She'd be gently pushing the door open soon with a tray of goodies, and complete disregard for the fact that I'm on a diet or may have been asleep. There was no sleeping once Stacy was awake. She created a symphony of bangs and whirs when she started on a masterpiece meal.

"Ma'am, did ya not hear me callin'?" she asked as she kicked my door open. She deposited a tray with two teacups, fruit, and different sweets onto my bed.

Stacy Johnson was the roommate of my dreams. We'd been roommates since our freshman year in college. It was quite evident that neither of us liked to change. She liked things neat, didn't have people traipsing through our loft at all hours of the night, and could cook her ass off. She was discreet and could lock down a secret so hard she'll forget it. If you told her something was vault or G-14 classified, you knew it was secured. Hell, sometimes I had to remind her of what I revealed just to discuss it.

Stacy was the party planner/chef extraordinaire of our group of friends. We all loved to try new things or the latest cuisines she was dabbling in. Get-togethers were her opportunity to hock her wares. She was the owner of her own catering company, Island Fairy, and a part-time celebrity chef, as well. I put on twenty-five pounds since we moved into this loft. Stacy said I needed those pounds because it wasn't healthy for a full-grown woman to weigh less than one hundred pounds. Shea had other ideas, it seemed. Stacy was the sweetest person I knew. I loved her from the first moment we met.

Stacy considered herself a demisexual. She was one of those people who had to have a powerful connection before she felt attracted to a person. She prided herself on being an equal opportunity lover. Her words, not mine! I was raised in a devout Christian home. We went to church on Wednesday, Friday, and twice on Sunday. *Whew!* But Stacy was a better person than half of the so-called Christians in our church. We hit it off, and that's all that mattered to me.

Stacy was statuesque at five feet eight inches and had a body most women pay to own. Her curves were dangerous, honey, and ought to come with a warning. Her skin tone was deep and rich chocolate. Most of us mortals have to buy our highlights from (my fave) Fenty beauty! She gave new meaning to the phrase *melanin poppin*. Her oval-shaped face was framed by a majestic Afro, like the crown atop Zulu Queen Nandi's head. Stacy's big sleepy eyes and full lips created a megawatt, infectious smile. She had high cheekbones and reflective brown eyes. She was slim-thick with an ass that announced itself before she entered the room. I always told her it cried out to be smacked. And I never hesitated to do so when the mood struck me.

"Smack That" by Akon was our ass-smacking theme song! I sang and smacked while she twerked and whined her body. Good times, man! She said if I ate more, I'd have a backside like hers one day.

Stacy had enjoyed cooking since childhood. She learned from her grandmother. You'd think as much time as I spent with my Grams, I'd know how to cook, but, no! Stacy knew I enjoyed sweets with tea because I was a "weird American."

"You eat biscuits with tea, not cookies," she once told me. Amazingly, she always knew when to make sweet treats for me. Rainy days were on the top of the list.

"Ignore you? No, child," I said, mimicking her accent.

"You got jokes," she said, mimicking my drunken Chicago accent. We giggled.

"So, whatcha thinking 'bout?" she inquired knowingly.

"Oh nothing," I said smugly. Stacy knew I did most of my introspection on rainy days.

"Don't, *oh nothin'* me! I know how you get on rainy days. Seamus on the brain."

"He texted me this morning. He saw a text notification from you asking if I was sure it was love."

"Well, did you tell him?" she asked.

"Girl, no! You know I'm a punk. Besides, I don't want to ruin our friendship."

"Chil', nothin' ruins a friendship faster than lying," she said, with her accent on full blast. "You need to tell that man how you feel before someone swoops in and snatches him up. You know these hoes are dry, parched, and thirsty for a man like him. Money, brains, looks, bawdy...shall I go on?" She code switched mid-sentence. Sounding better than any African American working for a Fortune 500 company, and I loved it!

I laughed because I knew she was right, but I couldn't take the risk. Shea and I had a relationship that was different from anything I had experienced before. We had "us" days. Those were days when it was just us from sunup to sundown. I'd spend the night, and we'd veg out. We took trips together. We had a BFF date night. Hell, we even shared a dog! Yes, we shared *a dog*. He knew me, the real me that I had only let Stacy and my close girlfriends see. The man saw me sans makeup in a silk head wrap!

"Y'all may as well be bonin'," our friend Rho said during one of our late night, wine-induced truth sessions. "He's seen behind the velvet curtain! You let that muhfucka see you in a bonnet!"

Rokuko Kobayashi, or Rho, was the resident Hood Rat of our group. It's a mouthful, for sure. She inherited the nickname, Ro Hoe, in college. Anyone else calling her that might get cut. She was sick with a switchblade! It was our nickname for her, and ours alone. Although now, it sounded like a shorter version of her full name.

Her father was Japanese and French while her mother was Korean and African American. She spoke four languages. And was known to curse you out in all four. Although Rho got flack for cultural appropriation, she understood the struggles we faced on multiple levels. Growing up, she was told she wasn't Black enough, Asian enough, or White enough. However, she was the only one of us who could genuinely flow from one culture to the next seamlessly. We defended her without question because we knew her. Stacy and I experienced Colorism regularly, so we genuinely comprehended her struggle to fit in any society. We all ascribed to the "not enough" sentiment, which was so prevalent in America. That's why we defended her so fiercely.

Rho had expanded the horizons of our little friend-family. She spent summers in France, Japan, and occasionally Korea. She introduced us to so many aspects of her multicultural background, from food to art and music. Who the hell knew K-Pop and K-Dramas were so addictive? I, personally, loved when she chose the cuisine for our international dinners. We loved trying new things together. Honestly, our little crew was very eccentric. We accepted one another and loved one another. That's probably why we fit together so well.

All of my friends knew how I felt about Seamus. He and I were closer than I'd ever been with any man. I couldn't bear losing the closeness. I was so deep in the friend zone though. I guess I'm a glutton for punishment.

"Girl, you are playing with fire," Stacy said.

"I know," I said solemnly. "But why should I ruin a great friendship for what could just be a crush?"

"You know this is more than a crush. Honestly, I think Shea feels the same way. I see how he looks at you when you aren't paying attention. He feelin' you like you feelin' him."

"I hear you," I said, looking at her.

"I'm not gonna push you...today," she acquiesced.

"Thanks, Stace. I know you get tired of my constant obsessing, but I appreciate you listening. Truly!"

"No worries! I'm here for you, sis," she said as she climbed in bed to eat breakfast while filling me in on the foolery our friend, Rho, had gotten into recently.

"Did Rho tell you about her threesome?" Stacy quipped, giving me a sideways glance.

I almost spat out my tea! *Almost.* Not on these Egyptian cotton sheets, Bitch!

"Threesome?" I choked out.

"Yes, girl! She told me last night while you were out with Seamus."

Seamus should've been called 'shame' because, well...

"It's a *shame* how you treat these girls!"

"It's a *shame* what you did with those twins!"

"You did what in the mascot uniform? That's a damn *shame!*"

"Three bitches fighting over you! You ought to be a*shamed!*"

"It's a damn *shame* how Professor Beddingford stutters whenever she sees you!"

You get the point.

Back to the threesome!

"I can't!" I squeal. "Rho is a mess! So, dish!"

"She hooked up with triplets she met on Tindr!"

"Three sisters? What the—" I started, before Stace corrected me.

"Brothers," she said, side-eyeing me. "*Again.*"

"Gahd da—" I started.

"No cursing!" Stacy said, laughing.

"Girl, I can't deal with Rho! Who the hell—heck, bangs not one, not two, but three brothers?"

"She said she had dicks in every hole!"

"No, no, no!" I hollered, as I hopped out of bed. I covered my ears while jumping up and down. "No, *ma'am!*"

Stacy was cracking up.

"Girl, she sent pictures!" Stacy pulled her phone out of her bra then scrolled through the text messages. She found a picture and turned her phone to me. I stopped jumping to study the cell phone Stacy handed me. Sure enough, it was a photo of Rho, reflected in a mirror, taken by one of the fine-ass Tinder triplets. She had one in the pink, one in the stink, and one in her mouth. I couldn't lie, I was a little aroused by the picture. However, I couldn't fathom having all of my holes filled at the same time.

"First of all, this is *not* a threesome, it's a foursome! Second, is that a heart-shaped birthmark?" I asked as I handed the phone back to Stacy. "Rho is officially the freakiest person I know. Triplets!" I said, shaking my head while picking up my cup to finish my tea. I grabbed one of the treats Stacy baked once I settled back onto the bed. I tucked my legs back under the covers as I listened.

"No, it's not a threesome. She tried to argue me down that since they share the same DNA, it should only count as one man!"

"Bitch, what!" I said, spraying crumbs across my lap. "Sorry..." I said, regarding my crumb-spray cursing. Stacy waved me off unbothered.

"Yes, girl! I met her in the middle by letting her call it a threesome. But for all intents and purposes, our girl had a foursome. Now that's some hoe ass shit!"

"Language," I laughed.

"There's no other way to say that darlin'! And yes, she has a heart-shaped birthmark on her butt. You know what, she has officially earned the title of the freakiest. I'm into some kinky things, but anal is where I draw the line," Stacy and I exchanged glances as we chowed down for a moment.

I pondered the picture some more before asking about Tish.

Tisha Michaels joined the group our junior year, after she cursed out a male professor in front of the class for assuming she was only in college looking for her M-R-S degree. She lit into him, then filed a formal complaint. The professor ended up getting fired. It wasn't what she said to the professor but how she said it. She cursed him out like an old Black grandma. She put combinations of curse words together like someone swept her foot with a broom or opened an umbrella in the house.

Tisha was very fair-skinned with freckles dotting her forehead and the bridge of her nose. Her nose was long and slender. Her waist-length hair was the palest blonde with flecks of gold in it. Her bluish grey, almond-shaped eyes were framed by long soft lashes. Her full lips were the palest pink. So pink they almost blended in with the skin on her face. She wasn't a striking beauty, but she knew how to accentuate her best qualities. With makeup, she looked like Jessica Simpson. Tish was petite, but her breasts were unusually large. She knew it too. The first time I saw her topless, I thought she didn't have nipples.

"Of course, I have nipples! They're called ghost nipples. I call this one Boo," she said, pointing to the right one. "And this one Hoo!"

"What the hell is a ghost nipple?" I asked, laughing at her choice of names. This term, ghost nipple had me Googling *breast* in the dressing room of the lingerie shop we were in. She explained her nipples' lack of melanin as I Googled.

"Wait! What color are your nipples?" she stopped and asked curiously.

"The same color as my lips. Brown," I said flatly, never looking up from my phone.

"Lemme see!" she said under her breath. "I've never seen a black woman nude."

"Really?" I said as I set my phone to the side. I lifted my top to show her mine.

"Wow!" she gasped. "They are brown...well, more of a pinkish brown. I expected them to be darker. Do they come darker?" she asked with wide-eyed curiosity.

"Yes," I said, laughing as I readjusted my clothes. "They come in a variety of browns."

"I've always felt odd because my nipples are so light. The first guy I had sex with got this weird look on his face when I took my bra off. I don't take it off anymore during sex," she said shyly.

"Seriously?" I asked. "What does the color, or lack thereof, have to do with anything?"

"I don't know. It just makes me feel better," Tish spoke so low I had to strain to hear her.

Tish had a lot of little quirks. They were endearing, though. My favorite was her aversion to tanning. To this day, she is one of the lightest white women I've ever seen. I thought she had an aversion to the sun, but she said she didn't want to end up looking like old leather when she got older. She took whatever the sun gave her but didn't overdo it by going to tanning salons or laying out. Tish looked like the quintessential Midwestern girl. Sweet and innocent to a fault. She didn't like hearing about Rho's conquests and didn't share when we were having those types of conversations. Come to think of it, I believe I'm the only one to ever see her fully naked. Sometimes, she made me feel like she wanted to experiment with me sexually or something. She always said she was "strictly dickly" when I asked, but I still got a vibe.

Her body was toned because she studied dance in college. She had tricked me into taking a few classes. I learned that I sucked at ballroom. I had talked Tish into double majoring in dance and business. She took my advice and was grateful she'd listened. She worked as a General Manager of Whole Foods until she saved up enough money to open her first studio. She now had several dance studios throughout Chicago and the suburbs. She taught everything from ballet to contemporary dance to cheer. She was the best dancer in our crew. She couldn't twerk like Stacy, but she did it better than me!

"Does Tish know?" I asked smugly. Tish was our resident prude. I might have been a virgin, but I wasn't ignorant of the inner workings of a sexual relationship, nor did I judge my friends for their sexual conquests. They didn't judge me for my lack thereof, either. But Tish was different!

"Rho swore me to secrecy. You know Tish ain't bout that life," Stacy responded.

"Hell, I mean heck, I'm not either, but it seems to me that sex is best when you don't limit yourself—at least that's what I get from our convos. Tish probably only has sex in the missionary position!" I said jokingly.

"She acts like she wants to jump your bones," Stacy said, laughing.

"She says she strictly dickly," I replied.

"I bet if you gave her a chance, she'd bump bellies with you," she said thoughtfully.

"I don't see that or three dicks happening," I stated. I thought Tish was attractive and all. But I didn't see myself eating at the "Y." Stacy and Rho had both been with other women. It's like, who hasn't, in this day and age. When I think about all of the abuse pussy takes, I'm instantly turned off.

"Three dicks," she repeated, shaking her head. "That's a little too open, even for me. No pun intended!"

"One dick is too open for me!" I said, laughing at her comment. "I can't even bring myself to have regular sex with one person, and she's double penetrated and giving head!" I said as I stood up. I picked up the now-empty tray, once filled with goodies, toted it out of the room and down the hall to the kitchen.

"I know, right?" Stacy agreed as she followed me out of the room.

This was our rainy Saturday morning tradition. I didn't know what we were going to do when the other got married, maybe FaceTime or Facebook Messenger one another. I was very thankful for Stacy. In college, I studied Financial Management, and she was studying Hospitality and Business. I always thought she was brilliant for double majoring. She knew she wanted to be a chef and felt her degrees would give her the education she needed to run her own culinary business. We didn't know then that we'd be successful businesswomen still looking for love in our thirties. Our dreams were to be married by this time, but our careers took off in our twenties, and we pushed having families to the back burner for success.

I was the youngest Chief Financial Officer in my company's history. Winchester & Wiles was my first choice for an internship while in college. They only gave out five summer internships. Finding the right professor to write my letter of recommendation was hard. However, my Accounting professor, Dr. Edward Greyson, was good friends with the CFO at Winchester & Wiles. He not only provided me with a letter of recommendation, but he vouched for me with his friend, Silas Jameson. After graduation, they offered me a position. Jameson had taken me under his wing because he said he saw himself in me. He felt my mind was sharp, and my work ethic was second to none.

As an analyst, I was always given the hardest projects to manage. I worked hard, rarely took vacations, and completed tasks weeks ahead of schedule. Jameson personally recommended me to the CEO, Ralston Winchester, and his partner, J. W. Wiles. They were skeptical because of my age, but Jameson told them they'd be fools to pass on me. He knew I was being headhunted by some of the top consultancy firms throughout the U.S and Europe. He lost a few friends along the way for selecting me as his successor.

My parents had money but felt it would build character for me to pay for school myself. Best believe I never failed a class! As one of my graduation gifts, they paid off my undergrad loans. My postgraduate loans were so close to being paid, though. I helped Stacy with a budget to save and pay off loans since we were sharing a home. She learned the hard way that Sallie Mae doesn't want a piece or a part of her money. She wants it ALL! She got her loans out of deferment and improved her credit score all at the same time. Winning! With the help of Darren Wilkerson, my pro football playing ex-boyfriend, she reached other celebrities in need of catering or personal chefs.

Finances was a sore subject, at first. But I told her I didn't want to bear the burden of her lousy credit moving in together. After our tiffs over her mismanagement of money, we agreed to always uplift and help one another. It was a sisterhood that propelled us into the positions we were now in. We shared a four thousand square foot loft overlooking Lake Michigan. It wasn't that Stace and I couldn't afford our own homes. We just loved having someone to come home to instead of going back to empty apartments.

We put our blood, sweat, and tears into renovating it to both our likings. Our loft was very modern. We both love the aesthetics of clean lines and minimalistic space. We decided to leave the brick walls, ductwork, and light fixtures exposed. We painted the walls white, went with hardwood floors, and added rugs, pillows, and accessories to soften our space. We decided not to add very many sheetrock walls, reserving those only for our bedrooms. We added extra insulation to avoid hearing one another through the walls. No one wants to listen to their roommate's moans of pleasure, especially if they weren't having sex. Additionally, Stace got her dream kitchen, and I had an office with amazing views and a killer closet.

Most people assumed we were lesbians in college because Stacy dated women occasionally. Naturally, the rumor proliferated once we bought a home together. I won't pretend like I didn't use her orientation to my advantage, often. Sometimes, you need to keep the raggely, yes raggely, men and women away. Stacy didn't mind. She said, "Sistas gotta look out for each other." We were closer than best friends. She was the sister I never had. I shared every single thing with Stacy and Seamus, except for how I felt about him.

I rinsed the dishes and methodically put them in the dishwasher. I walked back to my room to prepare for my day. I past Stacy, now tucked into one of our two oversized grey accent chairs, creating meal plans for her clients. I knew she was comparing inventory and making ingredient lists for purchases. She had a registered dietician on her staff that she worked with for those of her clients on restrictive diets. They'd be meeting on Monday, so she was doing leg work now. We each had our individual Saturday routines, as well. Otherwise, our lives were pretty dull. I usually did yoga or a spin class in the mornings, then do some work if we weren't kicking it with the crew.

Sunday was primarily reserved for church and dinner with my family at Gram and Pop-Pop's house. I was raised Baptist, Southern Baptist to be exact. It didn't matter what my week, or Saturday, consisted of. I knew I'd better have my butt on the pew next to my mama and daddy come nine-thirty am, or there'd be a thorough tongue lashing from my mama.

"The Lord has been too good to you for you not to drag your little narrow tail to the church for worship," she'd chide. Dr. James didn't play.

Since I skipped my exercise class to chat up Stacy, I decided to go into the office for a little while instead of working from home. I knew I wouldn't get any work done if I stayed home. Stacy and I had already ratcheted up the foolery before we got out of my bed. I made my way back to my room then padded into my bathroom. My bathroom followed the same aesthetic as the loft, except I decided to use a different countertop. I fell in love with Red Dragon marble and insisted on having it.

My bathroom was mostly white, with lots of metal and glass. I had a soaker tub centered in front of a large window. The all-glass shower took up the rest of the wall and had a rain shower head that jetted from every angle. With one switch, I could envelop myself in color therapy. I don't remember why I chose this feature because I have never used the lights or all of the nozzles. It was a bitch to clean, which is why we went in on a maid service.

I stood in front of my mirror and examined my face. I had some minor breakouts from cheating on my diet and drinking too much pop. My heart-shaped face, accentuated by my widow's peak, framed my small features. My cousins all said I had a Michael Jackson nose. Not the original but the first surgically-enhanced one. My eyes were light brown with flecks of green and were framed by naturally long eyelashes, a family trait. I had high cheekbones and pouty full lips. I knew I only got more attention from men than Stacy because I was a lighter complexion. My curls, in comparison to her kinky coils, made me look more "exotic," as the brothas would say. Cars, plants, and animals are considered to be exotic. I get so tired of people, my people, asking me *what I am* or *what I'm mixed with* when I'm just plain old Black. Yes, my mama and daddy both Black too. We are such a diverse people. I just wish we'd shed the Colorism that runs rampant within our community.

I am a Molotov cocktail of my parent's DNA. My mother, Dr. Paulina James, was light-skinned with hazel eyes. I got her long eyelashes, full, heart-shaped lips, but missed all of her height. She was taller than me by four inches. I was slender and petite like my Grams. Mama had hips and a booty, though. She always said she didn't want to look like her Aunt Maezelle.

Earl Rhys James, my father, was a stark contradiction from my mother. Mama called him Rhys because she says he doesn't look like an Earl, until he pisses her off. He was the dark to her light. Eyes, hair, skin color, you named it and was as dark as Black people came. Blurple is what he called himself. Anyone who said blue light doesn't look right on darker complexions lied. Old pictures of him and my mother, in dimly lit blues clubs bathed in indigo and violet, made his skin look like butter. My father was six feet and some change. He would never tell you exactly how much.

"Taller than you, Mae," He'd quipped as he patted me on the head.

"Seriously, Daddy!"

"Yes," he added.

He had a smile that could light a room and a laugh that was second to none. You always knew where he was because it was so boisterous. His sense of humor was sharp, as well. I never played the dozens with him. It's safe to say, I looked like my mama, except the booty. I got me some sun, though. My melanin is slightly popping!

I stared at my image a little longer. I could see the changes taking place since I had begun working out with Seamus. My stomach was more toned, and my thighs were more muscular. *Ok, Shea! I guess you do know what you're talking about!* My skin is a caramel color and smooth. I had been in the sun a lot that summer and was quite darker than my standard buttery pecan color. The tan accentuated my newly acquired muscles. I was digging it. My breasts were a bit larger than I wanted, but I shall not complain. My C cups were natural, not enhanced. My waist was small and I had some hips. You'd think I'd have some ass around the back. Nah! I had a nice butt, according to Seamus, though. He said it didn't look ridiculous like those reality stars who insist on stacking large asses on stick-thin legs. It was proportionate to my thighs and quite firm. According to him, it was "ass-tronomical." When I pushed myself at the gym, Shea didn't hesitate to smack what I did have as encouragement. *I can't say I mind that at all!* I giggled to myself.

I had a subtle hourglass figure, but I looked like a prepubescent teen, at times. My arms weren't Angela Bassett toned yet, but I am working on it. Auntie Angela got BAWDY for days. I was five feet, three and a half inches. I stretched that shit to four inches every chance I got. My hair was long, but I kept it in a messy curly bun on the weekends. I didn't wear it down at work because a mentor once told me men sexualize it and won't see me as a professional. I don't know if I still believe her, but I developed the habit of wearing it up.

After I finished surveying myself, I stepped in the shower and let the water carry my morning thoughts down the drain. I grabbed my shower oil and worked it into my skin. I thought it was an after-shower moisturizer when I first purchased it. Then I read the bottle. Reading is fundamental. It was an emulsifying cleanser. My shower is never slick or oily when I get out. What more can a chick ask for? I rinsed my skin then reached for bar soap to work on my sensitive parts. Call me old-fashioned, but I still feel the need to clean my jiggly bits with soap. I hopped out of the shower to towel myself dry after another rinse. I hated having to get out, but time was slipping by quickly.

I made a mental note to put my soaker tub to use soon. I traipsed into my closet to pick out something to wear. Renovating my closet was one of best the things I did after we moved into the loft. I took some space from my bedroom to widen the closet. I then spent three weeks installing shelves, drawers, and mirrors. Once I got it looking like I wanted, I spent another three weeks using an Asian method to find clothes that brought happiness. Stacy said only crazy people thanked their clothes before they got rid of them. I was hooked on the little Asian woman who introduced the method. I even had her books. Don't judge me. We're all at different levels, and you aren't on mine, okay! If you went into Stacy's room, now her clothes were folded and in her drawers standing at attention. Thank you very much.

Additionally, I took full advantage of the light coming in through the windows in my bathroom. I loved using the natural light to apply my makeup. But today was a makeup-free day. I quickly threw on some jeans, a white Notre Dame t-shirt, and some green leather Converse to match the shamrock. My go-to shoes on a rainy day. The Asian method makes finding something to wear oh-so-simple. I don't sleep on brilliance! I walked over to my nightstand, put in my favorite hoop earrings, and grabbed my Apple Watch and iPhone off the charger before I left my room. I grabbed my Off-White jacket, keys, and bag as I headed toward the door. I ran back to my nightstand and grabbed my laptop then doubled back to the door.

"Bye, Stace!" I yelled over my shoulder.

"A'ight den," she hollered back. I chuckled.

It was early afternoon when I stepped into the elevator. "What the entire fuck," I gasped. My nostrils were assailed by a fragrance hanging thickly in the air. One of the male residents of our building must've bathed in cologne because the aroma hung in the air like mist on a densely foggy day. It reminded me of my ex, Darren. He used to dip his entire body in cologne too. Not this much, though. *Gaaaaht damn!* The elevator descended to the parking garage coming to an uncharacteristically easy stop. The lift in our building usually rumbled to a jarring halt, not today though.

"They must've done some work on it," I mused aloud to myself.

I stepped out of the elevator and walked to my car happily. I slid behind the wheel and sank into the soft leather seats of my black Audi A8. Jason Statham, from those *Transporter* movies, had me in my feelings about him and this car. I vowed that when I could afford one, I would treat myself. And treat myself I did! I pushed the start button, and it leaped to life with ease. Oh, how I loved keyless entry and push start.

I babied her by only driving her a few days a week and on special occasions. I let it idle for a moment before putting it in gear, pulling out of the garage and onto the rain-washed streets of Chicago. I loved this city. I grew up in the suburbs, but since college, Chi-Town has been home. Summers here were hot, and winters were cold and windy as shit. They don't call it the Windy City for nothing. The wind, or Hawk as we called it, kicks hard than a motherfucker. Carmex or Vaseline is a must! Fuck the dumb shit. I don't fool around with all those wimpy lip balms in the winter. Your lips will crust over and have you looking like you have *gonoherpesyphilaids!* Yes, all of the STIs.

I made my way to Willis Tower through traffic. Between the tourists and those who trekked in from the burbs, traffic was ridiculous. With the addition of the rain, the roads were trash. Chicagoans know they can't drive. I ain't shame, though! New York, ATL, LA, Houston…even little ass OKC…all in the same boat! Crazy ass drivers fucking it up for the ordinary people.

"Hey Siri," I sang.

"Yes, beautiful," Siri responded in a male voice with an Australian accent.

You damn right! I have Siri call me 'beautiful' because I like to hear a man call me beautiful every once in a while. Plus, the female American Siri has an attitude. I couldn't strangle that bitch, so I switched it up. Don't judge me.

"Play my hip hop playlist."

"Your wish is my command, beautiful."

"Siri, I love you!"

"I think you're pretty great too."

Siri is my muhfucka!

I took my hip hop seriously. Dad used to DJ to pay for school. He met my mom at a house party where he was DJing. He had everything from the Isley's to Big Pun. I loved that we could vibe over the music. The last time I was home, he was listening to Migos. He never ceased to amaze me.

"Triumph (feat. Cappadonna)" by Wu-Tang thumped through the twenty-three speaker *Bang & Olufsen* system. I loved this song! I once had a classmate tell me this song made him pay attention in biology so he could understand what the RZA was rapping about in his verse. I was about thirteen or fourteen when this song came out. I could still remember dancing to it at a school dance.

BARS!

The crew often got into heated debates about rappers, lyrics, and the like.

"Shiiid, you smoking crack if you don't think Inspectah Deck's verse isn't some of the hottest bars ever recited. Wu-Tang forever!" I'd shout, putting my Wu-Tang "W" in the air.

"Right!" most of the fellas agreed, except Seamus.

"His verse isn't my favorite. It's nice, but the RZA's verse gets the top spot to me!"

"Ah," I shouted, waving him off with a drunken hand. "What do you know!"

"Go to bed, *Féileacán*," he said gently.

"Speak English, man," Stacy said, teasing Shea.

Out of all of our friends, I was the only one who took an interest in the languages Shea and Rho spoke. Most times, I was being nosey and just had to know. In this instance, I was the only one he told what the Irish word meant. Shea had called me by the moniker since our junior year. He had come back from visiting family in Northern Ireland over the summer. Privately, he said I metamorphically emerged from a cocoon like a butterfly. The glow up was real! I thought it was a sweet endearment. He alternated between the Irish and English versions of the word.

Another heavy bass-filled track thrummed out of the speakers as I steered the vehicle onto South Wacker Drive. The valet walked over to the car and opened the door for me. I grabbed my things before I disembarked my personal party bus. The other valets turned to see who was getting out of the car. I got some surprised looks from the newer valets, but the regulars knew what's up.

"Aww shit, Ms. James!" shouted Daniel. "Whatchu know about DMX!"

"I'm a hip hop head, Daniel. You ain't know." I shot him a wink before I headed into the building. One of the other valets ran to grab the door for me. "Thank you," I nodded to him.

I could hear Daniel explaining to the other valets how I was the youngest CFO W&W ever had. I heard a lot of "shits" and "for reals."

"She the sista that normally comes through here being dropped off in the Benz," Daniel said.

"That's the same person? Man, she must be hella-paid. That's a brand new Audi A8," the other valet said.

"Yeah, man, they love her up in here," he informed them.

If they only knew all of the hard work and sacrifice it took to get where I am, they'd know it was more than just "love." I knew many of the members of the Board of Directors resented the fact that I was so young. The partners told me I brought youth and a fresh perspective to the position. I couldn't forget some femininity and color too. They encouraged me to let them know if I got any flak from the old heads. I never had to, because the ones who had a problem either retired or rolled on to new jobs! Winchester & Wiles had seen twenty-seven percent growth within the first quarter with me as Chief Financial Officer. Nothing like making old white men some money to prove your metal.

The company bore the expense of a personal driver for me, which I gladly used during the week because Chicago traffic ain't no joke. I liked to drive myself on the weekends because I didn't want my employer to clock my miles. They didn't need to know my location 24/7.

As I walked through the glass doors of the firm, I waved to the security guard, George. "Hey, Mr. George! How you doin'?" I sang whimsically.

"Hey, MJ! I'm good now that I see you," he flirted jokingly.

"Aw, Mr. George, stop it." I blushed and waved as I made my way to the elevator. He was a friendly older Black man. He made me blush every time I saw him. George was our weekend security. He was two years from retirement and had begun to work a deviated shift to afford him the ability to take care of his wife, Shirley. She recently suffered a stroke and was recovering, but George wanted to be there for her. I admired that about him.

"A'ight now, Mr. George. I'll holla," I shot, as the elevator doors closed. I loved being able to be myself on the weekends. Having to code switch day in and day out was taxing on the mind, at times. George was himself twenty-four hours a day, seven days a week, though. His use of current-day vernacular endeared him to all of the corporate brothers and sisters who had to switch things up once we hit the doors of Winchester & Wiles. He knew the latest slang before most of us thirtysomethings did. I think he had a grandson who lived with him and his wife. Either way, George was as cool as a breeze.

I got off the elevator on the 47th floor and walked casually to my office. Jared, my assistant, had left notes on each of the files I found on my desk. I made a mental note to give him a raise and a bonus this year. Usually, he'd be here with me, but his sister was getting married this weekend. I turned on my laptop and let it boot up. I knew this could be a bad idea, but I remembered I needed to print out some Internal Audit and Expense reports on the DN&P account. I knew one of the partners was expecting the figures for an audit we were performing on the company. I usually left that to the associates in my department. However, this was a multibillion-dollar account, and I didn't want any mistakes.

I grabbed a bottle of water and an apple from my mini-fridge and started to peruse my files. I diligently worked, making a note of oddities in need of research, numbers that didn't match up with projections. I was mulling over an expense report laboriously when I heard a notification from my phone. I picked it up and saw that Seamus had hit me up. I noticed the time as I unlocked my phone.

"Crap. I've been here for hours."

Chapter Two
SOMETHING IN THIS LIQUOR

Bing! Bing!
Shea: Need you to come over!
Shea: Now!!
Me: Can't. I'm in the office doing some work.
Shea: 911! Please!!!
Me: Story?
Shea: Maeve! It's Max...hurry!
Me: I'm shutting it down... 😩
Shea: Just hurry!
Me: On my way!

I sent a text to the valet stand to have my car brought around, then saved my work, shut down my computer and loaded it, and numerous files, into my Burberry Ambrose briefcase. I moved briskly through the office to the elevator after locking up. The elevator glided smoothly down to the first floor. I exited, stepped out swiftly, and shot a goodbye over my shoulder to George. I walked through the door being held open by Daniel, past the valet stand. As the valet exited my car, he handed me my keys.

"Have a good evening, Ms. James!"

Am I being Punk'd? I swear the new valet looks just like Jason Statham...
NAH!

I shook off the notion as I slid behind the wheel, settled my things in the passenger seat, buckled up, and then pulled off.

"Siri, play my Afro Beats playlist."

"As you wish, beautiful."

Davido's silky smooth voice sang into my ears as I pulled off.

Seamus lived north of the city in a quiet community. I often wondered how his neighbors felt about a bachelor living there, or the fact that his circle included a host of non-whites. I loved to see the look on their faces when we were all out in the front joking around before we went inside or when we have barbecues. My thoughts drifted to what had Seamus so spooled up as I headed toward I-90 West.

Traffic was mild for a Saturday evening. Regardless, I was amazed at how quickly I arrived at Shea's neighborhood. Usually, the rain slows down traffic, but there seemed to be hardly anyone on the road. All of the Saturday night revelers must have been on the "L." The urgency of Shea's text spurred me to push the Audi a little harder too. I got off the Interstate and made my way to his house through the sleepy, manicured urban area. This was how the Upper Crust lived. I turned into his community. I used the security key fob he gave me to get into his gate. It seemed the universe needed me here with the utmost swiftness. My mama used to say "utmost swiftness" all the time when I was younger. I still liked it.

I parked in the drive and headed up the landscaped walkway to his front door. Seamus' home was an indication of his wealth. It was definitely too much for a bachelor. Lord, the sidewalk seemed to go on for days. His house was a little under twelve thousand square feet and had enough room to fit my loft in it multiple times. He said he needed privacy and didn't care that it was just him in the house. He said it was the home he would one day bring his wife to and raise a family in. Even though he was a ladies' man when he procured it, none of his conquests ever had the privilege to dawn the doorway. He usually took those birds to his downtown penthouse. So many flowers were pollinated by my bachelor BFF there. I chuckled to myself, thinking about his antics. Oh, the stories I'd heard!

I climbed the steps and rang the doorbell. I could never seem to remember the code to the door, though. Besides, I didn't feel like digging through my bag to find my phone, where the security code was stored. Shea answered the door with blood on his hands. He looked disheveled and irritated. This was definitely his *why the fuck didn't you use the code* face.

"What the hell happened?" I asked, searching his face frantically.

"It's Max," he said gravely. "Follow me." My heart dropped. *Not Max!* Shea turned around and ran up the stairs in the foyer.

"Max," I muttered softly, as I followed him up the stairs to his room, unsure of what I might see.

"Max," he whispered, pointing as he walked around his massive bed.

On the far side of the dark, quiet room was Max. He was lying on his dog bed, covered in blood and breathing laboriously. Our boy, Max. My heart sank. *Shit! What have I walked into?*

"Seamus, wha-what happened? Why didn't you take him to the vet?" I asked with angry concern.

"He…uh…he got off the leash to chase a squirrel and got hit. Mrs. Carter, down the street, is just sick about it. I let her know it wasn't her fault."

Who the fuck carries a dog up the stairs in a situation like this? I thought.

"Shea. We have to get him to the vet. He might have a chance," I pleaded before I got a good look at his injuries. He wasn't going to make it.

"MJ, I brought him up here right before I texted you. He's not going to make it," Seamus said.

"Don't," I started. "There's blood everywhere. You should've taken Max to the vet!"

"I know, but…he—he's not gonna make it," Shea murmured as he knelt down near Max, who was barely breathing.

I sat down opposite Shea and gently lifted Max's head onto my lap. This wasn't responsible dog ownership, but hell, what would I have done in the same situation? He wasn't going to make it. *Fuck! Fuck. Fuck. There's blood everywhere!*

Max looked mangled, and he could barely breathe. A moment later, he looked at us, nudged my hand close to Shea's, and then closed his eyes. The last breath escaped him shortly afterward. Even the dog knew I loved this man.

We were overcome with emotion. The *tears*, man!

I used to be one of those people who didn't understand how one spent thousands on a dog trying to save him. Looking at Max, at this moment, I realized I would've given anything to restore the life that quickly faded from him. *Shit!*

I didn't want to move. This was our baby.

Our tears subsided momentarily, and I gently moved my hand from Shea's. I stood, finding my footing unsteadily. Shea got up to assist me. Our eyes locked. *Damn it!* We embraced and cried some more.

"I'll go make some tea," I said, finally breaking away.

"Thanks," Shea said. He was rubbing my back, because he knew I didn't do well with death. He stepped back to let me leave. I made my way back downstairs to the kitchen and searched for the tea to no avail. I traipsed back upstairs.

"I can't find the tea, Shea," I said softly, peeking my head into the room.

"Oh," he sniffed. "I moved it to the cabinet near my coffee bar."

Seamus was curled up on the floor next to Max. The image of the two of them caused a soft sigh to escape my lips. It was hard to believe this was the same dog who was so full of life and bounding through the house the last time I saw him. I had gotten Max for Shea as a housewarming gift, when he moved into his house four years ago. Max was a cute little ball of fluff, which had grown into a massive one hundred-sixty-pound English Mastiff. We named him after the main character in *Gladiator* because it was Shea's favorite movie. Shea's favorite part was when the lead role finally revealed his true identity.

I'd seen the movie, so many times I could quote it backward and forward. We had so many memories involving Max. Bath time was always guaranteed to be hilarious. Max didn't hate baths, he *abhorred* them. Ten thousand square feet is a lot of space for a dog to run and hide from a tub. I was able to coax him out of his hidey holes, though. I gave the best treats and the best belly rubs. Bathing Max was not a one-man job. Shea had added a dog grooming station to the laundry room after Max turned one. Big boy was not having any of it. Shea refused to have Max groomed and avoided bathing him until Max stunk to high heaven.

"You can't smell him?" I asked once.

"Dogs and men stink," he had said. "Who can tell where his stink ends and mine begins?"

"No truer words have ever been uttered, sir," I said woefully.

I knew what needed to be done... That bath ended with all three of us soaking wet on the floor of the doggy shower. I smiled at the memory. We cried a few times, but we laughed much more as we reminisced over our departed pup's antics.

Max had earned some nicknames over the years. The best was the nickname "beast" from our friend Jesús. He housesat and watched Max for Shea while he was away on business. Shea said every night there was a call about something heinous that "the beast" had done. He ate a fly swatter and pooped all over the kitchen floor, hid Jesús' phone, stole food from the table, got loose, chased a squirrel, and brought the carcass to Jesús as a peace offering. The worst of it was when Max dug up a portion of the backyard. He was so muddy Jesús had to give him a bath. Zeus, our nickname for Jesús, said it took longer to clean up the mud puddles left by the fleeing dog than Max. He ended up calling me to come over so he could get some rest. It pissed Zeus off that Max was a perfect angel for me. Needless to say, he never watched the beast again. We had been beside one another silently for a while when Shea lifted his head to look at me. I put my hand on Max's head and said, "Rest well, boy." Shea and I drank in the bitter cup of grief at that moment. Our boy was gone. Maximus Decimus James-McGhee was gone. Shea stood slowly, never taking his eyes off of Max.

"We have to bury him," he said somberly.

"Sweetheart, I think it's illegal to bury dogs in the backyard. You gotta take him to—" my voice cracked. "We need to take him to the vet." "No," Shea said. "He should be here with us.

"Shea," I pleaded. "It's illegal. Let me take him to the vet. I understand if it's too hard for you to come with me." I knew I had to suck up whatever issues I had with death and be a rock for my best friend. I stood up and moved to stand in front of Seamus. I lightly touched him on the arm, and he looked down at me.

"Seamus," I said softly, "let me take him. I promise I'll come right back."

"Ok," he said, after a long pause.

I watched him gently pick Max up, then followed as he took Max downstairs to the garage. I ran in front of him, grabbing the keys to his SUV, hitting the lift door before opening the door leading out to the garage. Shea placed him in the back of his Range Rover. It was a good thing I parked on the other side of the driveway. I noticed Shea had grabbed Max and his bedding. How he managed to grab Max's bedding was beyond me. I'm sure glad Shea had a rubber mat in the back of the Rover. Although, I'm sure he would've spared no expense to have the carpet detailed or replaced.

"I'll be right back," I said.

I drove about ten minutes north of Shea's neighborhood to Max's veterinary clinic and went inside to get help bringing Max in. Thank God it was a twenty-four-hour clinic. A few of the vet techs on duty cried when they found out I was bringing Max in to dispose of his remains. He was such a ham! All of the ladies in the office loved him. I explained what happened, filled out paperwork, and paid for the disposal. Max's vet was on duty and came out to speak with me. She gave her condolences to me, and Shea, as well. I received a few hugs of comfort, then walked out. I climbed back into the driver's seat of the SUV and lost it again. I cried... hard.

I finally gathered myself together and steered the Rover back to Shea's house. I saw him in the window, waiting for me to return. I parked in the driveway next to my A8. I knew Shea hated cars in the driveway, but I was drained. I pulled the blood-soaked liner out and dragged it over to the water hose on the front corner of the house. His front yard was huge. I sprayed all of the blood off then set it against the house to dry. *Who the fuck is gonna steal with all of the security Shea has in this big ass house?* I put the hose back, then made my way back into the house. Seamus was staring blankly out of the large picture window in the formal living room when I let myself in. Amazingly, I remembered the code this time. The number came to my mind with such ease it surprised me. It's incredible how things come back to you when you really need them. I locked the door and walked over to where Seamus was standing. I moved his arm to step into his personal space, then placed my arms around his waist.

I saw the ice ball in the glass and heard it clink as he moved his hand to allow me to tuck into him. He had used his Macallan Japanese ice ball maker I had given him for Christmas. He poured himself some sort of brown liquor. He hadn't had a drink in over a year, since he started eating clean. I took the glass out of his hand and took a large swig. *Scotch.* It warmed my chest and went down smooth. Macallan. I handed the glass back and hugged him tighter. Seamus typically took his liquor sans ice. He must've needed to fill the time while I was gone. I usually used the ice baller for myself. I wasn't a scotch girl, but I loved the gadget and the look of the clear ice ball in my glass.

"Stay here, tonight. I need the company," Shea asked, his voice was husky and low. "Not that I'm scared. I've just never slept here alone."

I looked up at him and nodded.

"I'm gonna go take a shower. You good?" Shea asked softly as he massaged my neck with his left hand. *When had he moved his hand to my neck?*

"Yeah, I'll straighten up a bit," I offered. Shea leaned down and kissed my forehead before I loosened my grip on his waist. He turned, making his way into the foyer then up the stairs. I watched him leave as I finished his drink.

While Shea showered, I cleaned as much of the blood off the floor in his bedroom as I could. *Thank goodness for hardwood floors.* I put the towels and blankets he had used in a trash bag. I figured I'd just have to buy him some new linens. I didn't want to look like a serial killer taking them to the cleaners. I went to my room, down the hall, to clean up. After my shower, I rooted around in my drawers to find PJs. I found underwear, but clean pajamas eluded me. *That's odd*, I thought. Then I remembered, I had taken all of my dirty clothes home to wash them.

"Why didn't I do them here?" I asked myself aloud. *Dumb ass!*

I dashed down the hall into Shea's room to grab some pajamas or something. I was standing in my underwear when he came out of the shower, draped in nothing but a towel. We locked eyes. Neither of us looked away. I drank in slowly how he looked standing there. His hair was a mess of wet curls. The water made the hair on his chest lay entirely in one direction—down. And you know, I followed it to the dick print under his towel... *Shit! He's holding!* He wasn't quite dry, so the water beaded in all of the right places. I allowed my eyes to take the slow trek up to the perfection that was the Adonis belt and abs. He had been working hard to sculpt in the gym. I knew he had bawdy, as Stacy would say, but damn! He should've been on the cover of *Muscle & Fitness* or *Playgirl*. For real. The contrast of his tanned skin and the stark white towel was insane. I didn't realize how dark he'd gotten over the summer. He was absolute perfection. Just as I felt the lust starting to warm my body, he spoke.

"I'm sorry. I didn't know you were in here," Shea said, as his eyes wandered slowly up my body. *What the fuck? Is he drinking me in? Homeboy is giving my body the same attention I gave his.*

"No worries. It's not like you haven't seen me in a bikini a million times," I said, as I broke off my staring to pull open a second drawer to search for one of his t-shirts.

"The gym has been doing you well, *Féileacán*," he chuckled softly. "And see-through lingerie is not the same as a bikini." I felt my cheeks and chest flush hotly. I completely forgot that my underwear was sheer. I had dashed into his room, thinking I had plenty of time since he was still in the shower.

Dammit, I thought, as I pulled on the first shirt I found.

"Really, Shea," I said embarrassed.

"Don't cover up for my sake," he chuckled. "I've already seen the good wee bits." I looked at him, and he winked. He made his way over to the dresser where I was standing, dripping water in his wake.

"I just cleaned the floor, Seamus. Get dressed." I needed some space! I closed the drawer and quickly left the room. I made my way to the kitchen, where I promptly filled his copper teapot with water. I turned on the stove, waiting for the flame to lick up before I put the kettle down. As the water was heating up, I wandered to the laundry room. I found some clean sweatpants in the dryer and put them on. I went back into the kitchen to turn off the stove and empty the teapot. *Don't cover-up. What the fuck?* I thought. I needed a stiff fucking drink. I swung by the wet bar in his den and poured myself a double shot from the first decanter of brown liquor I found. *I really, really need a stiff drink.* I drank it down quickly. I poured myself another shot, single this time, then drank that one as well. I refilled my glass with a single shot the third time, contemplating if I should down that one too. Nah! As I filled a second glass with a double shot. Fuck, the scotch had him staring at my body, I was sure.

I wandered into the den and set the glasses down on the glass cocktail table. This was my favorite room in the entire house. It was all masculine décor. For starters, it was floor to ceiling mahogany library panels. It smelled like Shea because he spent so much of his downtime there. The room had tray ceilings with inset canned lights. The central light fixture was crystal, yet it had chrome lines and angles. It lent to the masculine vibe. When the light fixture was illuminated, it appeared to have a flame floating in the middle of it. I loved the library paneling on the walls but above the fireplace, Shea had mounted a monstrously large 90-inch television above the mantle. *So gaudy!* The wooden floors were hand-hewn teak, imported from Africa. Anchoring the room was a large cream Alpaca fur rug. He had chosen two matching cream tufted sofas and added pillows of various textures and sizes. He promptly corrected me when I called them couches—"They're sofas."

Most times, the pillows ended up on the floor or thrown at various members of the crew when we were all in here together. Shea had multiple pictures of family, our group trips, and awards on the shelves. He was an avid reader of military history, strategy, and autobiographical works. On the side of each sofa was a large Annie Selke St. John oval basket, which contained Sherpa and Mink blankets. Those had to be the only feminine items in the room apart from the fresh flowers on the mantel. Shea said he kept those for me, Stacy, and our other female friends. But I knew he used them when we weren't there because they all smelled like him.

I picked up the iPad lying on the couch opposite the cocktail table and pulled up the room I was in. Shea's house was a technical masterpiece. The iPad controlled everything from lights to the fireplace to the room temperature. He monitored cameras and food stored in his pantry. It took me months to learn it. I set off the alarm a few times, trying to figure it out. I turned on the fireplace and put on some music. I wasn't in the mood to watch television. The fire and the music came to life as if synchronized. The first few strains of a slow song came through the speakers. Those shots had me feeling right! The pain of losing Max was almost numb.

I was curled up on the sofa when Shea finally came in, dressed in grey sweatpants and a v-neck white tee and oblivious to how sexy he was. Men have seriously got to stop pretending like grey sweatpants are not the equivalent to women's lingerie. Hello...I could see his Eggplant Friday! I held it together as he came over to the couch—sofa, I was resting on. He leaned down and opened my legs to fit himself in between them like the missing puzzle piece. His body was warm and smelled like vanilla and citrus. He positioned himself in such a way that allowed him to rest his head on my chest.

"Uhhh... Excuse you. I was comfortable—" I started, before Shea interrupted.

"Shhh..." he whispered.

"Shea, you are taking liberties that are not authorized," I fussed. "Go get on the other sofa."

"Leave it out, woman," he growled softly, using Irish slang in his full brogue. I knew he wanted me to stop fighting him, so I hushed.

Another slow song played in the background. My body began to heat up, and my nipples hardened so tightly they hurt. I could tell the liquor had warmed my blood, as I lifted my hand to Shea's hair. I ran my fingers through his soft, damp, dark curls. He smelled so fucking good. I tried to remember why I was there and to tamp down all of the lust that was creeping up. We laid on the couch, quietly, for so long that our breathing became synchronized. A few songs played before I spoke again.

"Hey," I said softly.

"Mm-hmm," he said. We made eye contact, and I gestured to the cocktail table.

"Drink?" I asked, referring to the drinks on the table. Shea sat up to check my handiwork and chuckled.

"Good job, Butterfly," he said quietly.

Shea swallowed his scotch in one gulp before picking mine up. He handed me the other glass. I sat up and followed his example. We were trying to numb the ache in our hearts for Max. I don't know how many drinks Seamus had before I joined in, but I was feeling nice. I wasn't a big drinker, so I had to keep telling myself to chill.

"Feel like talking?" I asked.

"Not really. I needed some company," Shea said quietly.

"Ok," I said nervously.

"Am I too heavy, Butters?" he asked in a whisper. His words were perfumed with the honeyed orange scent of the liquor.

"I'll let you know if I can't handle it," I said, instantly regretting my words. It didn't matter what was going on—my best friend unearthed every double entendre! He sat up with the most devilish look in his eyes.

"Will you, now?" he asked, looking up at me with a twinkle in his eyes and a devilishly boyish grin.

"Alright now," I said sarcastically. "Simmer down. I'm not one of your birds."

"Nope, you're my main girl. Best girl. Only girl," he slurred.

Only girl? Shit! Don't do anything stupid, Maeve James. This is not the time to profess your undying love. Just be supportive, I thought to myself as I twirled one of his curls between my fingers. This was one of those times that Shea gave off the vibe that he wanted to be more than friends. He had reached up, locking his hands under my shoulders. He pulled me down further on to the cushion and pressed his full weight on me. I felt his cock press against my lady parts. I wondered what he'd feel like inside me. His head was resting next to mine in the crook of my neck. He had to know this was very intimate. *Surely, he isn't using the liquor as an excuse to—nah.* I shook off my thought. I relaxed fully with Shea lying on me. I had dreamed of being with him like this often.

Oh MY God! I screamed internally. *What fucking playlist is this?* Every song elicited sexual thoughts.

"Thank you for coming," Shea rasped. His accent was thick right now. It made me laugh a little inwardly.

"No need." He hadn't noticed the song. *Thank you, Lord!* I thought.

"You're always there for me. That's why I love—having you in my life," he mused.

"Seriously, Max is…was just as much mine as he was yours, Shea. He will always be our baby."

"He was mostly yours, though," he rumbled softly. "Remember how he always tried to leave with you when you came by? You would've thought I was abusing him."

"Yup," I said with a light chuckle.

"What about that last bath?" Shea asked, sitting up just enough to look at my face.

"*Stop the lights,* I was thinking about that upstairs. That was a mess! All three of us got a bath that day," I giggled.

"You had just gotten your hair done. You were low key pissed OFF. I think he knew, too."

"Low key? Try high key pissed off. It was funny at the moment until I saw my head. Lord, that dog brought me every toy in his…" I looked over at his basket of toys in the corner and instantly choked up. Max had brought me toy after toy to apologize. I sobbed.

"Don't cry, *arún*, please," Shea whispered. He shifted, so his face was directly over mine. Shea rested partially on my body. He used his other hand to wipe my tears away. He leaned down to kiss my eyes then pulled back to look at me.

"Don't cry, *álainn*. I can't take it," Shea pleaded.

"I'm sorry," I whispered.

I looked up at Shea, and the gravity of how we were positioned hit us both at the same time. I'm not sure if it was the liquor, but there was an ache in my heart that stirred. I believe he felt it too because he leaned down slowly like he was going to kiss me. I pulled my arms up around his neck and looked deeply into his eyes.

What am I doing? What is HE doing? What in the world are we... my thoughts raged!

"Shea...I—" His kiss silenced me. I felt his full lips urging mine to part, to allow him the access he craved.

Our lips dripped of honey citrus-flavored liquor. I parted my lips, and our kiss deepened slowly. As we kissed, I began to hear the falsetto strains of an R&B crooner song. I felt his tongue flick across my lips. I wound my fingers into his curls and pulled him in. Time slowed down, then stood still. The singer's falsetto was taking us some place we'd never been before. We were best friends, drunk best friends, laying on his big ass couch kissing like our lives depended on it. As the kiss deepened, I wrapped my legs around his waist, pulling him into me. He sank in, cupping my derrière as he grinded his hardness into my pelvis. His hand snaked up my shirt to fondle my breast. Fire ran down my stomach directly to my sex. My nipple responded to his touch by tightening when his thumb raked over it. *Why is the universe playing games with me right now?* The playlist was the sexiest shit I'd heard in ages. Straight fire. It was making me want to do all sorts of things. *Crap!* I must've accidentally played his "Knock 'Em Down" playlist. Maybe it tapped into his subconscious because he seemed to be on autopilot. All

I could think, with him pressing me into the couch, was S—E—X! The liquor was ruining our judgment. I wanted to be like this with him, but this was not the right time. I didn't stop, though. We kissed for the remainder of the song. Our tongues slow danced as we gave in to the feeling. I pulled back when the song ended...for a moment.

"Shea, we need to stop."

"Do we? Really?" he questioned softly. "You are so very...beautiful. Seeing you in lingerie made me want to fuck you," he murmured against my lips. *Whoa. My Gawd!* He was really, really drunk.

"Shea, you don't know what you're saying right now," I said softly.

"I know you're beautiful," he slurred. "Your eyes, your mouth, your breasts...your...body. That see-through lingerie and this fuckin' scotch."

"How much scotch did you have?" I asked ardently.

"Three, no...," he paused. "Yeah, no, four doubles," he slurred. He leaned in to kiss me again, but I moved my face.

"No, Shea," I said. "Stop. Sweetie, you've had way too much to drink."

"Your mouth...tastes...so fuckin' good, Butterfly." *Was this liquid courage? Did he really feel this way?*

"Shea, we need to stop before we do something we'll regret," I said reluctantly.

"I seriously doubt either of us will—" he hiccuped. "Regret it," he murmured softly against my lips.

Why the FUCK are we stopping? my body screamed. The Bad Bitch in my brain was screaming at me, *Bitch, he's drunk!* I screamed back, inwardly, *Do you really want your first time to be with your drunk ass best friend? No, so simmer down!*

"Seamus!" I stiffened at the thought.

"I'm sorry, Butterfly...forgive me...," he slurred.

"No worries, Seamus. Let's just get some rest," I said softly.

"Damn, this song," he growled.

"Yes, and this entire *feckin'* playlist," I whispered.

He heard the playlist. I truly believed those songs were the devil's work! I unfurled my legs, allowing Shea to roll onto his side behind me. We spooned as he draped his arm across my waist.

"You're my *álainn Féileacán*," he murmured as he pulled me in closer and drifted to sleep. Either my Irish was rusty, or he just called me his beautiful butterfly. *What the fuck, Shea? Do you like me?* I laid there for a while, thinking about what had just happened. Was it the alcohol? Was it the killer combination of this playlist and liquor? Did he really want to kiss me…fuck me? More importantly, would he remember this? *Ugh…Fuck my life* were my last thoughts before drifting off to sleep.

I woke up the next morning with Shea resting comfortably behind me. His arm wrapped tightly around my waist. He had pulled a mink blanket over us at some point during the night. Drunk but considerate. *Why couldn't this be our lives?* I wondered. *Are we going to discuss the kiss?* I shimmied myself out of his grasp and made my way to the kitchen. I rifled through the cabinets, pantry, and refrigerator, looking for food to prepare. I settled on my famous banana walnut waffles, eggs, and sausage. We deserved waffles after the night we had. He woke up about an hour later and made his way to the kitchen. I had set plates on the bar and already dug into my waffles, when I saw his face.

"I had syrup?" he asked in astonishment.

"Yup," I said with a mouth full of buttery waffles.

"Is that on the list of recommended foods?" he questioned.

"Nope!" I said, almost spitting my entire bite onto the counter. We laughed.

"I wasn't too much trouble last night, was I?" he asked.

"You were…something," I said in between bites.

"What does that mean?" he raised an eyebrow and asked quizzically.

"You'll have to check the security footage," I said, laughing.

"That bad?"

I rolled my eyes, wondering if Shea would ever check the cameras. I chuckled at the thought of him watching it. I'm sure he'd be horrified to see how he—we had behaved. I spent most of that Sunday there, and he never broached the subject. I called my mama to explain why I missed church. She was sad to hear about Max. She knew I had gotten him for Shea. She sent her condolences, and said we could borrow her King Charles Cavalier Spaniel, Inky, if we needed company. Inky was as bad as the day was long. No one was gonna take her up on that offer. Shea laughed and thanked mama for the invite. He said he'd take her up on it sometime.

"Lies," I whispered to him.

Shut it, he mouthed back.

I stayed until Sunday evening. Shea and I went back to his man cave after cleaning the kitchen. We watched a movie—*Gladiator*, you guessed it. I arrived home at around seven o'clock that evening and ate dinner while I conveyed to Stacy the day's occurrences.

Chapter Three
TRUTH OR SCARE

Bing!

Me: Ugh, I think I have the flu.
Shea: Me too, MJ.
Me: This is all your fault. Idk why you let me drink out of your glass.
Shea: You drank out of my glass? When? Last Saturday?? I was so gone... 🎃👻

I was more than sure it was the kissing, not the drink, that infected me. Hell, maybe one of the vet techs at Max's doctor's office had it. Either way, I felt run through.

Me: Uh, yeah. Now I feel like death. DEATH, Shea!
Shea: Sorry, Butters! 💀 Forgive me?
Me: Maybe if you bring me some soup 😷🥣
Shea: Seriously?! 💀
Me: Stacy's in Trinidad and Tobago with her family. I don't wanna infect anyone else...AND this is your fault!
Shea: Your mom is a DOCTOR! 🧟
Me: SHE didn't get me sick, germ bag.
Shea: Princess. 🧟

Me: Bow down and bring my soup then. 🍲
Shea: I'm not leaving when I come. Make room.
Me: The couch is free.
Shea: So is the bed. 😏
Me: Don't think so, peasant
Shea: No bed, no soup....
Me: I look like 🧟‍♀️ no joke!
Shea: It's all good.
Me: 😫😩😫
Shea: On my way! LOL

Shea showed up with enough supplies to last through a zombie apocalypse.

"Move over," he said gruffly.

"Ugh, I don't want to. Make do. It's a California King," I said. I was achy and cranky. I didn't want to share my bed, but he had brought me meds, soup, tissue, cough drops, and orange juice.

"Where are your clothes?" he asked.

"It's too hot for PJs," I said matter-of-factly. "You've seen me in a bikini before."

"Maeve, you are burning up! When was the last time you checked your temperature?" Shea asked angrily.

"Uh," I murmured, "it was 103° the last time I checked. I have a fever."

"A hunnert an' tree," he yelled in his thick brogue. "We'll recheck it in an hour. If it doesn't go down, I'm going to make you take a cold shower," Shea said with concern.

"Dude, can you not? Ugh, you sound like Dr. James. She said she was going to take me to the ER if the fever didn't break," I said.

"Your mom *is* a doctor," he said as he handed me some Tylenol. "Here, take these."

"I just wanna sleep—in peace!"

"Dammit, grouchy! I'm trying to help!" he barked.

"I'm sorry, I know. I-I don't feel well," I whined.

I took medicine with some orange juice and went to sleep. I was awakened to Shea and my mom lowering me into a tub of cold water. I was so confused.

"Wha-what's going on?" I asked. My body hurt severely.

"Shea took your temperature while you were sleeping, and it was 104.3°. If it doesn't break, we are going to the ER," my mother said. She looked very concerned, as did Shea.

"Mama, I'll be ok. I just need to get back in bed," I whined.

"Maeve Alena James, sit your narrow tail down in this water. Shea is sick too. I have half a mind to make the both of you get in here! He doesn't need to be lifting you. Now, sit on down," she fussed.

"Mama, seriously. I'm *not* decent," I protested.

"Child, it's not like he's never seen a woman before. Be still, baby girl."

I stopped resisting when Mama called me baby girl. She only called me that when she was worried. Mama left the bathroom and came back with a large bowl of ice from the kitchen. She dumped it into the water slowly, but it didn't seem to have much of an effect. The water felt warm against my fevered skin.

I was so tired and so achy.

The next morning, I woke up in the hospital. I was overcome with fever. Mama was in the recliner next to my bed. Shea had somehow finagled his way into the hospital bed across from mine. I took in the space and was blown away. The room was expansive. *I didn't know when your mother is the Chief of Surgery, they put you in the presidential suite.*

"You're ok, baby girl. You're in the hospital," Mama said quietly. "We couldn't get your fever to break so we called an ambulance. The doctor said it's a good thing we brought you in. There have been twenty-seven cases of flu and pneumonia that resulted in death in recent months. I don't know what I would've done..." her voice trailed off.

"Thank you, Mama. You take such good care of me," I said as I placed my hand over hers. I mouthed *thank you* to the chucklehead across the way, as well. He winked. I was in the hospital for seven days. I was on a steady dose of Tamiflu and breathing treatments every four hours. My dad had come by several times to check on me.

Rhys James was an engineer working for a government contractor. He had retired from the military and took on contracting work three days out of the week. Dad said Mama put him to work while at home. That way, he could golf four days and get out of the honey-dos. They were annoyingly cute, but I wanted what they had—lasting love.

My assistant, Jared, had come by the hospital to update me on the DN&P account and to assure me he had everything under control. Mama promptly shooed him out of the room when she came in, though.

"Winchester and Wiles are going to let her rest," she retorted.

"I tried to tell her, Dr. James," said Shea.

"Snitch," I yelled across the suite at him. He shrugged and chuckled.

"Mama, calm down. He was only informing me of progress on an account and letting me know he had it handled. Plus, I'm about to go crazy in this room," I said.

"You are going to sit here until the doctors say you can leave. No work, missy!"

"Yes, ma'am."

I could hear Shea snickering from his side of the room.

"Why are you still here, boy?" I asked, annoyed.

"Keeping you company, Butterfly," he said smugly.

Mama laughed. I turned over. Sleep was the only thing that gave me respite from Shea's foolishness.

On the seventh day, I was released to Shea's care. My mom had actually co-signed Shea's shenanigans. The flu-pneumonia combo had done nothing for my temper. I was cranky during the drive to my house. Shea stayed another week to make sure I was eating and drinking like I should. If he hadn't been in bed with me the day he came over, I might have died.

"Honestly, I thought you had wet the bed," he said jokingly. "And I'm surprised Dr. James didn't flip her Southern Baptist wig when she found out we were in bed together."

"You told mama you were in my bed? Have you lost your mind, man? What did she say?" I asked.

"She said she was glad I came by to look after you," Seamus said in amazement.

"Will wonders never cease," I said in awe.

Dr. Paulina James did not believe in premarital sex, shacking, or the like. Her overlooking her daughter was in bed with a man blew my mind.

"She likes me," Seamus said proudly.

"I can't for the life of me figure out why," I said laughing, as I threw one of the pillows at him.

"You know, throwing pillows is the international signal of pillow fights," he said wickedly.

"Seam—no! I'm sick," I said, feigning weakness.

"Oh, no," Shea said with a glint of challenge in his eyes.

"Don't. You. Dare…" I started jokingly. Before I could finish my sentence, he threw his entire weight on top of me and pummeled me with the pillow I had previously flung at him.

"Shea, stop," I squealed. "You're gonna break my bed! You're gonna kill me. I'm still recovering."

"You have to be taught a lesson!" he said in between his laughter and pillow attacks. When the pillow pummeling stopped, Shea was lying on top of me like the night after Max's death. His face changed. His eyes changed. I couldn't read his expression.

"MJ," he started. "I need to tell you something." *Oh no, where is this headed?* I thought.

"I have feelings for you that I can't explain. Its more than friendly, but…" Shea's voice trailed off.

"Seamus, I feel the same way. I have for a while now. I didn't want to—" I said breathlessly. Shea cut me off.

"How long, Maeve? How long have you felt this way? Were you going to tell me?"

"Seamus, I was afraid you wouldn't feel the same and…I didn't want to ruin our friendship," I said softly.

"How long, Maeve?" His tone grew harsher.

"Years," I said, holding his gaze.

"Wow." Shea's eyes widened. "That long?"

"I don't know. I felt like it was a crush at first, but it wouldn't go away."

"Wow...I can't believe you lied to me," he said.

"I was confused, friend zoned—wait...lied? I never lied to you," I said in a halted manner.

"I asked you if you had feelings for someone after seeing the text from Stacy. You said you were talking about an ex. You lied." He got up from the bed and walked to the window slowly. He rubbed his face as he stared outside.

"Shea, I was afraid. I wanted to tell you, but the time never seemed right. I thought maybe after the night Max—wait...you have feelings for me? You never said anything either," I said pointedly. I got up and walked close to him but stopped short. He turned to face me.

"I didn't realize it until I saw you lying unresponsive. Seeing you sick, thinking of you not being in my world...that's when it hit me. But you-you've known all this time." His voice trailed. The silence was deafening. I wanted to reach out to him.

"I met someone, Maeve," he said flatly. I began to sweat and breathe in short, shallow breaths.

"Really?" I asked softly. Jealousy pulled at my heart forcefully.

"Yeah, we've been seeing each other for a while now. I haven't brought her around because I wanted to be sure of how I felt about her. I proposed to her three weeks ago."

"You're lying! Why didn't she come to see you in the hospital?" I asked chuckling.

"I'm not lying. My fiancée was in Germany visiting family. She wanted to come home, but I told her not to worry." He was convincing.

"Wow." I paused for a moment, stunned. "Wow...okay. If you're happy, then I'm glad."

"Knowing how you feel changes—" he began.

"It changes nothing, Shea. If you loved her enough to propose and felt she was the one, then it shouldn't make a difference," I stated.

He walked over to me and pulled me into his embrace. He leaned down to kiss me, but I stopped him.

"Don't. I don't want to do this with you if I can't have you. This is my fault. I should have told you how I felt. Stace said someone else would snatch you up," I said with a cold chuckle. "She was right. I thought we—I had more time."

"Butterfly, I want to know what we could be," he said softly. His breath was soft against my cheek. I looked up at him—seeing the turmoil in his eyes hurt.

"You are actually engaged," I said in disbelief trying to push away. "You made a commitment to her. You are hers," I said quietly.

"We could..." he trailed off.

"We don't know what this could be, Shea. You don't know if you love me. You only realized you had feelings for me a few days ago. You should know by now whether you love your fiancée. After all, you did propose. You-you should probably go before—"

"I can't," he said before crushing my lips with a kiss. *God, I love this man*, I thought. *Maybe it's because I can't have him...anymore.*

Our embrace tightened as the kiss carried us away. I forgot about Shea's nameless fiancée, letting the kiss take us higher. I felt him walking me backward to the wall. The cold sheetrock chilled my back, but it didn't put out the fire our kiss had ignited. His tongue parted my lips, devouring my mouth passionately. Shea had complete control as his hand slide through the strands of my curls. He tightened his grip on my hair and pulled my head back to give himself more access to my mouth and neck. Shea's hand explored my body. I felt his hand under my butt as he lifted me. My legs instinctively wrapped around his waist. My arms tightened around his neck. We stood there for a moment, locked in one another's embrace, drinking one another in.

Shea stepped back from the wall, and I clung to him like fresh dew on the grass. I felt him move us from the wall to the bed. He set me gently on top of my covers. I fell backward as he pressed his full weight into my body. Our kiss deepened, each exploring the other's mouth and body in desperation. I ground my hips into him and felt his desire. He was hard…and huge. His erection pressed against me as hard as my nipples poked at him. His hands trailed along my face and neck. He was starting a fire that would consume us both if we didn't stop. *Fiancée!* my mind screamed. *Ugh!*

I didn't want to cause him to cheat on his fiancée. I had to stop, but my heart didn't want to end this bliss. His kisses were like sweet nectar. Now, I was like a bumblebee seeking the nectar he provided. He tugged my pajama shirt off, undid the clasp of my bra expertly, then pulled my arms free of the straps. His wanderlust was unsatiated as his hands traveled from my breasts to my thighs and ass. He lifted me, grinding himself into me. He moaned "Butterfly," and it sounded like music to my soul. I needed to stop, but his touch set my body on fire.

"Seamus, stop," I said, quietly pulling away.

"Butterfly," he moaned softly in my ear.

"Please, Seamus," I said as I turned my face.

"Why, Butterfly?" he pleaded. "Am I hurting you?"

"I can't. *We* can't. You're engaged. I don't want my first time to be like *this*…with someone else's fiancé."

"Wait, what?" he said, confused. "You're a virgin? How am I just now finding this out? You and Darren never…" Disbelief spread across his face.

"Never," I confirmed. Shea stood up as though someone had thrown a bucket of cold water on him and walked over to my window. I followed.

"I thought everyone knew I was a virgin. Plus, you know my mama. Can't you hear her saying, *all premarital sex leads to is diseases, babies and hellfire*," I said sarcastically. I could still remember the grotesque pictures of the various STIs my mother had shown me during our "human nature" discussion. My mama was a handful.

"I would've been obligated to marry you had I taken your virginity," he said with a smile.

"My daddy—and his shotgun—would agree," I said jokingly. "On a serious note, I know you're a good man. I couldn't live with myself if I caused you to be unfaithful. I love you too much."

"You love me?" he asked.

"Yes. Honestly, I hoped this was a crush. But I feel like I always knew," I confessed. "But...you have a whole entire fiancée, that I have never met, out there."

Funny how you know things when your options have been taken away.

"I'm sorry, Butterfly," Shea said gravely. "I shouldn't have kissed you."

"No, you shouldn't have, but what's done is done." I blushed a deep crimson.

"I wish you had said something sooner," he sighed.

"Would it have changed anything?" I asked, searching his eyes.

"Don't know," he said.

"I should've said something, Seamus."

"You're right...you should have. We are friends, Butterfly. We would've discussed it had you said something," he said.

"Don't co-sign," I smirked. "I didn't want to lose what we had. I had hoped you'd remember the night Max died...or at least looked at the security footage."

"Are you serious, why?" He implored.

"Because you kissed me then too," I confessed.

"And you didn't say a freaking word? You're killing me, Smalls. You're *killing* me!" he growled.

"I'm sorry," I repeated again.

"Stop saying you're sorry. Just stop! Why did you keep all of this to yourself?" he asked angrily.

"It's not my fault you didn't remember," I said angrily.

"Girl, you are seriously killing me!"

"I was tipsy, you were drunk. I figured it was the music or something—I don't know! This isn't all on me," I said. I felt beads of sweat begin to form on my nose and upper lip.

"No, it's not. But dammit," Shea said thoughtfully. "I wish things were different. I made a commitment...you understand that, right?"

"Do I have a choice?" I asked gruffly.

He looked down at me. We held each other's gaze for what seemed like an eternity.

"You are spectacularly beautiful, Butterfly. I'm sorry I didn't act on it sooner."

That was the last thing Seamus said before he walked out of my bedroom that night. I reached over and grabbed my pajama top off the floor and put it back on. Holy crap, I had a full conversation with my shirt off! I stood there still for a moment, thinking about all of the times I could have told Shea how I felt. My grandmother always said, "A closed mouth don't get fed, baby. You gotta tell folks whatchu want." Damn us and our closed motherfuckin' mouths!

I picked up my phone and went to my home security app. I locked the doors, turned off the lights, and set the alarm. I placed my phone on my nightstand and laid down. I cried into my pillow until I drifted off to sleep.

My dreams took me back to the day of Max's death. Shea was lying on me, and I was playing with his hair.

"I'm gonna miss him," Shea said.

"I know."

"I remember the day you gave him to me," he said stoically.

"Like yesterday."

"I'm gonna be all al—"

"You have me, Shea." I cut him off. He was directly over me.

"What are you saying, Butterfly?" he asked softly.

"I'm saying I love you, Seamus. I'm in love with you." He closed his eyes and sighed. When he opened them again, they were a brilliant bright green color. Beautiful.

"I love you, too, Butterfly," he sighed. He lowered his head until our lips met.

His face shattered into a thousand pieces, and he was gone. I woke with a start. I could still feel his touch, smell his fragrance on my sheets. Seamus, my best friend, my Shea, was gone.

A DAY LATE

The morning after Shea left, I called Stacy to tell her he was engaged. She didn't tell me that she had warned me. Instead, she listened and offered to come home, but I didn't want to pull her away from her family in Trinidad and Tobago.

"So how did he tell you?" Stacy asked quietly.

"He had brought me from the hospital a few days before, remember?" I asked. "He stayed over for a few days to make sure I was eating and following the doctor's orders. He said something slick, and I threw a pillow at him. Well, next thing I know, he's on top of me tearing me up with that pillow."

"Wait, what?" Stacy squealed. "On top of you? Come again?" Stacy was cracking up.

"Stace, can you let me finish?" I started laughing too. "He came to himself and told me as he was getting up that his behavior was inappropriate and apologized." I knew I was lying, but I couldn't tell her just yet.

"Then what?" she asked.

"He said he had something to tell me and said he had a fiancée. I told him I was happy for him."

"Girl, you are better than me. I would have slobbed that *foine* jokah down while he was on top of me! Damn his fiancée! She ain't you, she ain't been down for him like you," Stacy exclaimed.

I cackled at her reaction. I could envision her acting it out and could hear her little nieces giggling in the background to her antics.

"It's gon' be a'ight, girl," Stacy said confidently.

After our phone call, I deleted all of my social media accounts. I didn't want to risk seeing the man I loved booed up with his fiancée. The thought brought fresh tears to my eyes. *Why had I been so stupid? Why didn't I tell him like Stace had asked me to do?* This was horrible, and I had no one to blame but myself. Stacy texted me later on that day saying she had learned that Seamus' future wife was a marketing exec named Chelsey Robinson. Stacy could social media stalk better than anyone I knew. She saw a man in the parking lot of Walmart once, and by the time we made it to the highway, she knew his whole pedigree, who he was friends with, his blood type and whether he was dateable by our standards (no convictions or crazy exes, baby mamas, or lousy credit).

Stacy sent over several pictures of the perp in question. She was a tall leggy blonde who was intelligent, talented, beautiful, and well-spoken of in the circles we ran in. She would make a good wife. The last time I had seen or heard from Shea was October. Time passed slowly without him. I celebrated Thanksgiving, Christmas, and rung in the New Year quietly in my loft. Mom and Dad tried to coax me out of my misery by offering to come over. I wasn't in the mood for company, though. I loved that Stacy had reached a point in her career that she could take extended absences while her business continued to thrive. However, I missed my girl! Tish and Rho had come through a few times to check on me. They saw Seamus had changed his status on Facebook to engaged. They came with wine, chocolate, and snackage!

I hadn't heard from Shea in over three months. The holidays came and went without so much as a card. I had assumed it would be a slow fade, but he cut me off like the Soup Nazi on Seinfeld. *No soup for you!* How did we go from friends who spoke every day to not speaking at all? I wanted to call him on several occasions but didn't. Mainly because my Grams always said, "If a man wants to talk to you, he will make time." I decided to take her advice. We didn't text, FaceTime, or workout together anymore. I missed him like crazy but wanted to give him a chance to make a life with his future wife. I was snapped out of my introspection by my phone buzzing. It was Seamus. *Think of the devil, and he will appear...or call.* I answered the phone on the third ring.

"Hello."

"Hey Bu-Maeve, how are you?" He sounded professional. *Damn, my government name? I'm not his Butterfly anymore,* I thought. I swallowed hard before I responded.

"Hey, Seamus. I'm ok. Did you need something?"

"Uh, yeah. Chelsey, my fiancée, wanted me to check with you to see if you'd be available to be a part of our wedding. I didn't tell her about, well...you know."

"Wow, Seamus. Just...wow." I was flabbergasted. "Of course you didn't tell her. You have some nerve. It's not enough that you're marrying someone else—you want me to watch too," I said with indignation.

"Bu—Maeve, I wasn't—I-I didn't think about it like that. We thought you'd be happy for us since we've been friends for so long. I wasn't thinking. I didn't want to upset... ugh. Forgive me."

"We? Really? You don't call in three—nope! Who asks another woman to be in her wedding and hasn't been formally introduced? You've got to be freaking kidding me." I paused to collect myself. "It's cool, Seamus. If you can look me in the face and marry another woman knowing I love you..."

"Maeve, don't," he said sternly. "You haven't been introduced because I was trying to sort things out. I told her you were in Singapore on business. That's why you haven't met."

"Secrets and lies," I said. "What a way to start a marriage."

"I will tell Chelsey you are otherwise engaged and can't make it," he spat angrily.

"No, the fuck you won't, Seamus! There's nothing I'd rather do more than support my best friend on the most important day of his life. So, what would the future Mrs. McGhee have me do?" I said curtly. He was quiet for a moment.

"Had you said something years—years ago—this could have poten-tially been avoided. A closed mouth doesn't get fed, Maeve." *My grand-mother's words. Touché.*

"You put me in the friend zone years before you saw Stacy's text, Seamus. I was in there so deep that you didn't notice me there until I got sick. Yeah, I should have said something, but being your friend was better than having nothing...which is what I have now. I haven't heard from you in months, and when you do call it's because your fiancée asked you to."

I knew what I had said stung him, but I wanted him to feel the emp-tiness I was feeling. I wanted him to know how I ached every day in his absence. There was silence on the line once more. I could hear him breathing, composing himself before he spoke again. I knew he was upset, but so was I.

"I wanted you that night, and most nights since, Mae-," he paused to compose himself again. "Let's be clear, I did put you in the friend zone, but that doesn't change the fact that you lied to me! Besides, I wasn't trying to be in a relationship back then—none of us were. Our careers were taking off, and life was totally different. Had you said something, we could have discussed it. You lied, Maeve. I can't—I don't want to do this with you right now...it's too much," he said. I could tell he was going through the emotional gambit. But, he wanted me. I wondered how his fiancée would feel if she knew that. Ugh, I hated men! But I wanted him too. He filled my dreams almost every night.

Boss up, I thought to myself.

"That's fine, Seamus. Let's not talk about it...again. When do you plan on talking about it—your 25th wedding anniversary? You not talk-ing about the feelings you may or may not have for me should make a great foundation for a new marri—ugh, I can't. Just answer the damn question, Seamus," I said.

"What question, dammit?" he retorted.

"Seriously, Seamus," I spat. "What does she want me to do at your wedding?"

"Let's just forget it," he said.

"Let's not," I retorted.

"You really wanna do this, Butterfly?" he asked.

"Oh, now I'm Butterfly. I asked, didn't I?" I said sarcastically.

"Ok, Maeve, ok. She wants you to be the Best Woman," he said tersely.

Now, I was silent. I was expecting to be an usher, bridesmaid, or some other foolishness. Best Woman. That had me shook. I would be planning his bachelor party, helping him choose tuxes... and handing him the wedding ring he would place on her finger.

Boss up, I told myself again. *Boss ALL the way up.*

"I'd be honored. I wouldn't want to let the future Mrs. Seamus Aidan McGhee or my best friend down. Best Woman, it is, best friend," I said rudely.

"You are something else," he said dryly.

"What do you think about Vegas for the bachelor party, huh? Does Vegas sound good to you, best friend? Strippers, prostitutes—the whole nine," I snarled.

"Now, you're being a..." his voice trailed off angrily.

"Hmm? Don't mince words now, best friend. Isn't this what you wanted? One big happy family? We can forego the hookers—I wouldn't want to upset BAE. I'll keep you posted," I said sarcastically before I hung up on him.

He called back. *Of course he did.*

"What, Seamus?" I said dryly into the phone.

"We need to talk...face to face," he said flatly.

"I'm pretty booked up for the next few weeks. Check with my assista—"

"Chelsey would like to meet you for dinner this weekend. I figured you could stop by a little early and we could hash some things out then," he cut me off.

"I don't mind meeting the woman who captured your heart, but *hell* no to stopping by early. The last time we were alone, I ended up topless. I don't think the future—"

"Stop it! You enjoyed every minute of being topless. If I weren't protecting your virtue, I would have—" he stopped abruptly. "Listen, I'm not going to play these games with you, Maeve. If you aren't up for the task, then say so, and I'll ask one of our other fucking friends."

Oh, snap, Seamus is not playing with me today!

"I'm more than up for the challenge, Seamus. You did say you wanted me that night, and what was it? Oh yeah, most nights after that. Don't play with me, sir. I'll make you cheat on your girl, then call her from your phone and tell her I knocked you down," I said matter-of-factly.

"You talk a good game for someone who's never had the immense pleasure of riding my cock, or any other cock for that matter. Don't get it twisted. You can't run with this very big dog," he said boldly.

"Seamus Aidan McGhee, do I sound scared?" I asked confidently. "I didn't get where I am in life by bluffing. I said what the *fuck* I said! You of all people know this."

He was silent.

"Send my assistant the details for this little soirée, boo. I'll see you soon." I chuckled as I hung up the phone.

Ugh, what have I gotten myself into? Can I really watch him marry another woman? Can I really be the temptress I threatened to be? Why do I do this to myself? I thought. *Me and my big mouth...*

Dear God, please help me not to make a spectacle of myself. Amen.

After my brief prayer, I texted Stacy.

Me:	Seamus called
Stace:	AAAAAAND?!? 😩
Me:	He asked me to be his "best woman." Said his fiancée thought it would be a good idea.
Stace:	You told his stupid 🍑 no, right?!
Me:	I agreed
Stace:	🤬🤬🤬

Stacy didn't text back for a cool minute.

Bing!

Stace: Why, Maeve?? Why would you do that to your-
         self?! You're in LOVE with him. You KNOW you
         can't watch him marry another woman.
Me: If he can do this, then he isn't who I think he is.
Stace: Sweetie, he's marrying another woman. He's
         not hiding anything from you. He is exactly
         who he says he is, Maeve. Don't do this. Call
         him back and tell him no. Please...

Ugh...I need to tell Stacy the truth.

Me: Can't...
Stace: 😕😑😕
Me: I'm having dinner with them this weekend.
Stace: You have GOT to be effing kidding me. 🔫
Me: 🔫
Stace: Girl
Me: Brown liquor and Kleenex 😵
Stace: I got you, babe!
Me: Thx

Stacy didn't know Shea and I had discussed our feelings when I was
sick. She wasn't aware I had told him I was in love with him and that I
was the one to push him away. I was too ashamed to tell her what really
happened that night. She had been right, though. Seamus was more
upset that I had lied about my true feelings than anything else. I had
also pushed him into Chelsey's arms. I knew Stacy wouldn't be judgmental, but my pride was wounded.

Chapter Five
DINNER WITH THE HAPPY COUPLE

It's good to have friends, I thought. I had called my ex, Darren Wilkerson, the day I had spoken to Shea to ask for this favor. I needed a boyfriend—not a real one, but someone who I could trust to help me with my shenanigans. Darren never really liked Shea, but he loved me as a friend. He understood loving someone who didn't return the feeling. Darren was a complete asshole when we dated in college. In an attempt to get me back after cheating numerous times, he confessed that he was fucked up and didn't know how to love anymore. His high school sweetheart had done a number on him when he was being recruited his senior year. She had gotten pregnant, hoping he would marry her before leaving for college, but the baby was his friend's. He was in love with her and that broke his heart. When he arrived at Notre Dame, he was quite the dawg on campus. Girls threw themselves at him left, right, front and back. Sometimes, they were two and three at a time. His rep was so bad that he began to matriculate over to our campus to pick up ladies, since Chicago is only a hop, skip and jump from South Bend. That was how the two of us met. I thought he was *foine*! My friends couldn't stand him because he was a lady's man. I was so naïve. I didn't know football, so I didn't know him. I had only had one other boyfriend. Darren strung me along for two years, cheating on me the entire time with any and every chick in a skirt. It was Shea who finally had enough and walked me over to the dorm where Darren's rumored side chick lived. There he was, looking like the peacock he was, strutting around with another girl on his arm.

I didn't act unseemly. I locked arms with Shea and strolled past Darren without speaking. Darren and I talked about the incident later that night. He said he had urges and it was hard trying to be faithful with sex being offered to him day and night. Since I wasn't giving "it" up, I felt what he was saying and empathized. My friends said I was naïve to forgive him, but it wasn't like I was taking him back, so I let it go.

Darren went to the Dallas Cowboys first round of the NFL draft. We didn't speak for years afterward. When he got picked up by the Bears, he called to let me know he was back in town. We had drinks once and kept in touch via text or occasional calls. He was slowly becoming a great friend now that he had matured. I let our past be water under the bridge. My friends not so much! I had stayed in touch with Darren over the years and given him financial advice. I had put him in touch with a friend who helped him ink a lucrative endorsement deal. He said he was eternally grateful because I ensured he'd have money after his playing days were over. I had thought about having him name his firstborn—girl or boy—after me. So, pretending to be my boyfriend was a small favor. I wasn't courageous enough to show up without a date. I didn't want to see Seamus and Chelsey all booed up and me being the lonely third wheel. I was playing with fire, but I had an agenda. I had some surprises up my sleeve. What could go wrong?

As requested, Shea had sent Jared the details of the dinner. It was supposed to be casual, but I had other plans. I had been working hard the remainder of the week trying to get ready for dinner. Saturday morning, I had taken a "me day" to prep for that evening. I had gotten my hair done that morning, a hot stone massage, facial and a mani-pedi. I looked positively radiant. I wore my hair straight and let it hang down my back. I was wearing black a form-fitting Givenchy LBD with a gold zipper down the back. I paired it with black Christian Louboutins, red lipstick to match my red bottoms, large gold hoops, a small black

Fendi clutch, a black leather motorcycle jacket, and my Running back for the Chicago Bears ex—Darren. He owed me a few favors. Fortunately, he was still single and had time in his schedule. The Bears were in spring training, but he was free Saturday night. I drove to his downtown loft, and we rode to Seamus' house together in his Giallo Horus Lamborghini Aventador.

We arrived at Seamus' gated community, and I handed Darren the entry fob.

"You still have his key?" Darren asked.

"He didn't ask for it, and I forgot I had it until I was switching purses. Don't judge."

"Not at all, love," he said jokingly.

"Darren, you know—" I started.

"Hey, I'm prepping for my role. I know what it is," he said, patting my leg reassuringly.

"Thanks," I said.

We strode up to Seamus' door and were greeted by the beautiful Chelsey Robinson. She was wearing her hair up in a sleek ponytail with understated makeup. I, on the other hand, was snatched, honey! Her eyes were the palest shade of blue but were friendly. She was wearing a navy blue, silk maxi dress with large multicolored flowers. She was naturally slim and tall, so her nude ballet flats brought her down to my size—in heels.

I felt terrible, for a nanosecond, for how I planned to behave, but this trick had my man…Game on!

"OMG!" she sang in a nasal voice. "You are beautiful!" Her vocal frying rivaled that of many pop culture celebs.

"Thank you," I said. "You're quite the stunner yourself!"

"Come in! OMG. You didn't have to get dressed up on my account. Didn't Sheamy tell you it was a casual dinner?"

Shea-my? Did she just add a "my" to his nickname? Ugh! I was going to clown him the next chance I got.

"My assistant must've missed that part. No worries, I'm comfortable in heels."

Darren cleared his throat.

"Oh, this is my date—" I began. But before I finished, Chelsey went into full *stan* mode.

"Oh my freaking gosh! OMG! You're Darren Wilkerson!" she screamed. "Sheamy, you didn't tell me Maeve was dating Darren Wilkerson!"

"That's because I didn't know," he said dryly, as he came around the corner from the formal living room into the foyer.

Darren placed his left hand on the small of my back for support.

"Seamus," Darren said, extending his hand, "great to see you again."

"DW, haven't seen you since our college days. Looks like you put on some weight, Big Guy." Seamus said.

"Yeah, you know, the NFL will do that to you." Shea looked from DW to me like we had betrayed him.

"Maeve. Good to see you again." He smiled and leaned in to kiss my cheek.

"All's fair," I whispered in his ear before he returned to his full height. He chuckled.

"Indeed," he said, acknowledging the challenge that had been thrown down.

"Dinner isn't quite ready," Chelsey said, "but we can start with drinks in the living room." She directed us to follow her. I didn"t know how Shea tolerated her voice. It drove me crazy to hear professional women speak in that manner. However, I had learned in some of my business dealings that rich men loved it. Some even deemed it sexy. Maybe that was the appeal—hold—she had on my friend. Darren followed Chelsey, but Seamus stopped me.

"Let me get your jacket," he offered.

"Uh, sure," I said, turning my back to Shea so he could assist me.

"You look—and smell—delicious," he whispered intimately into my ear. The feeling of his breath on my skin sent a chill down my spine and caused me to have goosebumps.

"Two can play this game," I said softly as I shimmied out of my jacket.

"What?" he said, feigning innocence.

"Careful. The future missus might not take to kindly to your behavior," I said as I brushed my backside against his crotch. I turned to see him bite his lip. *Challenge accepted, baby!*

I left him standing there as I found my way into the formal living room. Darren was sitting on the couch looking just as handsome as the day I met him. He sat directly across from Chelsey chatting away. She had herself folded up on the loveseat with her feet tucked under her with her shoes on the sofa. Just no home training.

I sat next to Darren and crossed my leg, revealing the underside of my thigh. Instinctively, Darren placed his hand on my thigh and rubbed the exposed flesh methodically. Seamus did a double-take at the sight. He shook it off and joined Chelsey on the loveseat directly across from us. We chatted about work, current events, and other bland topics.

"So, Maeve, how did you and Darren meet?" she asked inquisitively.

"College," Seamus inserted. "They were a modern day Romeo and Juliet, Julia and Julie—" Chelsey swatted his thigh.

"Don't be rude," she scolded.

"Darren had a few dalliances, but things have changed," I asserted.

"Yeah, I ran into her a few months back, and we've been kicking it ever since," Darren said confidently.

"Where was this?" Seamus asked bluntly.

"Singapore," I said flatly. Seamus choked at the remark and stood up.

"Does anyone else need a drink?" he sputtered. He took our drink orders and left the room.

Touché, bitch!

"He was filming a commercial there. I walked past the set with some clients and saw him. He came over and chatted us up. We exchanged numbers then."

"I messed up back in the day, but I told myself if I ever got the chance with her again," he said looking down at me, "I wouldn't let it pass me by."

"I was there for a few months like Shea said. Darren came to see me during his bye week," I said to Chelsey.

"Bye week...didn't you have the flu or pneumonia then?" Seamus asked as he came back into the room with our drinks.

"Hm, you must be mistaking me for someone else?" I quipped.

"I distinctly remember you having pneumonia last fall."

"Nope. I was in Singapore when you proposed, remember?" I said, goading him.

"I guess you were," he acquiesced reluctantly.

Chelsey and Darren looked at each other and shrugged. Shea and I were in a staring contest. He knew I was lying, but it was his butt I was covering. Why was he trying to be a dick about things?

"Maeve," Chelsey finally interjected, "that is so romantic! Do you all have any pictures?"

We reached for our phones victoriously.

I'm definitely going to have to give Jared more vacation time to go along with his raise. He had photoshopped pictures of us all over Singapore! There wasn't a landmark he left unvisited. He had us kissing in the Gardens by the Bay. He had Darren lifting me up over his head on the beach in Sentosa and stuffing our faces at Hawker center. I looked at all of the pictures and wished I had actually done those things. It was fun to rub Seamus' lie in his face, though.

Darren and I just gushed and gushed about our time together.

"I see," Shea said dryly as he flipped through the pictures Chelsey had shown him.

"What about you guys?" I asked Chelsey.

"Oh, it isn't nearly as romantic as your reconnection in Singapore," she said.

She recounted how they had met, their dating, and the proposal. She and her business associates had pitched an idea to Seamus. Downplayed and low key. She was just now meeting most of Shea's friends. I was the first one. We heard the timer go off in the kitchen. Saved by the bell! Chelsey and Seamus went to get everything prepared.

"Our fake love story sounds a hundred times better than their real one," Darren said in my ear. I chuckled.

"Yeah, they're getting married for real, though," I said softly.

Darren turned my face to meet his gaze.

"What's meant to be, will be," he said genuinely. "You can't force him to love you. Life is lived moment by moment. Just live."

I looked at him and nodded.

Seamus came into the room and saw our tender moment. He started to walk away when Darren looked up and saw him.

"Hey...uh, dinner's ready," Seamus said.

Seamus knew our little act was a ruse, but he couldn't say a word. Had he not lied to his fiancée about me being in Singapore, none of this would even be possible. Darren and I laid it on so thick there were moments when Seamus looked genuinely jealous.

Meanwhile, Betty Not-So-Crocker was in the kitchen, burning the house down. Chelsey fancied herself a gourmet chef. *Bless her heart.* She had prepared pork medallion in a balsamic plum reduction sauce. She paired it with oven-roasted potatoes, carrots, parsnips, and broccoli. The sauce must've cooked too long because it was bitter. *Very* bitter. The vegetables were burnt and somehow undercooked at the same time. The tenderloin, if you can call it that, was dry—like the Sahara dry. There wasn't enough wine to wash down the unpalatable concoction she had thrown together. We soldiered through each, finding ways to compliment her meal. We went through several bottles of wine that night. We were five bottles in when I kicked off my shoe and began to rub Shea's leg under the table. He hadn't given much indication, except a stern look, that any mischief was going on. At one point, he reached under the table and gently squeezed my foot. He noticed my toenails were painted red to match my lips. He looked up at me agonizingly. He couldn't stand up because he was fully erect, and his erection was straining against his pants. I felt it lurch each time my toes grazed the tip. He was mine...for now. As I stroked his cock with my foot, I was overly friendly with DW. I laughed at his jokes, touched his arm occasionally, and dabbed his mouth with my napkin.

The dessert saved the day! Chelsey had gone to a local bakery and picked up a sampler platter. We were just all grateful she didn't try to make us stomach any more of her wretched cooking. I felt terrible, genuinely, for Seamus. I bet he was wondering what he had gotten himself into since she was definitely going to need lessons. The only other option was to hire a chef—which I didn't know how he was going to because it would definitely hurt her feelings.

"This was lovely, Chelsey," I said as I stroked Shea's ever-hard cock. "We have to do it again, sometime."

He didn't miss the double entendre. Shea flashed me a look that conveyed a meaning only I would understand. He was going to get me back. But as Kanye said, "How Sway?"

I smiled in response to it even though my heart leaped in anticipation.

"Chelsey, why don't you let me help you clean up?" Darren offered.

"No," Shea said calmly, "Maeve and I will clean up. You all go on out to the patio. We'll be out shortly."

Oh!" Chelsey exclaimed. "That sounds lovely! I cook, you clean!" She stood and kissed him on the forehead.

"Don't be too long," Darren said as he stood and followed Chelsey out through the patio doors. Shea waited until they were out of earshot before letting me have it.

"What the hell is wrong with you?" he whisper-screamed.

"What?" I said as I placed my foot back into my shoe and stood.

"You are treading on thin ice, MJ!" he said, still whispering.

"I didn't come to play with you, Seamus," I said under my breath.

I started clearing the plates and silverware. I turned to walk into the kitchen and dropped a fork accidentally—on purpose. I turned to look and Shea was watching me. He had spared everyone from seeing his substantial erection by holding his napkin over his lap.

"Oops," I said breathlessly. I bent forward to pick up the fork slowly, allowing my dress to ride up my thighs just enough to enable Shea to see a small portion of my garter belt and thigh highs. I stood back up slowly, then sauntered into the kitchen. I made sure each step had a little runway model hip-thrust.

He was shook!

I was in the kitchen scraping the plates into the trash when Shea finally came in with the wine bottles and glasses. He set the glasses on the counter next to the sink then put the bottles in the recycle bin in his pantry. I looked at him, searching his face. Tension rested in his expression, causing his jaw to clench slightly. He walked back over to the sink and began to stack the dishes.

"I'll wash, you dry. Where are the gloves?" I said sweetly.

"Laundry room, in the closet with the cleaning supplies," he said tensely.

I went into the laundry room, slipped out of my panties, grabbed the gloves from the closet, then went back into the kitchen. I slid my panties into Shea's pocket, put on the gloves, and began to wash the dishes. He reached into his pocket to see what I had put in it. He chuckled when he recognized what he held in his hands.

"Maeve, I warned you," he whispered. I winked in response to his threat.

We washed the dishes, then cleaned the kitchen and dining room in silence. Shea gave no indication that he was angry or otherwise bothered when we re-joined our dates on the patio with wine.

"So, Shea," Darren said, "how do you like living out here in the boondocks? I bet you see all kinds of wildlife out here."

"I see all sorts of things on my security cameras," he said smugly.

I choked on my wine, sputtering and coughing like a madwoman. Darren gently patted my back, trying his best to help. Chelsey dashed into the house, then ran over with paper towels from the kitchen. Shea sat quietly in the corner, amused by the ruckus he'd caused. I shot him the dirtiest look ever. *Shit!* He *had* seen the footage. He was not playing fair at all!

I apologized to Chelsey for making a mess.

"Don't worry about it. Are you ok, though?" She was genuinely concerned.

"I swallowed wrong. I'm ok," I said. Shea found a double entendre in that, too. I hated that I loved that man. The rest of the night went on without a hitch. We sat outside on the patio and regaled Chelsey with stories of our college antics. *Poor girl,* I thought. She was so sweet, and here I was trying to take her man. I thought about stopping, but his remark about the surveillance cameras would not go undiscussed.

It was getting late, so we said our goodbyes then left. Darren was such a great guy and had really matured since our time in college. He was even working on a Ph.D. He said he wanted something to fall back on after his playing days were over. He loved academia and wanted to teach when he was done. Shea and I had settled on master's degrees because our thesis nearly killed us. Chelsey didn't have a post-graduate degree. She said she had no intention of going back to school. Darren was going to make someone a good man someday. As DW and I drove back to his place, we were joking about Chelsey's struggle meal.

"How do you not know your food is nasty? She ate that mess like it was the best thing ever made!" Darren said.

"I know, right? We drank five bottles of wine and didn't get drunk because that dry biscuit she called a pork tenderloin soaked up all the liquor!" I cackled.

"Did you see your boy trying to scrap that reduction sauce off of his meat?" Darren was laughing so hard he had tears coming down his cheeks.

I was doubled over laughing, remembering Shea trying to slyly scrape it off.

"There wasn't any salt and pepper on those crunchy raw ass veggies either!" Darren said through laughter.

"Right, olive oil and some sprigs! My question is, how were they burnt and raw at the same time?" I was in tears now, too.

"We always say white people don't season their food, but hers—hers was seasoned with hopelessness and despair!"

"Anguish and gloom paired with a melancholy reduction sauce!" I hooped.

"Burnt Pterodactyl nuggets and dried unicorn horn would've been better!" Darren hollered.

"Darren, I can't." I was laid over against the door in tears. "Unicorn what? Boy, you are stupid!"

When I told Darren that Shea threw the leftovers out while we were cleaning the kitchen, he had to steer the car over into the shoulder. "Lawd, Jesus!" he howled.

He laughed so hard he had trouble seeing straight. We sat on the side of the road laughing for about five minutes before we pulled ourselves together. I don't think I had laughed that hard in ages. I was so glad I had on waterproof mascara. I would've looked a hot mess otherwise. I couldn't wait to tell Stacy about the meal. She was going to clown for real. We finally made it back to Darren's place, where I retrieved my car and headed home. It was nearly midnight when I made it back to my loft. I called for Stacy when I walked in, but she wasn't there. She had left a note on the mirror in the entryway saying she was out and wouldn't be back tonight. She signed it with a happy face, which was usually her indication that she was getting some. I couldn't keep up with her conquests. I think she was dating an Asian chick or was it an Italian guy? She'd tell me in the morning when she got home. I dropped my purse and keys on the table under the mirror before kicking off my shoes. I picked them up and padded down the hall to my bedroom. I reached the door to my room and was jolted still by a familiar fragrance—Shea.

UP IN MY ROOM

S hit! Shea was in my room, and he smelled delicious. I flicked on the light before walking in. We looked at each other for a brief moment.

"What are you doing here, *Sheamy?*" I inquired.

"You invited me, remember?" he said. He chuckled, undaunted by the challenge in my voice.

"I don't recall doing so, sir," I was getting annoyed. He reached into his pocket, and my heart sank. *My panties.* He pulled out my lacy black thong and raised it to his face. He closed his eyes, inhaling my scent.

"Oh, but you did," he said cocksure. I walked past him into the closet to put my shoes into the Sterilite box I stored them in. I placed them on the shelf, trying to act like the sight of him with my panties wasn't the sexiest thing I'd ever seen. My heart was beating fast, but I kept my breathing under control.

"Shea, I am tired. Go home to your fiancée," I said flatly, trying not to convey my nervousness.

"Chelsey doesn't live with me. She went home shortly after you all left. I came to discuss your offer, Butterfly." He meant business. He closed the distance between us too swiftly for my comfort. Caught off guard, I began to back up. His eyes let me know he meant to collect on whatever it was he perceived that I had offered. *Don't be scared now.* I stopped retreating.

"Turn around," he commanded, "and hold your hair." I turned around slowly, grabbed my hair, and twirled it into a thick twist. He started unzipping my dress. I pulled away unconsciously. My actions were met with a single rip down the back of my LBD. Arousal and shock flooded me instantaneously. *What the entire fuck?* I thought. He was definitely replacing that bad boy. Designer attire wasn't cheap. His hands were warm against my skin. His touch sent shivers down my spine. I tried to twist out of his grasp, but he held the tattered edges of my dress fast. When I stopped moving, he pushed the ripped sides off of my shoulders, letting the torn garment to tumble to the floor. I looked down on the heap of fabric, aghast. I was standing there, facing the wall, in nothing but a bra, garter belt, and thigh highs. *Where is he going with this?* I thought. *He cannot possibly believe I meant to have sex with him.*

"Go put the heels back on," he whispered seductively in my ear.

"Shea," I started.

"Put the heels back on," he demanded.

He stepped back, allowing me to walk into the closet. He swatted my ass hard as I started to walk away. I sucked in my breath through my teeth. It stung yet gave so much pleasure at the same time. I sauntered into the closet to pull the Sterilite box off the shelf. I took the lid off, then put the shoes on the floor. I stepped into the shoes before replacing the top and placing the box on the shelf and returning to where Shea was standing. His gaze cascaded down my body fluidly. I let him take in the length of my body. I relished his approving scrutiny. I didn't wax often, but I was glad I had taken Rho up on her request to get laser hair removal. He sucked in his breath when his eyes rested at the meeting of my thighs.

I knew he liked what he saw. No man had ever seen me like this, not even DW. What were we doing?

"Turn around...slowly." His voice was low and commanding.

When my back was to him, he unhooked my bra. He pushed the straps off my shoulders, letting it fall to the carpeted floor. It landed with a soft thud. He stepped back again to garner another look. *Approval.* I was nearly naked in front of my best friend. Honestly, I didn't care. He was here with me, and that's all I cared about.

"Butterfly, you've been a bad girl. Punishment is in order," he said with sheer delight. Shea reached into his pocket to fish out my panties. He brought them around to the front of my body then traced a line, from my navel to my nose, with them.

"Your scent makes me want to do nasty things to you, Butterfly." I breathed in the scent of the panties he had brought to my face. "Move your hair." I obeyed by twisting my hair and pulling it over my shoulder. He then used the panties to stimulate each of my nipples while he kissed the back of my neck. I moaned softly.

"Shit," his voice rumbled in his chest. "I don't like being challenged," His voice was rough with desire. I felt myself getting wet with desire for him. He lowered my panties to my clitoris then began to rub them in a circular motion.

"Shea..." I moaned.

"Yes, baby?" He inquired.

"Please don't," I begged. "Why are you doing this?" I moaned as he continued to caress me.

"I'm returning the favor, baby." With his free hand, he began to pinch, flick, and pull softly on my left nipple.

"Seamus, please..."

"Say the word, and I'll stop," Shea offered seductively.

Silence.

"Do you want me to stop?" he asked again.

"No."

"Do you want more?"

"Yes," I pleaded breathlessly.

"Tell me what you need, Maeve."

"You."

"If you weren't a virgin, I'd fuck the *shit* out of you," he sighed hard. "You have to be taught a lesson, though."

"I'm not afraid," I said haughtily.

"You should be," he groaned in my ear. "I *fuck* bad girls—like you."
"Then fuck me," I said. *Where did that come from?* I thought.

"Put your hands on the wall," he demanded. I let go of my hair to press both hands into the wall beside the door leading to my closet.

He began to whisper filthy things in my ear.

"Do you really think you can handle this dick? Are you sure you want me? Deep inside you…ripping you open…Thrusting deeper and deeper…Shit, shit! Your pussy is so wet, Butterfly. So, so, wet.…You smell delicious. I bet you taste as good as you smell. Would you like to taste yourself…"

He took my panties from my clit to my mouth. I parted my lips then he put my panties in my mouth. He quickly went back to work on my clit. *Shit, I'm going to explode,* I thought.

"Good girl, Butterfly. Imagine your wetness all over my cock…I wonder if you can take all of me. Ten inches, Maeve. Ten inches deep inside your tight little pussy."

Smack. He swatted my ass again.

"You need to be taught properly. You don't know when to stop, though, Butterfly. I wanted to fuck you on the table…In front of your *friend.*"

Smack.

"That's for bringing DW to my house."

Smack.

"That's for playing with my cock under the table. I warned you…"

Smack.

He was bringing me to the brink of a fantastic climax. He was skilled, very skilled, with his hands. His index and middle finger were expertly working my clit. I was beginning to lose control. I felt my orgasm beginning to stir.

I tasted the wetness he had created. Clit. Nipple. Ass smacking. Dirty talk in my ear. I leaned my body into his, enabling him to suck my neck, ears, and back. My body ached for him. I was ready for whatever he was willing to give me.

"Did I tell you to move?" he growled. Put your hands back on that fucking wall. I warned you, Butterfly…"

I knew he was aroused by the bulge I felt pressing against my ass.

"This is how you made me feel earlier," he murmured in my ear. "Remember that."

Then, without warning, he pulled away. What was he doing? *Don't stop. I'm so close.* I took my panties out of my mouth and threw them to the chaise next to me.

"What are you doing?" I pleaded. "I'm so close."

"I warned you," he said.

"Warned me," I repeated.

"That's what I said," Shea retorted.

"Wait, what?" I was confused.

Realization of what this was hit like a wrecking ball. I turned around to lean against the wall.

"Are you…are you *serious* right now? This was for revenge? You have me damn near naked, finger fucking me with *my* panties—for revenge? You're an asshole, Shea!" I was trembling with rage.

I walked into the closet to grab my robe. I put it on, tied it up then sat on the chaise near where we had been standing. I felt beads of perspiration on my lower lip and the tip of my nose. *How could Shea do this to me?* I thought. I knew I had tempted him at his house earlier but not like this. Shea didn't say a word. He picked my panties up off the chaise and swiftly tucked them back into his pocket. He had no remorse. He enjoyed this immensely. Payback for stroking his cock under the table with my foot. Had I done this very same thing to him? Was he this aroused at the dinner table in front of his fiancée? Shit!

"Don't play with me again," he said as he left my room.

I sat on the chaise for what seemed an eternity. I needed a hot shower to relieve the ache between my legs. I stripped out of my clothes and rushed to the shower. A short while later, I heard my phone.

Bing!
Shea: Can I call you?
Me: no
Shea: pls
Me: WHY?!
Shea: We need to talk.
Me: I have nothing to say

The phone rang. I answered.

"Do you ever fucking listen, Shea?" I yelled into the phone.

"Butterfly, I'm sorry." He sounded genuine.

"Too late," I snarled.

"For what it's worth, I rubbed one out in the car. I got caught up. I didn't expect you to let me—want me to do those things. I got caught up with it all. Your panties, your fucking body, you asking me to fuck you," Shea rambled.

"We keep saying things can't happen between us, yet things keep happening between us," I growled at him.

"You're doing something to me, Butterfly."

I knew he was vulnerable at that moment, but I was steaming mad. I had tried to finish what he started in the shower, but all my traitorous body wanted was to be with him. I was aching for fulfillment.

"Shea, I was wrong for what I did at your house. It was disrespectful, but you weren't going to cum in your pants!" I yelled into my phone.

"That's where you're wrong. I was very close. Your feet, the polish, the way you moved against me made me want to come," he revealed.

"So, you wanted to teach me a lesson. I get it…but you've seen me naked, Seamus." I was seething with anger.

"Yes, I have seen you naked. I don't regret it either. I don't know what I'm feeling. I know I'm engaged, though, Butterfly."

"Fuck that, Shea! Your actions speak louder than your words. I know you saw the security camera footage. Every time you let your guard down, I end up getting molested," I spat.

"*We* get molested, woman. You love to play the victim. We are both guilty. I did see the footage, and it shocked me. Only because, again, you didn't say anything. How did you expect me to know how you felt if you never said anything?"

"I am saying something now. If it were too late, we wouldn't have been in my room like we were…" my voice trailed off.

"I want you badly, but I don't want to break your heart. I don't know if I love you, Butterfly. I don't even want to go down that road. I'm trying to be honorable, but you keep forcing my hand," he said candidly.

"All I'm asking is that we have an open conversation, Shea. How can you marry another woman if there's the possibility that there is something—*anything*—between us? How?" I was losing my composure.

"Don't…" He paused. "You said you didn't want to know."

"I'm fine. I know what I said, but things are different."

"Now, they're different?" he said cynically.

"Yes, I know you're attracted to me. I know you feel what I'm feeling. I know you do."

"Is there a physical attraction between us? Yes, it's strong—I won't deny that I feel it. I'm committed to another woman, Maeve. Why are you pushing this? Don't make me the bad guy in this situation. Just stop pushing me…I guarantee you won't like me when this is done."

"What the fuck is that supposed to mean?" I demanded.

"It means, I will fuck you—very well—then marry Chelsey." His words stung.

"Do you really think you can do that, Shea?" I asked in disbelief.

"Absolutely fucking positive," he said flatly.

"We'll see," I said as I hung up.

Bing!
Shea: Don't do this, Butterfly.
Me: Kiss my ass, Seamus.
Me: I'm sending you the bill for my dress…

I went to retrieve my panties from the chaise. Gone.

> Me: I know you took my panties. I want them back.
> Shea: Come get them.
> Me: Think, I won't? 😜
> Shea: I'm betting on it. 😏
> Me: 🖕🖕🖕 asshole!!!

I put my phone on silent then threw it on the nightstand. Fuck me, then marry Chelsey. Shit! I was impressed. I had never seen this side of Shea. The Bad Bitch in my brain had lost her ever-loving mind. *Yes,* she said, *let him fuck us—well! Fuck, yeah! What that dick do? Better yet, what that mouth do?*

"Fuck!" I yelled aloud.

This wasn't going to end well.

Chapter Seven
THE FITTING

It had been weeks since I had spoken to Seamus. Honestly, I was doing better than I had expected. Darren and I were chatting regularly. When he wasn't training or practicing, we were on FaceTime or texting. He was becoming a great friend. I told him how badly Stacy had talked about Chelsey's dry pork loin, then relayed how Seamus had shown up at my loft that night and all of the fallout. He was supportive and recommended I change my security codes to avoid future incidents. That boy was a genius!

"I love it! He ain't my favorite person, but he got game." He laughed.

"Don't remind me," I said, thinking about that night.

"Ok, so you're telling me he watched the security footage of y'all goin' at it, and he didn't call you?"

"Yes, sir!"

"He's the real MVP!" Darren said jokingly—snickering at the foolishness, too.

I told him what happened when I got home after the dinner party.

"Wait," he cackled, "witcho own panties? I may have to try that shit! I'm aroused just thinking about the sight of you with yo' panties in yo' mouth! You know, that's some freaky white people shit for ya! When did you have time to take them shits off?"

"Shut up, Darren!" I giggled. "When we were washing dishes...y'all were on the patio." I smiled.

"Ooo, girl, you is nasty! So, wait, you sat your nekkid ass on my Lambo seats? You paying to have my car detailed!" He rolled with laughter.

"I can't stand you! My ass is clean and disease-free, fool!" I laughed too.

Darren's laugh was the kind of laughter that made you laugh just by hearing it, sincere and hearty. You didn't know what was funny, but it was so heartfelt it got you.

"I don't know how he did it. There ain't no way I'd have walked away from yo' fine ass and beat off in my car! Nope, you'd have been deflowered that night!" Darren said, shaking his head into the camera. I loved FaceTime.

"I asked him to fuck me...that's the crazy part—I don't know where that came from!" I said seriously.

"That's them ovaries crying out from the darkness! They ready to have the cobwebs knocked off." He roared with laughter.

"Man, who you telling! This waiting for marriage stuff is killing me. But... I've gone this long." I snickered at Darren. He knew how to make me forget about myself and my circumstances.

"Shit, you'd be pregnant as we speak. Club woulda been shot the fuck up."

"Not shot up! Boy, you a fool!" I was in tears.

"I'm just saying." He chuckled.

"I hear you. Shea is trying to do the right thing," I said, shaking my head.

"The right thing would've been to tear that ass up! That's all I gots to say about that!" He laughed again.

"Agreed," I said, laughing wholeheartedly.

"You are agreeing, but I don't think you're ready. Losing your virginity to the man you love is big shit." he stated matter-of-factly.

"I know," I said.

"Honestly, MJ, I think if you continue to push him, you might end up hurt."

"You sound like him." I was irritated. "Why can't he just talk to me?"

"You pushed *him* away, remember? And now you want to talk? You aren't normally this wishy-washy, MJ. *You gon' have to* let him come to it. If he doesn't, then you'll have to face the fact that it wasn't meant to be between you."

"I know he has feelings for me..." I said.

I knew Darren was right, but my gut wouldn't let me leave it alone.

"Don't let the real things that have happened between y'all cloud your mind. Men can fuck a chick and be in love with another. That's the nature of the beast, MJ. Women, y'all can be in love with two men at the same damn time and not know which one you really want." He was really frank with me, and I appreciated it.

"Darren, I don't know what to do," I sighed.

"When will you see him again?" he asked.

"We have a tux fitting next week. Then we have to find a dress or something for me. You are coming to the wedding with me, right?"

"You don't even have to ask. Just call me Plus One, baby," he said. "For real though, play it cool when you see him. Don't provoke him. Let him see that you are giving him the space he asked for, and if it's meant to be, then he'll come to it on his own. Support him as best you can. You can do it, MJ."

"You're right. I'll try, but I can't make any promises," I said, smiling into the camera.

"A'ight then, I'll holla atcha later, Playgirl!" he said, laughing.

"Bye, D-Dub!"

My conversation with DW was good. He helped me see things from a man's perspective. I needed that perspective. I had to leave Seamus alone to let him come to his feelings on his own. If I pushed, I was going to end up heartbroken and minus a best friend. I was glad to have Darren to talk to about this situation. I still hadn't told Stacy. I dreaded how she would take knowing that Darren knew, and she didn't. It was eating me up inside, but I still couldn't bring myself to tell her. *I'll let her know soon,* I thought.

Weeks had passed since our last heated exchange, yet Seamus' words still rang in my ears. *I will fuck you—very well—then marry Chelsey.* The Bad Bitch in my brain focused solely on the "very well" part. What did it feel like to be fucked very well by Shea? *Shit, he also said he had ten inches of man meat,* she reminded me. *Yes, Bitch, ten inches of man meat in your tight little pussy.* I was horny as fuck. My ovaries ached! My clit throbbed when I walked, and the mere thought of his touch made it jump with anticipation.

I was just getting out of the shower when Stacy announced that Shea had arrived. I was running late. I scrambled to get to my robe which was laying on my bed. I could hear Shea's footsteps approaching as I made it to the bed. He opened the door before I could throw the robe around me. He stepped into the room, closing the door behind him.

"Shit!" I breathed vehemently. I had cursed more those last few months than I had the past three years. *What is happening to me?*

"Nice to see you again, Butterfly," he said softly.

"I swear I was trying to cover up before you got here. I'm running late," I said as I finished tying the robe around my waist.

"Mm-hmm," he said in disbelief. He walked over to me, never breaking eye contact. He reached for the belt to my robe. I tried to block him.

"Seamus, seriously, I swear…" I faltered as he undid the belt.

"You know what I told you the last time I spoke to you, right?" he questioned.

"Shea," I backed away, "I didn't do this on purpose. I don't have to lie."

"Hmmm," he said as he gazed at my bare breasts, "you smell good enough to eat." With one swift movement, he grabbed my thighs and had me in the air. Instinctively, I grabbed for his head and wrapped my legs around his shoulders. *What the entire fuck?* Seamus quickly found my clitoris, pulling it into his mouth. He sucked, licked, and lapped at it expertly. Head game *strong.* His mouth was so big, hot, and felt amazing. I couldn't help but moan softly.

"Shhh," he said, pulling away from me. "You don't want your roommate to hear, do you?" Before I could answer, he went back to work. I felt my clit swelling as he made circular movements with his tongue. He began to rock my hips into his mouth as he palmed my ass. My body was betraying me. I had planned to play it cool, be supportive like Darren had suggested, but my body was having none of it. I hadn't been able to orgasm on my own since he had touched me last. My body was not going to be denied again.

"I'm gonna fall," I whispered.

"I got you, baby," he whispered back, against my pussy.

"Shea, I'm gonna come," I moaned softly.

"Come for me," he murmured.

Undone.

Waves of pleasure began to sweep over me. I hadn't had an orgasm this intense in my entire life. I dug my hands into his hair, clinging to him for dear life. He continued to suck, pulling wave after wave from my body. The orgasm was so intense I started seeing stars. *Am I losing consciousness?* I had heard of women passing out after orgasming, but I never thought it was real. If this was what his mouth did, I was indeed out of my league.

I came to with a cold rag on my head. Stacy was seated next to me, patting my hand. Shea was sitting across the room on the chaise, looking like the cat who ate the canary—literally!

"Hey sweetie, are you ok?" Stacy asked.

"What happened?" I said.

"Shea found you passed out in the bathroom. He couldn't rouse you, so he called for my help. When was the last time you ate?" She was genuinely concerned.

"Um, yesterday," I lied.

"See, that's the problem. When I'm not around, you don't eat." Stacy got up from the bed, fussing. She left the room to go grab something for me to eat.

"Liar," Shea said with a chuckle.

"What was I supposed to tell her?" I retorted.

"How about, I passed out from pleasure?" Shea recommended. "Or, I came so hard I blacked out—oh, how about, the head was so good—" he laughed as I interrupted him.

"I genuinely despise you," I quipped.

"I warned you," he stated seductively.

"Seamus, I swear, before all that is holy, I didn't do that on purpose," I whisper-screamed.

"I believe you, Butterfly," he said plainly.

"Then why the fu—" I stopped when Stacy re-entered the room with half a sandwich and a small bowl of soup.

"Eat! You will not leave here until after you eat," she stated, looking between Seamus and me.

"Yes, ma'am," we said in unison. The three of us sat in silence as I finished the food.

"Make sure she eats while y'all are gone, Shea." Stacy was stern with her instructions.

"Sure thing, boss!" he said, smiling.

"Don't let me find out you didn't eat." She directed her fussing at me.

"I promise," I said between bites.

I finished my food then shooed both of them out of the room so I could get dressed. Shea was dressed in joggers, a sweatshirt, and Adidas Ultra Boosts. I decided to match his comfort level. I put on leggings, Darren's jersey, and my Adidas NMDs. I slicked my hair back into a low ponytail and threw on a fitted Bears cap. I topped the look off with some large silver hoops and my Apple Watch. On the way out, I thanked Stacy for taking care of me. We hugged, then Seamus and I made our way to the elevator. The doors closed in front of us.

"Why did you do that, Seamus? You made me lie to my best friend," I shot at him.

"I thought I was your best friend," he mocked.

"Don't play with me, you know what I mean," I fussed.

"I wanted to see what you tasted like. I was reminded of the last time we were together, when I saw you there naked," Shea said softly.

"You literally just said that you wanted some time to think. You can't keep doing this," I said softly.

"I know what I said, but when I saw you, it went right out of the window. You are beautiful, and your body is simply amazing. I couldn't help myself. You taste so fucking good, Butterfly," Shea said earnestly. His honesty was dangerous.

Before I could formulate my next sentence, he was kissing me. He backed me up against the wall of the elevator. His lips, his mouth, his tongue all dripped with the scent of me. *Shit!* I was getting wetter. I savored it for a moment longer before logic took over. Pushing him off me, I was breathless. *Shit!*

"See, this is what I mean, Shea. You want me to stop asking you questions, but you can't stop doing things when we're together," I said breathlessly, trying to compose myself. "You're making me fall deeper and deeper in love with you."

"I know," he began.

"You know? God, Shea! Let's just go do this fitting and be done with today," I said.

"Ok," he said flatly.

"Thank you…for earlier," I said shyly.

"No, thank you," he said with renewed confidence.

We met the fellas at the tailor's shop so they could all be measured for their tuxes. Being around them was always a good time. We had all known each other since freshman year of college. The first to arrive, always on time, was Sherm.

"Awww, shucks!" Sherm said as he came around the corner and saw me.

We slapped our hands from way down low then brought it back again, bumped fists twice. On the third bump, we opened our hands and acted like there was an earthquake. We held our arms out for balance and everything!

Sherman "Sherm" Myers was the resident clown of the bunch.

Anyone with the name Sherman Myers had to be funny! He was as tall as he was wide. He was a chocolate dollop of handsomeness, with brown eyes, a broad nose, and thick lips. He said the ladies liked his thick lips. His hair was cut low in a Caesar, with waves for days. Waves on swim! Sherm played defensive end on the college football team. He was an all-city, all-state, all-conference athlete, and an all-around great guy. Sherm had even played in the NFL a few years before a career-ending injury forced him out of the league. He coached a local high school team, and his favorite pastime was hosting football camps for the inner-city kids, with the hopes of keeping them off the streets or preventing losing them to gun violence. Sherm's second favorite pastime was teasing Tish because he said she cursed like an old Black grandmother. He said if he closed his eyes, she sounded like his grandma, Mabel. Come to find out, Tish's nanny was an old Black woman who used to take her to the bingo hall.

"Let me get some of that, kinfolk!" J-Boogie said as he came into the shop. We repeated the handshake and hugged.

James "J-Boogie" Reid had been the captain of the lacrosse team. We all thought that was the most bourgeois shit we'd ever heard. None of us had ever met a brother who played lacrosse, but he came from money—old money. His family had owned slaves. It was something he wasn't proud of, and it caused him to overcompensate for it all the time. He was always giving to Black Lives Matter or the United Negro College Fund. Not that this was bad, he always thought people, Black people, wouldn't accept him if he wasn't giving off the appearance of being ultra "woke." He had a home with us, though, so he didn't put on a show. His nickname was the result of us flipping "Bougie" into Boogie. He was tall, lanky and the highest of yellows. He had very Eurocentric features. If you didn't know J-Boogie was Black, you would assume he was a white man. His hair was light brown and wavy, his eyes were gray, and his lips were thin, but he had a strong, chiseled jawline. He was handsome and had all of the ladies lining up to date him when we were younger.

"Miss James, Miss James, *Miss James!* Girl, you know you are still the baddest on the yard!" Ellis hooped in his southern drawl as he came through the door stomping. We all laughed, dapped, and hugged.

Ellis Kennedy was a riot and came to us by way of Leland, Mississippi. He was country, loud, and the baddest thing on two legs. Ellis set records on the track at the University of Chicago that still hadn't been broken. He had even made it to the Olympics and won gold. Ellis was on the cover of every magazine from *ESPN* to *Sports Illustrated*. The man was so fine that he dated nothing but supermodels. He was an analyst for *ESPN* and did the sports segment on *WGN*. Ellis was caramel complected, like me. He wasn't tall, but what he lacked in height he made up for in speed and personality. Ellis kept his hair short and faded. He didn't like facial hair, so he kept it off. Without it, El didn't look a day over twenty-five. He was still fit, too.

"Hey, where's Zeus?" Sherm asked.

"He couldn't make it," Shea said.

"Oh ok. Well, let's get this show on the road, baby!" Sherm said.

"You ready to do this?" J-Boogie asked Shea.

"Yeah, I think so," he answered.

"You think?" Ellis chimed in. "Boy, you betta know! Otherwise, I'm gone need my money back for this custom-made tux."

We all laughed. I was absolutely sure the shop owner was wondering how Shea had come to know this rowdy bunch. The tailor's assistant had brought out champagne for us while the boys waited to be measured. The bubbly was flowing, and so were the stories. I was amazed at how much trouble the five of them had gotten into without my knowledge.

"You didn't need to know everything, baby girl!" Ellis said slickly.

"I'm glad I didn't. My ears can't handle the debauchery. Sounds like y'all were a mess!" I joked.

"Your boy was the worst," Sherm said, pointing at Shea. "Remember those twins?"

"Yeah, the foreign exchange students from down under!" J-Boogie chimed in, with his best Australian accent.

"Guys," Shea said, looking at me guiltily, "let's not go down that hole!"

"That's what she said!" Sherm, J-Boog, and Ellis all said in unison as they fell out laughing.

I was laughing so hard I almost choked on my champagne—even the tailor was laughing. Shea was beet red with embarrassment, but he laughed at himself. We had a time reminiscing about the good old days and catching up. We hadn't all been together since the last summer. We all lived close by and tried to get together once a month, but lately, life was creeping in. We all agreed that we had to get together more often.

I told the guys that I had some plans to do just that.

"A groomsmen poker night and maybe a spa day," I suggested.

"You know, Sherm is all about pampering himself," he said in the third person.

"I don't know about the spa," Shea said doubtfully.

"Boy, if you don't shut yo metrosexual ass up!" Ellis cracked.

"I know, right," J-Boogie offered. "And y'all say *I'm* the bougie one!"

"Thank you, El!" I said, "He acts like he doesn't live in the spa getting facials and waxing his eyebrows."

"Those are necessary!" Shea chimed.

"Man, don't make me get on you today," Ellis popped back at Shea.

Shea laughed. "A'ight, man!"

"So, baby girl, whatcha got in mind for us?" Ellis asked sincerely.

"All I wanna know is am I gon' look *good?*" Sherm butt in.

Laughter erupted again.

"Yes, Sherm, you gon' look good!" I directed my next comment to Ellis. "Mani-pedis, facials, massages, and haircuts by Taj the barber."

"Quit playing!" Ellis shouted. Taj Parker was the premier barber in Chicago. He cut hair for a lot of the athletes on the pro teams around the city.

"How did you get Taj? I hear he's booked months out!"

"Let me guess," Shea said, "Darren."

"Darren...DW from college? Don't he play for the Bears now?" J-Boogie asked.

"Yes, Darren arranged it as a favor to me," I answered.

Shea turned around and looked at himself in the mirror. Ellis noticed the exchange and took note.

"Suga, you dealing with him again?" Ellis asked.

"He's different, Ellis," I said sincerely.

"Yeah, man, he's pretty chill. I've had some dealings with him recently," Sherm said. "He's a good dude. He donated to my foundation and made several appearances for free. He wants to do right by the kids. My man is the truth."

"They're dating now," Shea said in irritation.

"What?" they sang in unison.

"Okay," J-Boogie said, "I see you!"

"Sounds like you mad, brotha!" Ellis directed at Seamus jokingly.

"Nah, nothing like that. I know Darren's not MJ's type—won't last," Shea said casually.

"What the hell does that mean, Seamus?" I retorted angrily.

"Whoa now, ma!" Ellis said. "Shea, you need to chill. Why are you trippin'?"

"I don't want to have to save her ass like I did last time." Shea didn't turn around. He looked at me through the reflection in the mirror.

"Your ass is out of line, Seamus!" I said, getting up to walk over to him. "We were having a good time. Here you go shitting on the fun." Sherm grabbed my arm and walked me out of the shop. He knew I was pissed.

"Whoa, Lil Bit," Sherm said, trying to calm me down.

"No, Sherm—he's out of pocket."

"Yeah, but you don't understand the history behind why he's pissy."

"I know, he is the one who showed me Darren cheating. I understand why he doesn't like him, but we all grew the fu—grew up. He needs to let it go."

"Lil Bit, this stays between us," he said, looking in my eyes. "Seamus had a thing for you back in the day. We weren't ever gonna tell you, didn't see the need. I think seeing you with DW again must've brought some of those hard feelings."

"Sherm, that's some old bullshit"

I was pissed. All this time, Shea was mad at me for not saying something and he was holding in this whopper of a secret. My anger was rekindled. *The audacity of his ass!*

"Calm down, girl!" Sherm was confused. "We know something is going on between y'all. So, spill it."

I ran most of the situation down for Sherm, minus the sexual stuff.

"So, he doesn't want to talk about his feelings at all?" Sherm asked.

"No, I was trying to give him some space like Darren had said."

"Wait, wait, Darren knows about this too? I'm lost."

"Ok, Seamus lied to Chelsey about where I was when he ghosted me last year. She thinks I was in Singapore. So, I asked Darren to go with me and pretend to be my boyfriend. Sherm, it's a mess."

Sherm hugged me to him and comforted me. Ellis came out to check on us, and Sherm ran down the details on what was going on to fill Ellis in.

"Man, you know I was gon' root that out! He ain't even acting like hisself," Ellis said softly.

"Y'all, I don't know what to do. It's killing me knowing that Shea's going to marry another woman, and to top it all off, I have to stand by him as his Best Woman," I said softly.

"Naw, baby girl, we ain't having that. He gon' lay it out before he walk down the aisle. Ellis gon' make sure uh dat!" Ellis said assuredly.

"He cheatin' himself if he doesn't figure out how he feels about you. He tryna bury it, and that seed gon' come up another way if he doesn't handle it," Sherm said.

"We gotcha gurl," Ellis said. "Now, come on back in here and have fun. Don't let him dictate how you act."

We made our way back into the shop and finished the fitting—discussing whether I'd wear a dress or something else.

"She a woman," J-Boogie said. "She needs to be in a dress."

"Man, sit yo old fashioned ass down over there!" Ellis exclaimed, pointing to the other side of the shop.

"If I may," the tailor interrupted. "Why not wear a fitted tuxedo? Feminine, chic and tailored to your curves."

"Man, that would be straight fire!" Ellis said. Sherm agreed.

"You would look like a G standing up there with all of us!" Sherm added.

"Ok, I can see that," J-Boogie said. "That's hot."

We all looked at Seamus. He was pondering the idea.

"I'd have to run it by Chelsey," he said.

"Damn, she already gotcha balls," Ellis said slyly. Seamus cut him a dirty look. They laughed.

"Don't you get to select what the groomsmen wear?" J-Boogie asked.

"I do. To hell with it...let's go with that idea," Shea said, smiling at me.

The tailor helped me out of my chair and up onto the small platform to be measured. We were all to wear in tuxes. Mine would be ultra, *ultra* slim. I didn't even have to wear heels if I didn't want to for the ceremony. I was going to be totally comfortable. Yes!

"So, what's the plan after this, y'all?" J-Boogie asked.

"We're having dinner and drinks at the University Club," I said. *I hope I won't be blaming anything on the vodka or the tequila tonight.* I smiled at the thought.

Chapter Eight
CLUBBIN' CONFUSION

The University Club was one of the more upscale spots in the city. It boasted some of the most opulent weddings and galas. Darren was a member, so he asked his assistant to book us a private room for dinner. I didn't tell the boys that, because I didn't want to hear Seamus' mouth. We made our way to Seamus' house to change clothes. I was glad I'd kept some clothes and toiletries there. I went into my room to get dressed for the evening, when I heard a soft knock on my door.

Shea opened it. "Can I come in for a sec?" he asked.

"Sure. What's up?" I inquired.

"I wanted to apologize for earlier. You were trying to make things nice for me, and I let my feelings get—well…anyway, I'm sorry."

"It's cool. I think we need to unwind and relax tonight. It may do us some good."

"Agreed. Hug it out?" Shea asked.

I raised an eyebrow. "Don't know about that, homie," I said jokingly.

"I'll behave. Scout's honor!"

"You weren't a scout, boy!" He strolled over and wrapped me up in his embrace. I hugged him back.

"We cool?" he asked, looking down at me.

"We cool," I said, looking up at him.

I was wearing a black pinstriped pencil skirt with a sheer black button-down top with a cute bow at the top. I added my La Perla Ambra bodysuit underneath to give it some umph! My outer layer was a Saint Laurent Calf leather moto jacket. I paired it with some high-heeled leather boots. My makeup and jewelry were subdued, and my hair was up in a high chignon. I looked damned good. Seamus' eyes examined me as I came down the stairs. He had chosen to wear navy slacks with a navy-blue button-down shirt and a Tom Ford Atticus jacket. He wore a navy Salvatore Ferragamo ensemble on his feet and waist, accompanied by a Zenith watch on his arm. He was definitely a sight to see, as well. I devoured him with my eyes when I thought no one was watching. *Shit*. He looked good enough to eat.

We took a group photo before piling into two black Chevy Suburbans and heading toward our alma mater. We pulled up to the University Club of Chicago and were led to our private room.

"I'm getting faded tonight," Ellis drawled slowly.

"Alright, now," Shea said addressing us all. "Remember, we can't get *bleedin' gargled*. We're meeting Chelsey and her friends later on."

"No, *you* can't get drunk, but we can!" Ellis said.

"It's not just dinner, guys. We're hitting the club later. We're meeting Zeus and the ladies then poker later on," I said, informing them.

"So, we're going out *too*?" Sherm asked, surprised.

"Yeah, baby!" I said. I stopped to do a twerk movement. I adjusted quickly as I caught Shea's disapproving eyes.

"You, my muhfucka!" Ellis said as he scooped me up swinging me wildly. I giggled.

"Can y'all act like y'all got some sense?" J-Boogie asked under his breath.

"J, shut yo ass up!" we all said in unison as El put me down. Even Shea was with us on this one. We were going to kick it, smoke some cigars, and enjoy our young lives tonight.

After we were seated, I began perusing the menu. Ironically, the menu consisted of pork medallions. This tickled me richly. We were sitting in the Princeton room. The space was large enough to accommodate multiple tables, but there was one table in the center of the room set for five, with cushioned leather high back chairs around it. The tablecloth was white linen with place settings consisting of beautiful china plates and crystal glasses. The walls were library panel from floor to ceiling. The room dripped of masculine elegance, luxurious and refined for the board and club members. I made a mental note to apply for membership. *I shouldn't have had to go through Darren to set this up,* I thought. He had helped a lot because he knew I was tortured dealing with Shea's impending marriage.

Our food came out after we'd done several shots of Don Q Gran Reserva de la Familia Serralles. We were all slightly inebriated by then.

"You spared no expense, huh, MJ?" Sherm asked.

"Nothing but the best for my BFF," I said, winking at Sherm.

"How much did them bottles cost?" Ellis asked.

"They were a gift from a friend," I casually responded.

"Let me guess, DW?" J-Boogie said sarcastically.

"Does it matter?" I replied, with a smile.

"Keep your secret, MJ," Sherm said. "I don't care how you got them." He picked up his glass and drained it.

"Naw now, the Gran Reserva was a limited release. I couldn't get my hands on any, so I'm tryna see if I can get the same hookup," Ellis pressed.

"Let it go, El," I said, looking from him to Shea, who let the conversation pass without adding anything to it. Undoubtedly, he knew where I'd gotten the Don Q. He raised his glass to me in cheers, then drained it.

Our waiter cleared the table as the fellas chatted about the upcoming events.

"This is a lot better than your girl's attempt at cooking, huh?" I said, referring to our meal while leaning over to Shea. I thought I was quiet, but when you're *bleedin' gargled*—or really drunk—you have no volume button.

"Wait, what?" Sherm said, turning from his conversation with El and J. "Yo girl cooks, Seamus?"

"Burns is more like it," I said to myself. The fellas howled with laughter.

"MJ, she can't cook?" Ellis asked

"Huh? My momma said if you can't say something nice," I snickered, "don't say anything at all."

"You already opened your mouth and inserted your foot," Shea said. He was annoyed.

"Shit, I was thinking it. Did I say that out loud? Well, damn...I'm sorry," I snickered again. I reached for my drink, and Seamus moved it.

"That's enough for you," he said, before downing my glass.

"Man, let her live. We're celebrating the big day. You're the man of the hour! Don't rain on her parade," J-Boogie said.

"She's had enough," Seamus said. He meant it too.

"Seamus, you know we got her. We won't let anything happen to her," Sherm said.

"Yeah," Ellis added, "chill." Seamus looked at me. I knew what the look meant. I was sure there'd be some ass smacking somewhere in my future.

"Excuse me, sir," I said to the waiter. "Can you bring me some coffee?"

"Yes, ma'am," he said as he turned on his heels to retrieve it.

Unfortunately, I had to sip coffee with my dessert. I was practically sober by the time we left the University Club. The hawk was kicking a little bit, but it was refreshing as we made our way to the bar. We met Chelsey, and her friends, at the XYZ bar of the W downtown for drinks. I noticed Seamus' mood had improved, so I imbibed and chatted up Chelsey's friends. They introduced themselves as Jen, Monica, Kayla, and Charity. They may as well have said their names were Karen, Carin, and Karyn. They were straight corn flakes. No frosting or marshmallows to liven them up, at all. Chelsey had surrounded herself with moderately attractive women. I bet she did it to make herself look better. They met in boarding school and had been friends since they were little. Their parents were friends as well, so their families had vacationed together. They were your quintessential rich kids.

"So," her friend Jen asked, "how long have you known Seamus?"

"Since college. We all went to the University of Chicago," I responded.

"He's dreamy, huh?" she asked.

"Uh, I guess," I said. *Where is she going with this?* I wondered.

"I noticed you looking at him. Are you into him or something?" *Ah, there it is,* I thought.

"Sweetie, I barely know you. You need to fall all the way back," I sneered.

"Chelsey's my best friend, so I'm very protective of her—and her boo. Don't get any ideas," she said smugly.

"Or *what?*" I said, looking at her as I screwed my lips all the way up.

"Well, uh—" she started.

"You didn't think that through, did you?" I asked boldly. "I'm Seamus' best friend, and I'm going to be in his life. I don't give a damn who comes or goes. I'm the constant. Got me?"

I didn't give her a chance to answer. I saw Jesús coming in the door and moved to greet him.

"Zeus! My man!" I shouted. "What's good?" I left Jen sitting where she was with her mouth hanging open.

"Ay, Mami!" he said as he swooped me up into a big bear hug. "*Es todo bien, ahora!* Ma said to tell all y'all *hola!*"

Zeus put me down. "Hey y'all, look who's here!" I shouted as I led him to the table.

Of all of the crew's men, Dionísio Gabriel de Jesús Navarro was by far the finest. He referred to himself as Chicago's finest by way of Puerto Rico. He was born in Ponce, PR, and came to the mainland after his father died. His mother was the only family he had in Chicago. Most of his relatives lived in New York. Zeus had an affinity for reggaeton and had introduced the crew to several artists like Ozuna, Tego Calderon, and Nesi, because he DJ'd to help put himself through school. We knew the parties he DJ'd were gonna be fire, and we never had to pay to get in.

He earned his nickname our freshman year when he tried to cuff me.

I promptly told him, "Return yo' big son of Zeus lookin' ass back to Mount Olympus and sit the fuck down," because he was disrupting the class. Our professor laughed so hard she had to dismiss class. Zeus didn't get it. So after class, I explained that his first name was similar to Dionysus, Zeus's son. Stacy and Rho started calling him Baby Zeus, and before long, we dropped the baby.

His mom, Marie Carmen, was mom number three to the crew. Zeus spent a substantial portion of his time tending to her and working to cover her medical bills.

The fellas all came over to dap him up, while I went to the bar to get him a rum and coke. We all had a drink that was *our* signature drink—Zeus' was rum and coke. Zeus had turned me on to Puerto Rican Rum on my twenty-first birthday in the apartment I shared with Stacy. He brought some homemade brouhaha called Coquito. It was a coconut drink made with coconut milk, condensed milk, and Don Q rum. He said it was usually served at Christmas. I was fucked up after my first glass. He had told us that some people put eggs in it.

"Like eggnog," I slurred quizzically from the couch.

"Yeah, but real *boricuas* ain't putting eggs in Coquito unless it's Co-quito bread pudding!"

Puerto Rican rum had been our thing ever since. I returned with a drink as Zeus found a seat with the other guys. Chelsey came over, kissed me on my cheek, and chatted me up. After about an hour at the W, we made our way over to the Shark Bar. We'd been frequenting that haunt since our college days. It had recently changed to a thirty and older club. We loved that we didn't have to deal with the younger crowd. It was mature, sexy upscale fun. It wasn't a dive, like the Guerrilla Bar.

"So," Chelsey said hotly in my ear, "I hear you're wearing a tux with the guys."

"Yes, we all thought it would be cool. Does that bother you?" I asked. I genuinely hoped I would never have to wear the thing, but if I had to, I wanted her to be ok with it.

"No, I think it's awesome!" Her nasally vocal fry was made worse with the alcohol. *What the entire fuck is Seamus thinking? Seriously.* "Cool," I said.

Chelsey told me Jen was her maid of honor, and the two of us should get together to plan some bridal party meet-ups. I didn't want to deal with Jen, but I didn't want to make waves either.

"Yeah, sure. I'll get Jen's number before we leave tonight. Are you all coming back to the house later?" I asked.

"We hadn't planned on it. Why?" she asked, looking confused.

"We were playing poker. I thought maybe Seamus mentioned— well...you can work that out with him. I'm sure the fellas won't mind," I slurred.

"I'll check with Sheamy!" she whined.

"Alright," I said.

The liquor was hitting me a little too hard for her vocal fry. The Shark Bar was crowded that night. We waded into the sea of bodies on the dance floor as Cardi B blasted through the giant speakers hanging from the ceiling. That was my shit!

It was hot, and we were packed in tight on the dance floor. I faced away from Shea as we danced. It was so dark and crowded that it was impossible for Chelsey or the rest of our crew to see us. His hand rested on my lower back as I bent forward to bounce my burgeoning ass on him when I got a little space. I felt the length of him as I slid up and down. I looked over my shoulder at him. His eyes were dark, but I made out his expression. Pure lust! I knew he wanted me, so I whined my hips on the length of his now-swollen dick. He pulled me up, wrapping his right hand around my waist. Our bodies were snug as we swayed to the rhythm of Cardi's banger. I reached up behind me to snake my hand around his neck. He let his other hand rest on my hip as he pressed himself against me. The DJ slowed the music down after Cardi's song ended. I heard the first few refrains of a Bryson Tiller song and began to head off the floor, when Shea grabbed my wrist, pulling me back. The dance floor was still packed, and we were extremely close when we began to dance. All of me was on all of him. I felt his rock hard cock against the softness of my abdomen. My panties were instantly wet.

Shea cupped my ass while bringing his right hand upward to my breast to flick my nipple. I tried to pull away, but he had a vice grip on my ass.

"Wrap your hands around my neck, Butterfly," he commanded.

"Shea, don't," I said, trying to pull away.

"Don't make me ask again," he whispered softly against my neck. I complied with his request. He grinded himself into me. The friction caused the bodysuit to ride up into my clit. *Shit! He's going to make me come right here on the dance floor with our friends nearby*. I tried to wriggle out of his grip.

"Maeve," he whispered in my ear, "I want to be inside you right now. I bet your pussy is so tight...so wet." He never stopped moving, flicking, grinding...*Fuck!* I leaned into him as I felt my orgasm about to unravel.

"This fucking outfit!" he whispered gruffly into my ear. "Fucking La Perla, Maeve. What the *fuck* do you know about La Perla? If I could, I'd take you into the bathroom...fuck you...then make you lick your own juices off my dick as you blow me." The visual I got from what he was saying made me come so hard.

"Seamus," I murmured against him as each wave racked my body.

"It's taking everything within me, Maeve, not to find a dark spot in this club to *buck*." I scanned my Irish slang mental dictionary. *Buck means fuck*, I thought. *Wait, he wants to fuck me?* This small tidbit of information sent me spiraling into an intense orgasm. Oh, how I wanted to *buck* him too! Another rush of pleasure hit as he continued his assault on my body. Seamus made me orgasm on that crowded dance floor like we were the only two people in there. *I want him to fuck me in the worst possible way*. I orgasmed through the latter half of "Exchange", and the beginning of Ella Mai's "Boo'd Up."

When I was finally able to stand on my own, Shea lifted my chin so I could look him in his eyes. They were screaming for relief. He led me through the crowd to the back of the club, to a stairwell. He led us upstairs. We reached the top of the stairs, then followed a dark hallway until we came to an exit sign. He opened the door and stepped out onto the roof, propping the door open with a nearby paint can. He didn't have to ask, because I willingly dropped down and began to unbuckle his Ferragamo belt. I undid his pants and pulled his engorged member from an underwear prison. I took him into my mouth, beginning my ministrations. I slid up and down the length of him, occasionally pausing to work his swollen tip. I was hungry for his orgasm like it was T-bone steak, cheese eggs, and Welch's grape. If you don't know, now you know. Yup, Biggie reference!

His moans were drowned out by the club noises and the street sounds below. He wound my now loose hair around his hand as he slammed his cock into my mouth. I don't know how I didn't gag. It wasn't long before he was coming in hot spurts down my throat. He tasted sweet. He didn't stop until I had swallowed every last drop of his ejaculation. He stood there with his cock in my mouth, momentarily savoring the last bits of pleasure before he pulled me up from my squatting position. As I stood, he tucked himself back into his pants and fixed himself up like brand new. He reached for the bottom of my skirt, hiking it up to my waist.

"I need to clean you up," he said, as he bent down and pulled my bodysuit to the side.

There was a chill in the air, but it was quickly forgotten once his mouth latched on to me. He licked up all of the wetness he created from the orgasms he had given me downstairs. I began to rock my hips into his hot mouth, when I felt the pull of another orgasm. *Shit, what is he doing to me?* My knees almost buckled when my orgasm washed over me. Shea going down on me atop one of the hottest night clubs in the city with the skyline shimmying off the lake in my foreground was sexy as hell. I gripped his shoulders for balance until all of the contractions from my orgasm ceased. Then, only when he was confident I was "clean," he fixed my clothing, stood, and kissed me passionately.

Chapter Nine
BREAKFAST & SHENANIGANS

A s I made my way downstairs, I scanned our section to see all of our friends still sitting in VIP. They were laughing and carefree. No one knew we'd slipped off. We danced a little while longer then made our way back over to our respective sides of the VIP.

I was sitting in the corner of the couch, people-watching and sipping my drink, when I noticed Zeus get up and leave. Shortly after, Chelsey headed in the same direction. *What's up with that?* My busybody senses were tingling!

I scooted past Ellis and ambled in the direction I'd seen them go. I got halfway down the hall when I heard a man and woman arguing.

"You need to tell him," the man was saying. He sounded angry.

"It's not that easy...this will hurt him," the woman said. She sounded conflicted.

"I don't want to lose you, and I'm tired of waiting. We need to tell him soon," the man ground out angrily.

I cut into the women's bathroom at the sound of retreating footsteps. I was chatting with the attendant when I saw Chelsey walk in. She was crying.

"Hey," I said, walking over to her. "Are you ok?" I asked, genuinely concerned.

"Oh." She was surprised to see me. "Yeah, I'm ok. I...I think Sheamy is mad at me." She broke into a fresh sob.

"What makes you think that?" I said, regretting I had asked her what was wrong.

"He seems preoccupied and he hasn't danced with me all night," she said, wiping at her tears. "Did he say anything to you when you talked with him?" she asked me.

"None of us are dancing, really," I said, turning to look at our full section.

"See, this is what I mean. I'm over here and he's way over there," she complained.

"He seems fine," I said. "Why don't you go ask him to dance?"

"I did earlier. He told me he needed to sit down for a while."

"Oh," I said nonchalantly, "well, give him some time. We've all had a lot to drink."

Shit! Maybe our impromptu sex-capade, coupled with our alcohol consumption, drained him. I sensed she was lying, but what was I going to do, accuse her? One thing I could say about this chick was she quick. She covered her tracks well. I couldn't really catch the man's voice, but I had a nagging suspicion it was Zeus and Chelsey who were arguing. About what, though? Tonight was the first time the fellas met Chelsey. *It couldn't be that,* I thought.

I rubbed her back then made my way back to our section thinking Puerto Rican rum was a motherfucker. I stood in front of the VIP section, waiting for the large bouncer to notice me.

"Oh," he said, finally looking down. "I didn't see you there."

"No worries," I said, walking through the entrance when he removed the blue velvet rope to let me pass. I walked up two steps and took a seat near Zeus. I surveyed the section for a moment. Everyone was engrossed in conversation, except Zeus—he seemed to have something on his mind. I noticed Chelsey leaning over the rail, chatting with her friends. Aside from Jen, her other three bridesmaids were unremarkable. They stayed to themselves, only speaking when spoken to directly. They weren't overly friendly with us, but I could tell by the way they interacted with one another they were great friends. *Why didn't she come back into the VIP section?* I pondered. I looked across our section and saw Shea talking with two men from a neighboring couch. He seemed to be having a good time. *Was Chelsey lying to me?* I wondered.

I leaned over in my seat toward Zeus and said, "Penny for your thoughts, *mi amigo?*"

"Huh?" he shouted over the music.

I wasn't going to repeat myself, so I said, "I noticed you staring at Chelsey. So, what do you think of her?" He paused for a moment, staring at me intently, trying to read any hidden meaning behind my question.

"She seems nice enough," he finally said. "What about you?

"She's cool. I'm still getting used to her voice, though," I said, looking at Zeus with a smirk.

He laughed, then changed the subject. We chatted about work, Max's death, and some other random topics. In the back of my mind, I made a mental note that he didn't want to discuss Chelsey.

Later that night, I wandered over to Jen, Chelsey's sourpuss Maid of Honor, to get her number. Jen was an inch or two taller than me with mousy brown hair, brown eyes, and was a bit portly. She and Chelsey were an unlikely pair. They were polar opposites in the looks department, and Jen was rough around the edges. We exchanged numbers and talked for a bit. Then she broke the number one cardinal rule when it came to Black women and their hair. Yup! This bitch put her hands in my hair. I wanted to choke her instantly. That night Jen had gotten WGW—White Girl Wasted. Apparently, the drunker she got, the hotter I became. She'd gone from threatening me to asking me if I'd sit on her face because well—

"You look like you taste so fucking good," she whined into my ear before sucking the diamond-covered lobe into her disgusting mouth. Her hand was wound in my hair as she pulled my face closer to her.

"Have you lost your *gaht damn* mind!" I yelled at her as I mushed her in the face to get her off me.

"Sitcho goofass down!" Ellis quipped as he moved her from my space and sat her on the opposite end of the couch. Chelsey was trying to help Ellis calm her down.

Security came over to make sure everything was ok. J explained what happened and told the bouncer that we had the situation under control. I ended up having to undo my bun because a portion of my hair was pulled loose when she pawed at me. I had my hair straightened for the day, so it was easier to manage. *This bitch just fucked up my look.* Shea noticed I was irritated after I finger-combed through my tangled tresses.

"You still look sexy," he said, winking at me.

What the entire fuck does he think he's doing? I thought. Chelsey was right next to me! I was so surprised she hadn't heard him. Jen was keeping up a commotion. She was still going on about how gorgeous I was when Ellis handed her some water.

"Calm down, girl, *damn*," he fussed.

We kicked it so hard at the W and the Shark Bar that the poker game was called on the count of drunkenness. I was so gone I crashed in my room back at Shea's house fully-dressed, shoes and all.

The house was quiet when my eyes opened. I was quite hungover, but the Bad Bitch in my brain was upon and at it early today. I laid their pondering our oral session on the club roof. I got up around 11 am and changed out of last night's clothes. I grabbed a pair of shorts and a t-shirt from my dresser. I picked up my phone and shot my mom a text apologizing for missing church again then wandered down to the kitchen.

To my surprise, Seamus was up preparing breakfast. I washed my hands and joined him. He was making French toast, eggs, bacon, and fruit. I grabbed the strawberry stem remover and a knife from the drawer. I then began peeling, chopping, and placing fruit on a platter. We worked alongside one another in silence. It was nice.

I needed some coffee badly. I found the Kona coffee in the pantry. We had fallen in love with it on our group trip to Hawaii. I made quick work of brewing a pot of strong coffee. I poured myself a cup, then Seamus. I added cream and sugar as he preferred it. We liked our coffee the same way.

"Thanks," he sang as I handed him a mug.

"You're in a good mood, what's up?" I asked curiously.

"I had fun yesterday. I think things went well. Chelsey was singing your praises too."

"Dude, how long have you been up? We were fucked up last night! I don't know how I made it to my room!" I giggled over my mug.

"Sherm tossed you in there. None of them were brave enough to get you out of your clothes." He chuckled.

"Except you," I said, side-eyeing him mercilessly.

"I'm not afraid of you, Lil Bit!" He had used the fellas' nickname for me.

"Tell me something I don't know."

I laughed and set my mug down so I could pull some plates, silverware, and glasses out of the cabinets. I placed them on the island in the middle of his kitchen, then grabbed the juice and preserves from the fridge.

"J-Boogie has gotta be the bougie-est joker I know. Who puts preserves on French toast?" I joked.

"I know, right!" Shea said. "Errbody else uses syrup!" Shea copied Ellis's southern drawl correctly. I was cracking up when the fellas joined us.

"What's so funny, Lil Bit?" Ellis asked suspiciously.

"Nothing!" I lied.

"Lies, lies, lies!" Sherm said. "I thought we were friends, Lil Bit!"

"Don't be like that," J-Boogie said.

"Nah, we were joking about the fruit preserves—"

"Mocking me!" J interrupted in feigned offense. "Don't knock it till you try it is all I'm gonna say!"

"Man, we eat syrup on ours," Seamus joked. "J-Bougie!"

J-Boogie threw the kitchen towel at Seamus while the rest of us laid over on the nearest hard surface laughing.

Bing!

I picked up my phone. It was Stacy.

Stace: What y'all doing?
Me: Bout to eat breakfast
Stace: And y'all couldn't invite me!
Me: Girl, ain't nobody gotta invite you. You know
         you're welcome to come.
Stace: Did you tell Tisha and Rho y'all was getting to-
         gether?
Me: Nah, last night was the bridal party meet up.
         Grab them and come on.
Stace: You ain't right
Me: 😂😂😂
Stace: OMW

I looked up from my phone to see all of the fellas staring at me.
"What?" I said, looking at them like they were crazy.
"Who was that?" Shea asked. "Darren?"
I laughed. "No, Stacy. She's picking up Tish and Rho. So, make some more breakfast, boy!"
"Oh, hell naw!" Ellis said. "I'm leaving ratch now!"
We all fell out laughing. Ellis and Rho had fought like cats and dogs since college. If he said the sky was blue, she said it was green. I had never seen two people go at it like those two. They were a constant source of serious hilarity for us over the years. Seamus and I exchanged knowing glances. It was about to go down!

Chapter Ten
THE TRUTH IS OUT

Twenty minutes later, we heard the girls come in. I ran to unlock the door after they called from the gate. Rho burst through the door, loud and boisterous, followed by Tisha and Stacy.

"We up in he-yuh! What's up, fellas? Ellis," she said disdainfully as she eyeballed Ellis. She came in and hugged everyone but Ellis.

"Gon' with that now! You ain't been here two seconds, and you already starting mess," Ellis sighed loudly.

"Are we gonna have to separate you two?" Seamus asked, his accent peeking through as he laughed. Rho and Ellis both looked at him like he was crazy, and he roared with laughter.

"Ain't shit funny, Seamus!" Rho and Ellis said in unison.

"Hey, y'all!" Tish squealed as she went around the room greeting everyone.

"Whaddup," Stacy said as she made her way into the kitchen. "Wat yuh doin' up in here,

Seamus?" she asked as she strolled over to the stove where he was. Her greeting was succinct. She had plans to do one thing, and one thing only, take over Seamus' kitchen.

"*Trying* to cook!" J-Boogie hollered from the corner.

"Shutcho ass up, J," Seamus hollered back. We all laughed except J-Boogie.

"Forget all of y'all!" he yelled over our laughter.

I looked around the room and was in pure heaven. It made my heart swell to see all of my old friends together again. We were only missing one person, Zeus. Stacy scrubbed in and took over Shea's kitchen. Within ten minutes, she was cranking out a stack of French toast.

"See, now that's what I'm talking about," J-Boogie said.

"J, we done told you once," Shea and Stacy said in unison.

"I know—shut my ass up," he said sullenly. "I hate y'all's asses. I can't even talk!"

"Stay in yo lane," Rho told him.

"Rho, don't start. I'm not Ellis. I will light yo ass up!" J-Boogie joked.

"Try me, boo!" Rho tossed back.

"So, Lil Bit, what's up with the bachelor party?" Tish asked. Before I could answer Rho chimed in.

"All I know is I'm goin'," Rho stated.

"Oh, no the hell you ain't," Ellis countered.

"We'll see!" Rho said with her hand on her hip.

"Yeah, we'll see a'ight. We'll see yo' dusty ass sittin' ratch here!" he countered.

"Y'all two need to screw one more time for posterity, hell. I'm tired of y'all!" Stacy shot at them then grimaced. She was supposed to take that secret to the grave.

"One more time?" Sherm asked. "Whatchu, you mean, Stacy?"

We echoed his sentiments. *When did this happen? Why didn't any of us remember it?*

Rho and Ellis clammed up. Stacy looked down, then at them. They nodded their consent for her to tell the story. So, Stacy regaled us with the twisted, torrid tale of how these two mortal enemies hooked up. Turns out, Rho and Ellis slept together sophomore year as some sort of stress relief from finals week. Since then, Ellis had been upset because Rho told him he had a little dick and no rhythm. He told her she had been run through and didn't have any walls.

"It's the truth," Rho stated when Stacy finished her story.

"Just 'cause yo pussy's the Bermuda Triangle don't mean I'm little."

"Bermuda Triangle!" I exclaimed.

"Yeah—dudes fall in and ain't never heard from again."

We hollered.

"Fuck you, you cave-dwelling bat. Grow some more dick and maybe you could satisfy a woman," Rho said.

"Bitch, my dick ain't little! I've had plenty of women who can vouch for that!" he said confidently.

"Crackheads and junkies don't count, asshole!" Rho flung back swiftly. We were hollering watching them go at it. Just like the good old days, man!

Shea walked over to the table with a mason jar and set it down. Everyone stopped and looked at him like he was crazy.

"A'ight, we said we were gonna stop cursing. So, the next one who does needs to drop some doubloons in the jar!" Shea said.

"Well, if that's the case, you need to dump your entire wallet in there," I said. "Your mouth is downright dirty when you're—" Before I could say *drunk*, he spit hot sarcasm in my face.

"Well, you would know, MJ," Shea responded slickly.

Bastard, you fucking bastard, I thought. I guess I deserved it. Gaht damn.

Everyone in the kitchen quieted down. The tension between Shea and me was palpable. I turned, walking out of the kitchen. I found my purse on the console near the front door, grabbed my wallet, pulled out a hundred-dollar bill, then walked back into the silent kitchen. With all eyes on me, I deposited it straight into the mason jar.

"Would you ever *cop on to yourself,* Shea! I swear, sometimes you're *as thick as a maggot, you buck eejit!* " I shot daggers at him when I finished berating him. He sighed in response to my Northern Ireland slang riddled tirade.

Everyone scrambled for their purses and wallets, pushing and shoving as they went, to find some cash—leaving the two of us in the kitchen alone in a staring contest. When they returned, they began cramming money in the jar.

"Spill, Seamus?" Stacy was the first to ask.

"Go on, big mouth," I said sarcastically. "Might as well tell 'em."

Shea recounted how he'd made me pass out. Stacy, Rho, and Tish's heads were all on a swivel in harmony when they turned to look at me.

"Bitch!" Tish said.

"Get yo little ass upstairs, now!" Stacy said.

"Make sure you put some money in the jar, bastard!" I said heatedly to Shea.

I turned and walked out of the kitchen. The girls followed me up to my room. I wasn't in my bedroom two seconds before Stacy hopped in my ass.

"Were you gonna tell us, Maeve?" she retorted.

"Yes," I replied sheepishly.

"Fuck that," Tish laughed. "He made you blackout, for real?"

"That's what the hell I wanna talk about," said Rho, clapping and smacking her lips. Stacy was visibly mad.

"Stace, I'm sorry. I was going to tell you, but things kept getting worse and worse! First, it was kissing, then he was fingering me, then making me pass out. And yesterday I—"

"Fingering you?" Tish asked. "Yesterday?"

"MJ, he's getting married, and you're fucking around with him?" Stacy asked. "What are you thinking?"

"Sounds like she's thinking about giving it up—finally," Rho chimed in.

"You need to spill it, sis!" Stacy ground out harshly.

I outlined all of the events that had taken place over the last few months. What blew everyone's mind was the fact that he had gone down on me with Stacy in the house, then pretended like I fainted.

"Damn," Rho added.

"And?" Stacy questioned incredulously, "There's more?"

I relayed the events that occurred the previous night at the club. I knew I shouldn't have been ashamed, but I hated that my friends found out what was going on like this. *Shit!*

"Wait, what?" Rho screamed.

"Seamus is cold-blooded, had me thinking you were hypoglycemic and shit. Y'all ain't right!" Stacy said.

"Girl, what was I supposed to tell you, I blacked out after getting licked down? I was embarrassed."

"I don't know if I'm madder at the fact that Darren knew, and I didn't or the fact that I was in the house while y'all were fuckin'!" she said laughing.

"We didn't have sex. It's just been oral and hand stuff," I started.

"That's the Whitish shit I've ever heard you say," Tish sputtered with laughter. "One, oral sex *is* sex! Two, you are crazy as hell for putting your panties in his pocket."

"And three! Sucking his dick, *and swallowing*, in the vicinity of his woman...that's some gangsta ass shit right there," Rho added.

"Do you love him?" Stacy asked.

"Yes," I answered, "I told him while you were in Trinidad."

"Wait," Stacy said shaking her head, "you told him before you found out about the fiancée? You lyin' ass troll! I should kick you down the *gaht* damned stairs. You should've told me then!"

"I know. I was too embarrassed to say it, though."

"Why in hell are you his Best Woman and not fighting to be *his* woman?" she asked.

"He has to want me to be his woman. He has all the information, but he refuses to talk about it."

"The Caucasity," Rho said emphatically. "He won't talk about it, but he eats you out every chance he gets?"

"He won't talk about how he feels. It's my fault because I pushed him away when he wanted to try," I said sullenly.

"Girl, fuck the dumb shit," Rho began. "He loves you. It's not too late!"

"Yes, girl, but is he *in* love with me?" I asked. "What pisses me off is that he made me feel bad for not telling him, but he did the same thing."

"Typical male bullshit," Tish said.

"A'ight, we have to get y'all to talk about this," Stacy said.

"Yeah," Rho said in agreement.

"Are you good?" Tish asked seriously.

"So far," I said.

"Let's go back downstairs. I'm hungry as fuck," Rho said.

I knew the fellas were downstairs discussing the same thing. Everyone knew what we'd been doing. I was embarrassed, but it wasn't going to change. When I walked into the kitchen, all of the fellas, except Shea, pretended to pass out. They threw their hands up to their foreheads and swooned.

"Fuck *all* y'all!" I said, pointing around the room. "I hate all of you—especially you!" I laughed as I looked at Seamus.

They all got a good laugh at my expense.

Sorry, Seamus mouthed to me from where he was sitting at the bar.

Me too, I mouthed back.

"You don't have anything to worry about, Lil Bit," Ellis said. He caught our interaction, leaned over and said to me, "If anyone knows how you feel, it's Rho and me." She nodded in agreement.

It felt good to clear the air. I felt like a weight had lifted. I had the support of my friends, so I soldiered on.

"So, bruh, you still gonna go through with the wedding?" J-Boogie asked. All eyes fell on Seamus. He swallowed hard, looked at me then to J-Boogie.

"I made a commitment. It's...I-I can't back out now," he said.

I wanted to cry but I held it together. I wanted to fight for him, but I felt it would be easier preparing my heart to watch the man I loved marry another woman. Deep down, I was hoping he'd change his mind.

"So, we goin' to Vegas for the party?" Rho asked, changing the subject.

"Now, don't start that, Rho," Ellis said. "We already said y'all can't come."

"*Y'all* ain't said shit," Rho barked back. "*You* said we couldn't, but you ain't the boss."

"Hold on, guys," I said. "This is Seamus' big hoorah. He should say who he wants to come. That being said—Seamus?" I threw the decision to him.

Ellis was begging and pleading for him to say no. Stacy, Tisha, and Rho were all pleading for him to say yes. Seamus looked at me in frustration, but I was not making that decision. It made me happy to see him squirm.

"Ladies, let me think about it," he finally said.

"Well, don't think too damn long. We need to buy tickets, Seamus!" Rho fussed.

"Rho, shutcho ass up," Tish fussed. "You're gonna mess it up for all of us!"

"Well, if they go, I'm not going!" Ellis issued his ultimatum to Seamus.

Seamus got a wicked gleam in his eyes. "Ladies, it looks like you're going to Vegas!"

The four of us were jumping around, giving each other high fives, and celebrating like we won the Super Bowl. J-Boogie and Sherm were happy, but Ellis was throwing an all-out hissy fit.

"It's like that, Seamus? After all we been through? Man, fuck all that! This some ol' bullshit!" He was genuinely pissed.

"El, they were coming regardless of what you said. MJ was gonna be the only chick there. Do you think she wants to spend the whole time with us?" Sherm asked.

"Yeah, even I thought they'd be coming with us," J-Boogie said.

"So, we ain't gon' be with them 24/7?" Ellis asked. The four of us swiveled on him and said, "Hell, naw!"

The whole room erupted in laughter. Ellis simmered down, seeming to be pleased with the fact that he didn't have to be linked up with Rho for the whole trip. I didn't really understand why he and Rho fought so hard. I was looking forward to Vegas. It was going to be the last hoorah for our little troop of single friends. The next trip would have an extra person...Chelsey.

"Hey," Sherm said, "where the hell is Zeus?"

"I was just wondering the same thing," Tish replied.

"Come to think of it," I said, "he's been MIA for a while now."

"He was acting funny last night when I invited him to stay here,"

Shea said, "but I assumed it was because of his mom."

"Ah, well, yeah," Tish muttered. Zeus' mom had been sick for quite some time. We all took turns going by to check on her or calling to see if she needed anything. She was in hospice, and things didn't look well.

"We need to go see her," Stacy recommended.

"I don't know if we'll have time this weekend," I responded. "We're going to be meeting up with Chelsey and her friends this evening. Bridal party 'team-building' event. You know, support the happy couple and all," I could feel my face balling up as I was speaking.

"Well, damn Gina, why you gotta make that face?" J-Boogie asked jokingly.

"Is it that bad?" I questioned. I was met with a resounding *yes* from everyone in the kitchen.

"Ugh, fuck all y'all!" I said as I got up to clear my plate. Everyone pretended to pass out—gasping *orgasmically*. I looked at Seamus and gave him the finger.

"I blame you for this foolishness, fucker!" I gave everyone else the finger too. Laughter erupted from the kitchen.

"Babe," Seamus said, "Chelsey called to cancel that this morning. Jen can't make it."

"*Babe?*" Stacy questioned.

"Shit," Seamus said, "I-I-"

"Well, I-I," Ellis mocked. We cackled some more. It was now Shea giving us the finger.

"Man, you need to figure that shit out!" Rho said.

"I know that's right," Tish reiterated. "Let Chelsey catch yo ass callin' her *babe* and it's gonna be something!" Stacy and Tish high-fived cackling.

The boys nodded in agreement.

"Why don't you two hang out tonight? You know, so y'all can talk? Figure this shit out," Ellis offered.

"Sorry, can't!" I said. "I promised Darren if I was free I would go to a benefit with him."

"Aw, this bitch," Rho said, throwing her hands up.

"It's cool," Seamus said. He looked disappointed, but I'd made a promise to Darren. He had been such a good friend. Lately, I felt like I owed him.

I was the first one to leave after we restored Shea's kitchen to its original glory. I went around the room, hugging everyone before I departed. Yes, even Seamus got some love. I had just enough time to get home, wash last night off me, and clean up for tonight's event.

Stacy was coming in from Seamus' house as I was rushing out to meet Darren.

"Oh, wow! You look beautiful!" she exclaimed.

"Thanks, boo!" I sang sweetly.

"So, is Darren an issue we need to discuss?" she inquired.

"Not at all, he's just a great friend."

"After you left, we all talked to Seamus to see where his head was at regarding you."

She laid it out for me. Seamus had feelings for me, but he had obligated himself to Chelsey. He reiterated what I said about not wanting to see where we could go and me pushing him away. *He laid the blame on me. What an ass!* He told them that if things were different, he would've definitely been down to see where things went with us. When pressed about our molesting one another, he chalked it up to a "weak moment of the flesh." He said he hadn't been intimate with Chelsey because she wanted to abstain until the wedding.

"Bullshit! *Moment of weakness*, my ass! I don't want to be his second choice, Stace. I deserve to be…" I paused to smooth my skirt." I can't get into this now. I will say this, if he wants to be with me then he has to choose me. I'm not going to beg him to be with me."

"I feel you. But if you're wrapped up with Darren where's the incentive for him to choose you?" she asked.

"I'm not going to put my life on hold hoping Shea gets it together. He's moving forward with the wedding, so I have to make other plans."

"Sherm brought up a good point," she added.

"What's that?" I inquired.

"He thinks you'll withdraw from the group—us—if Chelsey and Seamus are married," she said.

"I won't be inclined to hang out if they are going to be around, but y'all are my family. I'll need to get to the mind frame that allows me to comfortably be around him...them," I replied.

"Seamus said he'd withdraw before he'd let you do that," she stated.

"That's a nice gesture, but it isn't Shea who has the problem. Why should he suffer for something I caused?" I retorted.

"Y'all seriously need to talk."

"It takes two people to do that. I'm here and willing."

"He was willing to do that today," she said directly.

"I have plans, Stacy. I'm not going to drop them because all of a sudden Seamus wants to talk. Darren's been a great friend to me. I owe him some support," I retorted.

"Ok, ok," she said, holding up her hands. "Go see Shea afterward then. It could do you both some good."

"I'll think about it," I told her as I leaned in to hug her goodbye.

"Have a good time," she said as she hugged me tightly.

Chapter Eleven
LOST TREASURES

I stood quietly, pondering being around our friends with Shea and Chelsey. I shook my head. *Nope, I can't do it. He's mine.* I believed I was knit to him, yet if he married another woman, I knew I'd need time to unknit whatever my heart and mind had bound to him. I stepped out into the hallway and took a deep breath to compose myself. I didn't want to bother Darren with all of this foolishness. Tonight was all about him. I locked the door behind me before depositing my keys into my clutch. I made way to the elevator. I pressed the button and watched the numbers illuminate, indicating the elevator's ascent to my floor absentmindedly. Thoughts were still swirling in my mind when the door opened. Darren was standing there, holding a Tiffany gift bag and looking as handsome as ever.

"Hey, beautiful," he smiled, "I was just coming to get you."

"Aww, thanks! You're not too shabby yourself, sir! For *moi?*" I said, gesturing toward the gift bag.

"*Oui!* We can open it in the car," he said.

He offered me his hand and helped me into the elevator. We rode chatting about the events that took place last night. I told him how drunk I'd gotten. He knew I couldn't hold my liquor, so he was quite tickled to hear that I slept in my clothes. Darren tucked my arm under his large bicep as we exited the elevator. He escorted me to the car, where the driver opened the door. Darren then walked around to the other side sliding in to join me in the rear. He gave the driver directions to the gala, and off we went.

I was wearing a nude two-piece silk gown. The top was a long-sleeve mock turtleneck sheer crop with crystal and lace embroidery along the bodice with scalloped edges along the bottom. The skirt hugged my tiny curves like a Formula One race car and flared at the bottom like a mermaid's tail. I had worn the ensemble at my cousin's wedding, but no one at the gala knew that. Recycle and reuse was my motto, honey. I paired my dress with a nude Chanel clutch, emerald studs, and a round-cut emerald cocktail ring. They were gifts for the bridal party at said cousin's wedding. She married well! Darren motioned to the Tiffany bag then watched me as I opened it. I removed the tissue paper, placing it on the seat next to me. I fished the box out of the bag and opened it carefully. Inside the box was a dazzling Tiffany Victoria diamond bracelet. The marquise cut stones looked like tiny stars with a single round diamond in between each star. Brilliant. Beautiful. Shit—expensive!

"Darren, it's beautiful...but I can't accept this," I said, looking at him, searching his face.

"I didn't ask you to accept it. It's yours—without question." He meant what he said.

"Darren, I-I...you know I," I stammered.

"I know how you feel about Seamus. This isn't about him, me, or any of that. This is about you being a good friend to me and supporting me. You've done more for me than anyone else I know. I'm set for life because of you. My future children will be set because of you. So no, it's not an option to give it back. It's a thank you, from the bottom of my heart, for being a great friend to me. I've had it and had been meaning to give it to you for a while. I know I didn't have to. I wanted to do this."

"Darren, I don't know what to say...it's beautiful! Thank you so very much." I leaned over to hug him.

"Let me put in on you," he offered. I put the tissue paper and box back in the bag then placed it on the seat next to my clutch. I then handed him the bracelet along with my wrist. It was funny to see his large hands clasping the delicate ornate jewelry onto me, but he was more dexterous then I thought. He held my wrist gingerly. I looked from it to him then back to him. He was an amazing man.

"I can't believe you did this," I said.

"Believe it," he said.

"Thank you" I said as I smiled at him.

"You deserve this and more, MJ," he said earnestly.

I shook my head at him. "Why did you do this?"

He hugged me to himself. "I wanted to show my appreciation, that's all."

"Darren, you didn't have to do anything. I helped you because we were friends. I wanted you to know that I didn't harbor any ill will toward you. I knew you'd do well as the face of Mitsuyama's product. I had no idea the offer would be nine figures."

Darren turned to face me. "It's the fact that you even thought of me. You didn't suggest Sherm or J-Boogie, you recommended me. I knew then you didn't harbor any ill will toward me."

We arrived shortly after six in the evening. The venue, DuSable Museum of African American History, was alive with activity. It was beautiful to see all of the people dressed to impress. There was a private viewing in the museum before dinner was served at seven. After the driver let us out, Darren and I walked up a small flight of stairs before entering the museum. I had been here during the daytime, but there was something about this place at night that stirred something in me. Here we were dressed in our finery walking amongst relics from a period in American history that was so heinous. *Are we so far removed?* I thought. Darren and I recognized the significance. A photographer from one of the media outlets covering the event had taken several pictures of us. My favorite was one of us turned toward a nearby display case which contained rusted iron shackles. The photographer captured a candid shot of me moved to tears at the sight of the irons. Darren was standing next to me with a comforting hand around my waist. The photographer asked for permission to use it in his article. Darren and I both agreed as long as he sent us a copy.

Darren started A Better Tomorrow Foundation because he saw a need for mentorship among young African American males in the Chicagoland area. Their reach went as far as some of the south suburbs like Chicago Heights, Harvey, and Markham. He mentored several young men personally. He even started a scholarship program that provided full tuition to any of the area colleges and universities. He wasn't one of those athletes who had a foundation for namesake only. He was such a prolific man, and Chicagoans loved him. I was very proud of the philanthropic work he was doing and often donated to his cause. I liked putting my money where I saw it in action.

We dined on pan-seared Chilean Sea Bass with lemon caper dressing, sautéed green beans, and mushrooms. It was exquisite. I couldn't readily remember the last time I ate fish so flaky. DW's meal paled in comparison to mine. He was speaking, but I was so engrossed in my food I missed his question. I hadn't eaten since breakfast, I was famished. Dessert was a choice between chocolate bourbon cake or seasonal fruit marinated in a Grand Marnier reduction. I was slightly tipsy. Tipsy or not, I wasn't going to pass on chocolate. It seemed as though my glass was never empty. A bottomless champagne flute went along with a thousand-dollars-a-plate soirée. I also knew that alcohol loosened the purse strings. However, I didn't want to embarrass Darren, so I had one of the servers bring me a cup of coffee to drink along with my dessert. Several of the other women at our table did the same. The mayor's wife winked and said, "Wise choice, young lady."

"Thank you, ma'am," I replied between bites.

Shortly after dessert, Darren excused himself from the table. He was poised as he made his way to the podium to address the night's patrons. He spoke candidly about the struggles of growing up without a father figure, the rate of Black on Black crime and how it was rising in the local area. He spoke of gun violence and how organizations like his foundation were replacing guns with books. He encouraged the celebrities, athletes, and politicians in the room to give back. He told them if they didn't have the time in person, then to reach deep into their wallets to provide money for resources to help save the life of a young black male who was trying to survive and make it to where they were. He encouraged them to remember that most of them weren't born to the privileged rank the currently occupied. He thanked everyone on the board of directors and all of the donors for their continued support. His finale was met with a standing ovation. I had never been prouder of my friend, not even after learning he was a doctoral candidate. Darren had blown me away with his eloquence. I beamed with pride when he sidled up to me.

"You were amazing!" I praised him as he returned to his seat.

"Thanks, MJ! It means a lot." He beamed.

"Every unmarried woman in this room wants some of you right now, sir!" I said, nudging him.

"Girl, stop!" He grinned from ear to ear.

"Seriously, though, I'm so proud of you. You were so poised and eloquent. I thought I was looking at a senator up there. You were very Barack-esque! Very presidential, sir!" I gushed.

"You gon' make me get the big head!" We laughed while the applause continued.

People praised him for the rest of the night. In total, A Better Tomorrow Foundation raised over a million dollars that night. It was a great success and would be a great help in furthering their outreach work in Chicago and its surrounding area. We mingled and danced the night away. My thoughts often went to Stacy's suggestion to visit Seamus after I left the event. But I reasoned we both had work in a few hours. Darren and I left the event around one in the morning.

"MJ, you good?" Darren asked. "You look deep in thought over there." I turned from the window to look at him. He knew without me having to tell him what I wanted. He nodded, patted my knee supportively, and directed the driver to take me to Shea's house. He must've remembered the directions from our dinner date. I couldn't look at Darren.

"Hey," he said, "the heart wants what it wants, MJ. I didn't have any expectations from you, and I know how you feel about him. You know,

I got you regardless." I nodded. I couldn't speak. I was overcome with emotions.

We pulled up to Seamus's addition. He was awake and opened the gate for us. When we reached Shea's home, Darren got out of the car, walked around to my side, opened the door then helped me out of the car. Seamus was waiting at the door in the joggers he was wearing that morning and a white tank top. His green eyes were hooded, and I couldn't read his expression. His usually reddish-brown hair was darker in the moonlight. I accepted Darren's assistance, but my eyes never left Seamus. He looked so handsome at that moment. My heart wanted him—only him. I pulled Darren down to kiss his cheek and thanked him for the evening. I walked up the walkway to the steps where Seamus met me.

"Take care of her," Darren shot at Seamus.

"I will," he shot back.

Seamus closed the door behind us then stopped to take my appearance in fully. He stopped at my wrist. He picked up my hand like I was a piece of fine china. He examined the bracelet, fingering it lightly with his thumb, then looked at me.

"Did he give you this?" he questioned softly.

"Yes," I answered.

"Does this mean..." he began.

"No," I finished.

"Why did you come here, Butterfly?" he questioned.

"I needed to see you," I answered.

"I'm glad you came. I needed to see you, too," he replied sweetly.

"Make love to me, Seamus," I begged softly.

"Butterfly, you know—" he began.

"No expectations. Just me. Just you. Just us."

"Are you sure?" he implored. "Are you sure this is what you want?"

"Yes, I am," I said softly.

He leaned down, effortlessly scooping me into his arms. He walked slowly up the stairs to his bedroom. Once in his room, he placed me down gently on the bed. He took my clutch from my hands, placing it on a tufted bench next to the door. His room was large and expansive. The furniture in the room was big, as well. His bed was white tufted leather with pillows in varying sizes and textures. His linens, like mine, were all white. We had similar taste. We both liked a masculine yet minimalistic aesthetic. He had two marble-topped nightstands flanking his bed. He had books on one and a lamp, tray for his watch, succulent plant, and a picture of him, Max and I on the other one. I was touched. It was the only picture he had in his room. Our little family...

He had a sitting area near the fireplace in his room and a balcony overlooking the lake off the master. His closet and *ensuite* bath were off to the left. The décor was masculine, yet it left room for a feminine touch. His bride would be able to easily assimilate herself. His artwork consisted of black and white photos of Chicago sights—the Bean, Buckingham Fountain, Wrigley Field, Navy Pier, and the Skyline. I loved it. It had a calming quality. He picked up the remote to the fireplace and turned it on. It was glowing blue instantly. I was about to be the first woman he had naked in his home. The thought was unnerving. How would he bring Chelsey—Nope, I wasn't going to think about that now. *Not tonight*, I thought.

I didn't speak as he began to slowly undress me. He undid the zipper to the top of my gown. He pushed the garment off of my shoulders and down my arms before he laid it over the back of the bench where my clutch was sitting. "Nice," he said, regarding my nude La Perla strapless Allure bra. He made quick work of my skirt, as well. He let it rest on the seat on top my clutch. I was wearing the matching Allure garter belt, nude thong, and thigh highs along with my Jimmy Choos.

"You are exquisite, Maeve," he rasped softly while capturing me in his gaze.

I felt like I was truly a butterfly trapped in a spider's web. I didn't want to escape, though. He led me over to the chaise directly in front of his massive bed.

"Are you sure this is what you want?" he asked pointedly. I looked him in the eyes and nodded.

"Please speak your answer." His voice was raspy now. I could see the arousal in his eyes. He didn't leave any room for waffling. If I wanted him, I was going to have to verbally confirm it.

"Yes, Seamus," I affirmed.

"I think we need to talk first, Maeve," he said matter-of-factly.

"I don't want to talk," I said dryly. He chuckled softly

"Ok," he smiled, "take off the rest of your clothes."

I turned to face him then began to unhook my bra and remove the rest of my garments and shoes.

"Fucking beautiful," he stood taking in my body. "Take off my clothes." His voice was authoritative. *Did he speak like this to the women he fucked downtown?* I wondered. The thought brought arousal.

I pulled his shirt off before sitting in front of him on the chaise to untie the drawstring to his joggers. His erection struggled to be free of the soft heather grey fabric. I slid the waistband slowly down his sides. His erection stood at full attention when it was finally free. He stepped out of his pants and kicked them near his tank.

"Have you ever seen a man fully naked, Butterfly?" he asked softly.

"Yes," I answered, "but you are a rare specimen, Mr. McGhee."

His eyes closed for a moment. When he opened them again, I saw raw, animalistic hunger. I touched his cock with the tip of my tongue. He sucked in air sharply. I swirled my tongue around the thick head. I licked off the first few drops of pre-cum. He tasted so sweet. The head of his cock was pretty—were cocks pretty? If so, he was the supermodel of cocks! I took the head into my mouth slowly. His body tightened.

"Am I hurting you? Did my teeth..." I stopped.

"No, don't stop," he said softly.

I wrapped both hands around his waist, bringing him closer to me. I took his head back into my mouth, slowly allowing as much of him into my mouth as I could bear. His moans aroused me as they had on the roof of the club the last night. My mouth watered as I tasted him. I gripped him with both hands, working them around his shaft as I used my lips and tongue to bring him pleasure. I moaned as I moved from the head, licking down the length until I reached his testicles. I gently sucked them into my mouth, moving them around as I continued to work the head and shaft of his cock with my hand. He removed the pins from my hair, allowing it to cascade down my back. Then he wound his hands into my hair, pulling me back up to the head of his cock.

"Don't tease me," he pleaded.

He fucked my mouth exquisitely. His moans grew more intense as I gripped his ass, pushing him deeper into my mouth. I gagged a little. The sound aroused us both. He began to swell as his arousal grew stronger.

"Maeve, your mouth is splendid," he commented as he stroked in and out. His pace quickened as I began to bob up and down, while moving my hands in circular movements around his inflated member. With a groan, hot, sweet liquid spilled into my mouth. I hungered for it as though it were the nourishment I needed to sustain my life. His groans were intense and ragged. His thrusts began to slow as his orgasm ebbed. I had just given my second blow job, and from the sounds he made, I knew I did a great job.

"Impeccable." He chuckled softly. "I don't know if I believe I'm the only one you've ever done that with."

"I want you, Seamus. I'm not leaving until I have what I came here for," I said brazenly.

"Get in the bed then," he commanded, moving to the bed. He slid the covers back and got in.

I pulled the covers back on my side and joined him. He dragged his eyes up and down my body before pulling me to the center. He laid next to me and put his hand on my stomach. He was resting on his elbow, contemplating his next words.

"*Féileacán*, losing your virginity will hurt, but I will try to be as delicate as possible," he said thoughtfully.

"I know. I trust you'll be gentle," I reassured him.

He kissed me passionately as his hand explored my stomach, thighs, and hips. He moved slowly and deliberately—teasing me. My body was aching for him by the time he parted my legs. I was trembling with desire when he finally found my clitoris. He began to make circles with his thumb. He slowly inserted his index finger into me. I moaned into his mouth with pleasure. He moved from my mouth to my nipple, circling it with his tongue. I grabbed his head and ground my pelvis into his thumb.

"Slow down," he whispered. "We have all night." *All night! Are you supposed to go all night your first time?* I thought.

He was making me crazy with his slow circles. Just when I thought I couldn't take more, he inserted his middle finger into me. He was stretching me in preparation of receiving the ten inches he told me I probably couldn't handle. His mouth was everywhere, all at the same time. He managed to suck both breasts, kiss me, and manually stimulate me without missing a beat. We had been grinding at a slow seductive pace for quite some time before I noticed he had three fingers inside me. My body had come alive in response to him. He sat up for a moment, bringing the fingers that were once inside me to his mouth. He sucked my wetness from each finger one at a time. That was even sexier than him sniffing my panties.

He maneuvered himself between my legs to hover above me. His arms and shoulders looked so strong. His face was serious yet mysterious. It was a face I'd never seen him make, so I couldn't read it.

"I'm sorry," he said softly.

"Why?" I looked up at him in confusion.

He guided his member toward my wet entrance. Anticipation was building within me. *Why is he delaying?* I wondered. Then, with one powerfully swift movement, he was inside me. Pain lit my body up like Times Square. Unconsciously, my back arched upward from the intensity of it. Tears spilled from my eyes as I squeezed them closed. My mouth opened to cry out, but no sound came. That was why he was sorry. He knew how badly it would hurt. He lowered himself onto me until our bodies touched. We were one. He gently wiped my tears away and kissed both eyes. He kissed my forehead, eyes, nose, and mouth, apologizing after each kiss. He didn't move for a while, allowing my body to acclimate to this strange new invasion. *Fuck! Ten inches hurts like hell,* I thought.

"Butterfly." I opened my eyes to find him searching my face. "You are so beautiful."

I was silent. My body was still adjusting to the painful intrusion. His cock felt extremely hot within me. Was it supposed to be hot? It was so big!

He kissed me as he began to move slowly. I brought my hands up, wrapping them around his neck as I matched his movements, returning his kiss in kind. He was gentle while keeping his movements shallow. I felt my body enveloped by him like he was supposed to be there. He was so deep inside of me. I didn't want to think about anything but that moment, so I clung to him. I gripped his shoulders, rubbing his neck as he gently bit my neck. I did my best to mirror his movements. I felt pain, but the pleasure he was giving was more intense. As his movements deepened, I rose to meet them, matching the intensity. His hands were under my back, cupping my head and neck. He groaned my name with such intensity that it gave me goosebumps. He was giving me what I needed.

"Seamus," I cried, "you feel amazing." I moaned into his shoulder.

"You're amazing, Maeve."

He was so intense. His strokes were so deep. I could feel the head of his cock plucking at something deep within me. I felt the tension in the core of my being building, but it didn't feel like my regular orgasm. As we moved, the feeling intensified. I met him stroke for stroke—each one more intense then the last. Tension grew in my body as my orgasm, and whatever else I was feeling, began fully to stir.

"Seamus," I moaned breathlessly, "I'm so close."

"Come for me," he commanded as he slammed into my body.

The most intense orgasm erupted from my body. I was midway through the throws of it when pleasure, from whatever he was plucking, ripped through me. An ejaculation so strong tore through me. Wetness began to gush out of me, but I didn't stop thrusting against him.

"Oh, shit...baby, come for me!" he moaned in shock as he came deep within me.

I felt the heat from his loins pour into me. I remembered what it felt like when I had him in my mouth. This was more than I expected for my first time making love, but it was better than I ever imagined or dreamed. Our orgasm was so intense we didn't speak or move afterward. Sleep overcame both of us at the *decrescendo* of our mutual climax. I wasn't sure how long we drifted off, but we were still in each other's embrace when I woke up.

"Seamus, wake up," I said gently. He popped up in surprise.

"Did I hurt you?" he responded genuinely.

"I have to use the bathroom," I said quietly.

"Oh, hurry back," he encouraged.

I padded into the bathroom. I caught a glimpse of myself in the mirror. I looked well-fucked! I laughed as I walked past to the toilet. As I sat down, horror set in. We hadn't used a condom. What the entire fuck was I thinking?

Lord, Please don't let me get pregnant...Wait, I am on birth control. Whew!

I was happy I had let Rho's hoe ass talk me into getting birth control implanted into my arm.

"It lasts for five years. You can't be too careful, and you never know, girl!" she had reasoned. Rho be knowing! I washed my hands and crept back to the bed.

"Shea," I murmured, "I'm gonna go."

"No, the fuck, you aren't!" he rasped, pulling me back into the bed.

"We have work in the morning," I said, laughing.

"Fuck work," he smirked. "We are nowhere near done, baby!" He sat me down on his lap slowly.

"Ooh," I squealed as he slid his hardness inside me.

I sat squarely on his massive erection. He grabbed a handful of my hair, pulling my head back until my neck was fully exposed. Black women definitely don't mind their men touching their hair when he's fucking them right! Shea slowly began to kiss my body from my neck to the valley between my breasts. Then, one by one, he began to lick my nipples like they were ice cream. They tightened under his ministrations. He drove me crazy with pleasure. I braced my hands on his chest and began using my thighs to slide up and down his length.

"Slow down, *a rún*," he mumbled with my nipple in his mouth. "I want you to enjoy the sensation."

"I can't—I want you so badly," I whimpered.

"Baby, you are so tight. If you don't stop, I won't be able to contain myself. I'm not trying to get you preg—shit!" he said with a start. "Fuck me, I forgot a condom!"

I grabbed his face to calm him down.

"Shea, I've been on birth control since college. I know you've never had sex without a condom. We're ok! Now…back to work, sir!"

"Wait, what?" he asked sarcastically. "Why the fuck are you on birth control? Who were you planning on fucking?"

"Uh, Darren, duh! I started taking it in college!" I laughed.

"Is that right?" he said wickedly.

Shea tore into my nipples with a vengeance. He ravaged my breasts until I begged him to fuck me.

"Please," I begged.

"Who do you want?" he asked.

"Stop playing, Shea! You're all I've wanted since we were younger," I said shyly.

"Don't get shy on me now, shit! I wanted you too…so badly. Shit, shit." He was arousing himself too much by talking.

"Seamus, please—don't tease me," I whispered in his ear. "I've waited so long. Please…" my voice trailed off.

Shea grabbed my hips with both hands and began to lift me up and down on his cock. I wrapped my hands around his neck and kissed him deeply. *Fuck, this feels so good!* I could feel my clitoris rubbing against his body. He felt so good! He was pulling another orgasm from me, and I was ready for it. I could still feel the tenderness from my torn hymen, but the pleasure he was giving my body outweighed the discomfort. My body took over and began to work itself against Seamus as I rode him exuberantly. I was so close to an orgasm—so close. He laid back on the bed and I rode him like I had seen the women in do in pornos. His expression was so arousing. He liked what I was doing, and it spurred me on. This little virgin was fucking the shit out of him! I could feel my orgasm beginning to build. Just when I didn't think I could take any more, he said, "Come for me, *a rún*," whispering against my breasts.

I spiraled into the most delicious orgasm. He was holding back so that I could enjoy every bit of the experience. I collapsed onto his chest as my orgasm waned.

"Oh no, baby," he said. "I have to get mine!"

He sat back up and scooted us to the edge of the bed, then stood up. I wrapped my arms and legs around him. He gripped my ass tightly and began to thrust deeply inside me. I moaned into his ear how much I wanted him, how he made me feel, and, to my surprise, the dirtiest stream of commands began to spew from my lips.

"Fuck me! I want you to come deep inside me. Make me feel every inch of this fat cock in the morning!"

"Shit! Tell me how you want it then," he bantered back.

Before I could figure out what he was doing, he pulled me off his dick and brought the space he just filled to his mouth. He licked and laved my wetness like it was the best thing he'd ever tasted. He sucked me into another orgasm, then brought me back down to his throbbing cock, slid back inside me, and came so hard I could feel his legs tremble from the magnitude. He ground out my name, gravelly.

"I love you so fucking much, Maeve!" he cried out unconsciously at the conclusion of his orgasm. I was shaken!

"What the fuck?" I asked, looking at him in sheer confusion.

He stilled with the realization of what he had just said. He walked us back to the bed, situated me, then laid me down next to me.

I love you so fucking much, he had said. *He loves me! He fucking loves me!* What the entire fuck was I thinking? My Grams was right. My heart ached because I knew, despite his admission, he was still going to proceed with this wedding. Why hadn't I spoken up sooner? How was I going to watch the man, this man, marry someone else?

"Maeve, I-I…" his voice trailed off.

I threw off the covers and sat up.

Chapter Twelve
WHO PISSED IN YOUR CEREAL

I sat up, scooting toward the edge of the bed. "You love me so fucking much?" I repeated. "What the fuck was I thinking coming here?" I said aloud to myself.

I played myself.

"Maeve, I never expected to feel what I felt in at that moment. Shit, I didn't think…" he faltered.

"No, Shea, you didn't think," I retorted.

"Maeve, I gave you exactly what you asked for. You said you could handle it," Shea said.

"What I can't handle is your sex-induced confession of love." I twisted my hair as I spoke.

"Is that what you think? You think more highly of yourself then you ought, Maeve." He stopped pacing to face me when he spoke. I knew he was offended.

"Fuck you, Seamus." I clenched my fists into tiny balls.

"You know damned well that's not how I meant it." He held up a hand to silence me. "I can get good pussy anywhere. You should also know if I said it, I meant it," Shea replied angrily.

"How am I supposed to know anything when you won't talk to me?" I yelled back.

"You pushed me away, Maeve—or did you forget? Now, you want

to lay all of this on me," he growled.

"Your words shocked you! You're engaged, Seamus, or did you forget that?" I shivered. Shea paused his pacing to pull the comforter around me then spoke.

"I'm not gonna lie, Maeve, being inside you brought up some very strong emotions. I know you feel it when we make love. I don't know what to do with everything I'm feeling, and every time I try to connect, you push me away." His shoulders lagged as he spoke.

"I trusted you with my first time. I trusted you enough to finally tell you the truth. How can you say you love me and marry Chelsey?" I asked.

"It's complicated." He turned away after he spoke.

"Damn it, Seamus," I said softly as the fountain of my tears dried up. I left him standing there and went to my room.

Shit, why didn't I drive my own car here?

I slammed the door then locked it behind me. I rummaged through my drawers until I found some shorts and a tank top to put on. I could get in a short hour nap before I left. I was definitely taking one of the cars to drive myself home. *Work! Shit! I'm not going...not after this.* I changed into my clothes and climbed into bed. Tears began to flow.

I heard Shea pad down the hall to my door. He begged me to open it, but I ignored him. He apologized for being an ass. Said he didn't mean what he said. I knew he was sorry. I heard the pain in his voice, but I wasn't going to be a fool twice.

The next morning, I woke with a start.

"What time is it?" I grumbled aloud.

It was 8:00 am. I grabbed my phone and sent my assistant Jared a quick text to let him know I wouldn't be in.

Bing!
Jared: No problem, honey! I already have you on sick
         leave. 😊
Me: You. Are. A. Lifesaver!
Jared: Your schedule is free this week. Do you need

me to put you on sick leave for a few days?
Me: YES! Thank you!
Jared: You got it, boss!

I got up to see if Shea was still home. I padded down the hallway to his room, but the door was closed. My body ached from the paces Shea put me through the last night. *Nothing a long hot bath won't fix,* I thought. I crept down the stairs hoping I didn't run into Shea. I walked across the kitchen to the back of the house to the entrance to the garage. I grabbed the keys to the Range Rover then closed the door gently behind me. The only thing betraying my departure was the chime from the alarm. *The Benz is gone, good!* He must've gone to work that morning. I knew Shea wouldn't mind if I took his car, after all that transpired between us. I'd eventually bring it back when I could face him. I placed my things in the passenger seat and began buckling my seatbelt when I heard the garage door open.

Shit! Fuck my life, I thought.

Seamus pulled his Mercedes E Class sedan into the garage. Maybe he'd let me leave. I sat still for a minute, hoping I wasn't seen. He got out of the car, closed the door, then tapped lightly on the window of the Rover.

"Maeve, your foot's on the brake. I have some breakfast and coffee," he said sweetly. "Don't leave like this."

His tired eyes are sunken and flat. All of the spark once contained in them was gone. I got out of the SUV to follow him inside. I sat down at the table, watching him pull a plate out of the cabinet and pile bagels and pastries on it. My mouth watered and my stomach growled loudly. He turned to look at me, and we both laughed.

"Hungry?" he asked sarcastically.

"Yeah, losing your virginity is a workout."

Shea grimaced at my candor.

"Shit. I didn't mean...I—" I faltered.

"I guess you were gonna leave your purse and clothes here, huh?"

I shrugged in response. Some things were necessary for a clean getaway.

"Eat," he said as he set a plate in front of me.

He didn't have to tell me twice. I dug in before his hand left the plate. The sight of me chowing down must have tickled him because he turned back toward the kitchen laughing as he went. I watched him make his plate, grab the two coffees, then head to the table. He set my coffee down near my plate, careful to stay out of the danger zone of my mouth.

"Cream, three sugars—just like you like it."

"Thanks," I said sweetly.

"You're welcome."

We ate in silence, occasionally looking up at one another every now and again, then looking away. I pushed my plate away and said, "Well, now what?"

"I don't know," he said solemnly. "We fucked up, though."

"No, we fucked," I said matter-of-factly.

"Must you——"

"Yup, so now what?" I said.

Seamus stood up, pushing his chair in under the table. "Stand up," he demanded.

You already know I obeyed unquestioningly.

He threw me over his shoulder like a caveman, and I let him. He took us upstairs to his bedroom and into the bathroom. He set me down on the counter then walked over to the shower to turn it on. He returned to me, parting my legs to stand between them.

"I want you," he said calmly.

"Wanting each other is what got us in this mess," I answered.

"Let's take a shower," he suggested casually.

"What would the future Mrs. McGhee think of me showering in her soon to be *en suite*?" I quizzed sarcastically.

"I don't plan on telling her, do you?" he volleyed back.

"Maybe," I smirked.

"You won't," he smirked back.

"Why, Seamus? Seriously, why are you doing this? You are about to marry Chelsey in less than a month. Are you really content to just fuck—"

"We," he said, gesturing between the two of us, "made love. Now, shower with me."

I acquiesced.

With that, he began to undress in front of me. Once he was completely nude, he turned his attention to me. He helped me down off the counter to take my bottoms off. Taking my hand, he led me to the shower, closing the door behind us. The water felt good against my skin but stung as it ran across my lady parts. I winced.

"You ok?" he asked sweetly.

"Yeah," I replied.

I felt weaker than butter on hot popcorn. We really needed to finish our discussion, but the Bad Bitch in my brain had a one-track mind.

He began to wash me with a delicate touch. Did he think he was going to break me if he rubbed too hard or something? As his soapy hands went over my nipples, I could feel heat stirring within me. The slippery soap enabled his hands to glide effortlessly as he focused on his task. His hand slid down my stomach gingerly as he made his way to the achy bits, causing me to flinch.

"I'm sorry." He moved quickly and efficiently.

When he finished washing me, he handed the soap to me to return the favor. I began to imitate his gentle strokes. He was visibly aroused as I bathed his nether regions. My touch gave him goosebumps. I wondered if Chelsey's contact had the same effect. Shea reached up, grabbing the shower nozzle from its resting place. He brought it down and began to rinse the soap from our bodies. Shea replaced the showerhead, opened the door then led me out of the shower. He handed me a towel, and we dried off. Shea took our linens and placed them on hooks to dry, then escorted me to his room. He had replaced the linens from the last night. I'm sure I had bled on them.

"Shea," I said quietly.

"Hmmm."

"Are we going to talk about last night?"

"No, we're going to make love, then talk," he stated.

Make love, we did...

"I know you're sore. Lay down." He smiled sweetly at me.

Shea's tender care extended into the bedroom during our lovemaking. He went into the bathroom to retrieve some massage oil. Coconut oil-covered hands set my body ablaze with desire. He kneaded my achy flesh before we began.

"Turn over." His voice was soft yet commanding.

I obeyed him and was rewarded when he began at my temples, making his way down to my body. He really took his time on my breasts and nipples. I wanted to open my eyes, but pleasure lulled me into sleepy docility. Shea rubbed down my abdomen, passing my sex to my chagrin. He kneaded my thighs, calves, and feet with firm pressure. Finally, Shea returned to my neglected sex. By the time he finished administering my rub down, I was close to an orgasm. Knowingly, Shea murmured in my ear, "Come for me, baby."

"Fuck," I panted, unable to hold on any longer. He rubbed my body into submission, mounting me, he plunged deep into my depths.

"You feel so good," I moaned.

"Not as good as you," he growled in my ear.

His words caused my orgasm to burst from my sex explosively. *Shit! Am I squirting, again?* My gushiness caused him to lose control. His thrusts intensified as he pounded into me hard, fast, and relentlessly. I clung to him tightly until we collapsed into each other's arms, gasping.

"You are magnificent, baby," he whispered into my ear.

"Coming from you, I'll take that as a compliment," I whispered back.

"I love you," Shea sighed softly before drifting off to sleep.

Not again, I thought. I didn't have the strength to argue. I nudged the hulk of a man to roll off me, settled in next to him and fell asleep in his arms.

It was dark when I finally woke up. *How long did I sleep?* I wondered. Shea had left me alone in his expansive bed. I rolled over to the edge of the bed and sat up. I examined the room for something to put on. My eyes fell on his recently discarded shirt. I padded over to the garment, put it on, then walked briskly to the door. Hopefully, I'd find my bedmate somewhere in this big house. I wandered to his familiar spots, but he was nowhere to be found. I found the stairs leading downstairs to the indoor pool, gym, and sauna on the lower level of the house. As I approached the door, the smell of chlorine from the pool accosted my nostrils. I heard Shea swimming laps and Jay-Z and Kanye's song "Niggas in Paris" blaring through the speakers. I sat down on a lounge chair close to the door, watching him swim. The only light provided came from under the surface of the water. The sun had gone down, but the garden lamps put off a soft glow through windows opposite the pool. Shea's body cut through the water like a hot knife through butter. He raced as though he were on pace for Olympic gold. I watched him glide from one end of his pool to the other, turning and pushing off again back into the water. *How did he have the strength to come swim after getting no sleep and making love to me so ardently?* I wondered. I felt tiredness in my bones as I sat watching him. With hunger overpowering my senses, I rose from the lounge to trek back upstairs. I was almost to the door when Shea called my name.

"Maeve, wait!" he bellowed. He wrapped a towel around his waist, jotting over to where I stood. He gave me a quick forehead kiss, then held the door for me. "You hungry? I can whip us up something or order something on Postmates?" he inquired.

"Sure. Can we talk over dinner?" I asked as I searched his face.

"Let's talk after we eat," he chimed.

"Shea—" I started.

"Maeve, I want to enjoy our day. I know as soon as we talk, it's going to get turbulent. I need this time. Ok?" He chided.

I acquiesced, because I knew he was right. "Ok."

We settled on cooking. We pulled out the ingredients to grill chicken and roast vegetables. I worked meticulously chopping veggies while Shea seasoned the meat. It was funny to think that when we met him, he was a "salt and pepper only" kind of guy. *Now, look at him over there with the Lawry's.* Homeboy had even introduced his mother to it. I sighed softly to myself.

"What's with the sighing? You good?" he inquired.

"I was thinking about the first time you cooked for the crew," I started.

"Don't start!" he said laughing.

"Nah, you wanted to know. I find it funny that you got Lawry's and McCormick seasonings all up in your cabinets now," I giggled.

He washed his hands quickly and came over to my prep area. He grabbed me, wrapping his arms around my waist, then kissed my forehead gently as he had downstairs. I tried to push him off, but it didn't work.

"I was *slaggin' you.* Stop. Let me finish cooking," I giggled.

"I know I was a hot mess, but this," he said, referring to my chopping, "is not cooking. This is sous chef work!"

"Boy, I have a knife in my hand! Don't do me! You think just because you know how to properly season meat now, you're a chef?" I questioned. My sarcasm was not lost on him.

"You know I throw down in the kitchen, baby!" He laughed while biting at my lips.

"I don't know about that, baby!" I spat back, dodging his mouth.

He took the knife from me, setting it down on my cutting board then drew me into him.

"*Féileacán,* I love being like this with you. I feel more myself with you than I've ever felt with anyone else, not even the fellas." We continued to embrace as he spoke.

I was so tempted to question him, but I let it pass. He was right. This was a great moment. I knew I should relish it because this time next month, Chelsey would be here with him. *Shit!* I truly hated the idea of being the side chick. As though Shea sensed my thoughts, he spoke assertively.

"Ay! You are not my side chick. You are my best friend. I mean that," he said, lifting my eyes to meet his.

"Kinda feels like it, though," I said. "Here I am in the same kitchen she just made dinner for us in, cooking what feels like the last supper." I was so dejected. Shea leaned down and kissed me gently on my lips.

"Trust me, you will never be my side chick. Nor do I think of you as such. You are Maeve Alena James. The best of my friends. You and me...we thick as thieves, and we'll figure this out. I promise you. Now, let's get back to cooking." He spun me around, smacking my ass as he walked off.

"Get back to work!"

Shea turned on the hood above the stove before he placed the well-seasoned bird on the grill plate. Flames leaped up to lick the moisture from the meat then died down. The sizzle from the fire was extremely loud. I carefully added the veggies I had chopped and skewered after Shea flipped the chicken. I knew it wouldn't take long for them to cook. I just needed a little char on them.

I set the table while Shea operated the stove. I went down to his wine cellar to look for a lovely Sauvignon Blanc for dinner. Shea had a wine cellar beneath the butler's pantry. I padded down the stairs to the obsessive-compulsively organized wine cellar. I found a bottle quickly, then jotted up the stairs closing the door behind me, then grabbed two glasses from the cabinet. I set the wine on the table along with the glasses, then went in search of a corkscrew. It was in the drawer with his other miscellaneous gadgets. Who the hell needed a garlic press or a strawberry core remover? He had mocked Stacy when he saw those items at our house. *Well, looky-looky!* I laughed to myself at the thought.

I removed the cork and poured two ample servings of wine, allowing them to breathe while Shea made our plates.

"Let's eat outside," he suggested randomly.

"Um, ok," I grabbed my plate and utensils following him outside.

The fire pit was lit, and Teyana Taylor's "Gonna Love Me" played softly in the background. Shea had pulled a mink blanket from the living room and taken it outside for me.

"I wasn't downstairs that long. How did you do all of this?"

"I brought it out here while you slept. I thought it'd be nice to eat outside." Shea sat next to me, placing his food down to run inside to grab our wine.

"The chicken looks great!" I praised him when he came back out.

"Thanks," he said before picking up his wine to take a sip. He went through the task of swirling it to open up the bouquet. "South African?" he asked before reaching for the bottle to see for himself.

"Yes, I thought the occasion could use a delicious wine," I said quietly.

"It's not the last supper, Butterfly. I am not letting you go, trust me," he said plainly.

"So, what is this then?" I asked.

"Two friends having dinner. Like old times—" he began.

"This is definitely not like old times, Shea. We've seen each other naked, been intimate...*so* not old times." I shoved chicken into my mouth to shut myself up.

"Look, I know some things have...changed. That doesn't mean I don't view you as someone different. I don't know how to proceed, but I'm sure we can come to some sort of resolution. Do you want to stop being friends, MJ?" he asked pensively.

"It seems like it would be the easiest course. I'm definitely not going to be your jump-off or mistress." I paused to look at him. "So..."

"Don't. I would never put you in a situation that would compromise who you are or your morals. I need to figure it out. I don't know either, but I would gladly take whatever you give me."

I looked at him sideways. "My morals are already compromised. I've been intimate with—wait, what are you saying?"

"I'm not married yet. If you want...shit, I'm just going to speak openly. I want to see where this," he gestured with his fork between us, "you and me, can go."

I let his comment breathe before I began, "You knew me before, Shea. What's different? You've seen me naked? Taken my virginity? I knew what I got myself into by coming here last night. You told me what would happen. You are not obligated to—"

"Shit," he interrupted in a frustrated tone, "you gotta stop being wishy-washy, MJ. I am at a loss for how to proceed then because... you're killin' me, Smalls!"

"Shea, why are you even putting that bullshit on the table? I'm already the side piece. I fucked you while you were engaged. Historically, this isn't going to end well."

"Stop being such a fucking pessimist. I haven't even slept with Chelsey!"

"I'm a realist, Shea," I started before the reality of what he said sunk in. "You what?"

Shit, I remember Stacy telling me they haven't been intimate.

"It's like that, Ms. Just-Lost-Your-Virginity-Yesterday! You don't get that she wants to wait. It's because of you that I can even respect her wishes." That stung—slapped with my own hypocrisy!

"Fuck you, Shea."

"Seriously," he said. "I respect her boundaries because I have a phenomenal best friend who wanted to wait until she was ready to give her virginity to the person she was in love with. Surely, you can understand that?"

"I do...I hate myself for waiting until you were engaged to confess my love. I know I'm wishy-washy right now. I keep thinking about something my Grams always said," I picked up my wine and downed it.

"What's that, *a rún?*" He waited patiently for me to finish my drink then poured me another glass.

"Ill-gotten goods are ill-gotten gains." I set the glass down before looking at him.

"If I marry Chelsey, will you still come around? Can you honestly say you want to see that happen?" he asked again.

"I don't know what else to do, Shea. If we're meant to be together, then we will be. It's that simple. I probably will back away from you or remove myself from events, but I'll need some time. I deserve that, don't you think? Maybe I can find someone new—" I said before he interrupted.

"Find somebody new? Like who?" He slowly began shaking his head.

"You're mine. The thought of another man—no, nope, hell no!" He picked me up and carried me to the couch in the den where we kissed so many months before. It seemed like a lifetime ago.

"Shea, chill," I began. "I am not yours. You can't have Chelsey and me. I'm not yours as long as you still have her."

"I don't want anyone else to do to you what I do to you." He started rubbing my breasts. "Do you want another man doing this?" he asked as he kissed me seductively on my neck. "Or this?" he asked softly as he found his way under my skirt. He looked up at me, devilishly, "You aren't wearing any panties."

"No, I'm not, but that is not an open invitation to—" I was quickly silenced as two of his fingers found their way into my wetness. He pulsed his fingers in and out as his thumb made circular motions on my clit.

"Do you want another man doing this to you?" he asked.

All I could do was moan. I could feel an orgasm beginning to stir deep within me. Shea nudged up my shirt, taking my nipple into his mouth.

"Do you want another man doing this?" he demanded with my nipple in his mouth.

Minutes ticked by before I could muster, "Shea...please." My words were drowned out by the intense pleasure he was doling out to my lower body.

"Answer me, Butterfly," he pressed further. "Do you want another man touching you like this, kissing you like this, loving you like this?" *How can I answer when you are wrecking my concentration?* I thought.

"No!" I groaned as the orgasmic sensation he created spread throughout my body. My brain was caught in a loop as the word fell from my lips like water over waterfalls.

My orgasm barely subsided when I felt him press his engorged member into me. *Fuck, he felt good!* The sensation of him rubbing against my clit for a few minutes caused my body to quiver from another explosive orgasm.

"Shit!" I moaned. "I'm coming again!"

"Yes, baby, come for me," he moaned in my ear. He grasped my neck with his right hand and my ass with his left. He slammed into me until I was screaming from my third orgasm. "Give it all to me," he said in response to my whimpers and cries of ecstasy.

I wrapped my arms around his body and used them along with my legs to match his enthusiasm. We clung to each other as though it were our last night on Earth. Like our bodies knew this was what our hearts needed to tide us over. I cried his name as tears spilled from my eyes.

"Can you feel me?" Shea asked. "Can you?"

"Yes, Seamus, yes," I moaned in response.

He was moaning and groaning so loudly. The only sounds were the sounds of the playlist we were creating. It was music in my ears when he finally came. It was so guttural and primal. I felt hot liquid pour into me as he pounded down, driving hard into my flesh. He laid down, allowing his full weight to rest on me. We lay on the couch until our breathing and heart rates adjusted to a normal rhythm. Seamus shifted on top of me, preparing to get up.

"Hold up, Kemosabe!" I said sarcastically. "If you move a lot of liquid will spill out of me onto this couch. I don't think you want to fuck up your furniture like that."

"Right, right." He laughed as he tightened his grip on my ass. I clung to his neck as he lifted us both off of the couch. We looked down to survey the damage we had potentially done to his furniture. We didn't realize we were on top of a blanket. It took the brunt of our loving. We breathed a collective sigh of relief. He carried me out of the room through the house and up into the master bathroom. It wasn't until we were in the bathroom near the towels that he put me down. How was he still inside me?

"You have a grip on me so tight," he said like he read my mind. "I'm surprised I haven't slipped out yet!" Shea turned on the water in the sink, fished out two small face towels, and wet each of them for us to clean up with. The warmth of the wet towel on my labia felt soothing. I reached for the soap from the dish and slathered it in the towel. I went back to cleaning myself. I hadn't thought about how personal an act I was performing in front of Shea. I stopped when I noticed him watching me.

"What?" I inquired.

"Watching you makes me want to see you pleasure yourself. Show me," Shea said.

"Uh, no," I said, shrugging it off. "Besides, we haven't finished dinner, Shea."

"Dinner can wait," he stated matter-of-factly. "Seriously, your movements seem so delicate. Are you that graceful when you masturbate?"

"Delicate? Graceful? Uh, I'm just cleaning myself," I said, laughing. He took the towel from me and placed it on the side of his sink. He gently picked me up and sat me on his cold granite sink.

"Shit, that's cold," I squealed, jumping down.

"Babe, please!" he begged. "Show me." I thought he was teasing at first, but he was serious. "Ok, ok," I acquiesced. He picked me up, putting me back on the sink. I leaned against the mirror and began to rub my clitoris. I focused on my movements. Sheesh…I guess my actions were delicate. I continued to touch myself. I peered up at Shea to observe his response to my efforts. He was enthralled and stroking himself in concert. *Fuck!* This was sexy as hell! He leaned against the shower opposite of me. He was a little rougher with himself, but I could see that he was very aroused.

"I want to kiss you," he said softly. "May I kiss you?"

"Yes, Mr. McFormal," I answered him playfully yet ardently. I felt the fire awakening in me, and I didn't mind the extra stimulation. His mouth was warm and salty. He stroked his cock with one hand in addition to cupping the back of my head. I caught a glimpse of us in the shower glass. *Fuck!* I reached up to grasp my nipple between my thumb and forefinger. I squeezed and pulled at it softly. He pulled back to look at me, then reached between my legs to get a bit of moisture for his throbbing cock. I was so close. He pulled back to watch as my breathing became more ragged.

"That's it," he moaned. "Show me how good it feels." He leaned down to take my other nipple into his mouth. He pulled on it, sucking and flicking it with his tongue. He bit down, sending a sensation down to my clitoris.

"I'm so close, Seamus." That was all he needed to hear. With a swift movement, he picked me up then filled me to capacity. Within three strokes, I was coming all around his cock. I felt my pussy convulse and grip him tightly. My moans were his defeat. He filled me totally, coming deep within. As he began to maneuver in and out, I could feel him pressing what I thought might be my G-spot. The pressure was rousing another orgasm. It built quickly and rushed out of me in a powerful stream that hit Shea with force.

"Damn, baby," he moaned. He was leaned over me with his left hand holding him up against the mirror. His other arm was wrapped around my body. "You are such a gushy little one! I love it!"

As our orgasms subsided, we looked at each other, spent. My mind was made up that I needed to go home. I wasn't sure how he'd take it, but I needed to be in my own space to contemplate all that had transpired. I knew the crew was going crazy in our group chat, wondering what was going on, since they hadn't seen us in 24 hours.

We began to clean up ourselves, and the mess we had created, in silence.

"So am I a squirter?" I asked, breaking the silence a short while later.

"More like a gusher, although that last one does qualify as squirting. Either way, I am absolutely amazed at the frequency and quality of orgasms you've had since you lost your virginity."

"A testament of your skill?" I asked boldly.

"No, more like a testament to your desire. You may have been a virgin in the physical sense, but you definitely know your way around an orgasm. You are a receptive lover, MJ." I felt proud, oddly enough.

"Shea, I'm gonna go home," I stated firmly. "I need to rest and think about everything that's happened."

"I understand. I wouldn't let you get any rest if you stayed." He put the towels in the hamper then returned to where I was standing. He bent down to kiss me, then led me from the master bath. He watched as I threw on my clothes. We walked back through the house, taking the same path we that led us up to the bedroom. I paused at the garden door, looking at my half-eaten dinner.

"I can wrap it up for you," Shea said sheepishly.

"Nah, I'm gonna grab something on the way home." I turned, walking toward the garage entry. Shea reluctantly handed me the keys to the Rover. I didn't know when I'd set them down or when he'd picked them up. I reached to open the door when he grabbed my arm. I turned to look at him. It seemed as though he wanted to say something but was afraid. I raised my eyebrows in silence.

"I love you, MJ."

"I love you too, Shea," I said before he pulled me in and kissed me on the forehead.

I paused to look at him one last time before sliding into the driver's seat and buckling up. He stood in the doorway, watching me leave.

SUNDAY GO MEETIN'

Mary J. Blige's "Real Love" was playing on my throwback playlist. My phone synced via Bluetooth with the sound system of Shea's Range Rover. I sang along as I made my way to my loft. I floated home on the memory of our lovemaking. I made it to my building safely and pulled into my secondary stall, then texted Shea to let him know I made it.

Me:	I'm home.
Shea:	I miss you already.
Me:	I bet
Shea:	We will figure this out.
Me:	GN 🖤
Shea:	GN 🖤

Three sets of eyes greeted me when I opened the door. Stacy, Rho, and Tish swiveled to me, then down to my disheveled appearance.

"Freshly fucked," Rho shook her head slowly. "I know that look anywhere."

"Mm-hmm," Tish said with a sarcastic smirk.

"Spill it!" Stacy yelled before she ran to the kitchen to grab another wine glass. She poured a full glass of wine and held it out to me as she took her place, patting the space beside her. "Now then."

"Ladies, I'm tired. I really just want to go to bed," I began before Rho's boisterous voice cut me off.

"I bet you are," she added as she acted out as many sex positions as she could. "Come on, bitch! Inquiring minds wanna know!" We all laughed.

"Ok, ok, sitcho ass down!" Stacy said as I grabbed the glass of wine and laughed.

I placed my belongings on the chair nearest the door, took a sip from the glass, and sat. I confirmed my friends' speculations.

"Yes, we had sex. Yes, it was…" I closed my eyes for a moment, recalling the many, many ways he had brought me to orgasm. "Good. And yes, he is as skilled as we all thought he'd be." They squealed.

"No, he's not calling off the wedding."

"Why the fuck not?" Tish chirped angrily.

"Yeah," Stacy and Rho agreed in unison.

"I don't want to be the reason they split up," I reasoned.

"Fuck that! Shea is *your* man, Lil Bit!" Rho exclaimed. Stacy and Tish agreed.

"I'm wrong as fuck for sleeping with him knowing he's engaged, and y'all know it! Don't co-sign this wack shit because I'm your girl. 'Cause if it were flipped, we'd beat Chelsey's ass," I said bluntly.

"Mm-hmm, that's right!" Stacy laughed heartily. "Remember, how we rode for you when Darren's ass got caught cheating?"

"See, that's what I'm saying. This shit ain't right!" I said emphatically.

"That ain't whatcha pussy said, though!" Rho screamed while Stacy and Tish roared with laughter. All I could do was laugh too.

"No, she quite enjoyed the experience," I said matter-of-factly. "That doesn't change the reality."

"Ok, so wait," Tish started. "Something ain't right in paradise, because he didn't turn you down. He fucked without hesitation, I bet!"

"He told me they haven't had sex yet."

"How you marrying a bitch, you ain't never fucked?" Rho quipped. "I still don't get that shit."

"He said she wants to wait till marriage," I told them.

Rho hopped up, running to grab her iPad out of her bag. She quickly pulled up Chelsey's Instagram and ran through the pictures.

"Girl, stop," she began. "This bitch done fucked err body she's ever been with and now—now she wanna wait until marriage? Get the fuck outta here! Something ain't right!" She furrowed her brow looking suspiciously at me. Stacy and Tish agreed.

"We all told him that when he said it yesterday morning," Stacy added.

"I heard she's a slut from way back—like middle school. Blow jobs in the stairwell and shit," Tish offered.

"Y'all all I can do is tell you what he told me," I said. "He said I should be able to understand."

"So, what the fuck are y'all gonna do? I know you ain't giving him up without a fight," Stacy said.

"I don't know, girl. I know I'm tired as shit. He wore me the fuck out. My brain is on auto-pilot right now. And this wine ain't helping the situation."

"Shit, we knew when you walked through the door, he fucked the shit outcho ass!" Stacy hooted.

"I hate you, bitch!" I hollered.

"Mm-hmm, *witcho hoe ass!*" Rho mocked how we sounded when we teased her about her hoe antics.

"Dead ass!" Tish slid off her seat onto the floor. The wine had gotten to us.

"Rho, I have one word for you—triplets! Witcho *hoe* ass!" I was laughing as I set my wine down.

Tish looked confused. "Wait, what did I miss?"

"Everything," I said as Stacy and I hooted and cackled.

"Fuck y'all," Rho said, trying not to laugh.

"Is someone gonna fill me in?" Tish asked.

Through laughter, Stacy grabbed her phone and scrolled through her texts. She found the video then handed her phone to Tish.

"Press play, bitch!" she hooted.

The sounds of sex began to fill the air. I ran over to peer at the video over Tish's shoulder.

"Gaht damn!" Tish and I screamed simultaneously.

It was one thing to hear about it, it was an entirely different beast to see clones fucking the living shit out of one of your dearest friends. The first brother was lying on an ottoman with Rho on top riding him—the second triplet inserted deeply into her ass from behind. His movements were barely visible. Finally, the third was standing to the side with his cock rooted to the helm down our friend's throat. He was the one filming the sordid affair.

The third triplet wound his hand into Rho's hair, fucking her with vigor, as she gagged and moaned with pleasure. The brother on the ottoman was sucking Rho's titties loudly and smacking her ass. Brother number two gripped her ass cheeks and spread her apart. We could see his cock spreading her entrance to a gaping black hole as he pulled out, exposing some pink flesh, then slammed back in. Visually, the short clip Rho had sent to Stacy was a lot to take in.

"Why the fuck did you share this?" Tish was clearly disgusted by what she saw.

"I didn't send it to you, asshole," Rho retorted sarcastically.

"Ladies," I slurred, "play nice."

"We had been talking about threesomes when she said that she'd had one recently," Stacy stated. "I've been asked to participate in one, and we were hashing it out."

"The closest I've ever been to a threesome is watching the series on the Playboy channel," I chimed in.

"See, MJ is—was—a virgin and she ain't as prudish as your ass, Tish," Rho spat. "This why I don't be telling you shit. Always trying to make a bitch feel bad for liking to fuck."

"All I'm saying is," Tish started, "you know what—I'm sorry if I make you feel bad for being you."

"Aww," I slurred, picking up my wine glass and draining it. "Now, hug it out."

"Shutcho ass up, MJ!" Rho said, laughing at me.

The ladies filled Tish in on all of their hoe antics then Rho mentioned that she was thinking of joining a sex club.

"I've long since thought you were a member of one the way you—" She looked away. "Fuck it, good for you!"

I couldn't imagine letting strangers do anything to me after what I experienced with Shea. *But hell, who am I to judge?* I thought.

We finished six bottles of wine before I made my way to my room. Good thing I didn't have to go to work the next day. Jared was a lifesaver for real! I peeled out of my clothes as I made my way to my bed. It was a pajama-free zone tonight. I woke up, slightly hungover. I spent the week reflecting on my situation, taking a few yoga classes, eating, and drinking with my friends. My diet had flown the coop when Seamus brought bagels.

Sunday came way too fast, and I contemplated not going to church, but I had to get the stench of sleeping with a soon-to-be-married man off of my conscience. I dressed in a white Christian Dior dress paired with silver metallic Jimmy Choo stilettos and matching clutch. My jewelry was simple—silver studs with a few Alex and Ani bracelets. I sent Darren a text to see if he was up for church this morning. He responded with a FaceTime call. *Typical Darren.*

"So how did your chat with Mr. McGhee go last week?" he asked casually. My silence was met with boisterous laughter.

"Oh shit," he sang, "did somebody finally give up the drawls?"

I laughed. "See what had happened was—" Darren was in hysterics. "Shut up, Darren!"

"I thought all you were gon' do was talk," he started. "Had I known he was gon' talk you outta yo drawls I would've taken yo fast ass home."

"It blew up in our faces and went downhill fast 'cause the wedding is still on, and our friendship is a clusterfuck!"

"Nah girl, I woulda called the fiancée and been like 'Richie, put yo mama on the phone! Look it, Linda," he could barely keep from laughing, "look it, I ain't neva comin' home!"

"See," I laughed at his *Harlem Nights* reference, "this is why I hate you!"

"No, this is why you love me," he responded casually. "So wait, is it just sexual, or does he have feelings? Wasn't that the purpose of going to his house?" Our conversation took a severe turn for a brief moment.

"He has feelings for me, told me he loves me and everything." I could hear DW spew coffee.

"What?" Recovering he said, "Ain't that what you want, though?"

"I don't want to start a relationship by busting up another one. I'm not that scandalous. Well...ok, I am so ashamed!"

"Right, 'cause you fucked that muhfucka so well he's willing to call off his wedding! Shit, as long as you two have been wanting each other, I don't see why you won't let him."

"Whatchu mean, Darren?" I said.

"I knew he wanted you in college. His bitch ass couldn't wait to snitch. He violated man code for you."

"True," I laughed, "I just thought he was a good friend." Darren was stating facts because even though Sherm, J, Zeus, and Ellis were my homeboys, they didn't say a thing.

"Nah, he wanted them sugar drawls for hisself!" he stressed.

"I wanna go back in time. I messed up," I whined.

"Too late, baby girl, he has already tasted. As we speak, that muhfucka's trying to figure out how he can wriggle out of marrying ol' dried pork, raw-but-burnt potato-looking, no-cooking ass Chasity and her burnt up reduction sauce!"

I was cackling through this rude as fuck—yet accurate—description of Chelsey.

"Did you say Chasity? I can't," I hollered. "Whew Lord!"

DW was running back and forth, head back, full-on guffawing. I was undone! Whew, I loved this dude. Why wasn't he a comedian?

"I can't deal with you! I'll see you at church, goofy!" I disconnected our FaceTime as I sprinted to the toilet to keep from wetting myself.

I arrived at church twenty minutes early and parked. Darren must've been right behind me. He pulled into the spot next to me. I waited for him to park. He made sure to park as close to the grass as possible.

"I don't want nobody denting my boo," he said, getting out of the car.

"You doing the absolute most!" I laughed.

We scanned the parking lot for my parents. When we found them, we walked arm in arm over to them. The parking lot was treacherous for a sista in stilettos.

"Hey, Mama. Hey, Daddy," I sang, greeting both of them with a kiss on the cheek. "You remember Darren, right?"

"Hey, Darren," my mama said, side-eyeing him.

"Hey, Big Guy! How do you think the season is gonna go this year? Aren't you supposed to be in spring training?"

"Hello, ma'am. Sir," Darren said. He gave both of my parents a hug before directing his comments to my daddy. "I think we actually have a chance to go to the playoffs this year, sir. We have a great roster, and we picked up some good recruits in the draft. I'm resting my wrist right now. I injured it in practice last week."

"What did the doctors say?" Mama asked inquisitively. She and Darren talked about his diagnosis while we made our way to our seats. Darren's attendance caused quite a stir. It took a minute for him to finally join us. He signed autographs and took pictures with a few of the younger parishioners and encouraged some teenagers to come to the free tutoring and mentoring sessions offered by his foundation. He sat as the organist began signaling the choir marching in to "Come, Thou Almighty King" by Reverend Timothy Wright. We went up from there! Their gold and silver robes looked good against the blue and cream of the carpet and pews.

The pastor's sermon encouraged us to stop sitting in Sin. *Does Jesus know?* I asked myself. *Of course he does!* He then proceeded to call out several types of sin people sit in—including fornication. *Whew!* I made a fast trail right on down to the altar call at the end of the sermon. Nope, no more fornicating. The flashbacks of our lovemaking hit so hard I felt like I was gonna lose my footing. *No! Not today, Satan. Not tomorrow either!* I shook off the images and pushed forward in the altar call to prayer. I went back to the pew afterward.

Darren leaned down and whispered in my ear, "Them flashbacks just about knocked you off your feet, huh?"

My eyes widened as I elbowed him.

"Shut up, fool! My parents might hear you!" We both stifled our laughter. Too late—Dr. James leaned over and looked at us both sternly.

"Children," she whispered severely.

We both put our heads down. I had to bite down on my inner lip, hard, to get the giggles to go away. We stood around for a little while, socializing with the other members of the church. A few of the mothers asked if Darren was my new boyfriend.

"No, we're just friends," we said in unison.

I let my parents know I'd meet them at Gram and Pop-Pop's house after I dropped off Shea's SUV.

"How did you end up with it?" My mother was quick.

"Long story—" I started.

"Well, make it short," she stated.

"Maybe later, Mama! He's expecting us any minute. Bye, Daddy!" Daddy waved.

"Indeed," Dr. James said. I knew she made a mental note. I kissed my mama on the cheek, turned and left. It wasn't odd that I drove Seamus' car. But he was usually with me when it happened. So, for us to break that practice was strange. Darren looked off in the distance, giving absolutely no assistance. He quickly joined in step as I walked off.

"Mr. Mouth-Almighty, and you can't offer no help?"

"I'm barely in your mama's good graces, and we just got outta church! You want me to lie and mess that up? Nope!" He chuckled.

"Jesus and my mama—two people no one ever wants to disappoint. You know, she ain't gone let this one go."

"Like a dog with a bone. Oh! Tell her you've had it since Max died, and he's driving the Benz."

"Darren, you are a G, but that won't work. Max died months ago."

"I tried!" He threw his hands up.

"She's gonna be back on it at dinner today. I don't even know what to say. You know I can't lie."

"I know you can't tell her you got dicked down either, so you better come up with something." Darren's sense of humor was so inappropriate, but it made him endearing to me. We made our way to Shea's house to drop off his car. A small part of me hoped he wasn't there. Darren waited outside while I pulled into the garage. As the garage door went up, I saw the Benz was there. *Shit!* I gathered my things, then headed to the house to drop off the key fob. I found Seamus standing there.

"Dammit!" I screamed. "You scared the shit outta me. What are you doing here?"

"This is my house, remember." *That fucking smirk. Ugh!*

"I know it's your house. I didn't expect you to be standing right here."

"I didn't want to miss you, Butterfly." His smile was sincere.

"Shea, you are not making this easy," I replied.

"I don't know what you mean," he said innocently.

He was wearing a tailored navy pinstriped Tom Ford suit with chocolate brown Salvatore Ferragamo double monk strap shoes. And the same belt I'd unbuckled on the rooftop just nights ago. Instant wetness. His shirt-tie combo was one I gave him for his birthday. *Shit.* He knew I liked it since I bought it to match the suit. He wasn't playing fair. I was sure he remembered how much I praised his appearance that day he bought it. Asshole!

"I was hoping you'd return the Rover this morning, so I dressed for church, but you didn't show. Is that Darren?" He looked over my shoulder to the driveway.

"Yes, he's giving me a lift to—" before I finished speaking, Seamus moved me to the side and trotted out to greet Darren. What was he gonna say? What were they talking about? *Shit!* Where was Darren going? I ran out, but it was too late. Darren gestured for me to call him, laughing as he drove away. *Why is this so fucking funny to him?* I thought. Maybe because now I was the cheater, and he had a front-row seat to the shit show. I rolled my eyes.

"Come on," Shea gestured to the Rover. "We can take the SUV since it's already warmed up."

"Dude, my mom is already asking why I have your car. If you show up, it's definitely gonna be a shit show! Why did you tell Darren to leave?" I half-fussed, half-whined.

"Calm down, love," he started.

"Don't call me that!" I yelled.

"A'ight, Maeve." He hugged me. "Let me grab my jacket, and we can head to your grandparents' house. We'll get our story together on the way."

Chapter Fourteen
DINNER AT GRAM'S

We arrived in Chicago Heights almost an hour later. My grandparents lived in a modest home, where they raised four kids. My mom was the only one who lived close to them. My two aunts lived in Indiana and Michigan. My uncle lived in Oklahoma. Grams cooked every Sunday and expected anyone in town to show up to eat. The only thing she asked was that we inform her of who was coming so she had enough food.

"It'll be ok," Shea spoke softly. "Remember, after the bridal party meet-up, we all came back to my house. You didn't have your car because you arranged for cars to chauffeur us that night. Or just tell her you were busy at work and couldn't—"

"She knows I took the week off," I cut him off.

"You took the week off and didn't tell me?" he said, sounding slightly offended. "I took the week off too. We could've gone away or something...to talk."

"We don't need to be alone, Seamus," I began. "I don't want to be the other woman."

"I postponed the wedding, Maeve," Seamus said softly.

"What? Why?" I implored. "Please tell me it's not because of this... whatever this is, between us. Darren said you'd do this. Fuck me!"

"Chelsey agreed. She said she had cold feet, as well. We pushed it to

September," he said, looking at me intensely. "What exactly did Darren say?"

"Something about you trying to find a way out of marrying no-cooking ass Chasity," I told him without thinking.

Seamus' laughter boomed throughout the SUV. "No-cooking ass, Chasity, huh? His words or yours?"

"Shit, I didn't mean to say that part." I blushed. "Postponing isn't canceling or calling off. You still intend to marry her."

"It gives us some time to figure out a few things. It's the best I can do." He placed his hand on my exposed thigh. My skin prickled under his touch.

"What are we going to tell my mom?" I changed the subject.

"Tell her you and Jen got into a fight at the club, which is true, causing me to be upset that you caused drama at our meet up. Then, I was busy at work, and today was the only day feasible to bring it."

"Why am I the bad guy?" I grumbled.

"Because it's better than telling her we made love and you spent the night," he stated.

"You are so right!" I laughed.

When we arrived, Shea got out of the car and came around to my side to open my door. We walked up to the house then went around the sidewalk to the back entrance. People rarely went to the front door. My grandparents' formal living room was reserved for their company, not us kids. I opened the screen door and walked upstairs. I could hear voices coming from the kitchen.

"Go on into the dining room, baby," Grams said without looking up from the stove.

"Um, what?" I asked. We never, and I mean never, ate in the dining room.

She put the spoon she was holding down, lowered the lid on the pot, then turned to face me. *Oh shit.* She was about to light me up—until she saw Seamus behind me.

"Well, hello there, Mr. McGhee! How you been? Come give Grams a hug!" He stepped around me and over to my grandmother. *Thank God!* He saved me from getting chewed out.

"Hey, Grams. You are looking as beautiful as ever." Shea's brogue was shining through.

He was giving her that Irish charm he was famous for.

"What am I chopped liver?" I griped.

"Didn't I tell you to take yo butt to the dining room?" Grams fussed. "I thought that football player was coming for dinner," she said, hugging me.

"Shea offered to bring me since I had his car," I explained. "He'll take me home."

"Well, now, maybe someone can tell me why you had it in the first place," my mama voiced from the doorway. Seamus launched into the concocted story as he walked over to hug my mama. She seemed content with it.

"Why did you mush that child in the face, Maevie? I know I taught you better," she rebuked.

"Mama," I declared, "she said something inappropriate before sticking her tongue in my ear, and she messed up my hair!"

"Oh, say no more." Mama's tone was understanding. "I'd fight if someone messed up my hair too!" Seamus and Grams laughed. I loved how she skipped past the tongue in my ear and went straight to messed up hair.

"What's all the commotion about in here?" Pop-Pop said, coming around the corner from the dining room. "Y'all gon' keep on jaw jacking in here or can we eat?"

"Oh, hush, dinner's ready. Get somewhere and set down," Grams fussed at her husband.

Pop-Pop walked over to greet Seamus. "Come on, young fella, tell me whatchu been up to since I saw you last."

The men made their way to the dining room as Grams, Mama, and I followed with food. Grams prepared baked chicken, green beans, mashed potatoes, creamed corn, and fresh rolls. Daddy was sitting at the table, trying to pretend like he hadn't stolen a roll.

"You just can't act right, huh?" Mama asked sternly. "You know we were coming with the food."

"Don't fuss at me," he fussed. "Your daughter and her friend kept us from eating on time. Fuss at her!"

"Daddy, your own flesh and blood. How are you gonna throw me under the bus like that?" I was laughing as I went around the table to greet him and Pop-Pop. I took my seat next to Seamus, seeing how I was the only one still standing.

"And where is DW? I wanted to see if he'd get me some tickets. Seamus said he's too busy to go to the games. How am I gonna get tickets now?" Daddy said.

"You are too much! It's good to see you again too. I'll ask him when I talk to him."

He was in rare form today. Seamus just laughed.

"Honey," Grams said to Pop-Pop, "will you say grace?"

Dinner was rocking along swimmingly until Grams asked Seamus about the wedding planning.

"Well, Grams, we've postponed it until September—" Seamus was in the middle of explaining when Grams interrupted.

"Have you come to the realization that you're in love with my grand-daughter yet?" she asked casually.

"Oomph, there it is," Pop-Pop said. "Time to go!" He and Daddy grabbed their plates and scattered. I dropped my fork mid-bite. My mother kissed her teeth and exclaimed, "Mama!" Seamus turned the brightest shade of red.

"Um-um," he stammered.

"Let me help you," Grams said calmly. "I know you two have feelings for each other. You're only postponing the inevitable. You love her, and she loves you. I would like to see her happy before I die."

"Grams, I care deeply for Maeve. After all, we are best friends—"

"Cut the bullshit, son," she interrupted again. "It's gonna take a long time for a little kitten like you to fuck an old cat like me!"

"Mama," my mother yelled, "please stop!"

"Paulina, put some bass in your voice then take yo' ass on in the other room if you don't wanna hear what I have to say." Mama glanced between Shea and me, then picked up her plate and left.

"Out with it," Grams demanded.

"Grams, I love your granddaughter, but I've committed myself to someone else. I've asked Maeve for time to see if there's something between us, but she feels like a mistress. She doesn't want to be the reason I break off the engagement." Shea was forthright and didn't mince words. My head was down as the story unfurled. I stared at the plastic-covered linen table cloth and wrung my hands, afraid of what my Grams would say.

"Mistress, huh? Well, she can only be a mistress if you've been with one another biblically. Are you saying you've been with my granddaughter?" Her voice was low. She completely blew me with that one—she was sharp for her age!

"Yes, ma'am, we've been intimate…but MJ doesn't want that to be the reason I break off my engagement. I hadn't been forthcoming with how I felt until recently, as well."

"Seamus, I know my granddaughter loves you. Otherwise, she wouldn't have laid down with you. You have some decisions to make, son. Just know if you break her heart, that's yo' ass." Sometimes, Grams spoke like she was the baddest bitch to walk the streets. I had heard stories about her fighting in her younger days but did she intend on whooping Shea? She used to tell her kids they'd better fight slow and let her win. I remembered her telling another lady in the grocery store to jump if she was feeling froggy. Hell, who knew? She may have some Krav Maga fighting stashed away.

She turned and addressed me.

"Stop being so got damned wishy-washy. You know you love this man. I ain't telling you to be a fool, but don't deny yourself a chance at happiness. You two need to quit screwing around and figure this out." *Pun intended.*

"Yes, ma'am," was all I could muster looking up from the table. I was no longer hungry. I looked at Seamus, and I could see the lust in his eyes. I knew I wasn't going home tonight. He had Grams' approval, and I think that was all he needed to hear.

"Can we come back in?" Daddy asked, as he leaned around the door frame.

After dinner, we moved into the living room for dessert and coffee. Grams made her famous sweet potato pie. I sat down on the couch with a crunch. My Grams' couch was still covered with plastic from the seventies. *I bet if she took the plastic off the furniture would turn to dust and blow away,* I chuckled to myself at the thought. The couch and loveseat were white with mauve roses with stems in various shades of green. Pop-Pop sat in a green velvet high back chair across from the love seat. Pictures of my family and artwork graced the walls. The end tables and coffee table had tiny figurines, old *Ebony* and *Jet* magazines on them. She always kept a small crystal bowl filled with little candies on the coffee table, as well. The Steinway upright piano, where I'd taken lessons, still sat across from the couch. My Grams accessorized everything from the blinds to the carpet to match the rosy shade of the flowers. It was overkill if you asked me. However, old Black women were the queens of the pop of color. I felt at home when I was there.

"Seamus, I think it's best if I go home," I said softly.

"What are you afraid of, Maeve?" Shea whispered.

"I don't want to get hurt."

"Give me a chance, Maeve."

"This has the potential to be very messy."

"Only if we let it," he said softly.

"Can we just go?" I whispered.

"Yeah." His voice was flat.

Seamus earnestly asked for a chance with me. I'd wanted this for so long, but then there was Chelsey. I knew I'd be devastated if my fiancé did this to me. I'd already given myself to him, entangled myself with this man. *Are we selfish?* I wondered. *Dammit, Darren said this was going to be hard.*

We stayed at my grandparents' house for a little while longer before we said our goodbyes. We pealed ourselves off of the plastic covered furniture, then headed to the car. My grandmother admonished Shea to remember what she had said. He nodded before kissing her on the cheek. We rode in silence, each pondering my grandmother's words. I couldn't believe it. She was actually pushing us to pursue a relationship—despite Shea's impending nuptials. She knew I was no longer a virgin and didn't judge or condemn me. God, I loved her so much, but how could I follow my heart? Shea was engaged.

"Shea, part of me thinks you're doing this because you don't want to see me with anyone else." I folded my arms over my seatbelt.

"I don't want anyone else to do the things I've done to you. I am in love with you, and I'm still trying to figure this out." He looked at me, and I knew he was honest.

He headed to his house. I didn't protest because I wanted to sort this mess out. I rode quietly, thinking about what he'd just said. I relived how my body came to life when he touched me and the pleasure he'd given me in just a week. *Is lust clouding my judgment? Shit!* This was an impossible situation.

Seamus continued, "I'm not *some* men, Maeve. I've been your best friend for over a decade and having been inside won't change that."

My body responded to his last words because, shit, let's face it...*I enjoyed him being inside me!* I felt the wetness between my legs and my nipples drew up so tightly they caused discomfort. I wanted him inside me again. Allowing delicious images to creep in, I licked my lips at the thought of his cock inside me and squirmed at the sensation that stirs between my legs.

"You good?" he asked. He watched me intently. I saw his eyes wander down my body and rest on my breasts. Upon seeing my rock-hard nipples, he sped up. I knew there wasn't going to be any talking when we made it back to his place. My essence buzzed with anticipation because I knew he'd fuck me—well.

We barely made it into the house before his hands were all over me.

I hadn't been out of church four hours, and there I was, breaking that promise I had made at the altar. *Damn!* I didn't stop, though. His lips felt amazing. We deposited keys, purse, church program, wallet, and jacket in the mudroom before our kissing led us around the corner to the counter in the laundry room. *In the laundry room?* I questioned myself. The Bad Bitch in my brain answered, *yes, in the laundry room!*

Seamus didn't even bother to unzip my dress or remove his clothing. He pulled my dress up under my arms, exposing my bra, then slid my panties to the side. My hands were braced against the countertop as I turned around to kiss him. He gripped my neck gently while undoing his buckle and pants. I wanted him inside me, desperately. Finally released, Shea bullied his way inside of me, as we sighed with relief upon entrance. *Yes!* This was what we both wanted. His left hand made its way up to my nipples. He pulled the fabric of my bra down to release my breasts. With his thumb and pinky, he stretched to work both nipples. *How the fuck is he able to reach so far?* I thought. I let my head lull against his shoulder as our kiss deepened. I was lightheaded and giddy.

"Your hair smells like a tropical breeze, Butterfly," he moaned into my mouth as he continued to thrust into me. Shea broke our kiss to place his index and middle fingers into my mouth, gathered some moisture, then lowered them to work my clit. I cried aloud in delight.

"Oh, Seamus!"

"Again, Maeve," he demanded. His pumping intensified as I breathlessly fulfilled his request.

"Seamus!" I said breathlessly.

"Again," he ordered.

"Seamus..." I breathed out softly.

"You're so...fucking...wet! Shit," he moaned, "I don't know how much longer I can last, Maeve."

"Then come," I responded as I pushed back against him.

"You first," he dropped his head into the nape of my neck, mumbling about my hair and the fit of his dick inside me.

I focused on the way he felt inside me. It felt like I was pulling him back inside of me. My body was literally pulling him back in as though fighting his departure. I pushed back and rode his cock with as much intensity as he was using to push into me. Our bodies were slapping loudly like…like applause! Motherfucking applause. Enthusiastic fucking. He still hadn't come yet. I could tell he was fighting to hold on for me. *Damn!*

The sensation, coupled with his never-ending hand movements on my clit and nipples, caused me to unravel. I screamed out his name as I came. My back arched so hard I felt his shoulder on the top of my head. Pleasure exploded from my body in swells traveling up through my navel into my face and scalp, then down to my arms, hands, thighs, calves, and feet. My cries were buried under the crushing intensity of his kiss.

"Mmm," I moaned into the kiss ferociously.

"Dammit…*SHIT!*" Seamus grounded out as he pulled away from my lips for a moment. We continued on like this for several minutes before he shifted his focus.

I felt his mouth move across my cheek, ear, then down to my neck. He sucked gently yet fucked me roughly. The juxtaposition of it was mind-numbing. His body was hot and hard against me. He gripped my breast, biting down on my neck and fucking me harder and harder. The tip of his cock was creating pressure on my g-spot as he sheathed his massive organ into me repeatedly. A second orgasm threatened to erupt with the force of Mount Vesuvius. *I'm going to decimate his cabinets, our shoes, and the floor,* I thought. My eyes searched for something, anything to use to save us. I spotted a towel on the counter and reached for it. It was the only hope we had of not destroying our clothes.

"I'm coming again," I warned as I slammed the towel over the hand stroking my clit. My timing was perfect. Seamus' hand was trapped when the hot liquid exploded into the cloth. I leaned back into him as he wrapped his arm around me for support. He didn't stop pounding into me, though. Our bodies worked in concert together to bring our lust to fruition. Our cries were a symphony in my ears. We rode the waves of ecstasy to fullness. Our pumping and thrusting eventually came to a stop as our orgasms waned. I braced myself against the counter. Seamus brought his hands to rest outside of mine on the countertop. I knew I didn't want this with anyone else. Chelsey was still his fiancée, and, in a few months, this very well would be her. Tears welled up in my eyes before rolling down my cheeks. I tried to stifle a sob, but they began to shake my body.

"Maeve," Seamus questioned softly, "are you ok?"

"One day...this will be you and-and Chelsey."

"Dammit, Maeve! I am still inside you," he growled angrily.

Shea stretched for another towel and used it to clean himself. He stepped back, letting out a long, exasperated sigh then continued, "Why the fuck are you torturing yourself like this? I'm here, with you, right now."

He readjusted my bra and my panties, pulled my dress down, smoothing it over my skin. He pressed his body against mine, burying his face into my hair, then inhaled. I felt his breath, still ragged, on my skin. It sent chills down my spine.

"All I know is you consume my thoughts. This past week I couldn't get you off my mind. You are the only woman I've made love to within this house. If you think I can bring another woman in here after what we've shared, then you don't know me."

"You said this is where you want to bring your wife to raise a family. What am I supposed to think since you haven't broken off your engagement? I'm confused, Shea. Things between us aren't the same. How do I know you won't do this same thing to me?"

He spun me around with rage in his eyes. "What the fuck does that mean? Do you really think I'd hurt you or betray you if we were together?"

"You know what it means, Shea. We're both acting out of character." I looked up at him. "I want you for myself. It's not selfish of me to ask you to figure out if it's Chelsey or me you want. I already feel like a whore..." I looked away.

I felt anger welling up inside me. Shea cupped my chin, turning my face, urging me to look at him.

"Why do I make you feel like a whore?" he asked rhetorically. "You know I take the women I fuck downtown."

"I've heard about your exploits, remember? I got an ear full from the friend zone! This—what we just did—was not making love. This was fucking. Pure unadulterated fucking, Seamus. We barely made it into the house. You didn't even take my clothes off. I'm not an expert, but that was not making love." I knocked his hand away.

"Yes, but don't act like I treated you like a fucking whore and don't throw being friend-zoned in my face. I bet you masturbated to the stories I told wishing you were the one I was fucking."

"Asshole!" I spat, pushing him away from me. I was embarrassed because he was right, though. I touched myself as he told me about his wild exploits. I hated him for being right and myself for being so fucking predictable.

"Get your shit and get in the Benz," he said abruptly. His energy shifted. I couldn't read his mood. I turned to gather my items, then headed out the door. *Is he taking me home?* I wondered.

I turned back. "Shea, I—"

"Car! Now!" he answered brutally.

I heard the car start as I turned the doorknob and stepped out into the garage to discover the door was still up. *Shit, we didn't even close the garage door! What if Chelsey had come in?* I slid into my seat and closed the door. Shea got in, put the car in gear then backed out of the garage letting the door down behind him.

"Don't you say a fucking word," Shea said before I fixed my mouth to ask where we were going. I stared out of the window, trying to gauge where we were headed by the direction he steered us. *Home! He's taking me home.* My heart dropped. *This is what I wanted, right?* I had told him he needed to sort things out with Chelsey and that I didn't want to pursue anything with him until he did. Maybe that's why he was taking me home. I continued looking out of the window at the L tracks, which ran for miles. We passed several stations with people waiting for trains going into the city and out to the suburbs. I imagined myself getting on the train heading home. I didn't want to be in his presence. I shrank into my seat closer to the window. He got off the highway five exits before mine. *Now, I'm confused. If he isn't taking me home, then where the fuck is he—his apartment!*

"Shea, no," I protested as the realization hit me.

"You need to be shown, Ms. James," he snarled.

Ms. James? What the hell! What did I get myself into? I thought as panic set in.

"I'll scream this bitch down if you don't take me home! Right fucking now!" My voice was booming in the car. The soundproofing was definitely second to none. Shea didn't flinch or maneuver the vehicle off course.

"Scream, and I'll give you something to scream about." His voice was barely above a whisper. "You need to know the difference between how I treat you and the women I've fucked. I'm gon' to show you better than I can tell you," he said calmly.

Chapter Fifteen
THE PENTHOUSE

We pulled up to his building, where the valet promptly opened the door. Before I exited, Shea put his hand on my wrist. "Sit," he commanded, then left the car.

He walked around the rear to my side, then extended his hand to me. I looked up into his eyes. They held a stern look as if to say, *don't embarrass me.* I took his hand, allowing him to help me out of the car before being led across the sidewalk to the door, held open by the doorman. "Good evening, Mr. McGhee. Ma'am," he sang.

"Good evening, Francis." Seamus led me through the foyer of his apartment building while greeting the staff that was in the area. I kept my head down and tried to stay in step. When we were safely in the elevator, he turned to me.

"Love doesn't exist where we're going. You are mine, and I will do with you as I wish. You will yield to my will, or there will be consequences and repercussions. Do I make myself clear?"

His voice was harsh, but he was giving insane sexual energy. I had masturbated to the thought of being the woman he dominated here. He told stories, let details slip, and responded to the questions I asked. Did he want me to know about his prowess? Did he want to bring me here before today?

"Yes."

"Our safe word is butterfly. You will address me as Mr. McGhee. Do you understand?" His tone was relaxed yet compelling.

"Yes," I said breathlessly. *Damn!*

We stepped out of the elevator into the foyer of his penthouse. It was a very masculine space. The furniture, floors, and curtains were all dark. The art on the wall was strikingly sexual. Every picture was of the female anatomy. Who had posed for these pictures? Was it one woman or many? Who was the photographer? Had he captured these images? What had I gotten myself into?

"Get on the floor," he instructed.

"What?" I said as his words pulled me out of my thoughts.

"I do not repeat myself, Ms. James. Obey or be punished. Now, get down on your hands and knees."

I did as I was told in confusion. Shea had never told me stories of women on their hands and knees.

"Head down and follow me." He walked toward the living room. The marble floors hurt my knees, badly, but I followed, nonetheless. I appreciated the heat radiating from them. He went through the living room and into the bedroom. His penthouse was by no means small. When I finally made it to the entrance, my knees and pride were severely bruised. I could feel tears welling up, but I bit my inner lip to quench them.

"Go stand near the bed and wait for further instructions," he stated.

I moved quickly toward the bed. Shea left me standing by the bed. I heard the elevator door open a second time, then I heard deliberate footsteps—a woman's footsteps—crossing the length of his apartment. A slow staccato on the Italian floors was maddening...then I saw her. *Damn, she's gorgeous!* I couldn't make out her ethnicity. She was taller than me but not quite the same height as Seamus. She let her garment slide off, then handed her trench coat to Seamus. She wore a black Dolce & Gabbana jacquard bustier, with matching garter and thigh highs. The lack of panties caused me to remix a Method Man verse in my mind. *No panties, no bra when you give it to me...yeah...give it to me raw!* She balanced precariously on daredevil black Prada peep-toe plat-form stiletto heels. Her exposed breasts were perched and sitting high. I wondered if they were real. Her tits were teardrop shape, full double D cup with large pink areolas. Her mons pubis, like mine, was almost bare. A single line guided the eye down to the split of her labia. Her pussy was not fat, but there was some cushion for the pushing. Her clit and labia hung down past her outer lips into her thigh gap. Her skin was slightly tanned, showing off her muscle tone. Her body was flawless!

Her jet-black hair was pulled up into a high chignon with a few es-caped tendrils framing her face. Her eyebrows were nicely arched. Her nose, like mine, was straight and upturned on the tip. Rounding out this goddess's face was a full set of heart-shaped lips, painted red to match her fingernails and toenails. Her makeup was natural, no over-the-top false eyelashes. She didn't need them because her lashes were long enough. Did I mention she was out of this fucking world gor-geous? She looked like she stepped out of some high-end brothel or fresh off a porn film shoot.

"Hello, Mr. McGhee. It's a pleasure to see you again." I heard him whisper something in response before taking her coat. "Ah! I see you brought me a present."

Her bright blue eyes sparkled with delight as she assessed me in a sweeping motion. *What the fuck did Shea just say?* I couldn't place the accent. Where the fuck was she from? I was instantly jealous, I was not her fucking present! Who did this bitch think she was? I turned to move, and she pounced.

"Mr. McGhee did not permit you to move. Did I?" Her voice was sharp and piercing. She meant business!

She covered the distance from the door to the bed in three long strides. Seamus was right behind her.

Before I moved or answered, I felt Seamus behind me. He drove me, face first, down onto the bed, then captured my wrists in his hand be-hind my back. *What the fuck?* my mind screamed. He hauled my dress up, then ripped my panties off roughly. I heard him tearing open a condom wrapper. He sheathed his cock, then bullied his way inside me. No warning. *What the fuck is the safe word again? Shit!* The woman leaned down, bringing her face close to mine. So close I felt her minty breath brush hotly across my cheek.

"I see you have a problem understanding simple commands," she began. "We are going to help your understanding, da'ling." *Russian! She's Russian—maybe German! Ah, fuck! This motherfucker is still fucking me! What the fuck is the safe word? Bitch, think!*

I was startled out of thought when she leaned in, placing her ruby red lips to my mouth. *What the entire fuck?* My mind was racing. I turned, but she pinned my head down with one hand then pried my mouth open with the other. She was squeezing my cheeks so hard it brought tears to my eyes. I yielded, allowing her to press her mouth to my painfully stretched mouth. *Oh, gaht damn.* She had put her mint, and saliva, in my mouth! I tried to spit it out. *Oh my fucking…Whew!*

"Suck it," Seamus groaned. *Bitch, what?* I peered over my shoulder at him, looking at him like he was crazy as hell. "Now!"

I complied for two reasons…First, he felt so fucking good inside me. Second, I still couldn't remember the safe word. Don't judge me…just yet.

She purred as she climbed onto the bed. Her hands roamed up my back then came to rest on the hem of my dress. She yanked it up further then palmed my ass cheeks like she was checking for ripeness. Seamus was groaning and driving into me wildly. The Russian bombshell lowered her mouth to my tailbone, then her tongue began a winding journey down the surface of my right ass cheek. She explored my backside like she was Sacajawea leading Lewis and Clark on an expedition into uncharted *ass* territory.

Well, shit! Jackpot! She found the spoils—my anus. I was mortified! I was fresh off fucking Seamus in the laundry room, but gaht damn! This bitch was officially nasty. Who licks an unfamiliar anus? I knew it was clean and disease-free, but shit! *Ok, Seamus wouldn't trust my ass to someone who wasn't disease-free, so I'm going to give her a pass…today!* I thought. *A'ight, I'm just gonna lean in here.* She licked and sucked my anus fervently, and you know what...the shit felt good! Feel free to judge now.

Seamus began alternating his cock between my pussy and her mouth. She gagged as she sucked him, allowing her saliva to flow from her mouth down the seam of my backside to my not-so-thirsty labia. Now, I couldn't tell where my wetness ended, and her saliva began. This was a lot for someone who lost their virginity just a few weeks ago. I rode the wave of pleasure he gave me until I sensed an orgasm begin to stir. I tightened around him as my clit pulsed. The onslaught of cock and tongue stopped when Seamus pulled out of me abruptly.

"You do not get to come until Ms. Petrov and I say you can, Ms. James," Seamus sang in mild amusement.

The Russian giggled wickedly. She released her grip on my ass to rake her nails along my arms then up to my neck. She leaned down to my ear to whisper seductively, "This is fucking, baby!"

Seamus released my wrist then flipped me onto my back. The Russian grabbed my hands, pinning them under her thighs before I even thought to move.

"Spread your legs, Ms. James," she purred.

Seamus made small circular movements with the tip of his cock before dipping inside of me again. While Seamus fucked me, Ms. Petrov began to palm my breast through my dress and bra. *They've done this shit before,* I thought. Their movements were too synchronized to not be second nature. *Shit, I'm still in my church clothes! Why can't I remember the safe word?*

"Open your mouth," the Russian version of Jessica Rabbit said breathlessly. I met her gaze. She meant business, so I obeyed.

She stuck two fingers into my mouth. "Suck!"

I sucked her fingers as she pumped them in and out of my mouth. She pinched my nipple tightly with her other hand. I grasped at her thighs, desperately trying to hold on as I was pounded into the bed by Seamus. Occasionally, she pulled her fingers out of my mouth to suck them. What she did next blew my fucking mind. She opened my mouth with both hands to let a string of saliva drip from her mouth down to mine. *This bitch! Fuck me!* Seamus watched us keenly. He was aroused by her illicit behavior.

"Swallow it, Ms. James," Seamus commanded. "Don't make me repeat myself!"

I swallowed reluctantly. Ms. Petrov's tongue was just in my ass, and I was trying not to gag! I knew it was my ass, but still....

"Fuck her harder, Mr. McGhee," she encouraged Shea in her thick accent.

This is some kinky Handmaid's Tale shit, I thought.

Oddly enough, my senses began to heighten, and I was incredibly aroused. Seamus went on for what seemed like an eternity before I felt my orgasm begin to stir again. When I started to convulse, Seamus pulled out. He paused for a few minutes then lifted my ass, folding me upward until my pussy was in the Russian's mouth. Yes, a bitch was flexible, and he remembered that small detail from one fucking yoga class we took together years before. She was feasting sumptuously!

Ms. Petrov's cunnilingus skills were immaculate. When Shea joined the feast, their tongues dance a beautiful tango between vulva, clitoris, and anus. His body was hard and hot when it pressed against me. I was not a lesbian, and I'd never been curious about sex with another woman, but this was fantastic. The sound and feel of the two of them bathing my undercarriage were maddening. I bet it looked like a kinky half-time acrobatic show! The Russian didn't stop devouring my pussy, though.

"Come for me, Ms. James," Seamus commanded. I obeyed with wicked enthusiasm after a few more minutes.

They supported my body as I went limp from the intenseness of it all. I could barely breathe with all of the fabric shoved up to my face. I probably blacked out a little. When the pleasure waned, the Russian concluded the assault on my clit to lower me back to the bed. Impatiently, Seamus sheathed his engorged cock into me. He pounded me until my orgasm was about to erupt, then pulled out quickly.

"Suck my nipples," she demanded in a thick Russian accent.

She leaned further over my body, so her breasts were parallel with my mouth. I hesitated briefly, contemplating the idea before I pulled her nipple into my mouth. It tightened as I flicked it. I grabbed the other one, guided it into my mouth, and alternated between the two large pink pearls. She moaned in response to my ministrations. I genuinely didn't know what I was doing, but I did my best. I licked the vestiges of Seamus' ejaculation off of her before she pulled away from my mouth, then lowered her lips to mine. Before our kiss could deepen, Seamus pressed his newly-hard cock between our lips. We moaned our excitement loudly in unison. His groans were exhilarating and punctuated the air. Threesome? Kissing a woman? Sharing dick? Who had I become? He looked into our eyes while he slowly pumped into each mouth. His strokes were slow and intentional. He wanted to savor this moment.

"Open your mouth, Ms. James," he ordered gruffly. It was my turn to receive his orgasmic reward, so I opened up willingly.

I swallowed his hot orgasm, not reserving a trace. Seamus stroked up from the base of his cock one last time. He wanted to give me everything he had to offer. I watched intently as a small amount of come beaded the tip. I sucked it off, which caused him to draw in a sharp breath. My lips were devoured as Russian Jessica Rabbit stole my gift.

"Take this fucking dress off," she demanded.

I had almost forgotten we were still in various stages of undressed. I sat up, reaching behind me to unzip it then pull it off. Ms. Petrov was on me before it hit the chair in the corner. She pulled my bra straps down my shoulders, unhooking the clasp in the front. Seamus removed his clothes, tossing them on my dress. The Russian bombshell sat back, watching us.

"You are gorgeous woman, Ms. James," she muttered. "I'm very pleased, Mr. McGhee." Seamus nodded his agreement to her.

"Lie back, da'ling," she rumbled low in her chest, gesturing for

Seamus to lie in the middle of the bed.

Her hands snaked gingerly across his body. Goosebumps rose along the path her hands took. She straddled his hips, leaning forward to give him access to her giant knockers. She rolled his head to the side, giving her access to his ears and neck. She inhaled his scent then nibbled Seamus' ear, stopping only to utter what I presumed to be Russian pillow talk. It made me wet with desire to watch. He addressed her tits again. This time giving them his full attention, flicking, sucking, and biting them delicately. She moved his hands so they rested above his head. Her kisses trailed from his neck down to each pectoral. The hot moisture from her mouth evaporated as she continued her trek south, kissing as she went. She kissed every inch of his abdomen, rimming Seamus' navel and making her way further south. She slid down, settling between his legs.

I was conscious of her every move, touch, kiss—and eager to see what her mouth could do. Our eyes latched, in wonder, as she gestured for me to move to Seamus' head. He wasn't hard when she took him into her mouth. I was positive we drained his energy with those first orgasms. For now, he seemed content to be used. I straddled his face, settling down onto his stubbled mouth. He snatched me from my musing as his wanton tongue suckled the pearl above my vulva's entrance. He pulled it into his mouth, rolling his tongue around it in small circular movements. I felt Seamus' mouth drift lower to my labia. He parted both lips with his tongue then pushed, deliberately unhurried, into me. *Fuck!*

"You taste good," Seamus moaned into my body.

I lost myself, grinding into his face. I grabbed his hair, the wall, the headboard, and then leaned back onto his chest. He supported my body weight with his hands until I moved to straddle him fully.

Seamus fisted at Ms. Petrov's, hair pulling pins from her chignon. Long, thick, inky black waves cascaded over her face onto his thighs and stomach. He wound his hands into it on either side, creating two makeshift ponytails, then fucked her face with reckless abandon. I looked down to see Seamus' face slick with wetness, my wetness. He rimmed my asshole with his tongue, fucking me deeper. I wondered how I tasted in his mouth as he laid waste to my slit and will power.

Seamus moved Ms. Petrov out of the way, then grabbed my hips, rolling me onto my back with ease. I braced myself on the bed as he straddled me, then slid slowly into my depths.

"You," Shea began, "are mine." His voice rumbled deep and low.

"Yes," I moaned.

"Ms. Petrov, I'm about to come. Bring your mouth to me, now," Seamus demanded.

She obeyed without question, scrambling to his swollen phallus as he withdrew it from my aching slit. He leaned back on the bed as Ms. Petrov leaned forward to drink him in. He came in her mouth, on her face, and my stomach. When he finished, she licked the remnants off my stomach before pulling my clit into her fiery mouth.

"Fuck!" I moaned. She straddled my face, then lowered herself to my mouth. Her clit felt large and fleshy. It was not nearly as long and thick like her tongue, but it was impressive. I pressed my clit into her mouth, kissing and sucking hers deeply in return.

"You like my fat pussy, baby?" she asked before rotating herself to face me.

"Mm-hmm," I moaned affirmatively.

Shit! What have I gotten myself into? I didn't eat pussy! The Bad Bitch within me was panting for more. Petrov's pussy was covered in wetness, fat, and throbbing. Hell, I'd already had it in my mouth, so I proceeded without further thought. She had given Shea and me so much pleasure and had received none in return. The Bad Bitch in my brain screamed, *Suck it up, baby!* This Bitch was gonna get evicted if she kept it up.

I licked the tip causing her to arch up to my mouth. I caught it in my mouth, and it was a fucking mouthful. Her labia hung from her pussy like curtains framing her smooth pink opening. I slid two fingers into her wetness, reaching up to feel around. If I was going to go down on another woman, I intended to make her come. I bobbed up on her giant clit while pressing into what I believed was her g-spot. I peered up at her to see if she was enjoying it. I saw Seamus buried to the hilt between her thick red lips. I should have been jealous but wasn't. It made me wet to see him, his length, slick from her saliva. She was getting wetter and wetter from sucking Shea's cock.

"I'm close...I'm so fucking close," Ms. Petrov said, tossing her head back. *Damn, that was quick,* I thought. I sucked fervently until I felt her clit pulse. The orgasm ripped through her, but I kept going until I brought her to completion. She tasted sweet like fresh melons. Her pussy tightened and pulsed around my fingers. It felt as though she were pulling my hand into her wetness. Seamus and I tag-teamed her body. He unsheathed himself from her mouth, leaning back onto the bed to admire my work. I sat up on my arms, looking at her in admiration where she laid.

"I want to taste," she said. "I bet it was wunderbar." She lapped the wetness from my lips and fingers, then kissed me deeply.

"Turn over, Ms. James," she said to me, peering at me through heavy, sated lids.

I rolled over on the bed, avoiding her wet spot. Her clit and labia were truly a sight to see. How was it that big? I made a mental note to ask Seamus about it later. She lifted my legs then aligned her massive labia to mine. Ms. Petrov slid her slick cunt over my own, and I met her thrusts in kind. We carried on as though Shea weren't in the room. We urged one another on. She released my legs to lay prone atop me and kissed me.

"May I come?" I said into her mouth as we kissed.

"We come together, Ms. James! Come, da'link, come!"

She slammed her mouth onto mine as our orgasms caught ahold of us. I grasped her hair, winding it around my hand. I bit her bottom lip as I continued grinding my hips into her. *Wow! I actually orgasmed,* I thought. This was fucking!

Seamus rolled out of bed, striding to the other side. He grabbed the Russian's feet with one swift pull as he yanked us down to the edge along with the duvet and sheets. His cock stood erect. I sensed the power of his thrust as his cock smashed into her. His strokes were unyielding, deliberate, and forceful. Ms. Petrov reached up, cupped my head, and brought hers down into a sensual kiss. Our tongues fought for dominance—she won. She sucked my tongue, reminiscent of how she had sucked my clit. Long pulls, letting her saliva run past her lips into my mouth. I am so enraptured with her kiss that I didn't realize Seamus had pulled out of her until he slammed into me. His cock was thick and pulsing. He fucked me even harder than her. She reached in between us to flick both of our nipples, while our clits grazed one another. I was spiraling fast.

He pulled out before I came, slamming back into her. He had us both begging and moaning for release. She came hard, arching her back. I drank in her moans, pressing my kiss hard onto her open mouth. She grabbed at the comforter as I took over, pinching our nipples. After her body relaxed, Seamus pulled out of her. His grip on my hips intensified as he thrust his cock, headfirst, into my deep end. I stopped kissing the satiated Russian to lay my head in the crook of her neck.

"May I come, Mr. McGhee? Please..." I begged.

He pulled out, ripped his condom off, then plowed back into me. Was that my answer? I came as my pussy gripped and convulsed around his cock, milking it as he came inside of me.

"Ah, fuck," he spat out, undone by what he had experienced with us.

Seamus pulled out of me, then collapsed on the bed next to us.

Have I always been this fucking freaky? I thought. How had I enjoyed this so immensely? I pondered the things I experienced as we laid there in sheer exhaustion.

CONSEQUENCES AND REPERCUSSIONS

Ms. Petrov got up and went into the living room to retrieve a bag, then went into the restroom. Shea followed suit. I watched him saunter to the liquor cart in his bedroom. The man had just satisfied two women, yet there he was looking like he could run a marathon. He made me think big dick energy was real. I heard Stacy and Rho say that about men we knew throughout our friendship. We were notorious for watching sporting events for the sole purpose of spotting athletes with it. Shea definitely exhibited all of the traits of BDE.

"Drink," he said, thrusting a cup into my hand. I swallowed the liquid in one gulp. It burned going down, but I pushed past it. He poured me another, making me drink it as well.

Scotch, his drink of choice, I thought as I swallowed the second drink.

"You're going to need it," he said, motioning his head to the doorway of the bathroom.

"Are you ready?" I turned to see Ms. Petrov in the doorway. I stared at her in silence, eyes wide open and jaw on the floor.

"Answer Ms. Petrov," Seamus said as he set my glass and the decanter of scotch down on the bar across from the bed.

Ms. Petrov wore a massive purple strap-on dildo. She had donned her daredevil heels again. I didn't remember her taking off her clothes or shoes, but a lot had happened.

"I'm not sure, Ms. Petrov." The Bad Bitch in my brain was screaming, *yes! Fucking whore*, I thought.

"Go lie down on the bed," she continued, "facedown, head toward the foot of the bed." Her accent was just as sexy as Seamus' brogue. I complied.

I heard chains and felt them work together, cuffing my ankles with padded cuffs. Ms. Petrov took the left side, and he took the right side. They moved in concert to lock down my hands. *Click. Click.*

"Under the bed restraint system," Seamus said as though reading my mind. "She's all yours, for now," he told his partner, then went into the bathroom.

I heard him turn on the shower then pad back over to the door to close it. *Fuck!* He was really leaving me alone with her and not joining us. He trusted her.

"On your knees," she purred. I complied.

I had just enough slack to get on my knees. It was funny how I was so obedient to a woman, this woman, I had only met a few hours ago. My body was alive, almost electric, with sexual energy.

"What do you want, Ms. James?" she purred.

"I want you to fuck me, Ms. Petrov," I suggested seductively.

"Not before you suck my cock," she growled.

She walked over to the foot of the bed. I watched her ass jiggle from the side. Trust me, it was the kind of ass that stopped traffic and turned heads. She stopped when she was standing directly in front of me at the foot of the bed. I opened my mouth to receive her cock. Usually, I didn't let strangers touch my hair, but this was different. Hell, her tongue had been inside me.

Her hands were wrapped in my hair while she pulled my mouth onto that purple monstrosity of a dildo.

"Sit and watch," she told Seamus after his shower.

He wandered over to the chair I had found him in earlier and perched. He studied the scene intently for a few moments before pouring himself another drink. Without warning, she spanked my ass so hard I yelled out.

"Silence, Ms. James," she responded, with another slap.

Fuck! She was strong and a shit-talker.

"Do you know the difference between fucking and making love?" she asked. "Answer me!"

Slap!

Slap!

"Yes, Ms. Petrov, I do," I moaned.

"Do you know how to be obedient?"

Slap!

Slap!

Both hands rained down on my ass simultaneously.

"Yes, Ms. Petrov," I yelped.

"I don't—" she began.

Slap!

"think..."

Slap!

"you..."

Slap!

"do!" she exclaimed.

Slap! Slap! Slap! Pleasure and pain blurred together.

Ms. Petrov gave me what we called in the Black community a *syllable whoopin'* that caused me to cry out with pain.

"Silence her, Mr. McGhee!" Ms. Petrov's words were sharp.

He stood slowly, allowing the towel to drop to the floor. He was hard as fuck. He took my chin in his hand when he stood in front of me. As they plowed me roughly from the front and back, I knew this was fucking. They didn't ask if it felt good, they didn't care. Ms. Petrov continued her assault on my hind parts mercilessly.

Slap! Slap! Slap!

The physical discipline and verbal review of my disobedient behavior didn't stop until Ms. Petrov reached her climax, twenty-eight ass-smacking minutes later. Her guttural cries reverberated throughout the room. Seamus swelled in my mouth shortly afterward as the remnants of his seed spilled hotly down my throat. They used me as a sex toy then left me wanting.

"May I please come, Mr. McGhee?" I was met with silence. "May I please come, Ms. Petrov?" I begged. Silence. They were silent for several agonizing minutes.

"These are the consequences and repercussions for not being obedient, Ms. James," Seamus said matter-of-factly.

"Mr. McGhee," Ms. Petrov started a moment later. "If she wants pleasure, let her get it by herself. Besides, I'd love to watch her try."

Her laugh was maddening. My body shook from the strain I withstood being held in one position for so long, but I didn't move. My suffering may have garnered a small bit of kindness from them.

"Hmm," Seamus pondered the request. "Alright," he said a short while later. They worked in accord to unchain me.

"Turn over on your back, Ms. James. I desire to see your lovely face as you come." Ms. Petrov's syrupy voice dripped with sexiness. She and Seamus sat on the bed, leaning against the headboard to watch the show. Unashamedly, I reached down to my swollen sex and began to delicately rub my clit. I rolled my nipple in my other hand.

"Fuck! She isn't shy! I like this one!" Jessica Rabbit-ov's interest had been peaked.

Ms. Petrov took off her mechanical cock then crawled alongside me. Seamus got off the bed and headed back to his perch, picking up his discarded towel. His eyes never left me as I worked myself into an orgasmic frenzy. Ms. Petrov decided to interrupt my pleasure quest to straddle my face.

Her movements were rhythmic and seductive. She palmed her breasts gently, rolling her taut nipples between her forefinger and thumb. I felt slickness on my face and fingers. I was so caught up in what she was doing that my orgasm snuck up on me.

"May I come?" I asked between licking her pussy, rolling my nipple, and stroking my clit. "Please?"

"Fuck, yes, Ms. James," she spoke as she rubbed her pussy into my face. I sucked her clit into my mouth and came undone as I heard her cry out through her orgasm. Her moans were low and guttural rasps. We moaned in concert over and over. *How am I this fucking horny?* I couldn't get enough of the Russian sex goddess. Her lips, tits, her round plump ass, her fat pussy, and even thicker clit! She caused all judgment to leave my mind—forcing me to push the bisexual boundaries I never knew I had.

"Ladies," Shea said softly, "it's getting late. I still have to get Ms. James home."

We turned to look at him as though he'd thrown a bucket of ice water on us. A smile spread across Seamus' lips. I pulled my fingers out of her opening to palm her ass with both hands.

"I want to fuck you one on one, Ms. James," Ms. Petrov said, turning back to me. "I bet we can have some real fun."

"Let me think about it," I said sweetly.

"I'll set up a group chat for you two. This way, I can keep track of your conversation, nudes, appointments, and such!" We laughed.

After showering, I went out into the bedroom and saw Seamus in a wing back chair in the corner. He was drinking something—scotch, I presumed. He motioned for me to come to him. I obeyed. I walked across the room slowly, stopping in front of him. He perused my body like he'd never seen it before.

"You amaze me, Ms. James," he started. "I expected you to use the safe word by now, but you've hung in there and taken all we've thrown your way like a champ." I remained quiet, mostly because I was processing everything that had happened in this loft.

We dressed after our showers and made our way to the elevator. Ms. Petrov pressed the third floor, and I pressed the lobby.

"Shit, you live in the building?" I asked, eyes wide. This was the first time I'd spoken since sex ended.

"Yes. Convenient, huh?" she responded. She stepped in front of me, leaned down, and planted another wet kiss on me. She kissed me from the penthouse to her stop on the third floor.

"I anticipate seeing you again, Ms. James," she said as her lips hovered slightly over mine.

"Me too, Ms. Petrov," I rasped back.

"My name is Katya," she purred. She turned and strode off the elevator, her fat ass jiggling seductively until she was out of sight.

I turned to look at Shea, smiling. He returned my smile, then said, "I didn't think you'd last. I thought for sure you'd tap out and use the safe word."

"The safe word escaped my memory once Katya shoved that mint into my mouth and you demanded I suck it," I said nonchalantly.

"How could you forget it?" he asked sarcastically. "It's my nickname for you."

Shit! Butterfly…the fucking safe word was butterfly!

"Fuck," I responded. Shea laughed as he led me through the lobby.

"Did you really forget the safe word, Maeve?" His tone was severe yet inquisitive.

"I wouldn't lie about something like that, Shea," I told him.

"I don't know how to fully process the things you—we—did tonight. I've never found a woman who would let Katya have her way." I gasped in surprise.

"Was that your first threesome, too?"

"Yes, my first real one, and it was fucking mind-blowing to say the least." He looked at me intensely.

"I wanted to make you happy. I thought about backing out, but sucking that mint was so intimate. All reservation just went out the window. It's like I was on autopilot or something."

I turned to look out the window for a moment. My brain needed to power down from the lust-filled encounter. The scenery blurred into dark shapes and shadows bathed in the pale moonlight. We rode in silence for a long time before Shea spoke.

"Do you think Stacy is home? I want to make love to you."

"How do you have the energy?" I looked at him with bewilderment. "I'm sorry, Shea. I'm sore and tired."

"Let's do lunch tomorrow, talk and whatnot," he implored.

"I haven't worked in a week. How about I let you know?"

He came around to my door to let me out looking dejected. I planted a sweet kiss on his cheek then dodged his grip as I ran to the elevator.

"It's like that, MJ?"

"Good night, Shea," I said through the slit in the closing elevator door. I pulled my phone out to text him.

Me: Text when you get home.
Shea: You know I will.
Me: Don't forget to set up our group chat. LOL
Shea: good night. ♥
Me: GN ♥

I stepped out of the elevator and made my way to the door. I unlocked it, stepped inside and pulled off my shoes. *Ah!* I deposited my purse on the table in the entryway, spotting the Post-It on the mirror. Stacy was off getting her some, too.

Me: Stacy's out for the night! LOL
Shea: I have half a mind to turn around!
Me: I'm exhausted...😬
Shea: Why are you teasing me?
Me: GN 💪♥
Shea: I really do love you, Butterfly.♥

Damn! I padded down the hall into my bedroom, peeled out of my clothes, placing them in the appropriate hamper then walked into the bathroom. I turned the tub on waiting for the water to get to the right temperature. I grabbed the Epsom salt from the cabinet and dumped two scoops into the water along with a lavender bath bomb. I quickly tied up my hair then wrapped my scarf around it. I went through my nighttime routine to clean my face, brush my teeth, and floss, then stepped into the tub. I turned the water off and relaxed. *Shit, I needed this!*

Just as I felt the tension leave my body, I heard my phone ring. FaceTime—from Darren. I reached for my phone off the shelf next to my bath. I answered it, lowering myself back into the water.

"Hey, Darren." *Shit, I sound tired.*

"Are you in the bathtub?"

"Yessir, it's been a long day," I rasped.

"You look like you've been rode hard and put away wet," he said.

"You don't know the half," I laughed.

He cocked his head, looking at me like *what the fuck!*

"Buckle in, muhfucka...it's about to be a bumpy ride."

I launched into the events following his departure after church.

"Yo Grams said wha-ha-hat?" he belted into his phone.

"I know, right?" I laughed. "She wasn't playin' today!"

"Shit, in essence, Grams said fuck Chelsey!" Darren's interpretation was spot on.

"Instead, he drove me home and fucked me!"

DW was mortified, "You was still in yo' damn church clothes! Girl, you going straight to hell—do not pass go, do not collect two hunnit dollars!"

I proceeded with the story, going into explicit detail when relaying the penthouse happenings. I took us on an emotional rollercoaster describing my freaky bedtime tale. He sat dazed for a moment before he responded.

"Hello?" I thought the phone froze.

"Nah...Hold on a gaht damn...let me finish rubbing this out!" he said, swinging his head back and forth. "Ok, ok! Now, how big was her clit?"

"It was big,"

"Shit, that bitch on 'roids!" His laugh was exuberant and pulled me in.

"She was strong as fuck too!" I added, thinking about how she'd held my legs up during our halftime show.

"He found the female version of Nikolai Volkoff!" Darren said.

"Nikolai who, Darren? Who the fuck is Nikolai Volkoff?" I giggled into the phone.

"Google it!" he continued. "See, this is what happens when you wait your whole fuckin' life to give up the drawls!"

I did a quick search to find out about Nikolai Volkoff.

"A WWF wrestler? Fuck you, Darren!" I laughed.

Darren had three older brothers. That had to be how he remembered this dusty ass wrestler. *Was WWF even still a thing? It's WWE now, right?*

"Whew...fuck!" he sputtered before continuing his thought. "Let me say this though, you are freaky as hell! How you go from being a virgin to getting down in a threesome—where you're eating random Russian pussy? Do you even know her name?" he quizzed me.

"Uh," I paused, looking stuck. *She told me...Fuck!*

I didn't plan on telling Darren her name, though.

"Darren," I fussed. "If I could tell you I would, but Shea's very private."

"I'll tell you what, you gone have me searching for Russians who look like Jessica Rabbit—with fat asses!"

"I can't do this with yo' ass! Good night!"

I hung up on him, giggling and sinking further into the tub, relishing the last bit of warmth.

I heard the front door open and the alarm chime.

"Maevie," Stacy sang.

"I'm in my bathroom," I sang back.

She deposited her items at the door. She headed to the kitchen, grabbed wine and glasses, then made her way to my bathroom.

"The doors open, honey!" I shouted.

She padded through my room into the bathroom, setting the Moscato down on my counter to open it. I opened the drain to let some of the cold water out then turned on the faucet to refresh the tub with hot water. It was gonna be a long night. Stacy turned, handing me a glass, then settled down on the floor, propping herself up on the cabinet directly across from me.

"How long have you been in there?" she asked.

I looked at my Apple Watch. "An hour," I reported, then sipped the wine.

"Whatever the fuck for, Maevie?"

"I was telling Darren about my day and lost track of time."

"Ok, I'm getting tired of being second to Darren, woman!" she remarked over her glass before taking a long drink.

"You wouldn't have been second had your ass been home," I said smugly.

"What the fuck happened, Maeve?" She squinted at me, furrowing her brow, feigning anger.

"Seamus and I had a threesome—long story short," I said nonchalantly.

Stacy choked on her wine, looking at me in disbelief. The water felt hot enough, so I turned it off. I was thankful we invested in a tankless water heater. Hot water on demand, bitch!

"What the entire fuck?" she responded, through unblinking eyes.

"Girl, it's a *long* story...we gone need more wine."

"Seriously?" She searched my face for the lie.

"Seriously," I replied.

"Spill." She drained her wine glass before reaching up to bring the bottle down to where she sat on the floor. I rehashed the story I'd just told Darren. Bit by bit, I saw Stacy's mind being blown. I finished my first glass of wine. Stacy refilled the glass I extended to her.

"Get the *fuck* out of here!" she screamed when I told her about what Grams said. "Your Grams is a fucking G, yo'! We've been telling you fuck that bitch for a while now! What did Seamus say?"

I almost spilled my second glass of wine in the tub laughing at her reaction to her question!

"You are lying! Swear on Grams' sweet potato pie!" Stacy said. Her grip on the glass was so tight I thought she'd snap the stem.

"Sweet potato pie? Bitch, what?" I roared with laughter. Who the fuck swore on pie?

"Yo, Gram's sweet potato pie is the truth, Maevie! Swear on it, or I won't fucking believe you!"

"I swear on Gram's sweet potato pie." I replied with a straight face, all joking aside, so she knew it was real.

Stacy knew I was telling the truth, but something in her wouldn't let her believe fully.

"Bitch, you went to church with your parents today. So why—how— the fuck did you end up not only fucking him again but letting him drag you into a threesome?"

"Stace, I still don't know! Honestly, I've never seen a woman who looks like her. She was gorgeous. Her clit was...." my voice trailed off.

"I know—large! I'm pissed!" she remarked jokingly.

"Why?" I asked seriously.

"My dick appointment fell through, and now I'm all hot and both-ered by your freaky ass epic," She giggled.

"Girl, Darren was out of control. He called her Nikolai Volkoff and Natasha from Bullwinkle."

"Girl, Darren plays entirely too much."

"Who are you telling? He said he's gonna be looking for big booty Russians."

"Shit, me too, and I don't fuck with foreign women like that."

"That's what he said!" We were tipsy and giggling uncontrollably.

"Are you serious about seeing her again, without Seamus?" she asked seriously.

"I don't know. He didn't seem comfortable with it. After all, he was trying to teach me a lesson."

"He's an ass for that, really and truly. If he wasn't our friend, and I didn't know him, I'd say that was some abusive shit," Stacy said

"I thought so at first, but wasn't like that. I could've stopped it when I wanted—if I could've remembered the safe word."

"Maeve, you lost your virginity a few weeks ago. There's no way you should've been tossed into the deep end like that. I've been fucking since I turned nineteen. I still haven't had a threesome."

"Darren said something similar. In a way, I feel like this brought us closer," I said.

"No, ma'am. Seamus fucked two twins in college, remember? Nope!"

"It's different when the women don't interact with one another," I said, sounding so mature.

"Word, I get that. A'ight now, get your little ass out of the tub. You gon' be wrinkled!"

She stood taking my glass, setting it on the counter next to the empty wine bottle. She padded over to my cabinet for a towel then handed it to me. I stood up, wrapped the towel around me, then stepped out onto my plush rug.

"Don't let all of this overtake you, Maevie. It takes a strong mind to be submissive when it comes to that type of sex."

"I won't. Thanks for not judging me. This is, without question, G-14 classified."

"It goes without saying. This is not my story to tell. Unlike Rho, you are not the resident hoe!"

We headed back into my room, where I threw on a t-shirt.

"Are you sleeping with me?" I asked her.

"Sure."

She stripped down to her undies and t-shirt then joined me in bed. The wine was the perfect sedative.

We drifted off to sleep a little after midnight.

Chapter Seventeen
GOING...GOING

My alarm went off at seven am the next day. I picked up my phone and saw nine missed messages from Shea.

> *Bing!*
> Shea: GM, beautiful
> Shea: You up?
> Shea: Hello
> Shea: Babe?
> Shea: Is your "do not disturb" on?
> Shea: What the hell...
> Shea: Ok, hit me up when you wake up
> Shea: I miss you...hence the stalking...
> Shea: OK...LAST ONE! LOL
> Me: Sorry, I just got your messages. Long night...got sidetracked by a phone call and conversation with Stacy when she got in.
> Shea: No worries. How do you feel?
> Me: Sore...tired but good. I took a long hot bath, a few glasses of wine and two Advil.
> Shea: Did you tell Stacy about us?
> Me: Yes, she was floored but didn't judge. She gave me some advice.
> Shea: I trust it was good. She's never steered you wrong.

Me: I hop I didn't worry you.
Me: *hope
Shea: No. I wanted to talk, but it's all good.
Me: I'm sorry.
Shea: No worries. It's all good.
Shea: Have a good day at work. Don't forget my
         lunch proposal.
Me: I won't...you too! 🖤

I laid in bed, pondering the previous day's events. I remembered the promise I made to God, and my heart sank. Why was Shea so delicious? Why was it so simple for me to fall into him? I rested for a few moments before I got up, trying not to wake Stacy. She didn't stir, so I slipped out of bed, making my way to the closet to find something to wear. Comfort was the goal for the day's outfit. I forewent the stilettos for ballet flats. My thighs were seriously killing me. I found some loose-fitting slacks and paired them with a cute blouse. I over-accessorized to make up for the ballet flats. Maybe Jared wouldn't notice that I was low key.

Bright sunshine greeted me when I stepped out into the building. The city sounds blared about me, and I beamed within before greeting my driver.

"Hiya, Jim," I sang sweetly.

"Miss James," Jim smiled in return and nodded his greeting.

My old driver had retired recently. Jim replaced him several months ago. In my mind, I had imagined him to be prior military, special ops, or some shit. His physique made me think his training was intense and rigorous, yet his eyes bespoke an air of sweetness. Jim was a very handsome man. He stood a full head above Seamus and was the living embodiment of sexual chocolate. His skin was velvety brown with full lips and a broad nose. He dressed neatly in a black suit, crisp white shirt, and black tie.

Jim opened the door and took my bag. I settled myself in as he went around the back of the car. He was efficient but not much of a talker. I couldn't recall any personal information about him or his family. I assumed he was single because he didn't wear a ring. I rode in silence, taking in the sites of the city. Traffic moved along slower than usual, but Jim managed to get me to W&W ahead of schedule.

Jared waved while chatting into his earpiece when I walked in, but the look on his face told me he noticed the flats. I caught the stunned look on his face when his elevator eyes made it to the bottom floor. I laughed quietly to myself as I strolled past his desk into my office. I had settled in and was working on a few charts for my meeting with the partners later that afternoon when Jared strolled in with tea and a bagel.

"Good morning, MJ," he said smugly. I looked up to catch a devious smirk on his face. "Now, what could have possibly happened this weekend to have you in those hideous flats?"

"These are Tory Burch, sir," I said, laughing at his comment. I pushed away from my desk, walking over to my sitting area where Jared had set my bagel and tea. "Don't you start." I took a seat and sipped my tea.

"Ma'am, Tory does not belong on your feet unless she is walking you to your car at the end of the day. What would the commoners think?" he joked.

Jared dressed in the latest fashions. I knew I didn't pay him well enough to afford the designer labels he sported. I didn't pry into his personal finances, though.

"They will think we're all at different levels, and there's no room for judgment," I mused sarcastically before sinking my teeth into the crunchy cinnamon-flavored bagel.

"Oh, sweetie." He tilted his head to the side, looking at me like I was a charity case. "And I see you tried to accessorize to compensate for them."

"I think I look nice," I protested jokingly.

"I bet you do." He chuckled as he crossed one leg over the other then brought his hand to his chest.

"So, you're telling me," I began mildly offended, "this outfit doesn't look nice?"

"No, ma'am, let me clarify. I'm saying pearls, a broach, a scarf, and those shoes are too much. You look like Mrs. Doubtfire's niece." I balled my napkin up and threw it at him. "What you won't be doing is wearing all of that into your meeting this afternoon."

"But I—" He lifted an eyebrow in judgment despite my protesting.

"I don't have any other shoes," I began.

"Bottom left in your closet." He shooed me over to my closet.

"How the hell did all of this..." I looked up at him in disbelief.

"Mr. McGhee had it sent over this morning." Jared smiled at me slyly as I perused all of the clothing items Shea had sent for me. Giuseppe Zanotti heels, Dolce & Gabbana dress, Givenchy blouse, True Religion jeans, a Trina Turk jumpsuit, Alexander McQueen blazer—with accessories and shoes to match each outfit. I was flabbergasted and puzzled. What had prompted this? I made a note to ask him later.

"He sent the items along with a card. I put it on your desk." He gestured toward the desk. "I wish my best friend sent me gifts like this. Now, you don't have to wear those granny flats for the meeting." He laughed as he made his way back to his desk. *Fuck me! Jared knew Shea and I had sex! Dammit!*

The card, which I had overlooked, was underneath my work. How had I missed it? I picked it up and opened it.

Just because.

Love, Seamus

I placed the card back into the envelope and hugged it to my chest. It was very sweet. I reached for my bag and fished out my phone to call him. Shea was on the line when I put my phone to my ear.

"Hey, you." His voice was a low rumble like he was just waking.

"Hello, Mr. McGhee," I sang playfully into the phone. "I got your gift. I was calling to thank you."

"You know that's not necessary," he replied, sounding nonchalant.

"So," I paused to think about how I wanted to phrase my question, "what was the occasion?"

"I thought I'd replace the Givenchy dress, with interest. Do you like the other items?" he asked sweetly. I blushed deeply and took a deep breath to keep the memory at bay.

"Other items?" Puzzled, I began to look around.

"Top of the closet," he answered, "in white boxes with the black ribbon."

"Hold up," I said, placing the call on speaker before setting the phone down on top of my desk.

I had to step back to see the top of the closet. Sure enough, there were three white boxes with black ribbons. I grabbed my step stool, placing it in front of the closet, then ascended to the top. I still had to stand on my toes to reach the packages. I pulled them down, then went back to my desk.

"Shea, what is this?" I asked as I pulled the ribbon off of the first package.

"Open it and find out," he said, smiling through the phone.

I opened the box and removed the top layer of tissue paper to reveal a very sexy black bra with two sets of thong panties. The first pair matched the bra, but the second was an exact match to the pair he had torn off of me during our threesome. Heat began to rise in my cheeks and chest. My sex clenched at the memory of the last night. *You still owe me another pair,* I thought deviously.

"Shea—" I started before he interrupted.

"I think you should open the other boxes before you say anything else," he suggested sweetly.

I set the first box aside to work on the other boxes. The second box contained a red lacy bra with matching thong panties and a garter belt. The third box held a long black satin robe.

"Shea," I asked sweetly, "where do you think I'm going to be wearing all of these things?"

"New York. I have a business trip this weekend. I'd like you to come with me," he spoke softly. His voice was doing things to my body. I began to perspire, my nipples hardened, and my sex began to throb.

"I don't know if that would be proper, Seamus," I said slowly. "After all, you are still engaged."

"Maeve, you've been on vacation with me plenty of times. Why should now be any different?"

"Well, let's see," I began. "There's the new and problematic fact that we've been intimate with one another."

"It's not problematic for me," he stated.

"Seamus, I don't know if that's the best idea right now. I really need time to think." Reluctance coursed through every fiber of my being.

"I think some time alone together will do us some good. We can take in a show, shop, or stay in. I really don't care as long as I'm with you." Shea's words oozed sensuality.

The idea did sound tempting. Chelsey was still in the picture, though. I knew he said the wedding was postponed so they could work through some issues on both ends, but I hated knowing I was the issue he was working around. Seamus had acknowledged his love for me and was willing to temporarily forego marriage to see what lay between us. Why was I in such a quandary about it?

"I've told you I don't want to be a jump-off, Shea," I spoke in hushed tones.

"Maeve, I don't want to marry another woman if there's a chance for the two of us. I settled on being your friend, but I won't settle when it comes to marriage." His candidness took me by surprise.

Those revelations had me in a tailspin. I was uncertain how to proceed. My friends and Grams had encouraged me to fight for Shea.

But what if I'm not the woman he chooses in the end? I thought warily.

"I don't know, Seamus," I started slowly. "I'm so far out on a ledge…" my voice trailed off.

"Maeve, I'm right there with you. Don't you think I'm scared too? If I marry Chelsey, I'm going to lose you. Do you know what the worst part will be?"

"No," I answered softly.

"The worst part will be wondering *what if?* Things with Chelsey are…complicated, but I'm in love with you. I want to call things off permanently, but there are extenuating circumstances that prevent it right now. Let me ask you a question."

"Go 'head," I responded, intrigued.

"Are you in love with me?" he asked evenly.

"Yes," I responded in kind.

"I am in love with you too, Maeve. I'm laying everything on the line here. We can take things as fast or as slow as you'd like. Just, please say you'll come with me."

So there it was, but was it enough? *This is what you've wanted for a long time*, the Bad Bitch in my brain screamed. I had a gnawing thought in the back of my mind, though. Everyone knew the side piece rarely won...

The line was quiet while I pondered. Was he holding his breath?

"Ok," I responded.

He exhaled slowly before he spoke again. "You've made me very happy, Butterfly."

"So," I asked, "what are the details of this trip?"

"There's a Louis Vuitton duffle in the back of your closet. It contains the itinerary for the trip. We leave Friday evening after work. I didn't ask Jared what your schedule was for the week, but he said your weekend was free. We'll be back Sunday evening. We've both missed enough work. This is just going to be a relaxing weekend," he concluded.

I retrieved the bag he mentioned from the closet, finding the itinerary. I reviewed it before responding, "What if I had said no, Seamus?"

"I would've looked incredibly stupid," he laughed.

"You could never look stupid to me," I responded.

"Are we still on for lunch?" he inquired sweetly, changing the subject.

I pulled up my calendar for the next week, then responded, "I'm going to have to pass if I want to complete all of my responsibilities before heading to NYC. Honestly, it's going to be a very long week. Plus, I'm meeting with the partners this afternoon. I'll be in meetings most of the week. I have a full plate, but I promise I'll make it up to you."

"That's a promise I intend to see you keep. Alright, my love, I'll see you Friday," he said sweetly before we hung up.

I buzzed Jared over the intercom.

"Yes, boss?" he chimed cheerfully.

"If you're free, come see me," I said.

"Coming," he replied.

Jared tapped before opening the door.

"I need your advice," I said to him.

Jared and I had become close friends after our first corporate retreat. On the first free day, we decided to get some exercise. Unbeknownst to us, the resort exercise center doubled as a gym for retired superheroes. Those geriatric go-getters were lifting, squatting, and running rings around the two of us. *It was downright embarrassing.* Back in my suite, we shared a hearty laugh and agreed to never discuss what we'd seen again. That night we shared our life stories over a charcuterie board and several bottles of wine. Jared wasn't just an assistant to me. He was more like the little brother I didn't have and knew I needed. He endeared himself to me and everyone in my life except Rho.

"Sure thing, MJ," he smiled. "What's up?"

"I'm sure you've figured out that my relationship with Shea has...changed," I began. "It's complicated now."

"I've known for a long time that you've been in love with him—if that's what you're saying." He sat across from me with his legs crossed.

"You did?" I asked. "How?"

"The way you look at him, the way you giggle when you talk to him...he's in love with you too, MJ. Let me guess, you've slept together. Am I right?" Jared asked softly. He glanced back to make sure he'd closed the door to my office.

"Jared, how—" I started.

"I know Maison L'amour lingerie boxes when I see them." He smiled wickedly. "And judging by the outfits he sent, he's not only seen the goods, but he's sampled them too."

I blushed at his response.

"Well, shit and shove me in it," I said, tossing my head back as I laughed. "Is there anything you don't know, Jared?"

"I know you, MJ. Clothes, lingerie, and a Louis Vuitton duffle for a weekend trip said two things—you two fucked, and it was good!" He snapped twice, pursed his lips, and raised his eyebrow knowingly. "Your virginal ass must've put it down!"

"Wow," I said in shock.

"Girl, bye," he began, "you've never missed this much work or been seen in ballet flats at work. Your little ass is sore!" Pun intended.

We squealed with laughter. Jared leaned back on the couch.

"You don't know the half," I whispered while laughing. I leaned forward on the desk.

"Oh, trust me, honey, I caught sight of his print the day you sauntered your ass up in here in that black Givenchy LBD after your lunch date a few months ago. He's holding at least nine—no ten inches, easy!" Jared laughed, but he was very serious too.

Unconsciously, I said, "He ripped that thing off me after the dinner party!"

"Well, damn," Jared said, leaning in. "Do tell, Miss James!"

"Do you remember the pictures I had you make for me?"

"Singapore?" he asked. "I meant to ask you how that went. Go on!"

I relayed the details to Jared about the dinner, my panties in Shea's pocket, and what it led to afterward.

"Fucking hell," he said, sitting back in his seat.

"It's been a clusterfuck ever since that night. He's postponed his wedding and now…now he wants to discuss our future."

I leaned my face into the crook of my hands. Jared and I sat staring at each other silently.

"Well," Jared said, breaking the silence, "I know you're going to New York. That is your man, MJ. So, what do you want to ask me?"

"You already gave me your answer in so many words," I responded.

"Oh, you wanted to know if I thought you should go?" he reiterated my unspoken question. "Hell, you already knew what I was gonna say!"

He stood up walking over to my closet. "Let me tell you something, I don't know what queen picked these pieces," he said, "but her taste is impeccable. For that alone, I say go!"

"Why am I the only one thinking about being the side chick?" I snickered.

"Side chick?" He strolled casually, taking a seat in front of me. "Honey, Seamus has been your man for over a decade. Chasity is the side piece—ring or not! Are they even fucking yet? Seamus' dick sprang to life way too fast at the sight of you leaning over my desk."

I laughed in response to his comment. "No, they aren't."

"Shit, I know a sex-starved man when I see one," Jared exclaimed.

"This is why I love you, Jared," I replied.

"I thought you loved me because I was the best executive assistant ever," he said languidly.

"That too!" I rose and went around my desk to sit next to him in the accompanying chair. Jared and I discussed my outfits in-depth for a few minutes before he urged me to get up and try them on.

"Come on," he squealed. "I've been dying to see this jumpsuit with this Alexander McQueen blazer. Honey, these Giuseppe heels are to die for!"

"Jared, I do not want to get undressed in front of you, and we have a lot of work to do."

"You called me in here, despite all of the work we have, now get out of those fucking clothes." Jared ran to lock the door as I kicked out of my shoes and pants. I was happy I had worn matching underwear.

"Well, fuck me," he exclaimed. "I expected beige or black granny panties. What the fuck do you know about La Perla?"

"I'm reporting you to HR in the morning! Do you know Shea asked the same question?"

"I bet he did," Jared responded through peals of laughter.

"Someone was eventually going to see me in them," I replied. "Besides, you've met Rho."

"Yes, I have," he replied flatly, "and she's a hoe from way back."

Rho and Jared didn't get along. He said she was a loud banshee of a woman. He also said I needed to find a new friend every time she called.

"Be nice." My admonition was met with an eye roll. "She introduced me to laser hair removal, Lelo sex toys and—"

"La Perla," we said in unison.

"She's a hoe with great taste in sexual accouterments," Jared snickered.
"That she is," I said in agreement.

Jared styled me as I tried on all of the things Shea had sent over, except the lingerie.

"I'll have all of these items laundered and packed in your duffle by Friday. Is there anything else you'll need? I can grab it while I'm out at lunch," he said. I made a list of toiletries I'd need in addition to some traveling clothes. He knew I liked to travel comfortably.

I dressed, finished my slides, and made it to my afternoon meeting. I wore the Giuseppe heels at Jared's prodding. They were comfortable, surprisingly. I switched shoes as soon as I made it back to my office. I found several Adidas leggings, matching tops, and NMDs in a variety of colors laid across my couch when I returned.

"Great job, Jared," I sang through the intercom.

"I aim to please, boss."

My week seemed to zip by because I was busy from the time I arrived every day until the time I checked out. I worked overtime at home to make sure I didn't leave any work for Jared. He was getting the weekend off, too. The weekend was going to be a welcomed vacation from all of my labors. Jared and I had burned the midnight oil on several occasions. I had to come down on several managers in my department hard because they missed deadlines. If I was staying late, so were they. We had eaten so much take-out it was coming out of our noses. I let Jared go home early on Friday.

"Your duffle is packed, and a car will be waiting to take you to the airport promptly at four-thirty. Do not miss it! I want to hear about everything when you return on Monday," he said before leaving.

Bing!
Jared: It's 4:20 pm, log off and head downstairs.
Me: In the elevator, J!
Jared: Aww, my little bird has flown the nest. I'm so
          proud!

Me: I hate you! LOL
Jared: You LOVE me! Have a great weekend!
Me: You're right! 😭 You do the same.

Shea's driver was waiting for me when I exited the building. He took my duffle and opened the door. He closed the door then put my duffle in the trunk. I was dressed in the freshly laundered Adidas gear Jared had purchased for me. I was tired and quickly found myself asleep. The driver woke me up when we arrived at the airport.

"Mr. McGhee is already here. I'll have your bags taken and checked. Enjoy your trip, Ms. James."

With that, he was gone.

Chapter Eighteen
UNEXPECTED CHANGES

The flight to New York was uneventful. Shea had to prepare for a meeting shortly after we landed, so he was unable to enjoy our flight. I had hoped to join the mile high Club.

"If I didn't have this meeting," he began, "I'd give you a proper tour. Unfortunately, I need to go over these property comps and a few contracts. This deal has to be perfect. We'll have to separate as soon as we land. I hope you'll like the new look."

"You renovated it?" I asked. I knew it was a business trip, but I was really looking forward to spending time with him.

"Chelsey," he looked up from his work to gauge the look on my face, "renovated a bit. She has been staying there when she comes to town for business."

"I can't wait to see it," was all I said. He stared at me briefly, smiled, then went back to his work.

Well, this was gonna be interesting. I already felt like a mistress. They weren't even married yet, and Chelsey was renovating his properties. I couldn't believe I was seriously going to stay in the apartment he shared with his fiancée. I groaned inwardly at the thought. I watched *Lego Movie 2: The Second Part* on my iPad until we began our descent. I loved cartoon movies. Shea looked at me like I was crazy every time I laughed a little too hard at something.

The New York skyline remained breathtakingly iconic. The city appeared almost magical before you got down into it at ground level. I was never prepared for the catcalls, bum piss, or rudeness. Chicagoans were rude, but New Yorkers took that shit to expert level. When I was there last, I kept waiting for a loud voice to part the sky and say, "Finish him." Yes, I was comparing New York City to a violent video game. I loved it when they heard me speak. They'd look at me oddly then ask where I was from like I had spoken in some exotic accent. That tickled me.

We landed and, true to his word, went our separate ways. I loved big cities, but I never understood how New Yorkers dealt with the traffic. I wasn't driving, but it still gave me a headache. People slamming on brakes, darting out in front of cars, yelling explicit words in every language imaginable. Shea's apartment building was called the Rutherford and was built in the late 1920s. The pre-war structure added to the charm of the building. I was welcomed by the doorman and the concierge in the building.

"Ms. James, I presume?" the grey-haired older man inquired. "My name is Jasper Seaworth."

"Yes, sir," I replied. "It's a pleasure to meet you."

"Likewise, ma'am. Mr. McGhee instructed me to give you this elevator key." He handed me the key then proceeded, "The apartment is 17B. The landing is shared by two apartments. Mr. McGhee's unit will be the first one you see when the elevator doors open. Your luggage has been taken up ahead of you."

"Thank you," I smiled.

The elevator in the building was fast. I stepped off the elevator into a stately landing, which was warmly lit and nicely decorated. The aesthetic of the building fit Shea's personality. Most of the details were in the architecture. I rang the doorbell and was greeted by an older woman.

"Come on in, young lady." Her smile was warm. "I'm Lina Jordan. Jasper phoned to say you were on your way up. Are you hungry?"

"I'm Mae—"

Lina interrupted, "I know who you are, Ms. James."

"Well sure," I responded sheepishly, "Ms. Lina, I was hoping to eat with Mr. McGhee."

"Oh, I'm not sure if that will be possible. I don't expect him until later. I don't mind whipping you up something," Lina said.

Dejectedly, I responded, "How about a salad?"

"Is that all?" Lina asked.

"I'm not very hungry. I think I'll turn in early," I said softly.

We talked as we made our way toward the kitchen. I assumed that's where we were headed, anyway. I looked around for renovations, but I didn't' see any. Shea's home looked the same as it had when the crew had come for New Years a few years back.

"I can warm up some soup to go with your salad, if you'd like," Lina suggested sweetly.

I pondered. "That sounds good. What kind do you have?"

"Mr. McGhee had the chef make roasted tomato basil. I believe he said it was your favorite," she added.

"It is, Ms. Lina." I smiled at her warmly. "I'd love a small bowl of soup. Do you have some crusty bread?"

"Sourdough, if that's alright," she spoke as she ushered me over to the table and pulled out a chair. "Sit." Funny how, when she mentioned soup, I became instantly ravenous.

Lina set to work warming up soup, rinsing and chopping veggies for my small salad. We chatted as she worked. She told me about her kids, two boys and a girl, all of whom were out on their own, making her very proud. Her oldest son was a lawyer in Pittsburgh, her daughter was a nurse living in Newark with her husband, and her youngest son was a student at NYU. She gushed and gushed about their accomplishments. It was endearing. I wondered if my parents gushed about me this way, then I remembered Dr. James expected me to be great. It wasn't an accomplishment—it was an expectation.

I finished my dinner while chatting with Lina, then prepared to go to my room.

"No worries, Lina. I can find it. There are only two rooms, and I assume I'll be in the guest room down the hall," I said.

"Actually, Mr. McGhee purchased the upstairs apartment for the renovations. That's where you'll be staying," she informed me.

"Do what, now?" I was so confused.

"He recently purchased the apartment above his. I don't have all of the details, but I know your room is upstairs. There are a private elevator and staircase, as well. Follow me," she said, gently guiding me in the opposite direction. We walked back to the entry to a door that used to be the closet.

"Get out," I gasped.

We stepped onto the elevator and proceeded to the new space. So, this was what Chelsey did. The apartment had been gutted, and in the new space was another living room and several guest suites.

"This is where you'll be staying, Maeve," Lina said with a smile.

Utter amazement washed over me. There was a tan leather wall behind the teak bed to the left, built-in bookshelves with two upholstered chairs, and a table tucked between them under the window directly across from the door with views of Central Park and the city skyline aglow. Across from the bed was a neutral-toned sideboard neatly tucked under the television. The fixtures and bedding were white and gold. There weren't many decorative pieces in the room so as not to take away from the picturesque view from the window. It was definitely the showstopper—Central Park. Genius.

"This is absolutely stunning," I muttered to myself.

"Ms. James, I'll be leaving soon, so let me know if you need anything else. Also, Mr. McGhee will be home tonight," Lina added.

"Lina, thank you so much for taking care of me. I greatly appreciate it," I said before giving her a quick hug.

"It was my pleasure. I'll come by before I leave to check on you."

Lina left me alone to get settled in. I closed the door behind her and went to check out the rest of my room. There were two doors, one on either side of the bookshelves. To the left was the closet, the other door led to the bathroom. All of my clothes were in the closet hanging neatly. I found my shoes on shelves along with my accessories. My undergarments were in the drawers. The crown jewel of the room was the *en suite* bathroom. It was top to bottom marble. The fixtures came out of the wall, sinks were built-in, and the towels were on a shelf under the sink. The shower was so spacious. I decided to peel out of my travel clothes and indulge. My toiletries were neatly placed in the shower and on the counter. How had Lina had time to do all of this?

Midway through my shower, I heard the door open. I jumped, turning to see Seamus stepping in to join me.

"Shit, Shea," I swatted at him. "You scared the hell outta me. Where's Lina?"

"I told her I'd check on you and sent her home." He pulled me into his grasp. His body was hot against my backside. The steam of the shower intensified his scent—notes of citrus, juniper, and sandalwood assailed my nostrils. He smelled fresh and clean, without the benefit of a shower.

"I wasn't expecting to see you until tomorrow morning," I said. I turned to drape my arms around his neck.

"I couldn't let you spend your first night here alone," he said as he traced the lines of my face and kissed my nose.

"Oh, really..." I began, but it was clear he didn't want to talk. He leaned down to kiss me. I didn't mind at all. Our kiss spoke the words we yearned to say as it deepened.

Shea pulled away momentarily, then said, "I'm sorry I had to leave you." He leaned in, nibbling on my earlobe as he spoke. "I'm glad you're here with me."

I planted soft little kisses and love bites on his shoulder and chest. I allowed my hands to wind into his loose, wet tendrils. He tenderly cupped my rear, pulling me to him. His erection, ever ready to serve, stood strong.

"I need you," he said, lifting me gently, then sliding within the walls of my aching sex. He backed me against the cool shower wall, causing my body to arch against him. I instinctively wrapped my legs around his waist.

"Whew," I gasped.

He reached up and turned the shower head toward my back. The water was tantalizing as it ran down my breasts and in between our bodies. He proceeded to love me with long, deep upward strokes. I grinded my clitoris into his stomach hard while digging my feet into his firm buttocks for leverage. Holding me with one hand, Shea reached between us to pinch my nipple. The little mound reacted wickedly, sending sensations directly to my sex. I arched again, causing Shea to back up. Without stopping the assault on my body, he broke the grip my legs had on his waist, pulling both legs over his shoulders. Then with his free hands, he set to work on both nipples. I moaned into his mouth as his kisses crushed my lips. I knew I wouldn't last long like that.

"Fuck me, harder," I begged.

I had a tight grip on his head, bringing his mouth to mine in a passionate kiss. Our tongues flitted and danced with one another. His mouth slammed down on mine hard as he put both hands on the side of my body. He drove into me with abandon. Ecstasy washed over me as the water cascaded down our bodies, I was undone.

Shea's face was exquisite as he unraveled into orgasmic bliss. Our moans and cries were intertwined as our bodies slapped loudly together. I lowered my legs to rest in the crook of his elbows on either side as our lovemaking subsided. We silently basked in what had just occurred for a few moments, before Shea finally lowered me to stand on the floor of the shower.

"Way to wreck my shower," I joked.

"You're welcome," Shea said with a smirk. "I'm not done with you, though."

He was a master at curtailing my protests in the most wicked ways. He sat on the bench at the back of the shower, then pulled me towards him.

"Put your leg up here." He indicated the spot on his left side. I did so eagerly.

He pulled my clit into his mouth, reaching around to explore my anus with his index finger.

I sucked in through my teeth, enjoying the sensation.

"Put your hands on my shoulders to brace yourself. You may not be able to stand when I'm done with you," he said hotly against my thigh.

Carefully, I stood on the bench pulling him back to me. I threw my leg gingerly over his shoulder, giving him better access to my pussy. He reached between me and the wall to resume his work on my timid anus then slammed his mouth onto my clitoris. His tongue flicked and sucked my clit masterfully, then he darted his tongue into the depth of my slit. I tried to brace against the wall, but it was slick from the water and steam. I reached for his shoulder to steady myself as he brought his other hand up to my waist then rested his knee on the bench. It soon became hard to focus on anything. His mouth felt amazing yet the sensation of his finger, now fully in my anus, gave equal—if not greater—sensation.

I felt my knees buckle a bit at the onset of my orgasm. Shea managed to steady me, but as frenzy began to set in, I lost all sense of space, time and had no reference as to where the orgasm was taking me. Pleasure washed over me in hot, roiling waves. I pressed myself back to the wall, clinging to the head between my thighs as I cried out with excitement. A state of euphoria took over me—possessing my spirit, body, and soul. I gasped and writhed until, to my own disbelief, emotion sprang up in my heart, causing hot tears to stream from my eyes as deep sobs left my throat. My body lurched with each sob. I didn't feel Shea lower my leg, pick me up, or sit down with me in his lap. He embraced me, squeezing tightly. He stroked my face gently as he spoke. His words were lost as emotion occupied my thoughts. Slowly, I became aware of Shea saying my name over and over. His voice was tender yet laced with concern.

"Maeve."

"I'm sorry," I said. "I don't know what came over me."

"I know what overcame you, Maeve." He lifted my face to look him squarely in the eye.

"How do you know what overcame me."

"Do you remember the night I finally admitted my love for you?" he asked gently. I didn't want to be reminded of it.

"Yes, what about it?" I answered.

"That night, I felt what I believe you just experienced. Uncontrollable, unspeakable emotion washed over every fiber of my being." He paused for a moment before continuing. He swallowed hard then continued softly, "I knew what I felt for you...was love."

I tried to look away, but he held my chin fast. I felt sparks pass between us. A low electric current rumbled within his body, passing slowly to mine. Every nerve in my body was humming with desire for him at this admission. I swung my feet off of his lap, breaking the hold he had me in. I stood before him for a moment to allow him to take in the sight of my wet body glistening under the warm shower light. I inhaled deeply then straddled him. He placed his hands on my hips as I hovered above his semi-rigid shaft. I reached down, working him until I obtained the desired stiffness, then deliberately and painstakingly sank onto his quivering manhood. We exhaled together when we were one.

I cupped his face in both of my hands, stared deeply into his eyes, then placed my lips firmly on his mouth. I closed my eyes and began to rotate my hips, grinding into his pelvis. I continued to kiss him, closed mouth, as I swirled my hips deliciously on his lap. I continued until I worked us both into a fever. He pawed at my hips, trying to get me to ride him. I kept my pace purposefully slow for what seemed like an eternity. Finally, I lifted my hips until his length was almost completely unsheathed. He shoved me back down onto his cock. I lifted, again and again, still only offering him my lips, no tongue. He licked at my lips, almost begging me to acquiesce. Realization spread over me. He wasn't used to not being in control. Usually, the tables were turned, and it was I who relinquished control, begged for satisfaction and let him lead me to orgasmic relief. This time, I steered the vessel, keeping control until he finally lost it.

"Maeve, please," he pleaded softly against my lips, "don't torture me like this."

I quickened my pace as I rode the length of his meaty cock, kissing him harder and harder, not relenting in the torture I delivered until I felt my orgasm begin to stir. He drove upward into me savagely when I finally allowed access to my mouth. His tongue darted into my mouth wildly. Wrapping his arm around my waist, crushing my mouth to his with the other hand on the back of my neck, he fucked me senselessly until I cried aloud. My sounds were guttural and intense. I didn't sound like myself until words formed.

"I love you, Shea," I wept as another round of sensation began.

"I love you too, baby," he said before pleasure took away all of his words.

He leaned back against the wall, taking me with him when the pleasure we'd experienced subsided. I laid my head against his chest.

"You're going to be a little wrinkled prune if I keep you in here much longer," he said against my forehead.

"I don't mind," I said casually.

"Come on," Shea said. "Let's get cleaned up for bed." He rose, setting me down in front of him and kissed me softly. "Don't you ever withhold your tongue from me again."

"Or what?" I said playfully. Shea smacked me on the ass lightly, but since I was still wet, it stung a bit.

"Consequences and repercussions," he said with a wicked grin.

"I don't mind a little punishment, or don't you remember?" I asked.

"Wash, before I take you up on your request," he said, gently pushing me into the warmth of the water.

"That was not a request, sir," I remarked. I picked up my shower oil and began working it into my body.

"Oh, but it was, " Shea replied. He picked up my shower oil and eyed it oddly. "What the hell is this? Where's the soap? Don't you have any shower gel?"

"Try it," I looked up at him. "Hold out your hand. Don't be a baby—try it." He held out his hand as I pumped some oil into it. He brought his hand up to his nose to smell it.

"Smells good, not girlie at all," he said in a serious tone.

"It's unisex," I added. "Add some water, and it will lather up."

He did as instructed, lathering the liquid onto his body.

"What about my manly parts?" He was genuinely stumped.

"It works the same way as soap. It's safe for all of your manly parts, just get some more."

"And I'll be clean?" he asked seriously.

"I promise you will be fresh and oh so clean."

We washed and rinsed, chatting as we bathed. He provided more details about his business meeting. He opened the door to the shower and stepped out when he was done. He was dry when I finally stepped out. He handed me a warm plush towel.

"Towel warmer," he said to my impressed look.

"I see you, Mr. McGhee, I see you." We both laughed. I dried off and wrapped the towel around me to begin my nightly skincare regimen. He leaned against the counter with his towel wrapped around his waist. He picked up a few bottles to examine them.

"I feel like I shouldn't be watching this," he joked.

"Then leave, sir," I said as I exfoliated. He rose from his semi-reclined position and took a few steps to stand behind me.

"I enjoy being like this with you. I get a peek behind the velvet curtain. You are exquisite in every way, Maeve." He pressed his hardened cock into my buttocks.

"I'm clean, Shea," I giggled knowingly.

"But I'm hard...and I want you," he murmured.

"No more, sir," I said as I moisturized my face, body, and hands before I spoke again. "See, that didn't take too long."

"You're killing me, Smalls," he exclaimed. "I'm aching from watching you lotion yourself."

He led me out of the bathroom with determination.

"Where are we going?" I asked.

"To your bed," he said.

"Shea, I'm clean and tired," I pleaded with him.

"But...I need you," he pleaded.

"How about some head, instead?" I acquiesced.

"If I can't be balls deep inside you—I'll wait." He was really putting on a show.

"Oh ok, suit yourself," I sang sweetly. I bounded past him and hopped into the bed.

"Wait, no," he replied, giving chase.

We laid in bed and snuggled for a while before I drifted into a deep sleep.

Chapter Nineteen
GOING, GOING, GONE

wakened by the delicious scent of food, I rose, went to the closet, and donned my robe. I followed the heavenly aroma to the kitchen, where I found who I presumed to be Chef R'myka preparing to whip up some chocolate chip pancakes, fruit compote, eggs, and turkey sausage. There was even fresh-squeezed orange juice on the table, which was set for two. Shea was already seated at the table reading *The Wall Street Journal* dressed in Nike running gear and Air Zoom Pegasus 36 shoes.

"Good morning, Miss James," R'myka said when she caught a glimpse of me at the entrance to the kitchen.

"Good morning. Please, call me Maeve," I faltered. I had been giving Shea the once over when she spoke.

"I hope you like pancakes," she said sweetly.

"She loves them," Shea said without the benefit of letting me see his face. "Doesn't need them but loves them all the same."

"That's not nice," R'myka admonished. "She looks great."

"Thanks," I replied.

I picked up a napkin and threw it at him. Shea feigned annoyance with me. He folded his paper neatly, setting it to the side of his plate, then picked the napkin up from where it landed on the table. Shea gave me a once over before rising to greet me properly. He moved languidly over to me, planting a tender and inviting kiss on my lips. I wanted to fall into it, then realized we had an audience.

"Hey," I finally said, pushing back from his full lips, "are we going for a run?"

"I am," he replied. "I thought you'd still be sleeping." I scowled at him.

"You have time to change and get a run in. Breakfast should be piping hot by the time you all get back," R'myka said from the kitchen.

"Thank you! Let me go change," I said before darting back up the stairs. I went into my room and found the running gear Jared had purchased for me in the closet. I put on some undergarments, and my clothes, grabbed my Apple Watch and AirPods, then headed back downstairs.

"Ready?" Shea asked at my reappearance.

"Let's roll," I said sweetly.

We stretched outside of the building before heading up for breakfast. It wasn't a long run, but it felt good to stretch out. I studied Shea's body intensely as he went through his routine. His shoulders revealed striations of muscle as he pulled his arms across his chest one by one, and his sinewy thighs quivered as he crossed his legs for a deeper stretch. He worked hard on his physique, and it showed. I made a mental note to resume my exercise more when I got home. His pec and abs showed through his dry fit running shirt. Sweat outlined the peaks and valleys of his musculature of his back. His body enraptured me so I barely heard him when he spoke.

"You hungry?" he asked.

"Famished," I answered.

"So am I," Shea said. I picked up on the double entendre. Looking up at him, I smiled knowingly at his response.

"I'd like to do some shopping, take in a show, then go out to dinner," he said as we rode up in the elevator.

"Shea, we really need to talk. Did you schedule any time for that in your plans?" I placed my hand on his arm.

"Let's talk after we shower. Sound good?" Shea asked.

"So, no shopping," I responded incredulously.

My response was met with laughter. I wiped my hand on Shea's sleeve then joined in on the laughter. We stepped off the lift and smelled breakfast in the hallway. Shea opened the door and headed toward the kitchen. We found food laid out on the buffet opposite the dining room table.

"I just finished cooking," R'myka said with a smile. "I hope you all enjoy it. Will you be eating lunch here, as well?"

"Yes, we'll have a late dinner before our show tonight. Do you mind setting out some fruit and light snacks for us?" Shea asked R'myka.

"Not at all, sir," R'myka said.

Shea pulled out my chair. I sat then turned my attention to R'myka.

"So, Chef," I began. She interrupted, asking me to call her by her first name. "R'myka, Ms. Lina told me you make your salad dressing from scratch."

She chuckled before responding, "I do. However, I don't give out the recipe. This guy," she pointed to Shea, "told me to stop so he could work on a deal to bottle it."

Shea looked guilty. "It's a million-dollar idea!" he said flatly.

"Shea," I demanded, "I can't get it before you bottle it?"

"Proprietary rights—secret ingredients and such," he said in a thick brogue. "Nay, m' love."

"I hate you so much!" I feigned disappointment.

"I'll write it down for you before you leave, Maeve," she said sweetly, giving my shoulder a squeeze before returning to the kitchen.

She walked back out with a small bottle of Griffin's syrup. I squealed with delight.

"I promise to try the compote," I exclaimed, taking the bottle from her extended hand.

"You better," she said jokingly.

We devoured our breakfast. The spread seemed like it was too much, but we ate everything R'myka prepared. To my chagrin, the compote was so good I ate more of it than the syrup.

"Uh oh," R'myka said. "Did someone like my compote better than the syrup?"

"It's not that," I began. "I wanted to, uh…savor—yeah, savor! I wanted to enjoy it as it was masterfully prepared." She and Shea side-eyed me mercilessly. "Ok, y'all got me. But," I exclaimed, holding up a finger, "I reserve the right to put Griffin's on tomorrow's breakfast!"

They laughed at me.

"Drama queen." Shea stood up from the table. He moved behind my chair to help me up and said, "Let's go get cleaned up."

R'myka had prepared bottles of fruit-infused water for after our run. *I think I love her.* I hung back for a moment to speak to her while Shea headed to shower.

"So, R'myka," I said, "my best friend, Stacy, is a chef, also. She owns her own catering business. I think the two of you should link up. Are you interested in sharing your information with me?"

"I'm always interested in networking with other chefs," she started. "Thanks for thinking of me. However, I have a question for you."

"Shoot," I replied.

"I hope you don't find my question too forward, but I have to ask," she began. "I know Mr. McGhee has a fiancée. How can you, as a sista, knowingly fall into the mistress role? You seem like a professional sista who has it together." *There it is,* I thought.

I paused for a moment, scrutinizing her face. She seemed genuine, so I proceeded. "Shea and I have been best friends for over a decade. We're taking this time to see if there is something between us," I stated confidently.

"I hear you. I don't usually make a habit of dealing with messy women," she spoke candidly.

Touché. This does look messy as fuck, I thought.

"R'myka, trust me, I'm not a messy woman. I know how this looks, and honestly, I do feel like a side chick. I…," I looked down at my feet for a moment before continuing, "I didn't want to look back and have regrets about our relationship. I only want to find out if what we share is love or something else. With that being said, if you don't want to give me your information, it's ok."

"It's not that," she began. "I am finally making a name for myself, and I don't want to be associated with gold diggers. I appreciate the opportunity, but I like working for Mr. McGhee. I don't want things to get awkward considering I know his fiancée," she said tartly.

Well, damn, did she just call me a gold digger and a mistress?

"Let me help your understanding then. You are employed by Seamus, not Chelsey," I spoke slowly. "The only way things will get awkward is if you violate the non-disclosure agreement I know he had you sign. You know—the one that says he can traipse a million women through here, fiancée or not. Furthermore, I am not, nor have I ever been, a gold digger. I make enough money to sustain my lifestyle, and I don't need any of Seamus'. So, while you're still making a name for yourself, I've already made one—legitimately."

"I didn't mean—" she began before I interrupted her.

"Sis, don't let our Blackness cause you to forget you're at work, and I'm a guest," my voice was barely above a whisper, "Don't make me resent the fact that I considered giving your info to my already-established best friend"

She tried it for real. I hated having to gather people together.

"You know what, this isn't my business," she backpedaled. "Please forgive my rudeness." She knew Shea could ruin her if I told him what she'd said to me, I'm sure.

I paused for a moment to ponder her apology before turning the conversation back to a professional one.

"So, do you have a card?" I asked politely.

"No, not on me...but I can get my information to you before you leave. Again, I'm sorry for assuming."

"No worries. I understand how it is for Black women out there. In business, our reputation is all we have," I said, smiling politely.

"So, we're good?" she asked.

"Yeah, we good," I responded with a smile.

"I thought you were gonna cuss me smooth out," she said jokingly.
"Oh, don't think I wasn't. It was on the tip of my tongue!" We laughed.
"Can we keep this between us, please?" she asked.

"I'm never gonna stop another Black woman's bag, sis," I said sincerely. "But now, you know you're gonna have to come up off the compote recipe—in addition to the salad dressing recipe." I smiled slowly.

"I got you, Maeve," she said lightheartedly. "I got you!"

I was wrong for blackmailing her for her recipes, but a sista's gotta do what a sista's gotta do!

We hugged before I grabbed my water off the table then headed upstairs. I made my way down the hall to my bedroom to shed the sweat-soaked clothing I was wearing. I was thankful Shea let me bathe without interruption. I showered and dressed casually in jeans and a t-shirt. I padded down the hall and rapped on the door, waiting for his response.

"Come in," he said softly. Lina quietly gathered his discarded clothes, then made her way out of the room. Shea was sitting in an oversized chair near the window. His bedroom was set up similarly to the guest room, but it was a lot larger. He looked comfortable, lounging with his feet up. His laptop and a few files were next to him in the chair. The remote was on the credenza under a large mirror with an equally large TV inside it. I reminded myself to do that in my room. I hated the look of a large TV mounted on the wall. This way, it was hidden decoratively. The TV was tuned to *SportsCenter* on ESPN. He had the volume muted, but the captions were running along the bottom of the screen.

"Good morning, Ms. Lina," I said.

"Good morning, Maeve." She stopped near me. "Did you sleep well?"

"I did, thank you," I said.

"Did you get a chance to ask Chef for the recipe?" Lina asked.

"Yes," I said, "she said she'd give it to me before I left."

"Good," she said. She squeezed my hand gently, making her way past me to the door then closing it softly behind her.

"Are you up for some conversation, now?" I asked.

"I am," he replied.

"No sex?" I questioned.

"Just conversation," he assured me. "So what took you so long?"

"Chatting with R'myka," I smiled.

"What?" he asked regarding my smile.

"She called me a gold-digging mistress," I said, laughing.

"She—what?" His voice boomed throughout the room. "Her ass is as good as—"

Shea's jaw clenched tightly before he moved towards the door. I leaped in front of him, planting my body to prevent him from leaving the room. His face, and most of his upper body, was bright red. He was livid.

"No, it's not how it sounds," I began.

"How the fuck was it supposed to sound?" he demanded. *Shit*, I thought. *Why did I say anything?*

"Calm down, Shea. I got her together. She apologized for being unthoughtful and rude. It's water under the bridge now."

"Why would she say something like that to you?" he asked, trying to reason within himself.

"I asked her for her info to share with Stacy. She didn't want to get mixed up in our shit and have her reputation sullied," I said calmly.

"I'll sully more than her reputation," he spat angrily.

"No—you won't. I understand not wanting to have your name, as a business owner, attached to a scandal. You and I are a scandal. Chelsey will be a PR nightmare for R'myka if she found out she catered our little affair," I added.

"This is not an affair," Shea said, pressing toward me.

"Then what is it, Shea? Because it sure feels like an affair to me," I said.

"Listen, she was out of line for saying those things to you. I'm going to speak to her about being professional," Shea said.

"No, you are not. I promised her I wouldn't say anything to you, so let it go. I told you I took care of it," I said.

"What did you say to her?" he asked sincerely. "I hope you gave her the bees for poking the nest!"

"You already know," I laughed. "I told her she works for you, not Chelsey, and if she violated the non-disclosure agreement you had her sign things would get…awkward. I told her I've never been a gold digger and that I make my own money—and a few other things."

"A few other things, like what?" he asked. He moved until he was standing in front of me. His height forced me to crane my neck to see his face. Was he still brooding about R'myka's comments?

"Like none of your business," I said. He grabbed me around the waist them pulled me to the bed.

"Come here," he said. His tone changed from brooding to seductive.

"No," I said, pushing him off me. "You said talk…just talk," I reminded him.

"Can we talk while I'm inside you?" he asked softly while nibbling my ear.

"Mmm," I moaned. "No, you…promised." My resistance was failing. He rolled off me, pulling me with him to the top of the bed.

"Let's talk then fuck," he said. I rolled my eyes.

"Talk," I said. "No fucking!"

Shea took a deep breath before proceeding. "You keep calling this an affair," he said." I don't see it like that. No, I didn't call off the wedding, but for all intents and purposes, I'm single. So, this is not an affair."

"You have a fiancée, there are no circumstances that can cause me to overlook that," I said.

"It's a technicality," he started.

"A what?" I exclaimed. I sat up, staring at him like he'd lost his fucking mind.

"I can't go into details…you'll just have to trust me," he said sweetly. He pulled me back down.

"Why not, Shea?" I asked.

"I signed a non-disclosure agreement, so I can't talk about it," he said. I laid on my back and exhaled, staring at the ceiling.

"Is this like the NDA you had the twins sign back in college? They couldn't talk about it, but you told us all of the details," I said doubtfully.

I was amused at this point and also seriously beginning to doubt that he was going to tell me what the real deal was with Chelsey.

"No, it's real," he said sincerely. "All you need to know is that I love you."

"How can you say that?" I asked. "You are engaged... but circumstances prevent you from speaking about why Chelsey is a *technicality*." I used my hands to put air quotes around the last word.

"Yes," he said plainly.

"Get the fuck out of here," I spat. "We've already had sex. You don't have to try to pull the wool over my eyes. Just be honest with me."

"I'm not trying to pull anything over your eyes, except for your shirt..." He smiled devilishly then continued, "Seriously."

"Ok, let's approach this from a different angle," I said. "You've said you love me. Is that true?"

"Yes, I love you," he answered.

"As a friend or more than that?" I asked.

"Maeve," he began.

"Answer the question, Shea," I said. I was getting irritated.

"I've told you that I'm in love with you, Maeve. What more do you want me to say?" he said, sounding irritated. "I've told you my engagement is on hold. You need to figure out if you want to pursue something with me regardless of my current status. I can't do anything about my situation right now. It's this, or we stop fucking around."

"You brought me here under the pretenses of seeing what our relationship could be, now you tell me my only options are to be a fucking side chick or nothing," I said. I sat up to get a better look at his face.

"You are not a side chick," he said in an irritated tone. Shea furrowed his brow and pinched the bridge of his nose.

"So, can we go on dates, make our relationship Facebook official—"

"Don't be ridiculous, Maeve," he interrupted.

"I'm not ridiculous, Shea. Do you hear yourself?" I asked.

"I'm asking you to be discreet because the situation demands it. I'm telling you that you are the woman I want to be with," he said sharply.

"But we can't do so openly because you have a fucking technicality! That, my dear friend, is the very definition of mistress, side chick, jump-off, booty call, kept woman, *chatelaine*! Shall I go on?" I questioned harshly.

"You're being difficult," he said dryly.

"Do you hear yourself?" I asked again. "I already am those things, Shea. I don't want to sneak around, fucking you in secret, hoping that one day you'll figure shit out. If that's what you want, then I should go home now because I want more."

"I can't give you more, Maeve. It's a..." He paused.

"A what, Seamus? I've been your best friend for over a decade. Why can't you tell me what's going on? Who the fuck am I gonna tell?" I pleaded.

"Stacy, Tish, fucking Rho! I said I can't discuss it. Why can't you leave it alone?" He rolled to his back, clasped his hands over his eyes, and sighed loudly.

"I've never repeated anything you've ever told me in confidence. Ever!" I yelled. "This trip was a fucking mistake. You brought me all the way to NYC to ask me to be a mistress without the label."

"You are my best friend...we fucked. You're still my best friend." He sat up to meet my eyes.

"Seamus, we stopped being best friends the day we fucked," I said.

"Why are you changing the parameters of the relationship?"

"I didn't change anything. What are you talking about?" I asked earnestly.

"You said just you, just me—nothing more, nothing less. To me, you are my best friend. Making love didn't change that for me." He moved his hands wildly as he spoke.

"Things," my voice trembled with emotion, "things changed when you told me you loved me...I-I can't be your best friend when I want to be more than that."

"Maeve, I—" he began.

Before he could finish, the phone rang. He leaned over to pick it up off of his nightstand. It was Chelsey.

"I have to get this," he said.

"Whatever." I looked away.

"Hello," he said into the handset.

I heard a torrent of words, but I couldn't make out anything being said.

"Clause…" Shea paused. "What provision? I—there are no provisions," he grounded out harshly.

"I'll have my attorneys—" He stopped abruptly.

"It has to be you," I heard Chelsey say clearly. "He doesn't trust me to get it done." *Fuck! She sounds frantic.*

"Calm down, Chelsey. He doesn't give me orders. I'm on a fucking business trip." He looked at me, warily. "I can't leave in the middle of negotiations." I knew he was referring to me.

"Please, Sheamy," she whined. "Do it for me, for us…please!" Seamus stood up then walked over to the window. He peered out, exhaling softly.

"Call my secretary. Have her make the necessary travel arrangements. I'll see you…yes, as soon as possible," he sounded dejected.

He looked at the phone before turning to face me. "I have to go," he said.

His voice was devoid of emotion.

"I heard *for us*," I began. Tears threatened to fall at any moment. "But what about us, Shea?"

"I've told you I can't give you what you need. All I can offer you is—"

"You lied to me. All you ever wanted to be was best friends…with benefits," I said, dragging myself off the bed. I walked slowly to the door.

"Don't leave like this," he spoke softly. "Can we talk when I get home?"

"No, Shea." I stilled my voice. "You've made your choice."

"The choice was made for me, Maeve," he let his words fall.

"You knew what it was before we came here. You're a liar, Shea. I'll go pack," I said. I opened the door and closed it softly behind me.

He really chose her…over me. The Bad Bitch in my brain screamed for me to take what he could give, but I wanted more. I wasn't going to cry or make a fool of myself. I should've listened to him when he said he could fuck me—and marry Chelsey. I played myself.

I made my way to the guest room, picked up my phone and saw I had several missed calls. Darren had called an hour ago. I wasn't going to return any of the phone calls, but I needed someone to lighten my mood.

Darren picked up my FaceTime call immediately.

"Hey, boo," he sang sweetly. The look on my face must've spoken volumes because he sprang into overprotective friend mode. "I'll fucking kill him!"

"No, Darren," I said softly. "I did this to myself. I just want to come home."

"Give me fifteen minutes. I'll have a car there for you, and a jet gassed up ready to bring you home," he said sweetly.

"I can catch a commercial flight, Darren," I whined.

"Yeah, but you don't have to," he said softly. "Look at me."

I lifted my eyes to look at him. "Don't hang your head, you hear me? If he doesn't realize he has a beautiful and precious gem in his possession, then he's the fool, not you."

I sobbed softly in response.

"He said I changed the parameters, Darren," I said pitifully.

"Yes, you did, because Shea said he was in love with you. You can't make a man choose you. He has to want to choose you and love you the way you deserve to be loved," Darren said.

"I don't know what to do…" I began.

"Start by packing your things, then take the car I send to the airport. We'll sort everything out when you get home, I promise," he said. Darren sounded so reassuring.

"Ok," I said.

"See you soon, MJ." He smiled then ended the call.

I packed my things quickly then gave the room a once over to make sure I hadn't left anything. I slipped down the stairs quietly to find the car was waiting just as Darren had promised.

"I'm sorry I kept you waiting," I said to the driver as he opened the door and took my bag.

"Not a problem, Miss James," he said.

Darren sent a black Cadillac Escalade to pick me up. Who did he think he was picking up— Obama?

The flight home was without incident until we got back to Chicago. The pilot said we'd have to circle the airport for a bit until visibility became clear enough to land. He noted we'd divert to Milwaukee if it didn't clear up soon. I tried to watch a movie, but my mind kept drifting back to Shea. I longed to be in his arms, to feel his lips pressed to mine, to feel his body next to mine and to feel him inside me again. I day-dreamed about our lovemaking, but that wasn't helping my heart.

"We've been cleared for landing, at this time," the pilot said. "We will experience some turbulence as we break through the storm. It's currently raining in Chicago. Local time is a quarter after two p.m. We should be on the ground shortly, Miss James. Please prepare for land-ing."

I placed my iPad and phone into my backpack then stared haplessly out of the window during our descent. The plane bobbed up and down and shook ferociously. I tightened my seatbelt for peace of mind. At one point, I thought I'd be physically sick. Finally, we were on the ground. The landing was hard, but I didn't care. I couldn't wait to gather my things.

"Thank you for flying with us," said the flight attendant as I made my way to the door.

I smiled at her, and the pilot standing behind her. "Have a good day," I said.

I walked from the tarmac to the terminal. I didn't know who I expected to pick me up because I had forgotten to tell Stacy I was coming home. I stopped to pull my waterproof Adidas windbreaker out of my bag. When I stood up, I saw Darren waiting at the door looking for me.

"You didn't have to pick me up." I wandered over to him and dropped my bag.

He wrapped me up in a big bear hug. "Yes, I did! You hungry?"

"No, I had a huge breakfast. I just want to go home," I said. I smiled up at Darren.

"How about some Garrett's?" He smiled down at me.

"You always did know the way to make me smile," I said. Darren picked up my bag and led me out to his car.

He was in the Lamborghini.

"Where are my bags gonna go?" I asked.

"It has a trunk, asshole," he said sarcastically.

"My bad, Big Guy." I dropped both bags and headed to the passenger seat. "Crickey, get the bags."

"Ok, Mushu!" He referenced Mulan's trusty sidekick.

We both laughed.

The rain was coming down in sheets by the time we made our way to the highway. Darren drove slowly, but the rain was unrelenting.

"I should've driven the Escalade," he mentioned.

"Speaking of Escalades, who the fuck did you think you were picking up in NYC—Obama?" I joked.

"It got you where you needed to be, right?" he sparred back.

"Yeah, but—" I said.

"Yeah, but nothing," he said. "I didn't know how much luggage you took. Who knew you only took drawls with you?"

He knew his comment was slick. He eyeballed me, waiting for my reaction. I was about to respond when I saw a large semi-truck begin to swerve in the lane next to us. A small white car had darted in front of it then jammed on the brakes. The truck tried to maneuver into the other lane, but it was too late.

"Darren," I screamed! I pointed at the scene unfolding in front of us.

We were headed between the trailer's front and back wheels. Darren looked back to the road and began to make corrections. The car fishtailed wildly as Darren tried to get it under control. The rain was so heavy on the road that the vehicle began to lose traction, and we collided with the back end of the trailer. The scene unfolded in slow motion. The Lamborghini hit a guard rail then flipped into the air.

This can't be happening, I thought.

Chapter Twenty
HOME AGAIN

D rip.
Drip. Drip. Drip.

Something hit my face. I tried to reach up to wipe at the moisture. *Pain!*

I heard sirens. Searing pain tore through my body.

"I got a pulse! She's alive!" an EMT screamed over his shoulder.

"What about the driver?" I heard a woman's voice ask.

Darren, my mind screamed. "Is he...is," I strained to speak. "Is Darren ok?"

"Ma'am, you've been in an accident. We're working on getting you out of the vehicle, but your legs are pinned. I'm gonna need you to be as still as possible," the EMT spoke calmly.

I tried to turn my head to see Darren, but the rest of the car was gone. The EMT's hand was warm when it touched my hand. "Ma'am...ma'am, look at me! Focus on the sound of my voice."

I gripped his hand and looked into his eyes. His face was severe, but his voice didn't betray anything. He put something over my eyes, then I heard the sound of metal being cut. *Where is Darren?* I thought again. More pain followed as I felt myself being lifted out of the wreckage.

"Ma'am try to be as still as possible," the EMT said as I felt him place a neck brace around my head. "We're going to lift you onto this backboard. Try not to move."

The vice grip that held my legs released, then there was a buzz of activity to get me out of the seat.

"Darren," I tried to ask again, "Is he…" My throat was raw.

"He's on his way to the hospital," a reassuring voice said. "He's being treated for his injuries, ma'am. We're gonna get you into the ambulance, ok?"

That was the last thing I heard the EMT say, then darkness overwhelmed me again.

Days later, I awoke, bound to my bed by large leather straps. I jerked at them to no avail.

"They're for your protection," I heard a familiar voice say. It was my mama, Dr. James. "You're ok, child. You were a madwoman when they brought you in. You were screaming about Milwaukee, saying you should've gone to Milwaukee. You tried to get up to go look for Darren, so they sedated you and strapped you in."

"Darren?" I asked, "Is he…"

"He's in bad shape, Maeve. The doctors aren't sure if he'll walk again. His right arm is mangled from holding you into your seat. He's clinging to life right now," she said softly.

"I shouldn't have called him," I began, "this is all my fault." I wept bitterly.

"This isn't anyone's fault, Maeve. I need you to calm down baby, or they'll come sedate you again."

"Has-has Shea…" She grabbed my hand.

"Maevie, try to focus on your health, right now," she began.

"Dammit, Mom!" I fussed angrily.

My mother overlooked my language and gently replied, "You two are very blessed to be alive. The doctor said you can go see Darren when you're feeling up to it."

I smiled at her, then turned away. She gave my hand a gentle squeeze then sat down on the bed next to me. *Shea hasn't come,* I thought. My heart broke into a thousand tiny little pieces.

Later that day, my mother fussed profusely when I said I wasn't hungry.
"You haven't eaten in days, Maeve. I'll have your doctor insert a feeding tube if you don't eat something," she said calmly. I knew she wasn't fooling around.

Heartbreak had done a number on my appetite. However, Dr. James only had to threaten me once. I knew she meant business.

Later, the nurse came in with a wheelchair.

"Are you ready to go see Mr. Wilkerson?" the nurse asked.

"Yes," I said.

I endured the long ride from my room down to his floor. At the sight of Darren, tears sprang to my eyes.

"You have to hold it together," my mother said softly. "He can hear everything that's going on. He needs hope, baby."

Machines, tubes, and bandages around his head and arms made it almost unbearable. I remembered what my mom said though.

"Will you push me to him?" I asked.

When I got to his bed, I gently picked up his left hand. It was warm to the touch.

"Darren," I began, "I know you can hear me. Thank you for protecting me. I love you so much, my friend. I refuse to let you give up. I'll be here every day until you get better. I promise not to leave your side. You hear me?" I squeezed his hand and kissed it.

"Ah, Miss James," a male voice said as he came into the room. "You are a fortunate woman."

I turned to see who it was. The doctor came in and introduced himself. He had attended to Darren and me when we came in from the scene of the accident.

"I prefer blessed," I said to him.

"I'm Dr. Stevens. Did they tell you what Mr. Wilkinson did for you?" he asked, shaking my hand as he did.

"No, what do you mean?" I asked.

"Are you sure you want to know?" he asked.

"Yes," I said bravely.

"Well, young lady, you weren't wearing a seatbelt. Mr. Wilkinson pinned you to your seat as it flipped," he said.

"Are you serious?" I asked.

"The police said the car came to rest partially on the divider. Do you remember any of this?" Dr. Stevens asked.

"I remember looking to my left and not seeing him," I added. Darren was always telling me to put my seatbelt on. I felt horrible.

"That's because another vehicle, unable to stop, hit his side of the car—splitting it clean in two," he added. He didn't speak for a moment, giving me time to digest the gravity of what he'd just said.

I looked up at my mother. She had tears streaming down her face. *I truly owe this man my life,* I thought.

"He's an amazing man," I said finally.

"Yes, he is," the doctor agreed. "He's a fighter though. I'm sure he'll pull through this and be just fine. Maybe he'll even play football again."

"You think so?" I said hopefully.

"Know so," the doctor said. "You need to get some rest. Those legs need time to heal." He left the room after checking Darren's vitals and giving me a reassuring pat on the shoulder.

I went back to my room when visiting hours were up in the ICU. I intended to keep my promise, come hell or high water.

I was released from the hospital after another week, but Darren was still in a coma. It didn't seem fair that I was home recovering, and he was clinging to life. My mother wouldn't let me go up to the hospital until I was off my crutches, but I called Darren's mother every day while she was there. She generously put her phone up to Darren's ear and let me speak to him without fail. Afterward, we'd chat about his diagnosis and prognosis. She said his vitals were strong. I promised I'd come to see him soon. She encouraged me, like my mother, not to push my recovery on account of her son. She affirmed that she was there with him as much as possible.

Weeks went by, still no response from Darren. The news had run the story day and night, showing images from the accident. I turned the channel every time I saw it. The outpouring of love from Chicagoans was terrific, though. Outside of the hospital, there was a candlelight vigil for Darren and his unnamed passenger. It was moving to see those images. Our accident even made it to the national news. NFL fans across the country flooded Darren's social media with good wishes. The fact that this had happened to us was surreal.

A month after the accident, there was still no word from Shea. *How cold-blooded,* I thought. My mom and the girls took turns sitting with me. It seemed as though everyone was careful not to ask about him or mention his name. They kept me company, kept me laughing and smiling, despite my silent heartbreak. Some nights, Stacy climbed in bed with me while we binged shows on Netflix. Days and weeks ran together. My job was very accommodating. After a few weeks, I had Jared bring my computer to me, allowing me telework. Two broken legs were enough to make anyone go a little stir crazy.

Once my legs mended, I began physical therapy. I made my daily calls to Darren. I updated him on my life, the happy parts, physical therapy, and gave him blow by blow of the crazy Netflix show I had been watching. I told him I'd have my driver bring me up there to see him soon. His mom said his heart rate spiked when I told him that. So that was promising. He was still in there!

The first day I was able to see Darren, my heart leaped for joy. He had been removed from all of the machines, yet was still in a coma. I relieved his mother on Wednesday nights. She hated missing Bible study. While she was out, I told Darren dirty jokes, stories about work, and about my grueling physical therapy. I left the room when the nurses gave him sponge baths, but I applied lotion to his face, hands, and extremities. I helped the physical therapist with his exercises too.

Most importantly, I always thanked him for saving me and let him know that I never failed to get into a car without putting my seatbelt on. I held his hand, asking yes or no questions—hoping one day he'd squeeze my hand to let me know he heard me. Then, one glorious evening, while watching a Bulls game with him, he squeezed gently.

"Darren?" I asked, "Do you think the Bulls will make it to the playoffs? Twice for yes and once for no."

Darren squeezed twice! I screamed so loudly the nurses came running.

"What's going on?" the nurse asked.

"He squeezed my hand! He squeezed it! He's wrong about the Bulls, but he squeezed it," I yelled.

She smiled, then left the room. Darren's regular doctor, Dr. Li, came in a little later and began to check his reflexes. Then he took Darren's hand and asked, "Darren, can you hear me? Twice for yes and once for no."

Darren squeezed twice!

Darren's mother came in on the tail end of the examination and learned he was communicating with us.

"What does this mean doctor?" she asked.

"It means that he could wake up soon. There's are no guarantees, though. Just keep talking to him," he said reassuringly.

Darren's mama looked at me. "You didn't give up, Maeve. I sure do appreciate you for it."

"It's the least I can do, right Darren?" I said, directing my question to him. I grabbed his hand and asked him to squeeze. Wouldn't you know, that's precisely what he did—twice! He had jokes even in a coma.

Chapter Twenty-One
THE LONG ROAD HOME

I visited the hospital regularly for months. I tried to give Darren's mother a break as often as possible. There were days she slept at the hospital in her chair. I gave her opportunities to go home, rest, and get cleaned up. I brought her books to read and DVDs to watch. She was a huge fan of Westerns and old cop shows. Sometimes, I'd take her dinner and sit with her. She told me about Darren's father and late sister, Darlene. Her stories always kept me on the edge of my seat. Darren and his sister were a handful.

"Bad as the day is long, you hear me," Mama Wilkerson hooted.

I was doubled over laughing when we heard a voice come from the bed.

"Almost drove her to drink." Darren's voice was raspy and barely above a whisper, but he was awake.

Tears sprang to my eyes immediately. His mother screamed as she rushed to his bedside. I jumped from my chair, wiping tears from my eyes, and rushed out of the room to find his doctor. I explained what had occurred to the nurse on duty at the nurse's station. She rose and hurriedly follow me while another nurse got on the phone to call his doctor. There was a flurry of activity in his room. The sun had set before I finally got to speak to him.

"Don't try to talk, Darren," I said softly, rubbing his arm.

"I need to tell you something," he started. I handed him his water and let him take a sip. "I appreciate all you did for me," he took another sip, "and my mama. I heard y'all, and it pulled me back."

Tears streamed down my face.

"I blamed myself for the events that occurred that day. Had I not involved you, none of this would have happened, Darren," I said softly.

"Don't," he said, struggling to formulate his words, "things happen. Only God knows why."

"You were there when I needed you, so I wanted to return the favor," I said to him, wiping at my tears. "I got to hear all about you and your sister, God rest her soul."

"We were bad," he said, chuckling. "Mama always liked you. She was so mad at me when I—"

"Water under the bridge, DW. Imma tell you what though, we scared the hell out of our parents, and half the world, when the accident happened. Boy, they were outside singing and holding candlelight vigils for you, son." Chicago showed up for Darren to let him know they were pulling for him. I regaled him with all of the tidbits I knew. I grabbed my purse to get my phone. I hadn't looked at the pictures of the accident or any news stories. I was so happy my friend was alive. I wanted to share with him what we had survived.

"Do you want to see pictures?" I asked, holding the phone close to my chest.

"Have you seen them?" Darren asked hesitantly.

"No, I wanted to wait for you to wake up," I replied.

"Ok, let's do this," he responded.

I pulled up the email that contained the photos. Jared had warned me the pictures were horrific. His warning didn't do them any justice.

"Gaht damn," Darren said slowly. I flipped through the pictures of the portion of the car I was in.

"This is just my side, Darren," I commented. "Are you sure you want to see your half?"

He looked up at me from where he was resting on the pillow. "If you can do it, so can I."

I continued to scroll through the photos. It was a miracle we had survived. We finished looking at the pictures and sat in silence for a time.

"They said you almost lost your arm trying to keep me in the seat," I finally added.

"I'd have gladly lost the whole thing to save you, Maeve," he said as he placed his hand on my knee.

I laid next to him in the bed and hugged him.

"Thank you so much. I don't know what I can ever do to repay you," I said.

"You can name your firstborn after me," he said. We both laughed heartily.

"You got it, Big Guy!" I said, smiling up at him.

The door to his room opened, letting the light from the hallway in. The nurse came into the room, smiling at us.

"I hate to break up the party, but visiting hours are over," she said sweetly.

"Aww," we both whined.

I climbed out of the bed then wandered slowly over to my chair to gather my things. I had hoped to garner some sympathy from the nurse, so she'd give us a few more moments, but she was not budging. Reluctantly, I hugged and kissed Darren on the forehead, reassuring him I'd be back the next day. Then I allowed myself to be ushered from the room.

"Normally, I'd let you stay, but he really needs to rest," she said, squeezing my hand softly.

"I understand completely," I told her.

I left the hospital and headed home. I couldn't wait to tell Stacy about Darren. I wanted to tell everyone before they saw it on the news. As I drove home, my thoughts drifted to Seamus. I was still amazed that he hadn't called or come to visit me as I recovered. Seemed like I had heard from everyone this side of the Mason-Dixon. I received cards and flowers from people who were friends of Darren's—even the Bears organization reached out to me. My church and friends had been incredibly helpful. They checked on me and my parents daily. I couldn't say I wasn't bothered, because I was hurt that he hadn't called or texted me. I hadn't even heard from his parents. I was flabbergasted at how none of them reached out. There were days I had cried myself to sleep and others when I cursed the day his mother gave birth to him. I never asked anyone if he'd called or sent anything. Yet, I longed to hear his voice, feel his touch, and be near him, still. But he made a choice—Chelsey.

Oddly enough, no one mentioned him to me either. Had anyone heard from him? Was there something they knew that I didn't? Was he back in Chicago?

My thoughts subdued me until I pulled into my spot in the garage.

"Stace," I called as I opened the door, "you home?"

"In the kitchen," she sang.

I made my way through the living room into the kitchen. "Darren woke up!"

She spun around, running to hug me. "Are you shitting me?"

"No," I jumped into her arms. "He's talking, cracking jokes—he's him!"

She swung me around a few times as we screamed before setting me down.

"I'm so happy! I have never been so worried in my life," she said seriously.

"I don't know how I would have lived with myself if something had happened to him," I said solemnly.

"MJ, how many times do I have to tell you it wasn't your fault?" she asked, walking over to me. She stood in front of me and placed her hands on my lap.

"He almost lost his arm, I just.... It's a lot, Stace." I fought back the tears as I spoke.

"I know he'd have given that arm to save you," she said sweetly.

"That's exactly what he said," I cried softly. Stacy folded me into her arms and let me cry on her shoulder.

"Listen," she said to me as she rubbed my back, "he's awake. This is a moment to celebrate, not be sorrowful. What's really going on?"

"He hasn't so much as called, texted or emailed, Stace. I thought…" my voice trailed off.

"Ok, it's time for some honesty. Your mom asked us not to tell Shea about the accident. He has no clue about what happened. We wanted to tell him so badly, but she said you'd been through a lot, and you needed positivity to heal. So…we respected her wishes," she said, pushing me to an upright position.

"Wow," I said.

"I'm sorry. We shouldn't have," Stacy began.

"No, my mom is probably right. I didn't need all of the turmoil—foolishness—that was Shea and Maeve. It allowed me to focus on Darren," I responded.

"So, you're not mad at us?" she asked, searching my face.

"Not at all," I said, pulling her in for another hug. "I'm thankful for all of you. Now, let's drink a toast to Darren and life."

"Imma call the girls! We need to turn up!" Stacy shouted as she turned to retrieve the champagne flutes. "There's champagne in the fridge." I hopped down to collect it and set in on the counter.

She set the glasses down next to the bottle then raced out of the kitchen to grab her phone. In less than thirty minutes, Rho and Tish were at our house with chips, dip and plenty of alcohol. I sent a quick text to Jared, informing him of the day's events, requesting he not disclosed the info and notifying him that I wouldn't be in until Monday.

I woke up in bed the next morning with Tish's legs and arms wound around my body. *What the hell?* I thought. *Why am I the little spoon?*

"Tish, getcho ass off me," I fussed. She woke up and slowly untangled herself from me. "Why are you in my bed?"

"Rho took the guest bedroom, and I didn't want to sleep on the couch," she mumbled, rolling over.

"No, ma'am." I was mildly irritated. "You are hot as hell! I feel violated, bitch! Whose sweat is this, anyway?"

Before I had a chance to push Tish out of the bed, the door burst open and Rho rushed in. She ran, leaping into the air and landing soundly on top of me. The air left my body momentarily. She humped me and made sexual noises.

"Bitch!" I screamed when I finally caught my breath.

"Yes, you sexy motherfucker," she said as she fondled me through the covers and continued to hump. I was laughing at that point.

"Why Rho?" I asked, finally flinging her off me to the floor.

She landed with a thud. "Damn bitch, you strong as hell!" Tish and I leaned over the bed to look at her sprawled out on the floor.

"What the hell is going on?" Stacy asked from the doorway. "I heard moaning!"

"MJ and Rho were showing me some girl on girl action," Tish said as she pretended to rub her nipples and lady parts. Stacy and I were shocked at first, but we quickly dissolved into laughter.

Rho sat up, looking confused. "What I miss?"

"Girl," I said between giggles.

"You had to see it," Stacy replied.

They all climbed into my bed. We hadn't done that since our college days. The last time we'd all been in bed was when the girls were soothing me over my breakup with DW. We had moved the desk that separated our bed and pushed them together to accommodate all of us. The RA came up shortly after because the troll living next door complained. She was so shocked when she opened the door she closed it abruptly, mumbling how she didn't want to be aware of our sexual explorations.

"Why don't we do this more often?" Tish asked.

"Because you get weird," chirped Rho gleefully.

"I do not," Tish fussed.

"Yes, you do," Stacy and I replied in unison.

"No," Tish began, "the last time we did this, Rho stuck her finger in my ass! That's why I got weird."

"Bitch, *what?*" I turned to look at Tish.

"It wasn't your ass. It was the crack of your ass. There's a huge difference," Rho retorted in defense. Stacy and I sat up to look at Rho who was lying to my left.

"You's a nasty hoe," I responded.

"Who does that?" Stacy asked Rho. She was lying on the other side of Tish who was spooning me again. I squirmed out of her grasp. "Ma'am!"

"Something is seriously wrong with her," Tish responded as she laughed at me.

"Y'all remember that episode of the Golden Girls when the heat went out, and they all huddled in bed together?" Rho asked, completely ignoring our pseudo denigrating statements about her.

"Yeah," we said, wondering where she was going with this.

"I'm Blanche," she began, "Stacy, you're Sophia. MJ, you are definitely Dorothy, and Tish—"

"Fuck you, Rho," Tish said, giggling as she reached over me to swat at Rho for insinuating that she was Rose Nylund.

We all laughed at Rho, but was there some truth to her comment? Hell, Dorothy was always picking the wrong man or getting dogged. Was that my fate, as well?

"Why I gotta be Dorothy, though?" I turned to look at Rho, awaiting her response.

"She ain't get no dick," Rho said seriously then broke into a smile.

"Bitch, fuck you." I grabbed my pillow then pushed it over her head.

"Get her!" Tish yelled, cheering me on.

"A'ight," Stacy fussed, "knock it off before you accidentally kill Rho!"

"Thanks, Sophia!" Rho said, sitting up to catch her breath after I let her go. Stacy's pillow flew past all of us to smack Rho square in the face, causing her to fall out of the bed again.

"Damn," Rho hollered from the floor, "I deserved that."

Yes, she did!

We all called in sick, then spent the rest of the day binging the *Golden Girls* on my Amazon Prime account. Our *Golden Girls* marathon ended with me filling the girls in on the events of NYC and updating them on DW's.

The next morning, I went to see DW. He was sitting up, chatting with his mom, when I walked into the room. His voice was still halted and raspy, but he looked great. I greeted everyone with a hug before settling in.

"Hey, Big Guy," I said, finally making my way to DW. "I saw you this morning on the news."

"They couldn't let him alone for a second before they descended down here like hawks!" Mama Wilkerson was upset.

"ESPN will be here later on today. They want to interview both of us," he said, looking at me. He squeezed his mom's hand, pulling her down next to him on the bed.

"I really don't want to be on TV, DW. I'll do it if you want me to, though." I frowned, shaking my head at the thought.

"The spot can't be very long. The doctor is limiting how long I can speak to each media outlet," he said. "I'd really appreciate it if you were here."

I nodded my agreement and took a seat on the edge of his bed near his feet.

"How was the marathon?" he asked.

I told him about my time with the girls, about my errant eyelash and my pajama stash.

"I can't stand Rho," I told them.

"She's always been a mess. I wish I could've seen that eyelash on your neck," Darren laughed.

"I'm gonna run down to the cafeteria," Mama Wilkerson said, standing up. "I need some coffee. You want anything, Maeve?"

"No, ma'am," I said as she closed the door behind her.

"Ask Rho if she took any pictures," Darren said.

"I will not," I said, swatting his leg gently. "When does physical therapy start?"

"It started today. And I can't wait for another session," he added, raising his eyebrow.

"What's her name?" I asked, laughing at his friskiness.

"Tamela. I think I'm gonna marry her," he said gleefully.

"Marry?" I said, choking on my saliva. "She must be fine!"

"She is the total package. She didn't take any shit either. Strong and feisty—just like I like them." DW laid his head against his pillow for a moment.

"Oh, my," I said, raising my eyebrows.

"She'll be back tomorrow. I'll introduce you then," he said.

"God help her—she doesn't know what she's in for," I said to him.

I visited with him for about an hour, when the journalist from ESPN was shown into the room by Darren's mom.

"Now, don't push him. He already agreed to an exclusive, in-depth interview at a later date," Mrs. Wilkerson fussed.

The journalist introduced herself as Jasmine Brown-Hall, then proceeded to ask both of us a few questions. She was a blonde-haired, grey-eyed Caucasian woman with a small frame. She was two or three inches taller than me, in heels. Her cream dress stopped midcalf, showing off shapely legs. She was slender with an athletic build. She wasn't beautiful, but with makeup, she had a classic face for television. She set up a small camera behind her chair. The shot included me sitting in my chair, and Darren and his mom sitting on the bed. Jasmine asked a few questions, Darren's mom filled in gaps he didn't remember. He did a great job. His answers were succinct and to the point.

"Ms. James, how did you feel when you heard Darren speak after being in a coma for months?" she asked me.

"I was overwhelmed with joy," I started.

"She cried. Go on and tell her how you lost it," Darren joked.

We all laughed. "Yes, I did cry. It was shocking and it took us completely by surprise. We believed he'd wake up because he squeezed our hands when we asked him questions. It was a matter of time for us."

"What was the first thing you did after he woke up?" Jasmine asked.

"Darren and I looked at the accident photos together. It was surreal, to say the least. I can't recall much from the accident, so it's amazing to see them and know that we survived."

"It's been reported that Darren saved your life," she said.

"Yes, I had forgotten to put my seatbelt on," I began, recalling a bit of the accident. "I remember Darren joking about me not putting it on, then I remember him throwing his arm across my chest and pinning me into my seat. Everything went so fast after that."

"Would you say Darren is a hero?" she asked.

"Jasmine, I owe him my life," I said, turning to Darren. "I am eternally grateful for all of the love you've shown me. I hope I can show you every day how much I love you." I turned back to Jasmine. "The heroes that night were also the first responders, doctors, and nurses who worked quickly to help us both. I just thank God that we are here together today."

"I couldn't have said it better myself," Darren added.

"Well, thank you for taking the time to speak with us today. I know we have all breathed a collective sigh of relief that you're both alive. The road to recovery can be long for you, Darren. We at ESPN are pulling for you," she concluded.

"Thank you for being brief," Darren's mom added.

"You're most welcome, ma'am," she said.

I left shortly after the reporter did. Darren needed some rest, and his mother was on a rampage to ensure he got it. I didn't take offense to it because I knew it was true. Hell, I was tired, my damn self.

Darren stayed in the hospital another week for observation. He hired the cute physical therapist to work with him at his home, one on one. I stopped by after their sessions to chat with them occasionally. The two of them seemed to be getting along well. The progress Darren made pleased me. He credited it all to Tamela.

The ESPN spot aired later that day. My phone rang shortly after.

Chapter Twenty-Two
OLD AND NEW FRIENDS

"**H**ello?" I said. I usually didn't answer unknown numbers, but I wondered if it was another reporter looking for an interview. "Hey, Butterfly."

Shea's voice took the breath from my lungs. I looked around my office for someplace to sit quickly. I sank onto my couch. Jared was sitting at my desk, preparing for my upcoming business meeting with a CEO in London. I was stunned into silence.

"MJ, is everything ok?" Jared walked over to me with a concerned look on his face. I waved him off.

"Can you give me a moment?" I asked. "I need to take this in private."

"Sure," he said. Worry spread across his face.

"Maeve." I heard the concern in Shea's voice. "Is everything ok?"

"Um, yes," I replied finally. "I wasn't expecting to hear from you."

"Yeah, about that," he began, "I wasn't aware of your accident. Otherwise, I'd have—"

"Why are you calling, Seamus?" I asked softly.

"I wanted to call to express how happy I am to hear that you and DW are both doing well. I saw the report on ESPN," he said.

"Seamus, the accident was…" I paused for a moment to collect myself. "Months ago."

"I didn't know. My parents were shocked to hear about it, as well."

"Seamus, they live here. You mean to tell me they didn't see it on the news, read about it?" I questioned.

"Actually, they've been in Ireland. They went home to take care of some family business. They made it home this past week," he said softly.

"Oh," was all I could manage to say.

"I'd like to have dinner sometime if you aren't busy?" he asked.

"I've been spending most of my time with DW," I began.

"I gathered that from the news story," he said tersely.

"That was rather abrupt. Something bothering you, Shea?" I asked.

"Not at all. So…dinner?" he asked again.

"I don't think that's a good idea. I can't deal with a repeat of our last few encounters."

"We really need to clear the air," he said tersely again.

"It's pretty clear from where I am, Seamus," I said.

"Please," was all he said. Yet, it spoke volumes and pulled at a previously closed door in my mind.

I took a deep breath and slowly exhaled. "When?"

"Are you free this weekend?" he asked.

"I'm preparing for a business trip. I leave this weekend," I replied.

"Then, tonight," his voice pleaded.

"Fine, have your assistant contact Jared with the details." I hung up the phone before he had a chance to speak again.

What the hell was I doing? I'd been getting along well the past few months. *I need to call him back and tell him no*, I thought. No, he owed me an explanation for New York! *He doesn't owe me shit. He is not my man!* The Bad Bitch in my brain was quiet. *What the entire fuck?* She wasn't begging to have his mouth on me or his cock inside me. Damn, she was tired of us too! I chuckled to myself as the door to my office flew open. I presumed his outburst was because Shea's assistant called with the details of our dinner. Jared was standing in my office having a case of the come-a parts.

"What the fuck, MJ? Why are you meeting with that asshole? He didn't call, send flowers or check on you for months! You don't need him," Seamus McGhee is an asshole, who does not fucking deserve to be in your stratosphere. Please call him and cancel!"

I stood up and walked over to Jared. I took his hand and guided him to my couch, then closed the door to my office. I smooth my hair and skirt before heading back to where he was sitting.

"Jared, Shea was on a business trip when the accident happened. My parents asked everyone to keep it from him," I began.

"MJ, that accident was on every news station in this country. You really think with all of the technology we have today he didn't know about it?" he asked.

"Jared, all I can do is take his word for it." He started to speak again, but I shushed him. "I can handle this," I stated. I placed my hand over his.

"If he hurts you, I will personally fuck him up," Jared said softly.

"He already has, Jared. Shea can't do any more than what's already been done," I reminded him gently.

"I'm sorry," he said.

"No worries, Jared," I said.

We sat quietly for a minute before he stood up and walked toward the door.

"Would you like to pick up where we left off, MJ?" he asked.

"No, email me the files I requested and see what info you can dig up so I'm not flying blind next week," I said.

"Alright, boss," he smiled sweetly then shut the door behind him.

I didn't see or hear from Jared or anyone else until he called to let me know the car Seamus sent was downstairs.

"Were you holding my calls, Jared?" I asked.

"Yes, I thought you could use some quiet time this afternoon," he said over the intercom.

"Thank you, sir!" I said.

I gathered my things then made my way to the elevator. Jared walked with me, and we chatted about the billionaire CEO I was meeting with the next week.

"I heard he's fucking gorgeous," Jared sang. "Maybe you'll make a love connection!"

"Business, Jared," I said in a pseudo-serious tone. "I'm not looking to make any more love connections."

We parted ways when we stepped off the elevator. I took a deep breath then went outside to the car Seamus sent. I situated myself into the backseat and closed my eyes, offering a secret prayer for a peaceful dinner. Afterward, I rested my head on the seat rest and drifted off. The driver woke me when we arrived at our destination.

"Why did you bring me here?" I questioned the driver, realizing I was at Seamus' penthouse.

"Mr. McGhee directed me to bring you here. That's all I know," he said calmly.

I stepped out of the car as my phone rang. "What the fuck, Seamus?" I whisper-screamed into the device.

"I thought we'd have more privacy here," he began.

"More privacy for what? I'm going home." I turned to get back in the car, but it was pulling off. "You've got to be shitting me!"

"Just come in," he said confidently.

"No, I'll take an Uber home," I continued to whisper-scream into the phone.

"Maeve, I'm on the roof. Come up, have dinner…we'll talk then I'll personally drive you home?" he asked ever so sweetly.

I turned to find the doorman holding the door. "This way, Miss James." He extended his hand to lead me into the building. I followed him to the elevator and up to the top floor.

"You'll have to take the stairs up to the roof. They're the first door on the left once you step out of the elevator. Have a good evening." He smiled as the doors closed.

Fucking, Seamus! I was greeted by one of Seamus' security detail as I stepped off the elevator. He led me to the door, opened it for me, then closed it behind me. I presumed he'd be standing just outside the door until dinner was over and we returned.

"You look lovely," Seamus said as I stepped through the door at the top of the stairs.

"And you're a fucking asshole," I said when I was within earshot.

"Don't be like that, MJ," he chuckled.

"Explain," I demanded. Shea took my purse, backpack, and coat. He handed them to a young lady who appeared from the far side of the roof. There were a few other people milling about. I assumed they all worked for Shea.

The rooftop was beautiful. There were two seating areas under pergolas. Each pergola had three bronze light fixtures hanging from it. Topiaries flanked the sections on either side. The outdoor furniture wrapped around a fireplace. A driftwood cocktail table set between the couches. There were various potted plants about the roof line. A small table was set for two, and I presumed that was where we'd be dining.

"Let's sit," he said, placing his hand on the small of my back, attempting to lead me to the table.

"Not until you explain," I demanded.

"I planned to take you to dinner, but…unforeseen circumstances dictated that I change my plans," he offered.

"You knew if you told me that we were eating here, I'd say no," I retorted crisply.

"It's just us. There's no one here except us, waitstaff, and security. Technically, we aren't alone. Besides, I had to do it this way, MJ," he offered gently.

I sucked air through my teeth. "You and your unforeseen fucking circumstances. You just can't act normal. We've been seen out before, so why is it now weird for us to eat dinner together?"

"Chelsey knows about us."

His statement took the wind out of my lungs.

"How?" I asked, finally allowing him to lead me to our table.

He pulled out my chair for me to sit. He stepped around to the other chair and took a seat.

"Chelsey's father had me under surveillance…standard business practice—under the circumstances. The indiscretion was forgiven, but I can no longer be seen with you publicly," he stated.

"The wedding?" I asked.

"Still on as planned. That's why I asked you here tonight," Shea said.

"I'm confused," I frowned then looked up and around like I was being watched.

"We're safe here. I need to come clean about my relationship with Chelsey…" He paused. "But I have to ask you to sign an NDA."

"Are you serious?" I asked. I searched his face in confusion, but he was sincere. "Fine," I responded flatly.

The young woman who took my coat re-appeared with a folder and a pen. I read over the document then signed where indicated. She took the information and headed to the stairs. An older man brought us our meals then began to serve us. He placed our napkins on our laps and poured wine. He headed to the door once Shea affirmed that we are taken care of and no longer needed his services.

"Chelsey approached me a while back when I made a bid to take over one of her father's holdings. She told me she had visions of running the family business, but her father wouldn't hear of it. Her father said the only way he'd give in was if she married a powerful man like me. I thought this was odd, but I chalked it up to old-world bullshit. Chelsey didn't want to get married but agreed only if she could run the company. I had been eyeing the property for quite some time since I was looking to diversify my holdings. I didn't have any romantic prospects, so the situation was a win-win. When I discovered I had feelings for you, I tried to called off the wedding. Now, I have to go through with this deal," he finished.

Absentmindedly, I lifted the silver lid sitting on my plate and set it to the side. I didn't even care what was on the plate. I cut the meat gingerly and placed it in my mouth. I was a few bites in before I heard Seamus call my name.

"Huh?" I said, staring blankly at him.

"You're not gonna respond to what I've divulged?" he asked. His face was furrowed in annoyance.

I set my utensils down and tipped my head to reach an itch that was bothering me then responded. "What are you talking about, Seamus?"

"You can't afford me the common fuckin' courtesy of listening. Is the food that good?" his brogue was quite thick at that moment. His anger was kindled.

"Seamus," I said, gathering myself. "Why do you have to marry her?"

"Why is that important?" he asked.

I slammed my fists down on the table, rattling the dishes. "Damn it, Shea! Just back out of the fucking deal if you don't want to marry Chelsey. Why have me sign an NDA if you weren't going to tell me what's really going on? All this security and secrecy...Fuck!"

Seamus leaned back in his chair, furrowed brow, and pinched the bridge of his nose. I knew this spoke to his inner turmoil, but I didn't give a fuck at this point.

"When I purchased my parents' home, I learned my father wasn't the person I had always believed him to be. Dad is a founding member of an international crime syndicate. He had several offshore holdings that were used for money laundering. I was given the opportunity to join, but I declined. Since I declined to take his place, as a parting gift, they gave me one of the holdings. Before you ask, it was a gift I couldn't refuse. The business I'm trying to legitimize was his, and if anyone finds out about it, my father will be looking at thirty years federal time, for tax evasion and money laundering."

I sat down, staring at Shea in disbelief as he continued, "When Chelsey first brought the idea of us getting married to me, it was simple. Postponing the wedding, while continuing to purchase—*take* the company, angered Albrect Reichling, Chelsey's father. When he learned that I had called off the wedding, but still intended to take his company he was pissed off. He did some digging and learned about my father...and you. Reichling believes his honor has been insulted and he's now using this information to blackmail me. The easiest way out of the situation is to marry Chelsey. Maeve, he has documentation on my father dating back to the early eighties. I have no choice."

This was too fantastic to believe. I sat there staring at Shea in disbelief as he spoke. That was why he made me sign a non-disclosure agreement. Who the fuck would have believed me if I told them this farfetched ass fairytale? Criminal activity, blackmail, forced marriage. Who demanded a wedding over money in this day and age? Why the hell hadn't he gone to the FBI or the CIA?

Shock and panic hit me all at once. "How does this involve me? What does he know about me, Shea?" I managed to ask.

"He knows we've had sex and he knows I'm in love with you," Seamus added.

"How? Should I...be worried?"

"As long as I marry—" Shea began before I cut him off.

"Wait," I started, "Am I in *danger*, Seamus?"

"Yes, Maeve. Reichling is a very dangerous man. If I don't follow through with his demands, there's no telling what he will do," Shea responded softly, trying to soften the blow of the news.

"Shea, we have to go to the police with this information," I replied.

"And then what?" He began to show irritation. "I won't let my father go to prison, Maeve. If I involve the feds, the entire syndicate will be after us. I've weighed all of the options— this is the lesser of all evils. It's not like I have to stay married to her for life. Just long enough to acquire his company and make things look legitimate."

"Surely there has to be something else you can do besides marriage, Shea. As long as they have this over you, you're stuck," I retorted angrily.

Shea remained quiet, he looked out over the city as I spoke. The realization hit me suddenly. "You fucked her."

"To appease her... And I thought you were with Darren," he replied softly.

"To appease you! Don't you dare bring Darren into this." I stood looking for my things. "We almost lost our lives, and you were *fucking* Chelsey. "

"What was I supposed to think?" he retorted.

"Had you called, come by, asked, you would've known I wasn't *with* Darren," I snarled.

"That was a mistake, but I'm trying to keep you safe. Don't you get that?" he asked.

"I don't want to hear your fucking excuses," I responded, biting back tears. I was a ball of emotions.

"I never wanted to…" He didn't finish.

"I'm done, Shea. Where are my things?" I spat angrily.

Shea pointed to a bench near the ledge of the building across from where we were sitting. I walked over to retrieve my things, pivoted, and headed for the door leading downstairs.

"Don't leave like this, *Feíleacán*," Shea called from behind me.

I turned to face him when I spoke. "Don't call me that again."

I made my way down to the street, as Shea caught up with me. My usual driver was waiting in front of the building. What the fuck was Adjemi doing there? The driver spoke, "Miss James, I'm here to take you home. Mr. McGhee hired me as—" He was interrupted by Seamus.

"He's here for your protection. You may not want to hear from or see me, but until all of this is sorted out, you will have twenty-four-hour security. Not negotiable," Shea spoke sternly.

"That's what the police are for," I began.

"Dammit, I'm not going to argue with you." I knew Shea was getting agitated, but I persisted.

"How am I supposed to get Adjemi past Stacy?" I barked.

"Figure it out! Now, get your motherfucking ass in the *fucking* car!" Seamus yelled.

I looked at Adjemi, but he had stepped back and was looking down the street. The doorman had stepped into the building and closed the door. In the time we'd known each other, Shea had never raised his voice at me like that. I knew he was serious. I looked at Shea, who was red-faced and furious, and tears began to fall freely from my eyes. He pulled me close to him, looking around to make sure we weren't being seen. Shea let me cry into his chest as long as I needed it.

"You may never want to see me again," he spoke softly into my ear, "but I intend to keep you safe. Let me handle this, please."

"Fine," I said, finally stepping away. Adjemi turned to open the door as I walked toward the vehicle.

Before he shut the door, Shea grabbed it and said, "I love you. Despite how you may feel right now, I know you still love me, too."

I turned to look out of the other window as he spoke. I was hurt by the knowledge of his betrayal, but he was right...I did love him.

"Mr. McGhee mentioned round the clock security. Is that feasible?" Adjemi asked.

"Did it sound like I had a fucking choice? How am I supposed to lie to my roommate? This is an impossible situation," I barked at Adjemi. "I'm sorry."

"No worries. I'm sure you will think of something. I will go along with whatever you come up with," Adjemi responded.

I buckled my seatbelt then began to ponder reasons for a huge black man to suddenly be staying with me. Adjemi drove to my house in silence. He implored me to remain in the car while he performed a perimeter check. I was irritated, but grateful to be safe after all I'd just learned.

"Let's go upstairs, Miss James," Adjemi said when he returned to the car.

"Ok, if this is going to work, you'll have to call me by my nickname—Maevie," I informed him.

"Yes, ma'am," he responded.

"No, Adjemi," I retorted sharply. "Maevie."

"Maevie it is," he said.

I opened the door to find Stacy sitting on the couch. *Act normal, Maeve,* I encouraged myself. She looked up at me, then to the doorway. Her face never betrayed her thoughts.

"Hey, Stace," I sang. "This is my cousin, Jimmy. He needs a place to crash for a while. You don't mind, do you?"

"Nope," she responded, looking back down to her work, "not at all. Hey, Jimmy. I'm Stacy. Nice to meet you."

What the fuck? my mind screamed. No protests, no questions—nada. This may have been easier than I thought.

I looked back at Adjemi, who gave nothing away. "You'll be staying in the guest room, follow me." I led him to his room before speaking again.

Once in the bedroom, Adjemi finally spoke, "You think she bought it?"

"I'm not sure. That was a little too easy," I said, looking at the door.

"Well, let's see where it goes," he said, setting his bag down.

"So what's next?" I asked hesitantly.

"You'll give me a tour, go over the security system with me and get ready for bed," Adjemi stated as he walked over to the window, peering out to the street below. He looked at me momentarily before heading to his bag. "Where can I put my things?"

I pointed to the dresser and the closet. "I'll bring you some towels."

"Thanks, Maevie." Adjemi gave me a sympathetic look. "I'll try to make my presence in your life as seamless as possible."

"This all seems surreal to me," I confessed.

"As it should," he spoke candidly. "Mr. McGhee is very concerned for your safety."

"So you're aware of the situation?" I asked.

"Yes, he filled me in a few weeks ago," he said.

"Is that why you started driving for me?" I asked. I was fishing for more information then I'd gotten from Shea.

"No, I work for W&W, but I'm freelancing for Mr. McGhee. Since I was already driving for you, providing security was a no-brainer. I was Army Special Ops before I separated from the military."

Adjemi made me feel comfortable. He spent the rest of the evening acclimating to our home.

I had done a google search of Chelsey's father and found out he was the head of an organized crime family that made the American Mob bosses look like Mister Rogers. I contemplated my situation and prepped for bed when Stacy came into my room, closed the door behind herself, and spoke.

"So who the fuck is Cousin Jimmy, really?"

"Shit, I knew it was too easy," I laughed.

"Honey, boo! I know you don't think I'm that dumb. What's the deal?" She walked over to the bed and sat.

"I can't talk about it. I need you to trust me, though," I began before she interrupted.

"Oh, hell, no! I deserve to know what's going on if I gotta go along with Chocolate Thunder residing here," she said in a matter-of-fact tone.

"Shea called me today and asked me to have dinner with him. I went against my better judgment. Long story short, my life is in danger because of some illegal shit he got himself into. Adjemi—Cousin Jimmy—is my new live-in bodyguard. I understand if you don't want him here," I said, trying to keep the story as short as possible.

"Shit," Stacy paused momentarily to absorb what I'd told her before she began again. "Girl, no one was going to believe that fine ass man in there is your cousin," she laughed. "Did you forget I went to your family reunion a few years back? I'd have noticed his big ass!"

"Damn it! I completely forgot about that," I giggled. I loved Stacy for keeping things light. I couldn't take any more stress.

"Cousin Jim Bob would've been well fucked had he been at your family reunion," she joked.

We fell backward on the bed, giggling. My only desire was to confide more in Stacy, but the less she knew, the better.

Adjemi remained with us through the summer into September. During that time, Adjemi made me wonder on several occasions if he wanted to do more than protect me. It was the way he ushered me into the car with his hand on the small of my back, chance touches when he took my bag to load into the car or even the way he brushed past me in the kitchen or hallway. Each set my sex-starved body ablaze. I fantasized about sex with Adjemi often.

Adjemi was with me all of the time. He learned quickly to gauge my mood. Adjemi recommended working out to ease some of my tension. We ran together before or after work. Most days, he hung back to give me some space. Once, I had a complete meltdown. We had been running near Navy Pier when I bugged the hell out. People were outside walking dogs, pushing strollers, exercising, and enjoying the beautiful Chicago summer evening like I should have been doing.

It was one of many anxiety attacks I had been having lately. I felt overwhelmed and consumed. I had an all-encompassing urge to run away from Adjemi, Shea, work, home—everything. I felt as though the walls were pressing in on me, even though we were outside putting feet to the pavement. All I could do was run faster. To a bystander, it must've looked like Adjemi was chasing me. I ran faster and harder until it felt like I hit a brick wall. I doubled over in agony, straining and gulping for air.

"Hey," he said, placing his hand on my back. "What's going on?"

"I can't," I sobbed, "I can't keep doing this." My breath came in ragged as I spoke.

He rubbed my back softly. "I know it's not easy. I'm sure after the wedding—" I knocked his hand away to walk off. Adjemi was quick if nothing else.

"Don't," I began.

"Hey." He pressed his hand into my shoulder to stop my departure. "I'm sorry."

I looked up at the big Nigerian's face. His expression was soft and comforting. Tears threatened to fall again when he pulled me into his embrace. I wrapped my arms around his waist and cried.

Our exchange was cut short by a familiar voice.

"I pay you to keep her safe, not fondle her."

Shea stood a few feet away from us, scowling angrily.

We parted, then Adjemi stepped back. "I'll give you two a moment to talk." He stared at Shea unappreciatively for having the nerve to insinuate anything improper.

"Are you fucking him, now?" His tone was bitingly rude.

"What the fuck, Shea?" I asked incredulously. "Are you serious right now?"

"I find you locked in another man's embrace. What am I supposed to think?" Shea asked.

"*Would you ever cop on to yourself?* I haven't seen you in months, and you show up *acting the maggot*," I said as I turned to walk away.

Shea put out his hand to stop me. My body leaped to life as his hand came in contact with my stomach. He stepped closer, not removing his hand before he spoke. His voice was just above a whisper. "How am I not acting normal? I hate to think I'm annoying you, but I've told you before...you are mine, *Feíleacán.*"

"I've told you not to call me that," I said, pushing his hand away. "I'm not yours, Shea."

"The hell you aren't," he said in a hushed tone.

"Don't," I gritted out between clenched teeth. My hands were in tight balls at my side.

"I'm sorry," his voice softened.

"I was having an anxiety attack, and Adjemi was trying to help," I explained.

"This isn't easy for either of us, Maeve. All I want to do is keep you safe," he said sweetly.

"I get it, but don't make accusations, Shea." I looked at him intensely. He looked terse, tired— worried.

He reached out to lightly brush my hair out of my face. I closed my eyes as his hand trailed down my cheek.

"I miss you, *Feíleacán.* I'll figure out a way for us to be together, I promise." He leaned down, kissed my lips sweetly, then walked away.

"I miss you too," I whispered. I stood watching him leave for a moment. Adjemi tapped me gently on the shoulder.

"Are you ready to head home?"

"Not yet." I replied.

I stood there watching Shea until he disappeared from my sight.

"It's getting late, Maevie. Let's head back to the loft now," Adjemi suggested softly. His facial expression was all business when I turned around.

"Fine." I jogged off, leaving him where he stood.

My thoughts drifted to the kiss Shea gave me before he departed. I wanted to be mad at him for sleeping with Chelsey, but I knew I still loved him. I hadn't forgiven him, though. Adjemi kept pace with me on the way home.

"Are you ok?" he asked smoothly.

"Yeah," I panted.

We made it back to the to the loft slightly after dusk. The Shea sighting wore me out.

"You hungry? Let's order take out. What are you in the mood for?" Adjemi asked.

I turned to look at him. *Damn, that seemed to be a loaded question...*

"What do you have in mind?" I asked.

"I'm down for anything," he said suggestively.

If I didn't know any better, I would've sworn Adjemi was offering more than food suggestions.

I stopped short to ask, "Anything?" I raised my eyebrow at his double entendre.

"I am here for you," his words were gentle and inviting. The Bad Bitch in my brain perked up.

"You work for Seamus, Adjemi," I began before he interrupted.

"I work for Winchester and Wiles. I'm doing part-time security for you. Seamus was out of line for suggesting..." Adjemi cleared his throat before continuing. "His statement wasn't totally false, though."

"I-I," I looked down, scratching a non-existent itch at the back of my head. "So what are you saying?"

"I'm saying I'm here for whatever you might need. Listen, I know you're in love with him. I also know you're a woman...with needs." He looked around as he spoke, but his tone betrayed his attentiveness toward my needs.

Oh shit, she was wide awake now! The Bad Bitch in my brain sat at attention, salivating for this tall drink of water. Adjemi was absolutely correct, and it would serve Shea's ass right for fucking Chelsey. But what if the dick was good, and I liked it, a lot? It wasn't like I was cheating...

"Let's get Chinese and see where the night goes." I gave him a coy smile. Adjemi's face brightened.

Stacy wasn't home when we arrived. She had left one of her cute Post-it notes on the mirror. I giggled.

"What's so funny?" Adjemi asked.

"Stacy's out for the night." I pointed to the note.

"Is that right?" he asked. Adjemi grabbed my hand, leading me to my room. Our hands were wet with perspiration.

"We need to order food," I laughed.

"We will...afterward." The seriousness of Adjemi's tone caused my sex to clench tightly.

Adjemi led me down the hall to my room. He reached behind me to close the door, then slowly undressed us both before leading us to the bathroom. The shower was foreplay on steroids. After our shower, I threw on a robe, then tipped into Stacy's room to borrow a condom. I wondered briefly if she counted them. Hopefully, she wouldn't notice one missing from her stash. I went back down the hall to my room and paused outside the closed door for a moment. I was scared shitless, because I had never been with another man.

What in the hell am I doing? This felt wrong, but my body, and brain, were crying for release. What would Shea think if he ever found out? The Bad Bitch in my brain was not having all of my second thoughts. *Girl, did he think about you when he fucked Chelsey?* That was all I needed to hear.

I pushed the door open to find Adjemi standing at the window wrapped in one of my white towels.

"Hey," I whispered.

"Hey," he said back.

"I found a condom," I said, waving the spoils of my conquest for him to see.

"Good." He looked me in my eyes while he let the towel drop from his waist.

Oh, damn! The man was hung like a fucking horse—and he wasn't even hard yet.

"Uh, um-um," I stammered.

"I'll be gentle," he said. Adjemi beckoned me to come to him with his finger. I obeyed as sheer lust pulled me to him.

"I'm a little nervous. Shea's the only—"

"You're the boss, M" Adjemi interrupted, looking me in my eyes. The thought of being in control spurred me into action.

"Get on the bed," I ordered.

Adjemi followed my instructions by sprawling out onto my king-sized bed. He almost made it look small. I turned to walk over to the lights to turn them off. I desperately wanted to hide my shame. Did Shea fuck Chelsey with the lights off? *Hell no!* the Bad Bitch in my brain screamed. *Leave them on,* she offered.

I stopped in my tracks and untied my robe, letting it fall slowly to the floor. I heard a sharp intake of air from the man who occupied my bed. I turned around to find his thick shaft fully erect. He let his eyes wander up and down my body before closing them. When he opened them again, they were full of desire.

"Fuck me," he pleaded.

And fuck him, I did...

I placed the condom between my lips as I climbed into bed. I crawled slowly toward Adjemi, tearing it open in one movement when I reached his engorged member. I sheathed his cock then mounted him, allowing my sex to engulf him slowly. He let out a long sigh when I rested squarely on his midsection.

"I need this," I started. "I am fully aware, and I consent to sexual relations with you."

He chuckled, then repeated my sentiments, "I need this, and I too, consent to sexual relations with you, M."

"Do you think we should kiss?" I asked shyly.

"I want to experience all of you, but if you aren't comfortable—" I cut him off with an ardent kiss.

He returned my kiss with equal passion. He wrapped his arms

around me, pulling me tightly to his chest. I rose and fell onto his cock as he sheathed and unsheathed himself inside of me. His mouth devoured my lips, neck, and ears. I leaned up, giving him access to my breasts. They seemed smaller than usual in his large hands. Adjemi savored them as he rolled me onto my back. From that position, he took care not to crush me. His hips were more expansive than Shea's. With his full weight on me, my thighs pressed into the bed. He had deeper access to my inner folds. Adjemi was adoringly sweet and did not put demands on my body. He allowed me to set the pace. Our lovemaking was slow and sensual.

"You are so beautiful," he whispered, nuzzling into my neck.

I moaned in response, as slow waves of pleasure washed over me. "Mm, Adjemi, I'm coming."

"I feel it," he spoke softly.

Adjemi pulled out of me moments after I came, which confused me. "Turn over, I want you from behind." His voice sounded strained.

"What's the matter?" I asked.

"Nothing. I want to feel more of you, is all," he responded.

I adjusted myself to lay in front of him. He lifted my leg, bringing his cock to my entrance once more. Adjemi pushed into me slowly. I felt every inch of him stretching me open. His cock wasn't as lengthy as Shea's, but he definitely had more girth.

"Fuck," I moaned.

"Am I hurting you?" He paused to wait for my response.

"Don't stop," I pleaded.

Adjemi pushed deeper into my folds. He nuzzled into my nape speaking delectably filthy phrases into my hair.

"This ass, your tits, this tight pussy. You're about to send me over the edge," Adjemi began.

"So go over the edge," I moaned.

"I want to savor you." He bit into my shoulder softly. He pulled my body into him with one hand while gently choking me with the other. I let my leg fall slightly forward. He rolled me back onto his body, as I moaned his name softly.

"Adjemi," I cried out in pleasure.

"Yes," he responded.

"You feel so good," I murmured.

"You feel better, M," he breathed out. My sex clenched at the sound of his nickname for me.

"I can't last much longer," I groaned.

"I'm close, M. Don't hold back," his voice beckoned me forward.

I splintered into a deliciously slow-rolling orgasm. Adjemi came shortly after I began. Our groans were soft yet intense. I whimpered into his mouth as he pulled my head back to kiss me. His lips piloted me into another orgasm. *Fuck!* I didn't want this to stop, but I only had one condom. I made a mental note to purchase more condoms. I didn't want this to be our last time.

We hadn't even pulled the covers back, just fucked right on top of them. I laid in Adjemi's arms, spent.

A few hours later, I awoke with a start. I was under the covers, alone in my bed, naked. I sat up. I couldn't shake the feeling that I wasn't alone. I scanned the room for familiar shapes, calling on all of my senses. No unfamiliar sounds or smells. I got up searching for my robe. I found it at the foot of the bed and put it on, then headed for the door. A large figure opened the door, stifling my scream with a large hand.

"Don't scream," Adjemi whispered. "My security detail called while you were asleep. Someone was in the apartment. I need to get you out of here now. Do you understand?"

I nodded my head sharply.

"I'll stand guard while you throw on some clothes. Grab what you need, and we'll go," he whispered.

"I have to warn Stacy." My volume matched Adjemi's.

"Text her when we're in the car. No more talking—get dressed." He pushed me toward the closet.

I ran into the closet, grabbing some athletic gear and dressing as I searched for my backpack. I threw some essentials into it then made my way back to Adjemi. My heart was racing when I stepped out of the closet into darkness.

"The power has been cut. My men are waiting outside the door. We'll go down the stairs to the garage. We're taking your car." Adjemi's instructions were clear and concise.

"Is it safe?" I asked.

"Your car has been checked. It's safe. Listen, when we leave this room, I will be right behind you. Don't stop moving until we get to the door," Adjemi spoke in a reassuring tone.

"Ok," I said.

Adjemi opened the door, peering out before ushering me. I moved swiftly to the door, opening it when I reached it. The security detail outside looked to Adjemi then me. We walked briskly past the elevators down the hall to the emergency stairs. We entered the stairwell then began the descent into the darkness. It was eerily quiet—we barely made any noise. The three of us snaked through the lower floor toward the parking garage. The emergency lighting came on as we pushed the door open. I saw a dark figure step out from one of the support pillars.

"He's with us," Adjemi whispered.

My car purred to life as I laid down across the back seat. Adjemi got into the driver's seat while the other security detail stepped into a neighboring SUV. Our caravan, consisting of my car sandwiched between two large black SUVs, darted out of the alleyway. I frantically texted Stacy.

Me:	Don't go back to the loft! Danger!
Stace:	Is everything ok?
Me:	Someone broke in, security rushed me out.
Stace:	Holy shit! Ok, I'll stay here. Text me when it's safe!
Me:	I'm sorry! Will do!
Stace:	No worries, chica. Be safe!

"So, what's the plan?" I asked from the back seat. I wasn't sure where we were going but I saw the highway sign for I-90.

"I'm taking you someplace safe. I've contacted the police to let them know we've left the premises and that the power has been cut. They'll investigate, and call you with the findings," he said reluctantly.

"And Shea?" I asked.

"He has a need to know, but not until I know you are safe," Adjemi said softly.

"And work?" I followed up with another question. I had a job and responsibilities. But my life had become a string of unlucky occurrences since I'd slept with Shea. There were days I wished I'd remained chaste. Other days, I didn't think this was really my life. I often felt that I was in a terrible dream like I'd never awakened from the coma I was in following the accident. Here I was in the back seat of my Audi zipping down the highway along with not one, but two SUVs. This was a motherfucking nightmare.

"I will update Winchester and Wiles. I was obligated to let them know about the security threat since you are one of their shining stars." Adjemi's admission surprised me. I was hoping to keep my private life private.

"I'm a very private person, Adjemi. I didn't want my employer all up in the business." I was slightly pissed off, but I sensed his teasing.

"M, you know that all of the drivers for W & W are private security. Mr. McGhee is paying for the additional security though." I looked up to find Adjemi staring at me through the rearview mirror. I remembered adding private security into the W & W budget and the communique that the board of directors had to sign.

Fuck, I was so happy to be a part of the board of directors I would've signed anything.

Hell, it's hard for minorities, especially Black women, to see themselves in the same light as old, rich white men. That shit just didn't happen. We had to be more educated and work twice as hard for less while not compromising our morals. So, did I think I was ever going to use the security I set up for them? Hell no! Look at me now...using that shit like a motherfucker and appreciating the fact that we didn't settle for some cheap-ass, cut-rate company.

"Honestly, I never saw myself needing security. That's probably why I forgot," I answered, shaking my head. "So what's next, Adjemi?"

"I thought we'd take you to a safe house for a few days. Once we know your loft is safe, we'll head back to the city," he answered.

Adjemi and I rode for a long while with conversation peppered between our silence. It wasn't quite awkward, but it was slightly uncomfortable being alone again. Our intimate evening had been interrupted by ill-timed insanity. I never did get my Chinese food—and my stomach growling proved it. My body betrayed me every fucking chance it got.

Adjemi peered through the rearview mirror.

"I promised you Chinese food." He smiled. I returned his smile, hoping to reassure him that I wasn't upset.

"It's not your fault. How about a raincheck?" I proffered. He silently considered my suggestion. I noticed him checking the side mirrors before answering.

"I assumed tonight was a one-time thing, M." Adjemi put the ball back in my court.

Fuck! Tonight should have been a Netflix and Chill or Hulu and Do You type of night, I thought. Unfortunately, we never got to the Netflix and eat portion of the evening. I knew I wanted to have sex with him again, but I didn't want to look easy or man-hungry, even though I was parched.

"I don't think it counts since things didn't go as planned, Adjemi. Do you?" I bounce-passed the ball back to him. He looked up with a broad smile across his handsome face.

"No, but," he paused briefly, "it's not Chinese food that I want." His volume dropped a few decibels. "The thought of being alone again is making it hard for me to concentrate, M."

Our eyes met once more, causing my heart to flutter. There was no denying the sexual chemistry.

Is it more than tension relief? I wondered. Honestly, the sex was so bomb it had me contemplating more than just a one-time thing. I knew I said it was just sex, but I felt some kind of way when he spoke like that. I liked knowing I made him lose his focus, but in-house dick—dick that was supposed to be protecting me—could be trouble. I needed all of his focus to survive.

"Adjemi, I...um," I fumbled for the right thing to say when he cut in.

"Don't worry, M. I'm a professional. I know how to separate protecting you from pleasing you." Adjemi didn't look away from the road when he spoke. We rode in silence for a long while before I spoke again.

"I hope I didn't offend you. I know it's not proper for us to hook up, but I'd like to try again if it's alright with you." I glanced at the mirror hoping he'd look up, but he kept his face forward.

"You didn't offend me, but this—" Adjemi's response was cut short by my ringing phone.

"Shit! It's Seamus," I said looking toward the display panel in the front seat. Adjemi answered the phone before I contemplated the next move.

"Mr. McGhee, it's Adjemi," he spoke into the air.

"Why are you answering Ms. James' phone? Is everything ok?" Seamus spoke tersely.

"There was an incident at the loft—" Adjemi launched into an explanation, but was promptly cut off by an angry Seamus McGhee.

"Why the fuck didn't you call me? Is Maeve alright? What the fuck happened, man? Have the police been notified?" Seamus fumed.

"Someone broke into the loft, but my primary concern was getting Miss James to safety. We are on our way to an undisclosed location, Mr. McGhee. The police are investigating—"

Seamus interrupted once more, causing Adjemi to get visibly upset.

"Broke in? Is she ok?" Seamus seethed.

"I can hear you, Shea. I'm ok," I spoke up angrily.

"Take me off speakerphone, damn it," Seamus demanded, causing me to bristle with anger.

I turned the Bluetooth off from my handset and pressed the phone to my ear. "Yes, Shea?"

"Are you ok?" he asked softly.

"I'm fine, but do you have to be an asshole?" I asked indignantly.

"What the fuck am I paying for? I should have been notified," he seethed.

"I understand your frustration, Shea. But you're doing the absolute most right now, for real!" I yelled.

"Why the fuck are you defending incompetence, MJ?" Shea questioned.

"Incompetence? Are you fucking kidding me? It's because of Adjemi and his team that I'm safe." I was livid.

"Yes, incompetence! How the fuck did someone break in with a security detail in your fucking loft? What was he asleep, distracted—" He paused. "Were you fucking him?"

I sank into the plush leather upholstery of the Audi, stunned into silence. Seconds ticked by as I thought of an answer.

"Shea," I swallowed the ball of emotion lodged in my throat, "don't be ridiculous."

"Tell me I'm wrong, *Feíleacán*. Tell me you didn't fuck him. I'll wait." Shea's voice held all of the calm of a sleeping dragon.

"I'm not going—" I started, then was cut off.

"I can fathom slipping past the security detail outside, but there had to be one hell of a distraction to penetrate Special Forces within the house," Shea spoke softly so as not to be overheard by Adjemi. "Were you the distraction, *Feíleacán?*"

I picked up on his penetration innuendo. He picked up on my reluctance to speak. My reticence told him everything he needed to know, though. *Don't forget he got distracted by Chelsey! Fuck him, the Bad Bitch in my brain screamed.* Oh, how quickly she turned on Shea. Jealous much? Yes!

I hadn't been paying attention to our direction, but a familiar landmark caught my attention—Big Sable Point Lighthouse. *What the fuck are we doing in Michigan? Fuck!* It didn't seem like we'd been in the car for four hours. I had extended family in Muskegon, Michigan. The

James family had reunions there when I was younger.

"Answer me, Butterfly." Shea's voice brought me back to reality.

"I'm not doing this with you, Seamus," I replied sharply.

"Let me know when you're safe, Miss James," Shea quipped, then disconnected the call. His attitude irritated the fuck out of me. I knew he thought his earlier allegation was founded in truth when I refused to deny it.

"Is everything ok?" Adjemi inquired sweetly.

I sighed, looking up at his reflection. His almond shaped eyes showed concern and a glimpse of something more...jealousy.

"He asked if I distracted you," I answered honestly. Adjemi closed his eyes momentarily then returned his gaze to the road. *Shit!* We really allowed our mutual anger at Shea's earlier accusation of impropriety to cause our complacency.

In essence, we got caught lackin'!

Chapter Twenty-Three
BIG SABLE POINT LIGHTHOUSE

The police called the next morning to let me know they had caught the intruder, who wasn't some hired assassin coming to dispose of me in my sleep, but a young kid looking to score some trinkets to pawn to support his heroin addiction. Also, the power lines hadn't been severed. A repairman had cut the wrong wire causing an outage throughout the building.

I inhaled slowly, allowing the air to escape my lungs slowly.

A fucking false alarm. *What the fuck?* I thought, as I ended the call. You'd think a highly-trained security team would be able to tell the difference. I should've been appreciative, but I was irritated.

I laid in bed, mulling over the newly acquired information and last night's events, which had brought me to Ludington, Michigan. I crashed hard when we had arrived at the little cabin in the woods, not pausing to remove my clothes, shoes, or shower. Meanwhile, the men slept in two-hour shifts, leaving two men awake at all times. The aroma of freshly brewed coffee threatened to lure me from my little safe haven, but I didn't stray from the bedroom for fear of awkwardness between myself and Adjemi. I looked around at the furniture and accouterments in the brightly lit room. I had never been a fan of coastal interior designs. To me, aquatic animals weren't meant to be décor unless they were housed in a well-cared-for tank. A petrified wood headboard sat atop a sizeable king-sized platform bed. Heavy manila nautical rope had been looped through an anchor in the ceiling and held a smaller sliver of petrified wood where a short stack of books about Lake Michigan and the lighthouse sat neatly, and a small conch rested atop them. The wall opposite the bed contained three large windows which looked directly out on the lake. The walls and floors were light tones, lending to the casual mood of the room. A small shelf with artifacts and beach treasures was located near the door, with a TV mounted over it.

Who is watching television with this view of the lake? I thought, looking out the window.

I wanted to go for a run, explore the lighthouse again, and find some breakfast. But if the food didn't lure me out of my sanctuary, nothing would. I decided to take a shower instead. I rose and padded to the en suite bathroom to brush my teeth and wash my face. I looked haggard, but given the circumstances, it was expected. Adjemi had definitely put me through the paces before we had to make a mad dash for safety. As I brushed my teeth, my thoughts wandered to Adjemi. My body loved the way we felt making love. It was vastly different from my first experience. Adjemi was gentle and expressive, not demanding or controlling—the total opposite of Shea. Why was I afraid to face him then? The Bad Bitch in my brain piped up, *Guilt.*

I felt like I'd cheated on Shea. Yes, the same Shea with the fiancée. What the hell was my problem?

I quickly went through an abbreviated version of my skincare ritual. I was happy I hadn't removed my toiletry bag from my backpack after the NYC trip. I was surprised all of my belongings survived the accident. I used the tiny toiletries to clean my face and neck before peeling out of my clothes and stepping into the shower. The warm water soothed my anxieties.

"Siri," I called to my phone from the tub.

"Yes," Siri responded promptly from the bathroom countertop.

"Play Adele," I requested of the AI assistant.

"Playing Adele in Apple Music," Siri informed.

I washed and conditioned my hair, finger-detangling my strands, before putting it up into a half-dry makeshift bun, then focused on my body. I exfoliated and bathed my flesh using the last of the products in the tiny bottles. I reminded myself to buy some more Cowshed body scrub and shower gel when I got home. Rho had turned me on to the brand when she visited family in London a few years ago. I was ecstatic to find it in Chicago because it kept me from ordering and paying to have it sent from the UK. I loitered in the shower until my fingers resembled prunes. I toweled off, dressed in the hoodie and leggings I had thrown in my backpack, then made the bed. I didn't like sitting on the bed after making it, so I plopped into an oversized chair next to it. I texted Stacy afterward to let her know all was clear. Instead of texting back, she called.

"Hey, boo," I sang into my phone.

"Hey, Maevie," she sang back. "I have a question for you."

"Shoot," I responded.

"So, how was the dick?" Stacy said confidently. I heard her smiling through the phone.

"The wh-what?" I sputtered.

"The. Dick," she repeated confidently.

I inhaled sharply. "How did you know?"

"Someone broke in on Cousin Skeeter's watch. He had to have been distracted. Pussy is the only thing I can think of that could occupy his big ass long enough to miss the crackhead robbing us." Stacy's laughter was infectious, so I giggled with her.

"Girl, Shea figured it out too," I sighed.

"Shut up!" she screamed.

"Yeah, he called last night, mad as fuck about not being kept in the loop...among other things," I informed her.

"Well, if you didn't confirm or deny sexual intercourse took place, it's purely speculation on his part, at this juncture, Maevie," Stacy tried to cheer me up.

"My silence spoke volumes, sis."

"Have you spoken to Adjemi?" Stacy asked.

Before answering, there was a knock at the door.

"Yes?" I sang out, putting my phone to my chest.

"Are you decent?" Adjemi asked from the other side of the door.

"Yeah, come on in," I responded before addressing Stacy. "Hey, girl, let me call you back."

"Cool," she said before disconnecting the call.

Adele's voice sang the first verses of "Make You Feel My Love", and I shut that shit down expeditiously. I adjusted in the chair to address him.

"Hey," my voice cracked, "so the police called."

"Yeah, I got the update. Company practice is to take precautionary measures." Adjemi's large body took up most of the space in the door frame. "Can we talk?" he asked.

"Sure," I responded, trying to keep things light.

Adjemi looked very handsome in the morning light. He was dressed casually in dark wash jeans and a light grey crewneck sweater. My eyes fell on his full lips. The memory of them on my body made my stomach do flips.

"It's our modus operandi, M." Adjemi paused a beat to see if I had another question. He proceeded at my silence. "I owe you an apology. I allowed myself to be distracted, which put you in a gnarly situation." Adjemi seemed to be coming down very hard on himself.

"Adjemi," I interjected, "you don't need to explain yourself to me because I don't share Seamus' sentiments. We both got...distracted."

"Seamus was right—about the situation yesterday. I wanted to..." Adjemi looked past me out of the window. "I've wanted to be with you long before last night. M, you are a serious distraction."

I rose from my seat, making my way to where he stood. "I disagree." Adjemi let his head lull back as he laughed heartily.

"You're telling me you aren't a serious distraction?" He smiled devilishly.

He leaned down swiftly, picking me up. I wrapped my arms and legs about him as his mouth crushed mine in a heated kiss. My mouth opened to his as we lost ourselves in the passion. Adjemi slid one hand to the middle of my buttocks to support me as the other one went to my neck, pressing our bodies closer together. I knew he was walking us to the bed as I wrapped my limbs around him tightly. I allowed myself to fall into our kiss. My mind blocked out all intrusive thoughts as our tongues danced feverishly together. There was definitely intense sexual chemistry between us. To think, less than forty-eight hours ago, I hadn't really given "Jimmy" a thought.

His mouth tasted of hazelnut. I sucked his tongue, gently mimicking oral sex. His mouth watered, switching to a salty flavor. Arousal—pure arousal.

I came to my senses as his solid frame rested heavily on mine. If we didn't stop, we'd both need another shower.

"Wait," I panted heavily, "we can't."

Adjemi leaned up onto his elbow, looking down at me. "My point exactly, M. See how easily we're distracted?"

"Fuck." I allowed my head to fall back onto the bed. "I was thinking we'd need another shower." We laughed.

"I need to pull back, M. I can't protect you if I'm thinking about *this* all of the time," he said as he ran his hand down my body, sending a chill down my spine.

"What does that look like, Adjemi?" I asked.

"It looks like me moving out of the loft, allowing my team to do their job properly," he replied. Adjemi stroked my face delicately as his eyes drank in my engorged lips.

"Will I still see you?" I closed my eyes, knowing the answer before he gave it.

"I don't think that's wise. I need to run this detail from a distance. I'll put my best two men on you. That's in addition to the two outside the building."

"I trust you, so do what you need to do." I smiled, trying to be as nonchalant as possible. "Will we still talk?"

"I can't make any promises," he said softly. He stopped stroking my face, leaning down to kiss me again.

What the fuck am I tripping about? I thought. We fucked one time. It wasn't like this was a relationship. I wasn't gon' lie—the sex was phenomenal, and I'd grown accustomed to having Adjemi around. I got that he had a job to do, though. I was just hoping for a little diversion from the Shea conundrum. *Fucking Shea!* Instead of us being caked up right now, he'd gotten us into a life-threatening ordeal.

Adjemi rose from the bed and then made his way to the door before turning back momentarily. "We're departing shortly. There's food and coffee downstairs if you're hungry, M."

"Thanks," I said. I perched on the bed, with my knee raised, staring at the door after Adjemi pulled it shut.

Gaht damn, good dick is hard to hold onto these days, I thought.

Chapter Twenty-Four
BAD BITCH, WHERE?

everal weeks had passed since I'd seen Adjemi or heard from Shea. I had gotten used to the changes made to my security detail. The house felt weird with Adjemi absent. I never saw the men who secured the building, but I knew the full security detail set up shop in a building across the street from our home. Stacy and I had them on speed dial, though we had no need to use the number. My new driver, Trevor, was quiet. I attempted to learn more about him, but he was a closed book. There would be no repeat of the Adjemi distraction. Mike monitored our security system and cameras throughout the house. Stacy and I made sure to confine our nudity to our rooms. As much as I dreaded watching Shea marry Chelsey, I was looking forward to being free of Big Brother's watchful eye.

"Girl, it's weird without Jim Bob here," Stacy noted.

"I agree," I said, munching on a sliver of bell pepper. Stacy liked to cook with the colorful variety rather than the typical green ones.

"Give me those." She wiped her hand on her apron before removing the pile of peppers from my cutting board. "So, how was the sex? You know you never told me."

Never one to mince words, Stacy eyeballed me, laughing at my reaction to her unanticipated question. "Better than those peppers," I quipped.

She lunged for a kitchen towel to snap at me as I ran from her reach. "That's how you gon' play it, Maevie?" Stacy laughed.

"I'll tell you if I can have two more peppers," I bargained. Stacy quickly grabbed for two small slivers of bell pepper as my ransom. I gladly accepted payment, then opened the cabinet to pull down stemless wine glasses. I grabbed a bottle of Moscato and poured her glass before I launched into my sordid story.

"Ok, so…I had one of my panic attacks while running at the lake. Adjemi caught up with me and attempted to *soothe* me," I motioned air quotes with my free hand. "Shea walked up while we were hugging."

"Bitch, wait!" Stacy turned from the stir fry she was cooking in a wok to address me. "Hugging?"

"Yes, child! Shea must've been out for a run too because he walked up and flipped the fuck out," I added.

"I bet! He thinks you belong to him. Men fucking kill me," Stacy rebutted.

"I know, right? Shea accused us of fucking, which pissed us both off." I took a sip of my wine before continuing. "We argued—of course—then I left."

"Don't you miss the time before, you know?" She sighed knowingly.

"Yes, ma'am," I laughed. "So, on the way home, Adjemi confessed his…desires to me, and the Bad Bitch in my brain took over," I confessed.

"The bad bitch *where?*" Stacy couldn't contain her laughter. "Who?"

"My alter ego," I started. "Don't act like you don't have one."

"You mean like Lil Stacy?" she said, pointing to her nether region.

"No, that's what you call the va-jayjay. I'm talking about the shit-talking, uber-confident, sexy inner goddess you," I disclosed.

Well, damn! Maybe it is just my crazy ass that has an alter ego, I thought.

"Oh ok." Stacy was giggling at herself. "So my alter ego is Lucy, 'cause I get loose."

"Ok, bitch, I *see* you!" I hooted at the name.

"Now, we gon' have to work on your name, 'cause that shit sounds tragic." Stacy side-eyed me mercilessly.

The Bad Bitch in my brain was instantly offended. *No, she didn't!* "You tried me like a free sample," I barked at the offense.

"Don't get mad! How about Trixie? You always called yourself Trixie in college. Why isn't that your alter ego's name?" Stacy asked.

"Trixie?" I pondered the name. "You know what, Stacy? I forgot about that!"

Trixie was smart, sexy, confident, and flexible. It ain't trickin' if you got it—good pussy that is! And I know I got it. The Bad Bitch in my brain co-signed the name as she ran about thumping her chest like Queen Kong.

"Ok, sis," Stacy interrupted my musings, "back to the story!"

"Ok, so, on the way home, Adjemi professed his desires and recommended Chinese food and fucking, because we had needs! We were supposed to eat, check out a movie, and see where things went. Apparently, *Trixie* had other ideas," I smirked before taking a sip of my wine.

"See, that sounds so much better than that wordy shit you said earlier! Ok, Trixie, get it," Stacy extended her fist, and I met her in kind.

"Girl," I continued, "he was so tender and sensual. I wasn't expecting that."

"I can see that. Jim Bob was Special Forces, so I'm sure he had to learn to finesse shit, move slow, and be patient," Stacy concluded.

"That makes perfect sense, Stace. Don't get me wrong, sex with Shea is phenomenal. I guess I expected it to be...I don't know, similar in some aspects," I admitted.

"Seamus has big dick energy, so I always assumed he was into control—BDSM or some other kinky shit. So, when you told me about the threesome, I wasn't surprised that he was into that sort of thing, you know," Stacy reasoned.

"Agreed. Shea's told me some stories—" I began.

"Wait, what? He told you stories, and you still fucked him?" Stacy sputtered, choking on her wine.

"Shit." I shook my head, realizing I had never shared that with her.

"Aw naw, sis, I ain't letting that shit pass. *Spill*," Stacy demanded.

"Damn it, Stacy. I swore I'd never tell," I began.

"I'm not asking to know what he told you. I'm trying to figure *you* out at this point. This man told you in-depth details about his sexual encounters, and that didn't faze you? Did it turn you on? Is that why you wanted to fuck him? How much detail did he give?" Stacy's inquiring mind wanted to know details.

"Don't judge me, ok? Shea was very explicit. He sent pictures of the women he fucked, asked my opinion of them, described the deed at length." Shame spread across my face in a deep blush.

"Girl, that's some dominant-seeking-submissive grooming type shit." Stacy set her glass down on the counter next to the stove. She reached into the cabinet and grabbed two white plates. I turned to open the drawer to grab some chopsticks and pull off a few paper towels. We worked like a well-oiled machine to prepare our plates.

"I don't think so, Stace. I'm treated like one of the boys. That's friendzone behavior, not dom-sub behavior," I explained.

"Girl, you cannot be that naive. Me, Tish, and Rho are one of the guys too, but he ain't telling us that shit. Seamus was testing you—or should I say your level of freakiness. He sent you pictures of other women doing what?" Stacy quickly plated our food and grabbed her wine before heading out of the kitchen.

I followed her. "Most times, he forwarded nudes or videos...I feel stupid discussing this," I confessed.

"Please don't, you know I'd never judge you. It's just that you're new to all of this and Seamus...well, Seamus is—" Stacy couldn't help but laugh. "That muhfuckah is something else."

We walked past the dining room into the living room, taking seats opposite one another and setting our wine glasses down on the cocktail table before digging in.

I felt the urge to defend Shea, because I encouraged his behavior by allowing it. "I could've told him to stop the first time he did it, but...I craved the closeness. It was something."

"Maevie, didn't you think it was degrading for him to share those nudes? I'd hate for pictures I sent in confidence to be shared with someone—anyone—other than the person I sent them to," Stacy said sincerely.

"Does it cross lines? Definitely! I always deleted them, Stacy. I just wanted to be closer to him," I responded.

"Did you get off on them?" She stared at me over her plate, chopstick poised to place food in her mouth.

"Truthfully?" I asked shamefully. "Yes. The sad part is, I think Shea knew, and he got off on it too."

Stacy took the bite off of her chopsticks, shaking her head. "I ain't judging you, but that's some kinky shit."

"Look, I know it was wrong. I should've told him I didn't want to hear about his exploits. Listening to him describe how turned on he was, and the things he did to them, made me want to fuck the shit out of him," I stated.

"Yeah, and I think that's what he wanted it to do. And Adjemi?" Stacy inquired.

"He was different. He let me take the lead, told me how beautiful I was, and really made me feel...special. Twisted as it may be, I had longed to be one of the women Shea fucked. It was almost predictable, in a sense. With Adjemi, it was just different. Unexpectedly different," I finished.

I set my plate down, returning to the kitchen to get two trays and some respite from Stacy's questions. She definitely made me think about my feelings, my barely existent sex life, and the future. I took a beat to breathe before returning. Stacy took the tray I handed to her.

"I know it's not just sex with you and Seamus, Maevie. Adjemi throws something extra into the mix, though," she concluded.

"I haven't heard from Shea. Not a fucking word. Hell, I don't even know if I'm still in the wedding," I spoke as tears threatened to fall. "Adjemi was only meant to be a diversion—something to do when there was nothing, no one, to do. I hoped NYC would've changed things, but shit went downhill fast."

"Do you think you'll resume things with Jim Bob after the wedding?" Stacy smiled slyly.

"That's the hope. Casual, of course," I drained my glass before finishing my dinner.

I cleaned up after dinner then followed Stacy to her room, taking a seat on the oversized beanbag in her room while she peeled out of her clothes to prepare for bed.

"I'm glad you'll be with me at the rehearsal dinner. Hopefully it will be smooth sailing," I remarked.

"Hopefully," Stacy repeated. "I'm gonna take a bath. You coming?"

I was comfortable, but I got up, following her into her bathroom.

Stacy's room was a stark contradiction to mine. Mine was severe and stark, and hers was warm and cozy. Warm, rich, vibrant tones of orange, red, and gold covered the bed. She had pictures of her family in Trinidad and Tobago adorning the walls. Stacy had cookbooks and recipes on her shelves and the desk opposite her bed. She studied spice flavor notes and researched unusual pairings of wines and foods to make the dining experience more thrilling. I ran my hands along the books on her shelf resting on a leather-bound cookbook, *La Cuisineire Bourgeoise* by Menon. Stacy had been gifted the book when she went to Paris to study for one summer. The slightly brown pages gave off a musty odor when I opened it. I quickly put the book back after I noted the publishing date—1752. I wondered if the work should be casually left on a bookshelf. It seemed like the type of thing that needed to be kept in an acrylic box or a safe, not tossed on a shelf.

"Stacy, why is there a book published in 1752 just lying on your bookshelf?" I asked as I wandered into the bathroom. Stacy sat on the side of the soaker tub, waiting for it to fill with water and bubbles.

I always loved Stacy's bathroom. It smelled like a tropical breeze, and she kept an assortment of oils and soaps she brought back from her trips home.

"I forgot to put in back in the fireproof box under my bed. I'll do it after my bath," Stacy vowed.

"You do realize this is just the thing a would-be junkie robber looks for when breaking and entering, right?" I remarked.

"No junkie is looking for a two-hundred-year-old cookbook," she laughed.

"You're right." I joined in on her laughter. "I'm gonna let you enjoy your bath in peace. Hell, I need to take one my damn self," I added.

After my shower, I joined Stacy in her bedroom to continue the conversation.

"I should probably call him to figure out the wedding details," I suggested.

"Can you back out? See if you can," she countered.

"You sound like Jared. It's worth a try," I said. "Ok, girl, that wine got me feeling right. I'm gonna capitalize on this feeling and go to bed." Stacy laughed. "Good night, girl."

I padded down the hall toward my room softly. I wandered into the closet, looking for something to throw on. I dug through the drawers and came across a shirt that belonged to Shea. It was my favorite shirt to put on when I was at his house. It faintly smelled of him. I slipped into the shirt before heading back to my bed. My cell phone flashed, indicating an incoming message. I sat on the edge of the bed wondering who would be texting this late.

Bing!
Shea: Thinking of you...

I contemplated whether or not I should reply. My stomach turned flips, and *Trixie* was salivating. She was a man hungry whore!

Me: Ditto
Shea: I'm sorry. I had no right to accuse or judge you.

Shock spread across my face as I read his text. I sat looking down at my phone, wondering if he was alright.

> Me: You ok?
> Shea: Yeah, just really missing us.
> Me: Don't ponder US too long. It is what it is…

I was sure my response cut him. I was learning to live without him, and I didn't want to revisit the pain. Shea didn't respond for a while, so I set my phone down and climbed under the covers. My body relished the feeling.

> *Bing!*

I reached for the phone and unlocked it. I reminded myself to set up Do Not Disturb.

> Shea: I've been sleeping on a pillow from your room. It smells like you.
> Me: I'm wearing your favorite shirt.
> Shea: You swore you didn't take it. LOL
> Me: You knew I had it.
> Shea: It's cool…keep it.
> Me: Nah, I'll bring it to you. I need to get my things from your house soon.
> Shea: I don't want to think about that right now. Promise me you won't stop being my friend.
> Me: We haven't been friends for a while now, Shea.
> Shea: I don't believe that.
> Me: You're really making this more challenging than it has to be, Shea
> Me: I need time… GNite
> Shea: Wait! Can I call you? I need to hear your voice.
> Me: …

The phone displayed Shea's contact photo as his call came through. "*Dammit*, Shea!" I whisper-screamed.

"I needed to hear your voice." His voice was full of emotion.

I paused as I felt the raw emotion prick my heart. Tears streamed from my eyes.

"Shea, you are making this impossible for me," I sobbed into the phone. "This back and forth is killing me."

"I'm so...sorry," Shea's voice caught. "I'm having a hard time right now."

"Seamus," I tried to speak as another wave of emotion washed over me.

"I've been drinking, and...I lost Max, and now I'm losing you," Shea sobbed into the phone. "I'm all alone."

"Seamus," I pressed through the ball of emotion in my throat, "you will be married soon—"

"She's not you!" Shea's speech slurred.

"Shea," I began.

"She's not...I had it all, and I fucked it up." Raw pain permeated my soul.

"I will always love you, Shea," I began. "I can't make any promises for the future, though. Getting through the wedding is gonna be tough enough."

"FaceTime me," Shea pleaded.

I reached out, turning on the lamp next to my bed before pressing the screen to initiate a FaceTime call. Shea answered before it finished the first ring. He looked a hot mess—we both did.

"You are so beautiful," Shea wiped at the tears washing down his face. The sight of him, red-faced and disheveled, broke my heart. I covered my face and cried into the crook of my elbow.

"Why can't falling out of love be easier?" I moaned softly into my elbow as I slid my arm across my face.

"Is anything easy for us?" Shea said softly.

I laughed. "We look a mess."

"Do you remember the night we got Max?" he asked softly.

"How can I forget?" I smiled wearily.

"Remember how he howled when you tried to leave?" Shea's speech was still a little slurred. His smile was lopsided and goofy. Hot tears sprang to my eyes, recalling Max's pitiful little howl. We ended up sleeping on the floor of Shea's room. It was the only way to quiet the sorrowful wails.

"He rewarded us with sweet little puppy kisses the next morning." I smiled again.

"Max knew...he knew. That's why he always tried to keep you here...Sleep with me one last time?" he asked softly.

"How do you propose we do that?" I laughed.

"Prop the phone against the pillow next to you," he instructed.

I set the phone up, then responded, "Ok, now what?"

"Go to sleep, Butterfly," Shea spoke tenderly in Irish, while I willingly obliged—drifting off to sleep.

Chapter Twenty-Five
SWITCHED AT THE REHEARSAL

I knew the rehearsal dinner should be the night before the wedding, but I had been planning a weeklong bachelor party getaway in Las Vegas. *Who the hell wanted their parents and grandparents in the mix of their debauchery?* I had asked Shea and Chelsey early on to consider switching them. Surprisingly, they agreed to my request since money wasn't an object for either. Their families didn't mind spending a week in Chicago before the wedding either.

It was the night of the rehearsal dinner and I hadn't spoken to Shea in weeks, since the night we Face Timed. His absence left a void in my heart. My friends tried to cheer me up, but nothing worked for long. I wasn't a wreck, per se. Earlier in the day, Jared did his best to convince me to ditch the wedding once again. I chuckled at the thought, but I had seriously pondered the idea at one point.

It was the last hoorah for the crew, and I decided I didn't want to miss it. Besides, I had worked too long and too hard garnering favors from everyone I knew trying to make Shea's bachelor party a success. If I had known Shea was marrying Chelsey for the sake of business, I'd have taken him for drinks at his favorite strip club, The Roxx, or hired some strippers to piss off his neighbors. I chuckled to myself at the thought.

I dressed for the night's festivities in a myriad of designer attire. I swept my hair around to the left side and held it in place with pins. The style accented the sapphires that dotted my ears and neck. Chelsey had sent out a text to our group chat earlier in the week, requesting our footwear be neutral colors. *Who the fuck does that?* I thought. Her event, though, so I obliged.

"I'm almost ready, Stace," I shot down the hall to Stacy, since we were riding together.

"Shit," Stacy retorted.

"We have time, sis," I replied.

Stacy peeked her head into the door of my bedroom. "Oh snap, you look amazing!"

"Thanks," I turned, winking at her.

"Can I borrow some lotion? I'm out," she pleaded.

"You know where it is." I nodded to the bottle on the counter.

Stacy stepped around me, picking it up.

"You ready for tonight?" she asked.

"As ever," I responded coolly.

"Ok, I'll bring this back in a sec." Stacy smacked me on the ass as she headed out of my bathroom.

I applied the finishing touches to my makeup, then went into the closet to grab my Alexander McQueen Four Ring Croc clutch. Chelsey asked us to keep our shoes neutral, but that didn't mean I couldn't rock with that red crocodile bag. It was the pop of color my outfit needed. *A girl can't go wrong with a red lip and a red clutch,* I thought. I grabbed my phone and keys off the nightstand before making my way into the living room to wait on Stacy. I snapped a few pictures for Instagram at the window, because I felt myself—like Nicki Minaj.

"Ok, bitch," Stacy sang. "I see you!" She trotted over in a stunning yellow harem-style jumpsuit paired with a matching yellow shoe.

"Ooh, you're gonna get it! We're supposed to be in a neutral shoe," I said, imitating Chelsey's vocal fry nasally voice.

"*Fuck* that bitch," Stacy smirked. I howled with laughter at her cavalier attitude. Stacy didn't give two fucks about that text.

"You are a mess," I responded when I caught my breath.

"Do you really think she's gonna say anything to me?" Stacy asked sarcastically.

"I doubt it. You know I don't give a solitary fuck. I only obliged because I don't want to deal with Shea," I replied.

"Ugh, you right," Stacy quipped. "Let me change, then we can head out."

Stacy and I arrived at The Lakewood earlier than anticipated. We were forced to socialize with Chelsey and her bridal party before our girls showed up. Shea, Sherm, J-Boogie, Ellis, and Zeus arrived shortly after us. They looked dapper and appeared to be having a good time.

Leave it to Rho and Tish to be late, I thought.

Chelsey's wedding planner, Celina Withers-Blake, arranged for a quick rehearsal before dinner. I felt the practice would have served us better in Vegas, since that was where the wedding was going to be, but what did I know. The bridal party convened in a private area away from where the rehearsal dinner was being held. I was thankful I didn't have to practice walking in. Shea and I chatted politely about work and family while we watched the others run through the procession. Chelsey wanted her bridesmaids to be escorted in by the groomsmen. I didn't think she realized what she was getting into having Shea's crazy-ass friends walking down the aisle. The fellas' playfulness irritated the hell out of the Emily Post of event planners. At one point, Celina stopped the whole production to chastise Ellis.

"Mr. Kennedy," Celina exclaimed, "there will be no, and I repeat, no gyrating or getting *jiggy with it* in this entrance."

Ellis looked over at me like *come get this bitch before I do.*

I took my cue and began walking toward the confrontation. Celina wheeled around on me, putting her hand up to stop my progression. "Please take your place, Miss James. This is none of your concern."

"If you don't want to get cursed out," I stated, continuing to walk toward them, "you'll step outside with me."

I gently guided Celina away from El and escorted her out to the hallway. She was grumbling about being dignified and running a respectable business.

"We are on a schedule, Miss James," Celina started.

"Listen, I understand schedules and the like. The guys are just blowing off a little steam and having fun. Your comment about," I used air quotes, "getting *jiggy with it* was inappropriate and mildly racist, especially since the bridesmaids were getting jiggy too."

"I didn't see that," Celina stated.

"I bet you didn't," I said flatly. "We're all young, and we'd like to have a little fun. I promise you the wedding will be the dignified spectacle you'd like it to be. Please lighten the fuck up."

I left Celina standing in the hallway as I opened the door and said, "Alright, people. From the top! El, act like your mama raised a gentleman before I snap you in half."

I turned back to Celina, indicating that she had the floor. I winked to let her know all was well. She smiled, rejoining the rest of us.

"What the fuck did you say to her?" Shea asked.

"Calm the fuck down with the racist ass comments before I set it off," I responded with a wink.

When it came time to practice the vows, Jen's goofy ass recommended I stand in for Chelsey since it was bad juju for her to do it. I swore I'd never heard this rule, but I obliged. The minister ran through the vows while Shea and I squirmed.

"Then, I'll say, 'you may now kiss the bride' and present the couple—" Before the reverend could finish his instructions, Jen spoke out.

"Kiss!" she said jokingly.

Everyone—and I do mean everyone—whirled around to stare at her.

"Omg, Jen," Chelsey snarled, "what the hell's the matter with you!"

Did Jen know, too?

While all eyes were fixed on Jen, Shea brought both of my hands to his mouth and kissed them. My eyes met his as he dropped my hands and spoke, "Give it up for Celina! She finally got us together! Let's go eat!"

Everyone cheered in excitement. More importantly, no one had seen Shea kiss my hands. Jen was still beet red as we all headed out of the room.

"Maeve," Jen called after me, "Mae—"

"Jen," I said and pivoted to face her. "you've said enough."

Another bridesmaid walked up to drag her off. "Yeah, shut the hell up, Jen!"

Fuck, they all know. I planned to have a little chat with Chelsey before the night was over.

Tish and Rho showed up shortly after we finished the rehearsal. Rho's ass was wearing hot pink shoes, too. *This bitch,* I giggled. They were seated with Stacy and a few of Shea's single cousins from Ireland. The event space was decorated beautifully with soft lights and white silk fabric draped about the room. Round tables dotted the floor throughout the venue. Atop each table were large floral arrangements, crystal stemware, and white Hermes place settings. Lush greenery flanked seating areas around the venue. A slideshow of Chelsey and Shea played on two large screens on either end of the room while we ate dinner. They were pictures I'd never seen before. I prided myself on stalking their social media, and I didn't recognize any of the photos. For all intents and purposes, they looked happy, but Shea's recent drunken call spoke volumes. He played his role well tonight.

After dinner, Jen headed to the microphone to give her speech. By that time, she was a weepy, drunk ass mess. She spoke about meeting Chelsey, being best friends since they were kids, and all of the trips their families took together. It was sweet, but I was utterly over the bullshit. Someone was getting cursed the fuck out tonight, and she was at the top of the list along with Chelsey. I sauntered to the podium as Jen was finishing up. She mouthed *sorry* to me as she handed me the mic. I mouthed *fuck you* as I took it from her.

"Hello, everyone! I hope you all are having a great time." I paused, allowing the audience to whoop and cheer. I greeted Chelsey's murderous ass father with a nod, then turned to smile warmly at Shea's parents.

"Let's give the parents of the bride and groom a round of applause for throwing such an amazing party," I said sweetly. I had a sweet little buzz going at that moment. I had downed my Vodka and cranberry and took the flute of champagne being offered by the waiter before I began my speech.

"I've had the pleasure of knowing Seamus since we were in college." I faced Shea as I spoke. "I thought he was the biggest jackass on campus until I got to know him. Then I found out he really *was* the biggest jackass on campus."

Everyone laughed.

"Hey!" Shea exclaimed in fake outrage.

"She ain't lyin'," Ellis said.

"That's enough from the peanut gallery," I laughed. "Like I was saying. Seamus may have been the biggest ass on campus, but he has a heart of gold. For instance, he told us he was working out or playing basketball, but I knew he was sneaking off to work at the food pantry, tutor kids, or volunteer at the local animal shelter. Shea—Seamus is a closeted animal lover. It's because of that love I gave him the late Maximus Decimus."

"The beast!" our friends shouted.

"Yes, the beast as he was affectionately dubbed by Zeus," I said, pointing at him.

"Crazy ass dog!" Zeus shouted.

"You can still see his generosity through his philanthropic work with various charities throughout Chicagoland. It speaks to his upbringing and the wonderful parents who raised him. I am—we are all blessed to call you friend. Before we raise our glasses, I have a gift for Seamus."

He looked sincerely surprised as Celina had the gift brought in on a cart. The large white box was wrapped with a gold bow. Shea pushed his chair back and made his way around the table to the box. He removed the lid gingerly to peer in. Shea looked at me, then back into the box.

"You didn't," Shea gasped.

"What the hell is it?" Chelsey chimed in.

Shea reached into the box, pulling out a small puppy that was the spitting image of Max.

"Aww," Chelsey squealed, making her way to Shea and the puppy. Shea held the puppy aloft, examining him thoroughly. He was astounded at the likeness to Max.

"Oh, hell no!" Zeus exclaimed.

"Chelsey," I said, smiling at her, "I hope you don't mind."

"Not at all! He's gorgeous," she said, taking the puppy from Shea. Shea eyed me knowingly, because he recognized the significance of the gift. I was leaving him with a small part of me, a reminder of our life.

"To the bride and broom," I saluted as I raised my glass.

"To the bride and broom!" everyone shouted in response.

I set my drink down, heading to the restroom. Tears had begun to blur my vision, so that when Chelsey's father grabbed my wrist, it took me by surprise. I peered at him in disgust. "Take your hands off me."

"You're doing the right thing, Miss James," he said under his breath.

"You don't know what's right for me—or anyone for that matter. This from a man who's forcing his daughter to marry a man for money," I spat.

"One day, when you have a family of your own, you'll understand," he began.

"I will never understand what could make a parent leverage their child's happiness to blackmail another human being. You've caused nothing but grief since you came into my life. After this wedding, I don't ever want to see you again." I wrenched my hand from him and walked away.

I mentally crossed his ass off the list of people to tell off. I just hoped I hadn't put myself back in his crosshairs. I went to the bathroom farthest from the party, for a moment of peace. I checked all of the stalls before allowing the tears to freely fall. I didn't hear Shea's mother when she entered.

"Here you go, m'dear," Mama McGhee pressed some Kleenex into my hand, then began gently rubbing my back.

"Thanks, Mama McGhee. But I'd like to be alone. It's nothing personal," I spoke softly.

"I know y'do. This won't be takin' long, I promise ye. I wanted you to know you're always goin' to be my daughter. I'd hoped my son woulda seen the love ye 'ave for him before it was too late. I saw the way he looked when you presented him with the gift. It's killin' me to know he loves ye…and now, through no fault of his own, he's bein' forced into marriage to save his father," her accented speech was barely above a whisper, which made it more difficult to understand her.

"I don't know what to say," Stunned by her acknowledgement, I turned to face her. "I know Shea couldn't live with himself if something ever happened to the two of you."

"That's what makes this so much harder, *Feíleacán.*" My eyes widened at her use of Shea's nickname for me. "Don't be so surprised. It was my name for ye, to begin with, m' dear." She pulled me into a hug and let me cry a little while longer.

"I hope one day you can forgive us for stealing away your happiness," she said, pulling back from our embrace.

"There's nothing to forgive." I smiled at her.

"Let's get you cleaned up. Here, I brought your purse," Mrs. McGhee beamed.

"Thank you so very much," I said, turning to clean myself up. I didn't look too bad aside from the redness in my eyes. I was still a babe!

I picked my purse up off the cream marble counter and began reapplying my makeup. I was glad I'd brought the essentials with me. When we finally emerged, no one was the wiser of what had taken place in the bathroom. We bumped into Shea on the way back.

"*What's the craic?*" he asked, eyeing us suspiciously.

"Nothing…*just faffin' about* in the ladies' room," his mother responded.

"Do you mind if I have a word with MJ?" Shea asked his mother.

"Not at all. I'll see you later, m'dear. I think your father and I are about to leave anyway," she said, pulling her son down for a kiss.

"Dad offered to take Deci with you all. Is that ok?" he asked.

"Deci?" we both said in unison.

"Decimus," he responded with a smile. The significance wasn't lost on me.

"Tis not a problem, dear," she responded.

"Seriously, Shea?" I asked. He stared back like I was crazy.

"Well, I couldn't name him Maximus, so Decimus was the next logical name," he smiled.

I rolled my eyes, then turned to watch Mrs. McGhee walk away.

"What's up?" I asked.

"Are you ok?" Shea replied.

"Now you know you can't answer a question with a question," I said.

"Seriously, I saw Chelsey's dad say something to you. Are you ok?" he asked again.

"I'm fine. Nothing a stiff drink won't cure." I tried to keep things casual.

"I wanted to thank you…and talk about the significance of your gift," Shea began.

"There's no need for explanation, Shea. I wanted you to have—"

"A reminder of you," Shea cut me off.

"Listen, we were a part of each other's lives for so long I…um…fuck! Just focus on making some new memories with Deci and Chelsey," I stated.

"This is a marriage for convenience—nothing more, nothing less. I don't love Chelsey, Maeve," he said flatly.

"It doesn't matter at this point, Shea. I'm not participating in any impropriety. That's what started all this trouble in the first place. Don't worry though, I'm still gonna want time with Deci. I have visitation rights," I joked.

Shea chuckled. "Chelsey hasn't put him down since you gave him to me."

"Damn that! You better let her know what's up," I said sarcastically.

We headed back to the party joking about visitation rights, PetSmart being our drop off and pick up location. We stopped at the bar and grabbed two Vodka and cranberries each. I guessed we both planned on getting shit-faced that night.

By the time most of the guests left, we were adequately lubricated. The younger cousins, friends, and couples who had stayed had taken to the dance floor and were well into the groove of a serious party. I was chatting with Tish and Rho when I saw Chelsey head toward the bathroom. She looked suspicious.

"Hold up a sec." I locked on to Chelsey's movements with drunken laser precision.

"Don't start no shit," Rho quipped. She'd followed my eyes to my prey.

"What?" I responded innocently.

"I know that gaht damn look. Yo ass about to cuss somebody the fuck out," Rho responded.

"Why don't you stay here with us?" Tish said, trying to grab my arm.

I brushed her hand away, continuing on my trajected path. "Nah, man," I slurred, "I'll be good. Imma be right back."

"How many drinks has she had?" Tish asked Rho. She responded with a shrug.

Tish was genuinely worried, and rightly so. My girls knew the *hold up a second* look well enough to recognize it. It was second nature at this point.

"She ain't got on no shoes either. It's 'bout to be some shit. Where's Stacy?" Rho asked, looking around.

I waited in the corner to make sure no one else was in the bathroom. Just as I was about to head in, I was stopped by one of Shea's cousins. I chatted with him for a moment. I didn't want to be rude, but I didn't want to miss my opportunity to give Chelsey a piece of my mind. I politely excused myself from the conversation, feigning the necessity of the ladies' room. When I opened the door, I was accosted by the subtle silence. I thought she had left until I heard a soft moan coming from the back of the restroom.

What the fuck?

I went further into the bathroom, rounding the corner to see Chelsey's shoes under the last stall. *Those fucking shoes!* I crept further toward the closed door. I was thankful—and disgusted—that I didn't have shoes on. I crept closer to the stall, trying to remain inconspicuous. I peeked through the slit and caught sight of Chelsey.

With motherfucking Zeus!

I covered my mouth to keep from screaming as I retreated. I moved as swiftly and quietly as my little drunken feet could take me. My vision was blurred, causing me to run face first into Shea.

"Watch it," Shea snapped harshly as his drink sloshed onto his shoes. "What the hell is the matter with you?" he asked, before looking up to see it was me.

"I can't believe this shit." I paced, ignoring Shea, trying to wrap my mind around what I had just seen. "So it was *him* in the club."

"What the hell is going on?" Shea asked.

"What?" I asked angrily.

This bitch was still in the bathroom fucking his best friend. *That's it, I'll take him into the bathroom and confront them!* I thought.

"Bathroom—let's go in the bathroom," I said, grabbing at him.

"Maeve," he said, pushing me away, "we're at the rehearsal dinner. What the fuck happened to focus on making memories?"

"Fuck that, Shea. I need you to go into that bathroom with me right now—" Shea interrupted me by jerking away.

"I'm not hooking up with you here—my family is here. Have you lost your fucking mind? You had your chance." The realization of what he meant hit me.

"Had my chance? You sent me away then fucked Chelsey," I spat vehemently.

"Let's not forget you fucked your driver," Shea shot back.

"Well...now, that bitch is fucking one of your best friends," I responded smugly.

Fuck! Alarm bells went off in my head.

I turned to run, but Seamus grabbed my arm to prevent my escape. "Oh no, you don't." He grabbed my arm while whisper-screaming, "What the fuck did you just say?" His eyes were an intense green. I shook my head, trying to wrestle myself from him.

"Let go of me, Shea!" I stumbled, trying to get away. He threw his glass down to free his other hand. He grabbed both of my wrists, pulling me into his chest.

"You better open your fucking mouth and tell me what the fuck you mean, Maeve," he growled, holding my hands like a vice grip in one hand and my face in the other.

Shit, this hurts!

"Ask *that* bitch! Let me go, Seamus," I whispered back at him. I managed to jerk free of his grasp, then turned to run again. Of course, he gave chase—catching me quickly in the back hallway of the venue. Seamus had me pinned against the wall with my hands between us. Sherm and Ellis came around the corner and caught sight of Seamus shoving me.

"Aye man, what the fuck are you doing?" Sherm asked as he rushed to separate us.

"Man, you trippin'! Take yo' gaht damn hands off her!" Ellis yelled.

Sherm reached in between us to pull me away from Seamus. We tussled back toward the lounge near the restrooms. During the skirmish, Seamus grabbed my sleeve, accidentally ripping my blouse. Buttons flew off, revealing my bra and exposing my shoulder.

Flame, the fuck, on!

"Mother…fucker!" I screamed, managing to loosen my right hand from his grip. I swung at him, punching him in the face. Hard!

"Lil Bit, no!" Sherm finally wedged himself between us, but Shea still had a grip on my left wrist. The punch to the face renewed Seamus' anger. He lunged over Sherm, reaching for me. I was drunk, but adrenaline had kicked in.

"Dammit, El, get her arms! Seamus calm the fuck down! Lil Bit, stop!" Sherm yelled.

Sherm and Ellis worked in a concerted effort to separate us, but it wasn't working. I finagled my left hand from Shea's grasp then went on the offensive. I slipped out of Ellis' grip, sliding around Sherm as he stepped back to get better footing. In that gap, I managed to punch Shea in the stomach, causing him to double over. I grabbed his hair and attempted to smash my knee into his face. My knee connected with his shoulder causing him to fall wildly onto the couch in the lounge.

"Don't you fucking...touch," I slurred. I pawed at my clothing and spat. "This is Givenchy. You're buying me a new blouse, asshole." He was livid. He wiped his face, seeing blood.

"Fucking bitch!" he shouted as he tried to stand up.

"Get her outta here!" Sherm yelled over his shoulder at Ellis.

Sherm put all of his weight on top of Shea as he scrambled to his feet. Ellis grabbed me in a bear hug when I turned to look for my buttons. He rushed me from the area, moving quickly to haul me over his shoulder. Ellis ran through the party out of the doors of the venue. Stacy, Rho, and Tish caught a glimpse of us.

"I knew it was gonna be some shit," Rho said to Tish. "You ready to go?"

Tish nodded slowly.

"What the fuck?" Stacy shouted as she sprang into action. She hauled ass to grab my purse and shoes before heading outside. She reached the parking lot in time to see El's car fly past the entrance. She ran to her car, hopped in, and gave chase.

"No, fuck that El," I slurred. "His ass was outta pocket! Fuck him and that raggedy-ass, cheatin' ass, no-cooking ass bitch!" I went off.

"Wait, what, Lil Bit?" he asked. "You gotta calm down!"

"No, no, fuck that," I slurred. "Do you-do you see my blouse? Where are we," I hiccupped "going?" I looked around realizing we were in a car.

El's phone rang.

"Yeah, I got her...Did you see her drop his ass?" He spoke loudly into the phone.

"Shhh," I fussed in response.

He paused for a minute, then continued, "No, stop him! Tell Sherm to keep his ass there and calm him the fuck down! The wedding is a week away, and the groom and best ma—woman are brawling? This is some shit!"

He paused for another beat, then said, "J, just meet me at the loft. A'ight, bye!" Before El could set the phone down, it rang again.

I was still muttering about my ripped Givenchy blouse. "Twelve hundred fucking dollars. Silk…my buttons…funky bitch!"

"MJ, you gotta calm down," he said, attempting to talk over my insane ramblings.

"Fucking shoes…And I can't wear shoes…cum dumpster ass bitch," I muttered, flailing wildly, fussing at no one.

El tried to discern what I was talking about before he answered the phone again.

"Hey—" he started.

"What the fuck is going on, El?" Stacy asked frantically.

"Stacy, I'm not sure, but Lil Bit and Seamus got into a fight!"

"What?" Stacy screamed. "A *physical* fight?"

"Is that Stacy…gimme the phone," I yelled, pawing for the phone. El ignored me.

"Yes, an actual fight. I don't know what started it, but Sherm and I tried to break it up. They drunk asses were hard to separate, but ya girl held her own. She dropped Seamus like a pile of bricks!"

Stacy screamed again. "What?"

"Yeah, she decked him then punched him in the stomach and kneed him in the shoulder."

"Get the fuck outta here! Is he ok?" she said in shock.

"I don't know, but Sherm said it took him and two of Seamus' cousins to hold him down."

"Did you know she knew karate?" he inquired, half laughing. El was driving like a bat out of Hades through Chicago traffic.

"Karate…the fuck you talking about, El? Where are you headed now?" she asked.

"Yeah, never mind. I'm headed to your house. J-Boogie is too."

"Keep Shame the fuck away from her," she said.

"Oh, you ain't even gotta tell me. Old boy looked like he was gonna beat Lil Bit's ass for real, and that's not like him."

"They were both doing the absolute most," Stacy said, matter-of-fact.

"There's no telling what would have happened had we not been there," he said as though he were pondering it.

"I'm just glad you were," Stacy said. "I'll see you in a bit."

"Ok, see you in a few." El put the phone down then looked over to me.

Ellis and Stacy helped me upstairs and on to the couch. J-Boogie, Tish, and Rho arrived shortly after, then came upstairs.

"Ok, what the fuck happened?" Tish asked, walking into the loft.

"And why does Seamus look like somebody beat his ass?" J asked.

El and Stacy exchanged looks before El said, "Somebody *did*."

Ellis filled everyone in on what he knew.

"We heard the ruckus all the way in the dining room," J added. "I ran back there with his cousins after seeing you run out with Lil Bit. We piled on top of Sherm when he asked for help. Then I peeped Zeus coming out of the ladies' room, looking like he was either fucking or getting his dick sucked."

"What?" El and Stacy asked in unison.

"Yeah, that's when he asked what was going on. I was on the phone with you leaving before I could figure it out."

"I knew it was gonna be some shit," Rho added. "We were talking to her when she got that *hold up a sec* look on her face."

"Why did y'all let her go?" Stacy asked angrily.

"I tried to stop her, but you know how she gets when she gets that look on her face," Tish responded. "By the time we found you, we forgot."

"Wait," El said, scratching his head. "Lil Bit said something about Chelsey being a cheatin' ass bitch! Y'all don't think..."

"Oh, hell no," J started. "Zeus ain't did no shit like that!"

"But what if that's what MJ saw? Shit, she was drunk as fuck and probably said something to Seamus," Stacy said.

"They been arguing for months now. What the fuck is that about?" Ellis asked the others.

"They've been fucking for months," Stacy said dryly.

"Say *what?*" the men said in unison.

"Y'all remember the night we convinced him to talk to her, but she had event thing with Darren?" Stacy asked. They nodded. "Well, instead of talking, they ended up fucking...and have continued to fuck ever since."

Stacy continued to fill the crew in on everything that had happened, including Darren's accident, the trip to New York, and my torn romance with Shea.

"It all makes sense now," J-Boogie said. "So, if she saw Zeus and Chelsey..."

"It's gonna be some shit," Tish added.

"Do you think Seamus will believe it—considering the Darren thing?" Ellis asked sincerely.

Silence fell over the room like a dense fog.

I smiled goofily at everyone from the couch as they peered at me somberly.

"Well," Ellis said slowly, "we just gon' have to wait for Rhonda Rousey to sober her little ass up so she can tell us what the fuck she saw."

Chapter Twenty-Six
THE AFTERMATH

uck! My head hurt so badly. I grabbed my watch off the charger to check the time. I tapped the screen and a photo of Seamus popped up. It was nine-thirty in the morning. I laid back down on my pillow.

Holy shit! His eyes... What the hell happened last night?

My body felt like I'd been hit by a truck, but I couldn't seem to recall why I was so sore.

I heard Stacy padding down the hall.

She opened the door to my room, gingerly. "Good! I was hoping you were awake. So, what the fuck happened last night?"

Damn, straight to it then, huh?

I watched as she balanced a tray of tea, fruit, and some baked confections, along with cream and sugar. She set the tray down as she has done so many times before. She slid it slowly to the middle of my bed, careful not to spill the tea on my all-white linens, then sat on down on the foot of the bed.

"Stace," I began dreamily, "I wish I knew. All I remember is how Seamus looked at me and the color of his eyes."

Every time I thought about his eyes, I got sick to my stomach.

"Say *what?* The color of his eyes, what about it?" asked Stacy. I could tell she was confused.

"Seamus' eyes change color depending on his mood. Last night, they were the oddest color I've ever seen. I've never seen him look so angry," I said.

"I told you he's a green-eyed devil," she said jokingly. "Maeve, I'm sure he's pissed. I know you ruined their rehearsal dinner. After what happened, can you blame him?" she asked sympathetically.

"That's just it, Stace. I don't remember much about last night. It's a blur," I said.

"Ok, so...from what I heard, you were on one," she said. I covered my head with the pillow I was lying on.

"Whew," she said as she paused to take a deep breath. "I heard you whooped Seamus' ass."

I had a flashback of Seamus grabbing my arm and spinning me around. *Those eyes.*

I slowly sat up, placed the pillow on my lap, and looked out the rain-glazed window. My heart sank because I was sure Shea was pissed to the highest level of *pisstivity.* Yes, there are levels.

"Whew..." I shook my head. "I don't know *why* I would've done that!" I said.

"Well, let's start with your undying love and affection for the man," Stacy said with a smirk.

"I may have ruined...ugh, well, I'm sure I ruined a great party. I can't face Shea. I just can't! Girl, I just wish I could recall why I showed my ass like that."

"Maevie, the emotional dam finally reached its breaking point."

I reached for a cup of tea from the tray next to me. The hibiscus hit me on so many plains. Stacy knew it was my favorite. My grandmother always said there was nothing a good cup of tea couldn't cure. I didn't know if the rehearsal dinner qualified, though. Stacy always seemed to know what I needed when I was down. I took a sip and was immersed in the sweetness. I looked over the rim at Stacy, and she smiled.

"Good, huh?"

I nodded.

"We'll figure it out, I promise," she said as she picked up her cup and leaned against the white leather headboard.

"Wait, did you say I called Chelsey a cheating ass bitch?" I was startled genuinely, then had a flashback of her on her knees in the bathroom stall.

"Yes, why?" Stacy perked up and turned toward me.

"I remember her giving someone head last night!" I grabbed my head, trying to calm the pain throbbing in my brain.

"Girl, J-Boogie said he saw Zeus coming out of the women's bathroom looking like he'd just been fucked or sucked!" she said, then proceeded to tell me everything she knew.

"Shit! That's it! I know I was drunk as shit last night but, God as my witness, when I walked into the ladies' room, I saw Chelsey's feet under a stall. So I crept in, peeked through the slit in the door, and saw her giving Zeus head!"

"Shut up!" She processed what was just said then asked, "Ok, so that explains the 'cheating ass bitch' comment, but how did you and Seamus end up fighting?"

"Shit! Did he throw a glass at me?" I asked incredulously.

"El said he and Sherm heard glass breaking, but I can't tell you how it got broken," she added.

"I think that fool threw a glass at me, or maybe I threw it at him. I vaguely remember him grabbing me...asking what I meant. Why my drunk ass try to run?" I laughed at the thought. "He caught me and wanted me to clarify, so I said something like ask your bitch!"

"Girl, El said it took forever for him and Sherm to separate the two of you, but he said you knocked Seamus the fuck out. They were calling you 'Bruce Lee' last night."

"Wait!" I shouted. "That motherfucker tore up my Givenchy blouse!"

"Your shirt is the least of your concerns. Back to the story," she insisted.

"Oh," I said, "I took Taekwondo as a kid. I am—was a brown belt. Seriously, I thought he was gonna hurt me."

"Well, that shit came back with a vengeance!" Stacy exclaimed.

"Is he ok?" I asked, feeling like shit. I hated that I had possibly caused him pain. *Fuck!* In a matter of months, we'd gone from passionate love-making to threesomes to fighting!

"He's not gonna believe me." I looked down at my wrists. They had bruises on them. My arms had scratches on them too.

"You still have to tell him. Shit! We leave for the bachelor party later," she said in a low voice.

"I'm not going," I exclaimed.

"Maevie, you're the Best Woman. You have to go."

"Nope, hell no. No ma'am…fuck that." I got up and began to pace the floor. "Do you really think I'm gonna be at the wedding?"

Before Stacy could respond, my phone went off.

> *Bing!*
> Shea: We need to talk

"Shit, it's him!" I shouted at Stacy. "He says we need to talk."
"It's true, you do, Maevie," she responded.

> Me: I'm scared
> Shea: We were really drunk last night. I can't do this
>   over text.
> Me: I don't want to do this at all
> Shea: My house. Come alone.

"He wants me to come to his house…alone!" I spat out frantically, clutching the phone to my chest.

"Oh, hell no. He tried to fight you last night. You are not going there alone."

"Technically, he wasn't trying to fight me. He wanted to pull me closer," I remembered.

"Bitch, I don't give a damn. You have bruises…hell no!"

Shea: I want to clear the air before we leave this after-
          noon.
Me: You still want me to be a part of your wedding
          after what happened last night?
Shea: I still want you to come on the trip, but we need
          to clear this up beforehand.
Shea: Tell Stacy I swear on your Gram's sweet potato
          pie that I won't hurt you!

I relayed the message.

Stacy's laughter pealed throughout the room, and I joined in.

"Tell him I said we still have to pack, but I'll drop you off on my way to pick up the girls," Stacy said.

I texted him then headed into the bathroom to shower and dress. I threw on my white Adidas Tiro pants and a tank. I grabbed my Adilette sandals before heading back into the bedroom. I was amazed that Shea still wanted me to be a part of the wedding party. I wondered if he knew about Zeus and Chelsey...

Are you prepared to tell him what you saw? I asked myself. *What if he doesn't believe me? After all, I was very drunk last night.*

I was glad I packed before the rehearsal dinner. We pulled into Shea's driveway two hours after his text. I grabbed my bag and tossed Stace a reassuring glance before she drove away. I trotted up to his door, using the code to go in. I heard music, but there was no sign of Seamus. I dropped my duffle by the door, then wandered into the formal living room. I checked the den and kitchen, but there was no sign of him. *Please don't be in the bedroom*, I thought. I went up the stairs adjacent to the kitchen and wandered down to his master bedroom. I knocked softly on the door.

"Come in!" he shouted from inside. "I'm packing."

Oh, hell, no, I thought.

"I'd rather not. Can we talk downstairs?" He swung the door open, catching me off guard. I jumped back with a yelp.

"Shit, man, you scared the fuck out of me!" I bent over to brace my hands on my knees to catch my breath.

"Get your ass in here," he said, reaching for me. I pulled away, then followed him reluctantly into his room. He was wearing light grey Nike joggers. No t-shirt or shoes. I glanced down and saw his dick print— he wasn't wearing underwear.

"I think it's best if we talk downstairs," I said before turning on my heels and heading back down the hallway. I walked down to the formal living room, taking a seat near the door in case I needed to make a fast getaway.

"Seriously, MJ?" he said, giving me a *what the fuck* look as he joined me in the living room. I got a good look at him when he came closer. He had split lip and a hint of a black eye. I winced.

"Don't worry," he said, rubbing his lip. "I deserved it."

"Shea, I'm sorry. I don't know what came over me."

"I do—fight or flight. The bad bitch who took Taekwondo popped out and whooped my ass!" He laughed.

"Still, I hate that I hurt you," I said earnestly. I imagined Shea looked pretty fucked up last night.

"No worries," he said. His eyes twinkled with happiness. *He's actually happy*, I thought.

"So, what's up?" I was genuinely confused now.

"I wanted to apologize for shoving you last night." He smiled, and it melted my heart.

"Shea, I need to tell you something, and it's not good."

"Listen, you were drunk last night. I didn't take anything you said to heart. Drunk people say all kinds of shit."

"Yeah, well," I said, rubbing the back of my neck, "I *was* drunk— very drunk—but…" I stopped short. *Fuck!* He looked so happy. *Just tell him!* "I know what I saw. Shea, I saw Chelsey and Zeus in the ladies' room. She was giving him head."

Shea looked at me pensively before he spoke. "Maeve, *ye were fecking gargled* last night. Listen, I know you're jealous, but this is low even for you." His tone was low and unwavering.

Motherfuck me! He truly thinks I'm making shit up because I'm jealous.

"Ok, I agree I was fucking drunk last night, but I have nothing to gain from telling you this! I'm trying to help you out, asshole." I stood up, turning toward the door. Shea closed the distance between me and the door in a fraction of a second.

"You don't get to come in here and tell me *my* fiancée is cheating, with one of my best friends, then walk out. What proof do you have?" Shea said, his voice intense.

"You know me, Shea. I wouldn't fucking lie," I snarled back.

"You are accusing one of *our* best friends, so you better have some kind of fucking proof if you're gonna be making accusations like that."

"What color were Chelsey's shoes?" I asked him.

"What? Shoes? What the *hell* do her shoes have to do with this?" he quipped back.

"Everything, dumbass! She was the only one in the building wearing colorful shoes, besides Rho. She even made a big production about them. That kind of shit sticks in your memory 'cause if there's one thing I know—"

"It's shoes," he said flatly.

"You gaht damn right! So, you can best believe I know what kind of fucking footwear she had on—burgundy Krystal Du Desert Christian Louboutin with a big fucking bow and iridescent studs." I caught a much-needed breath, because I was hungover, my head hurt, and I was yelling.

"Ok, but what does that have to do with anything, Maeve?"

"Shea, I saw her on her knees in the stall!"

"So? She could have been throwing up!" He was yelling now.

Fuck! I need some water and a couple Tylenol.

"Yeah, and I guess she was using Zeus' dick to gag herself! Shea, I peeped through the stall. I saw him holding her hair back. So I saw her fucking face...his fucking face...their *fucking* faces! I know what the fuck I saw!"

"I don't believe Zeus would do something like that!"

"But you believe that I would lie to you after all that we've been through? Seriously?" I looked him in the eyes, but they were unwavering. He really believed I was lying. "You know what, Seamus...Fuck you. Fuck Chelsey. Fuck this wack ass, bullshit trip! I'm not going. Have a great life!"

I tried to push past him, but I may as well have been shoving a brick wall. He didn't budge.

"You're goin', and if it's wack, you planned it. Besides, you said nothing would make you happier than to be my Best Woman. Or did you forget?" I couldn't read him, his body language, or his tone.

"And you said you couldn't bring another woman back here after what we shared. So, I guess we are both some lying ass muhfuckahs!" I yelled.

"I plan on keeping my word. How about you?"

"How the fuck do you plan on doing that?" I regretted the words after they left my lips.

"We're moving into her brownstone until I can sell this place and my penthouse. Any other questions?" Shea asked smugly.

"Are you fucking kidding me? You've got to be fucking shitting me right now," I said, looking up at him.

"Dead ass. Besides, you've made all of the arrangements for the bachelor party. Now, you want to back out because I don't believe your bullshit story. That's not right." He was dense as fuck if he thought I was going on that trip.

"Seamus, I can give all of the details to Sherm or Stacy if you'd like," I said nonchalantly. "I'm not gonna do this witcho goofy ass! Move!"

"We'll spend a week holed up in this bitch before I let you back out," he said sarcastically.

"We've spent too much time together as it is, sir," I spat back.

"Don't act like you didn't enjoy every minute of it," he responded, grabbing his crotch.

I laughed at his comment. "Is that supposed to hurt my feelings? You act like I was the only one enjoying it."

"You were," he responded.

The comment stung, but I didn't let on. "Seamus, you did exactly what you said you'd do. You fucked me, and you're marrying Chelsey. I got what I deserved, but—"

"But what?" he snapped.

"I hope you like the flavor of your homeboy's dick 'cause you'll be tasting every time you kiss her. Oh, and he was *deep* down her throat." I humped the air like I saw Zeus doing to Chelsey's mouth.

"Jealous bitch," Shea spat at me.

"Who's hurt now, asshole?" I whispered as I pushed past him to sit on the couch, since it was clear he wasn't going to let me leave.

Shea followed me to the couch and parted my legs with his knee. I let him…only because I wanted to see what the fuck he was going to do. Shea leaned down, bracing himself on either side of my head on the sofa. He inched close to my face like he wanted to kiss me. We looked at each other for a long time.

"You talk a lot of shit, Maeve," his voice was barely above a whisper. "Don't play with me."

"Correction," I began. "Don't play with me. I'm going to leave with a clean conscience knowing I told the truth." He stared at me for a moment, contemplating his next comment.

Before Shea spoke again, the doorbell rang. We continued looking at one another like we didn't hear a thing. Our staring contest ended when the doorbell rang a third time. He pulled away from me to answer the door. I follow, hoping to make my escape.

"What the fuck is going on? Why y'all taking so long to get the door?" Sherm barked.

"Your friend here," I said, motioning toward Shea, "won't let me leave."

"She's trying to back out of the trip," he replied, matching my energy.

Sherm separated us, vocalizing his disapproval while pushing his way in. He looked at us with displeasure written all over his face. "Come on, Lil Bit! It ain't gone be the same without you. You gotta come."

"I ain't gotta do shit, but stay Black and die," I said flatly.

"Well, you're barely Black…more like beige," Sherm joked. My expression shut down his laughter.

"I'm not doing this with him, Sherm. He's pushing buttons, and I can tell you I'm about to pop…OFF!" I rolled my neck so hard I felt something pop. I clutched my neck working the muscles.

"You done popped off enough," he said, mimicking me. "Don't do it for him. It's our last group outing before everything changes. I guarantee it will not be the same without you. Please come!" Sherm hit me with the saddest puppy dog face ever.

I laughed, contemplating his request. I knew he was right, but I wasn't prepared for the shenanigans I knew would surely ensue.

Fuck me! I really don't want to deal with Shea and his bitch ass or that slut of a fiancée. I knew this was gonna indeed be our last hoorah because I was absolutely done with Shea.

"Ok, I'll go," I said before shifting my focus to Shea. "I'm going, but don't expect me to be there to help you pick up the pieces when this shit blows up in your face."

I pushed past him and headed back into the living room when Shea reached out to stop me.

"Don't be like that, Butters," he said softly with a hint of sarcasm.

"In your fucking face," I said smugly. Shea chuckled to himself as he watched me walk away.

"Blow up…what the hell is she talking about?" Sherm asked, looking at Shea cluelessly.

"*Gargled* ramblings," Shea said to him when he finally turned around.

"Drunken ramblings, huh?" Sherm said to himself. "Did you two assholes at least make up?" he asked seriously.

"Who you callin' an asshole?" I shouted over my shoulder.

"We good," Shea said casually.

"Speak for yourself," I said.

"Is it gonna be some shit?" Sherm asked. "I don't want to have to break y'all asses up again."

"Shit, you know I can handle mines," I said, smirking.

"You sure the *fuck* can, Lil Bit," Sherm said, returning my smirk.

Chapter Twenty-Seven
THE BACHELOR PARTY

We arrived at O'Hare after a lengthy ride, ready to head on our journey. I knew the trip was gonna be some shit, but I didn't expect it to start as soon as we loaded into the vans. I had a tremendous headache, exacerbated by Rho and Ellis' arguing. This time it was who sat where that set them off. At some point, I genuinely hoped they would figure out whatever "it" was between them because we were all tired of the noise. I pondered the situation with Shea and wondered if we'd be like Rho and Ellis one day—two bitter fools who really want to be together but can't get it together long enough to reconcile and be friends, or at least civil.

"You could've let me sit by the window. You always gotta be extra witcho stupid ass," El said, getting out of the black Mercedes Benz Sprinter we chartered to ferry us to the airport.

"Gaht damn," J-Boogie sighed. "Do you two fools always have to be at each's other throats? I'm tired of y'all's shit already!"

"Me too," we all griped in unison.

"If he wasn't a such a baby over a fucking seat, it would've been a peaceful ride," Rho complained.

"You could've just given me the seat, Ro-coo-coo! You heard me ask in the house before we left!" Ellis retorted out of sheer frustration.

"I wasn't the only person who sat at a window seat, Geritol. Per the norm, you singled me out!" she shouted back.

"Wait, Geritol?" I asked. I'd heard her call him many things, but "old" was a new one.

"Yeah, 'cause his dick looks like one of those big ass vitamins!" she said sarcastically.

Everyone was amused, except Ellis.

"My dick ain't small! Shutcho ass up, Sudoku!" We could tell that Ellis was frustrated at her "tiny dick" jokes, but he clowned her name just as much. It was a never-ending stream of little dick or crazy combinations of Rho's name.

"Geritol and Ro-coo-coo, shut both y'all asses up," Sherm finally said. He was tickled yet equally frustrated by Ellis and Rho, and tired like the rest of us. "No more fighting! Hell, no more talking, period!"

"Thank you!" we all screamed.

"Fuck y'all," Rho and Ellis said in a united front.

"Oh, now you two loudmouths wanna be on the same team?" Tish remarked pointedly.

"Please make sure you all gather your belongings. It's been a pleasure driving you. Thank you for the entertainment," the driver said. We all turned to look at him like he was speaking gibberish.

"Did he say entertainment?" Stacy asked Tish in amusement. Everyone laughed except me.

At least someone thought this shit was funny. I probably would have laughed if I didn't have such a pounding headache.

"Hey," Shea said, gently placing his hand on the small of my back, "are you ok?" I looked up at him. I could tell his question was genuine. His touch sent another spark through my body, which triggered flashbacks of our lovemaking and the private tenderness we once shared. I moved away slightly to stop the heat from spreading throughout my body.

"Uh, yeah. I just need some Tylenol and a nap. I can't shake this headache. The talkative twins didn't help the situation," I said softly.

Taking note of my body language, Shea stepped back. "I have some in my bag," he said sweetly, although somewhat concerned by my abrupt withdrawal from him. Was that hurt I saw in his eyes? Indeed not, since we were headed to Las Vegas for his bachelor party. He had let me know, unequivocally, nothing would make him happier than marrying Chelsey.

I watched him remove his bag from the luggage cart, and root through his black Salvatore Ferragamo soft leather duffle in search of medicine for me. Most of our luggage had already been placed on a cart to be taken in. He turned, looking up at me as he extended his hand.

"Here you go, Maeve." With that, something changed between us. I received the message he intended to send by calling me my actual name...no more Butterfly.

Did he sense me pulling away from him, from us, from all we'd shared?

"Thank you," I said, reaching for the bottle, careful to touch only the bottle.

I had to shut off those feelings. Pulling away was the only way I knew how to teach my body I couldn't have him and instruct my heart that he didn't want me. I pulled a bottle of water out of my backpack and took the medication. I handed the medicine bottle back to Seamus. He followed my suit when he retrieved the bottle— careful not to touch me. He sensed me pulling away.

My pain was self-inflicted, but it was a necessity. I slept with my best friend, who was engaged to be married. How did I think that was gonna end?

Seamus and I were the only two still outside of the terminal. I grabbed the handle of my bag to head in when he called my name.

"Maeve." His voice was heavy with emotion. "It doesn't have to be this way, you know."

"What way?" I responded, pretending not to understand.

"I know you're pulling away from me...from us," he started before I interrupted him.

"Seamus let me be clear," I paused to take a breath then proceeded.

"There is no us. You'll be a married man in a week."

"We can figure something out that doesn't have to end with you pulling away from me." His voice was low as he inched impossibly close. The pull between us was like two stars on a collision course. But colliding and becoming one, with his impending marriage, was impossible. The only other option was...a black hole. Disastrous!

"Seamus," I bit back emotion, "I don't want to get hurt any further. I can't—won't do the vicious back and forth with you. I can't be friends with someone who can't trust me."

"I know, Maeve." He placed his hand on my shoulder. "I need you in my life, though."

"I said what I said. Why can't you just let it go?"

"Can't we find a way forward? I'm begging. Please, don't pull away. Life won't be the same without you. Please," Shea implored, searching my eyes.

"I won't make any promises," I whispered.

"This is killing me—" Shea began before being interrupted by El.

"Bring y'all's asses on up in here so we can go!" he shouted. He had the unmitigated gall to be upset.

"El, shutcho ass up!" we both shouted back before putting our luggage on the cart.

The three of us headed to the terminal and onto the tarmac. Our friends were ascending the stairs to the jet as we began the short trek to the plane. I reached up to grab my head. The noise from the jet's engines was wreaking havoc on my headache.

"You good?" Shea asked, reaching out to pull me closer as he spoke.

"I'll be aight," I said, trying to pull away.

"Don't," Shea responded sweetly.

I settled into walking side by side until we reached the stairs. I boarded, pausing to take in the opulence of the aircraft, before heading toward the rear of the fuselage where I spied one of two couches occupied by J-Boogie and Stacy.

Everyone was chattering about the agenda, different shows they wanted to see, and how drunk they planned to be when we arrived at McCarran International Airport—the gateway to Sin City.

"Will one of y'all make sure Ellis has a window?" Stacy said jokingly.

"Right, right!" Sherm co-signed her sentiment.

"Do you all mind if Maeve lies down back here?" Seamus asked seriously.

"Are you ok, Lil Bit?" Stacy asked with concern. The boys were silent, but their faces betrayed their feelings. Everyone was concerned.

"Yeah, I'm still a bit hungover from last night. I just need a nap," I reassured them. "It's still game time when we land."

The flight attendant met me in the back shortly after she secured the door. She handed me a pillow and blanket, letting me know if I needed anything, she was available to assist. I set my backpack at one end of the sleeping area. I pulled out earplugs and my excessively expensive noise-canceling headphones. If I could get at least two hours of sleep, maybe, I'd feel better. As soon as I settled in, Stacy brought me her blanket, swapping it out for the one I had. It was a small mink blanket with a mauve border around a cream background. In the center was a mauve rose—her favorite.

"I can't," I tried to refuse, but she didn't give me the option.

"I don't need it, Maevie. Take it and rest. You need it more than I do," she insisted. Stacy turned to leave, but I grabbed her wrist, pulling her down for a hug.

"Thank you…for everything," I said with tears in my eyes.

"We'll grieve properly when we get home, sweetie." She hugged me tightly, then returned to her seat.

Seamus' eyes were on me. *Did he hear us?* He stared at me intently. Grabbing my phone, I set my alarm, turned on my quiet storm playlist, then drifted into the black hole.

We landed in Vegas and disembarked the plane, pausing to let Ellis pick his seat in our awaiting transportation before the rest of us loaded up. The trip to the hotel was quick and peaceful—no arguing from El and Rho, no contact with Seamus. I sat quietly as chatter hummed around me. I felt Shea's gaze on me, but I didn't meet it. Instead, I leaned against the window, closed my eyes, and allowed my thoughts to drift to a previous conversation with Shea. It was hard to fathom Shea selling his house. We had shared so many events and memories throughout the years there. I had hoped his home would be where we shared life. I had imagined it, fantasized about it, for so long. Now, it hurt deeply to think about how things would change after this week. *No reminders, Trixie* said, callously in the back of my mind.

"The agenda says we have free time after we check-in," Zeus said. "I think I'm gonna go down to the pool to check out the scenery."

J and Sherm looked at each other and at Zeus hesitantly, "We'll join you."

The crew wasn't quite sure what to do with the knowledge of Zeus and Chelsey hooking up. They had all hoped when Shea heard the news, he'd call off the wedding. Honestly, they were just as puzzled by his reaction as I had been. I hated that I couldn't tell them that Shea was being blackmailed into marrying her or that Shea's father was a fucking international criminal. We were all just holding our breath to see what this bachelor party had in store for us.

Stacy, Tish, and Rho wanted to hit the tables.

"I'm not up for all of that smoke right now," I managed to mumble. "I'm gonna head up to the room and rest."

"Ok, maybe we'll stay in with you until dinner," Tish said softly.

"It's whatever," I said, drifting back to my thoughts.

"What are you gonna do, Seamus?" Zeus asked.

"I'm meeting Chelsey to tour the venue and knock out some small details before next weekend." Shea's penetrating gaze was on me once again, but I still didn't move.

"Well, I guess I'll be heading to the pool with you fools then." El was the last to confirm his whereabouts.

"Man, what else were you gonna do?" Sherm asked jokingly.

"Man, I don't even know," he said slowly. "I thought somebody might wanna go see a show or something."

"We gon' go see a show a'ight!" Zeus exclaimed, as the boys laughed. Shea scampered to his appointment after we checked in. Upstairs, I let the ladies pick their bedrooms in our oversized-ass suite. It far exceeded my expectations. The view was so impressive that the room's furnishings paled in comparison. The mountains were always an unexpected juxtaposition to the flashing lights of Las Vegas.

"Hey," Stacy caught my attention. "We decided to let you have the master bedroom. It's the least we can do."

"Y'all don't have to do that," I started softly. "I really appreciate it, though."

"Do you feel up for a little chat before napping?" she asked slyly.

"I factored that into my nap time, girl." I giggled at her.

She grabbed the other girls, and they met me in my room. They sprawled across the king-size bed with abandon, waiting for me to begin.

"Y'all are so silly. I factored in some free time because I knew it was gonna be some shit. So, where y'all want me to start?"

"I wanna hear about what happened at Seamus' house before we got there. Sherm said y'all took forever opening the door," Tish said slyly.

"It isn't what you think. We had been fighting, and time got away from us." I told them about the rest of our conversation—how Shea didn't believe what I told him about Chelsey and Zeus, and how he called me a liar.

"Ok, wait," Rho began. "So you really saw them fucking?"

"Oral sex—mouth fucking—yes, with my own eyes."

The ladies gasped and went into *hell nos* and *what the fucks* but simmered down before I proceeded to tell them what I'd seen in the bathroom the night of the rehearsal dinner—shoes and all.

"I knew it was gon' be some shit!" Rho said.

"Right?" I said, knowing they were picking up what I was putting down. "I saw Zeus standing in front of her with his hands wound in her hair, fucking her mouth—hard! She was gagging and shit. I'm amazed she didn't have spit all down her dress."

"Dayum!" Tish said.

"So, you tell Seamus this, and he says you're lying?" Stacy asked in amazement.

"Yup, so I told him I wasn't going to come here, but Sherm guilted me into it. So here I am."

"What were y'all talking about before we boarded the plane?" Rho asked.

"He was saying he wants to remain friends and that all of the shit we've been through is killing him—blah, blah, blah," I stated sarcastically.

"Killing him? The fuck!" Rho said louder than necessary, to which I winced. "Sorry!"

"It's cool. I know I'm telling y'all some shit. My head hurts from all of the liquor I drank, and my body hurts from the fight. I'm in love with Shea, and I have to watch him marry that lying, dick-in-the-mouth whore. I can't figure this fuckery out."

They all gathered around and hugged me, offering words of affirmation and condolences. I knew they were there for me, but they couldn't take the pain away or bear it for me.

"This is gonna be a shit show!" Tish said when we ended the embrace.

"Not on my watch, sis," I replied. "I am gonna try my best to make sure this trip goes off without a hitch. I need you all to help me, though. If you see me getting upset, just step in or something. To top it all, I think my period is about to start."

"Aunt Flo *always* seems to throw a monkey wrench in our plans," Tish quipped angrily. Shit, you'd have thought it was her period she was mad at.

"Girl, yes!" Stacy and Rho said. We chatted for a few moments longer before Stacy suggested I get some rest before dinner.

The next day I awoke to light streaming through my curtains onto my pillow. From ninety-three million miles away, the sun was telling me to wake my ass up. I was still a little tired when I got out of bed, threw the curtains open, grabbed my robe, and wandered into the dining room. I found the girls eating and chattering about the night before.

"Did you hoes eat dinner without me last night?" I asked, in sheer disbelief.

"We tried to wake you," Stacy said.

"Yeah," Tish co-signed.

"Are you hungry?" Stacy asked as she got up to fix me a plate.

"Famished," I said, walking to join her.

"No, sit. It's the least I can do. How's your head?" Stacy asked. The ladies watched as I made my way to the table.

"Good," I sang.

"That's good because you looked like freshly shat *gachug baeseolmul.*" Rho smirked at her remark.

"Gat chi, what?" I tried to repeat, laughing. Where did she come up with this shit?

"It's cow shit," she translated. "You know, dung!"

"Uh, no, Rho. I don't know! How would I know that?" I asked sarcastically.

"Hmm, well, I guess you wouldn't, seeing how you don't know Korean." She went back to eating like she hadn't said anything.

"Shutcho ass up." Tish sat across the table staring at Rho in awe.

"Here, ya go, sweetie. I hope you have an appetite left after all of this cow-shit talk," Stacy tossed out sarcastically, looking at Rho like she was crazy.

Stacy set a plate of sausage, eggs, toast, and fresh fruit down in front of me, then seated herself at the head of the oval-shaped glass table. The dining room was decorated with modern furnishings and artwork. If I could've, I would've stolen the painting over the buffet. It would've looked amazing in my room. I made a note to look into abstract art for my bedroom when I got home. Redecorating might wash away all of the reminders of Shea since I couldn't sell my share of the loft.

"Did I miss anything last night?" I inquired before stuffing my face.

"Dinner was fantastic. We had to move it to Seamus' suite. We didn't wanna wake you, though," Tish said.

"Yeah, it was delicious! How did you get Chef Martín to agree to cook for us?" Stacy asked. She had told me he was one of her idols a long time ago.

"Amazingly, Jared knew a friend of a friend who dated him. He got the number and called to make the arrangements. I hate that I missed it." I was genuinely saddened.

"Don't worry! He said he'd be willing to do an encore performance for you at his restaurant later this week. The reservation has already been made. We were waiting for you to rearrange the schedule," Stacy said eagerly.

"She couldn't wait to tell you that," Rho said, laughing.

"Are you guys serious? That's awesome!" I exclaimed, clapping my hands.

"Shea brought Chelsey...so you didn't miss that," Tish said softly.

"Yeah, and Zeus looked like he was gonna piss his pants!" Stacy exclaimed.

"Bitch, what?" I screamed, spitting my eggs across the table. "Sorry," I said, scraping up egg bits.

"Yes, ma'am," Tish nodded. "Chelsey played that shit off so cold! Pretending like she vaguely remembered him. She didn't let on for one second that she knew him."

"Wow, I bet he didn't like that," I added.

"Nope," Tish said, "he was in a sour mood for the rest of the night. He even went to bed early when we all went down to hit the tables."

"Did Shea let on like he noticed it?" I asked without looking up.

"Not at all," Stacy answered. "He acted like everything was status quo."

"Dumbass," I muttered.

We continued to eat while they told me about their winnings and how much El lost playing craps.

"Well, shit, and shove me in it," I said. "I would've stopped at one hundred, but that fool kept going 'til he lost a thousand?"

"Girl, Sherm talked him off the table by agreeing to go see a show with him. Said he'd buy the tickets and everything."

We all laughed.

"Well, there goes my itinerary...now we all gotta go. It's not like El's gonna go hungry, though. That fool probably brought ten Gs to gamble with," I quipped.

"Try twenty," Rho said.

"Twenty?" we shouted.

"Yeah, he told me on the plane he was gonna double his money during this trip," Rho relayed. We all laughed, because he was already headed in the wrong direction.

"Enough about that fool," Stacy said. "The agenda says we're touring the Grand Canyon. Is that true?"

"Yeah, we're taking a helicopter tour to the Skywalk. I thought it'd be cool to do that and tour the Hoover Dam, too. Not on the same day, of course."

"Girl, you have this trip planned down to the minute. Is there any wiggle room?" Stacy asked.

"Everything is moveable. I just have to say the word, and the concierge will work miracles. He just about lost his mind when he heard Sherm, J-Boogie, and Seamus were gonna be with us. It didn't hurt that Darren had his personal assistant call to make sure we were cared for. They love him out here. He's a high-roller."

"Girl, what are you gonna do about DW? You know, he's in love with you, right?" Tish added.

"He's *not* in love with me, for one. He's dating his physical therapist. For two, we are—and always will be—good friends."

"She told you!" Rho pointed and laughed in Tish's face.

"Seriously?" She looked confused.

"Yes, Darren knows all about Shea. He knows shit you don't know because I don't want the judgmental bullshit you bring to a conversation," I retorted.

"Damn, Maeve," she said dejectedly. "I didn't know it was like that."

She pushed her chair back, threw her napkin down, and stormed off.

"Fuck," I mumbled. I followed Tish to her room, stopping her from slamming the door in my face.

"Tish, wait." I walked into the room and closed the door behind me. "I didn't mean to hurt your feelings, but you are so fucking judgmental. I saw how you were when Rho had her threesome, and I didn't want to deal with the same shit."

"I thought you and I were closer than that," she said, turning to face me. "Hell, you've seen me naked."

"What the hell does that have to do with anything, Tish?" I asked before relaying the information to her, and she was blown away. She asked questions and gave her honest, non-judgmental opinion.

"See, was that so hard?" I asked sarcastically.

"With you, no, but Rho does absolutely the absolute most! I swear she tries to gross me out." Tish giggled.

"Good. Now get ready! The van will be leaving shortly," I said over my shoulder before running across the suite to my room.

I noticed that Stacy had already stacked the dishes neatly for the maid. She was always so thoughtful of workers in the service industry. Yet another reason to love her more.

I was the last one to make it downstairs.

"Bout time, slowpoke," Shea shouted as I exited the hotel. I shot him a dirty look, but chuckled.

"Let's roll, people," I said, cutting the line to get in the van.

"Uh, no, ma'am!"

Everyone vocalized their distaste for my early morning rudeness.

"Blame Shea," I retorted over my shoulder as I took the same seat I had the night before.

For all intents and purposes, Ellis should have had a window seat, but we weren't with the shit last night, so we boxed him out along with Rho. We could be assholes, at times.

"Don't put your rudeness on me, Butterfly. This is all you!" Shea laughed.

"And I told your ass to stop calling me that," I retorted.

We leave the strip, making our way to the airport where the helicopter tours depart.

"Alright, people," I began. "Once we get to Amazing Tours, we will fill out waivers and be weighed."

"Weighed?" Rho questioned.

"Rhodan, shutcho ass up and let me finish," I quipped before continuing. "You will be placed on the helicopters according to weight distribution. We will not all be in the same bird, so get over it now."

Rho leaned over to Sherm. "Did Lil Bit just call me a *Kaiju?*"

"Yes, she did. Now, shutcho ass up," Sherm giggled under his breath.

"Thank you," Ellis replied sarcastically.

"El," I retorted, matching his sarcasm. "Let me hit you with a fresh *shutcho ass up* to start the day. I ain't here for your bullshit this morning."

Shouts of *amen* and *preach* erupted from the crew—even the driver joined in. We all turned to look at her—who gave not a solitary fuck—and laid over laughing.

"Well, damn," El said. "You muhfuckahs done did it now. Y'all done turnt the driver against me!"

"Naw, she's not with the bullshit today because it's just too damned early," Shea said, patting El on the back.

"Back to what I was saying," I interrupted, giving both men a swift side-eye. "There will be no swapping seats or complaining. Additionally, your Skywalk tickets have been pre-paid, so come hell, high water, or Sherm...yo' ass is walking, so suck it up right now."

"Sky-Skywalk," Shea stuttered. "Uh, I thought we were just going to look at the Grand Canyon?"

"Shea, I don't care if Sherm has to drag *yer Irish arse* across that damn crystal bridge...you going. So put your big boys drawls on and deal," I said, unfazed by his fresh terror.

"Damn, girl," J said, "you must've got some *good* sleep!"

"Naw," the driver said nonchalantly, "she ain't with the bullshit this morning." She peered up at my reflection in the rearview mirror, then directed her attention back to the road. We hooted with laughter at her comment.

"Show you right," I said to the driver.

I moved up to the front during the trip to chat with the driver once everyone went back to their previous conversations. Miss Eveline Jennings drove charter vans to put her son through college. I came to find out her son played basketball for Kennesaw State in Georgia. He wasn't on full scholarship, which meant she had to work this job and another on the weekends to help with books, room, and a portion of his tuition. I asked why he didn't go to UNLV. She said she wanted him to get away from some bad influences he grew up with, and she had a brother in Jonesboro, Georgia, who could check in on him often. We chatted for a little longer before I headed to the back to sit down.

"Thanks for sharing, Miss Eveline."

"No, thank you for asking, baby," she responded. "Most people don't care enough to ask 'bout my life. I'm just the driver, you know?"

"Yes, ma'am, I do. You'll see that we aren't like that."

I headed to the back and joined a conversation in progress.

"All I know," El started, "is I don't wanna be on a chopper with yo loud mouf ass."

"El, I know I told you don't start and to shutcho ass up. Ya heard?" I fussed.

"Ok, ok, Lil Bit. Imma let it go," he promised.

"I say we put him and Rho on a chopper by themselves," Shea said.

"How 'bout you shutcho ass up, Seamus," Rho jumped in with a head wag and a snap to Shea's face. "I'm sitting over here being obedient to the rules and minding my business."

I was tickled by Rho's comment and remained quiet because she shut Shea all the way down. He laughed and left her alone.

"Lil Bit, switch seats with me, for a sec, so I can chop it up with Zeus," Sherm said, who was sitting next to Shea. I'd hoped to avoid a lot of contact and conversation with him, but I agreed.

I wasn't sitting in the seat for more than three seconds before Shea put his arm around me, whispering in my ear, "Are you purposefully avoiding me?"

"Yes," I whispered back.

"Why?"

"Why what?" I responded.

"Maeve," Shea whispered sharply.

"I'm tired, Shea," I said softly, settling into the crook of his arm. "Let's have a good day."

"We'll talk later," he responded, then kissed me on the top of my head.

I searched the van to see if anyone caught his unconscious display of affection. Miss Eveline noticed, but didn't acknowledge it when I caught her eyes. I drifted off to sleep to the road noise and soft chatter of my companions' conversations. It wasn't a long drive, but I managed a power nap. Shea shook me softly, rubbing my arm to wake me. The shock of my hand resting on his erection was like cold water to the face. I sat up, removing my hand.

His body had betrayed him.

"Hey, we're here," he whispered. I peered around the van once again, hoping no one caught sight of where my hand was resting. Old Miss Eveline didn't miss shit! She smiled at my reflection once more.

"I'm sorry," I whispered to Shea.

"I'm not," he said to my surprise. *Well, damn.*

"You all can leave your things on the bus," Miss Eveline said as we pulled into the lot.

"Thanks, Miss Eveline." I smiled at her briefly. "Make sure you grab your IDs through."

We walked to the small building that housed Amazing Tours' business office and was greeted by a young brunette who perked up when she saw Shea walk in. He didn't notice her.

"Excuse me," she started, "may I have your attention?" We all quieted down. "My name is Misty Green. I'll need to have you all watch a short safety video before we begin. When you finish, you'll find clipboards with waivers on them on the counter over there." She directed our attention to the counter, running along the wall opposite the seating area. "Once you've completed them, I will weigh each of you over here," she said, pointing to the scale near the door we entered. When the video was over, we meandered over to the counter to fill out our waivers. Shea was the last to finish.

"I bet you work out a lot," Misty said sweetly.

"Not really," Shea responded flatly.

"Genetics, nice." She smiled up at him. He ignored her flirting, but she persisted.

"Will you be in town later?" she asked.

Damn, she's forward, I thought.

"No," he replied.

"What brings you to Las Vegas then?" she asked in a husky voice.

"My wedding," he said. "Are we done?"

Misty's cheeks reddened as soft chuckles fill the room. She wrote his weight down, then stepped back. She surveyed the room, but we were all looking in various directions trying not to make eye contact.

"Uh, yeah," she said dryly.

"Now, pick your face up 'cause it's cracked and on the floor," Stacy mumbled, barely audible enough for me to catch.

"Well, let me run these forms out to the pilots. I'll be right back," Misty said before rushing out.

We held it together long enough for her to get out of earshot before we started laughing.

"Whew, child," Stacy said, "I just about pissed my pants when he said *my wedding!*"

"Shea," I asked, "why did you do her like that?"

"I tried to ignore her, but she just kept on. Hell, she asked for that, and you know it," he said seriously. I shook my head and continued to chuckle.

"Welp," J-Boogie said, "this goes down as the worst brush off in history."

"She ain't his type anyway," El said.

There I was laughing at Misty getting rejected, and I'd been dismissed two seconds before her! My laughter dried the fuck up real quick. I thought for a moment. *Does Shea have a type?* I'd seen him date every variety of women. He did not discriminate at all. I had once seen him date an overweight blind woman. That fool said the sex was phenomenal, and he didn't see that coming. Shea was genuinely a mystery.

Shea winked at me when I looked up from my thoughts. Misty bounded back into the office, handing out our seating arrangements. Sherm, Stacy, Tish, and J-Boogie were in the first helicopter, while Ellis, Rho, and Zeus were on another aircraft. This left Shea and me in the last chopper, together.

"How the fuck does this shit keep happening to me?" I whispered to Stacy.

"You think you have it bad? Zeus is stuck in a chopper with El and Rho!" She couldn't contain her laughter.

"That's what his ass gets. I don't deserve this!" I whisper-screamed.

Slowly, each group began to board their aircraft and take off. Shea and I were the only ones remaining when our helicopter shut down.

"Guys, your bird is having minor engine trouble," Misty informed us dryly. "It's gonna be about twenty minutes before we can get it up and going again.

"Dammit," I muttered. "How does this shit keep happening to me?" I walked away, heading toward the shuttle.

I saw Miss Eveline and asked if I could wait in the van. She opened the door for me, then started the engine.

"Give it a second to cool off," she said, then looked over my shoulder. "Here comes your fiancé." I turned to see Shea.

"Oh no, ma'am. He's my friend."

"Friend?" She shook her head and chuckled. "I don't think so, sweetheart. You're in love with that man, and he's in love with you. Anyone with eyes can see that."

I stared at her with my mouth wide open. *Then why the fuck is he marrying someone else?* I wanted to retort.

"Don't stand there catching flies, honey. Catch that fine-ass man before he marries the other woman," she said before returning to the chair under the shade tree where I found her.

"You look like you've seen a ghost," Shea said as he walked up.

"No, but I think Ms. Eveline peeped our exchange and came to the conclusion that we're in love," I informed him, then turned to get in the van.

Shea grasped my hand, spinning me around.

"She's right." His truthfulness was like a daggers to my heart.

"Don't." I wrestled my hand from him before I entered the van.

He paused for a moment before joining me. He closed the door behind him, then sauntered over to where I sat.

"Don't what?" he asked.

"Don't start this shit," I replied.

"We're all alone in this air-conditioned van for twenty minutes. I can think of plenty of shit to start."

He stared intensely into my eyes before leaning in. *I know this fool isn't trying to kiss me,* I thought. *Motherfuck me, he is!* I moved my face, and his kiss landed on my neck. Wrong move!

He pinned me down, kissing my neck until I murmured softly. Fuck, his mouth felt so good.

I closed my eyes to the sensation of his warm mouth surrounded by the low scruff he'd allowed to form on his face. The stubble tickled my neck and cheeks. The feeling of his breath on my mouth caused my eyes to dart open. Before I could move again, he kissed me. His mouth was demanding entrance from me. I yielded, returning his kiss with vigor. *Dammit!*

Shea pulled me over onto his lap, dragging my dress slowly up my thighs, torturing me every inch of the way. He palmed my ass with one hand, ripping off my panties with the other. Our kiss didn't falter while he undid his buckle, his button, and unzipped his pants. His stiff cock was making it difficult for him to free himself. He struggled for a moment longer until I lifted up off his lap slightly. He found release from the fabric prison that held him fast, then rubbed his cock against my clitoris. I wanted him inside me so badly.

"Please," I implored.

"Please, what?" he asked, as his lips turned up into a smile.

"Seamus," I began but trailed off.

Before I could finish my statement, he pulled me down onto his erection. We sat for a beat, taking in the gravity of the moment. Our kissing stopped briefly as his head lulled backward. When he lifted his head, his pupils were dilated, causing his eyes to look slightly bluer. I was mesmerized.

"You are so fucking incredible. Do you know that?" Shea asked me in a low rumble.

I nodded cockily.

"Fuck me," he demanded.

I rose slowly from my seated position on his lap. I unsheathed him to the tip, then gently teased the head of his cock at my entrance. Shea grabbed my hips, pulling me back down roughly.

"Fuck me *now*."

"This isn't Burger King, Shea," I taunted.

"Don't play with me, woman," he said gruffly into my neck. *So demanding*, I thought. I started the descent down the length of his mountainous erection, rose, and repeated the motion of teasing him over and over.

Finally, he pressed me to his chest, wrapping his arm around my body. He grasped my left arm roughly. With his other hand, he pulled my dress up, tucking it into the same hand he was using to hold my arm. He clasped my hair with his free hand at the root, pulling my head backward.

"Stop babysitting my dick and fuck me, Maeve," he growled.

I moaned loudly at his words. I leaned down to kiss him while I writhed on his cock and grinded my clit into his stomach, searching for an orgasm. I wriggled my right arm free to wrap it around his neck, winding my fingers through his hair and kissing him ardently. I began to ride him furiously. He responded with an energetic thrust to match my intensity.

"Like this?" I asked seductively when I pulled back from our kiss.

"Mm-hmm," he groaned deeply. "Slow down, though. I don't wanna come before you!"

I kept going at a breakneck pace.

"Maeve, slow down," he said. He placed his hands on my hips, trying to slow my pace.

"Shea," I pleaded, "I need you."

"I need you too, baby." He released my hips, bringing both hands to my head. "I felt your hand on my cock while you slept earlier. All I could think of was this...fucking like this...I didn't care who was watching us either." My sex pulsed at his words. "Ah, shit...Maeve...wait." Shea felt my body respond to his words and struggled, losing his train of thought.

"Seamus," I moaned his name, breathlessly, "I want you so badly."

I was teetering on the brink of a much-needed orgasm.

"I know you're close. I can feel you tightening around me. Just let go, Maeve."

Every inch of me cried out for release as Shea pushed into me harder and faster, urging me to come. I knew he was fighting for control. His jaw clenched tightly, and the vein in his forehead bulged. His hands slid down my back to cup my ass as he lifted me up to drag me back down to push deeper into me. His hands were so big, so warm, so strong. *Shit, his cock feels so good!* I thought. It made me forget the lasciviousness of the act we were committing.

I felt his organ grow larger inside me just before he came. I cried out from the release of my orgasm at the same time.

"Maeve," Shea groaned, repeating my name like a mantra—searing it into his brain, over and over.

Our orgasmic musings continued as we climbed higher together. I leaned into Shea, overcome with emotion, until I felt the frenzied sensations ebb and subside. We were still for a moment basking in blissful peace—no fighting, no hateful words, no enmity.

"You're crying! Are you ok?" he asked, lifting my face to meet his gaze.

"No, Shea," I whispered hoarsely. "I'm not."

"Did I hurt you?" His voice was barely above a whisper when he searched my face.

"No. This is...overwhelming," I responded softly.

He inhaled deeply then began, "I—this—we probably shouldn't have done this but... I..." his voice trailed off.

"They know we're in here fucking," I said of the employees at the terminal.

"I don't care," he said. I moved to sit next to him, but he held me fast on his lap.

"Shea, I just heard the chopper start. We've got to head over to the tarmac. Besides, I don't want Miss Eveline to catch us in the act."

He paused for a second before he let go. I rose slowly before climbing off his lap. I reached under my seat for my backpack. I dug until I found the baby wipes, which I used to freshen up, handing Shea a few as well.

"Dammit," he said, looking out the window. We saw Misty making her way to the van.

We quickly cleaned up and gathered our clothing before stepping out of the van. We left Misty standing where she was as we strode past her towards the helicopter.

Chapter Twenty-Eight
Bird's Eye View

"**H**ey there, pretty lady," the pilot greeted me. "I'm sorry for the delay. I promise I'll get you to the party before this guy turns back into a mouse!" I giggled at the Cinderella reference. Shea looked confused.

"Mouse?" he questioned into his DC headphones as he positioned himself in the back seat.

The pilot and I laughed.

We flew toward the western rim of the Grand Canyon. I took in the beautiful view as the pilot pointed out various sites in the landscape beneath us. We chatted, asked the pilot questions, and took pictures. Our conversation was easy now that we'd gotten all of the tension out of the way. We arrived at our destination without occurrence. Our friends greeted us with questions when we arrived. We told them about the engine problems as we headed to the shuttle, which transported us to the Skywalk.

"Thanks for waiting for us, guys," I sang.

"Naw, Lil Bit," Sherm corrected me. "We waited on Seamus! We all wanted to see the look on his face when he walked out on that glass bridge!"

We chatted briefly about our respective flights and some of the things we noticed that others missed. Our friends began taking bets whether or not Shea would make it onto the bridge.

I turned to Shea. "I'll walk out with you if it makes you feel better."

Shea was a mild, sickly green color. "Um…I don't know if that will help."

"You poor thing." I rubbed the back of his shoulder to console him.

Our tour guide, Justin, met us to begin the tour. He told us about the history of the horseshoe-shaped bridge. We took time to learn about the western rim of the Grand Canyon before our guide led us through a crowd of people. At first, it wasn't apparent, but the bridge had been cleared for Ellis and Sherm, the celebrities in our midst. I walked out onto the bridge. The view was breathtaking until I looked down. Fear took me momentarily. I turned to look at Shea. He was terrified. I walked back toward him, grabbed his hand, and led him gingerly out onto the glass walkway.

"Don't be afraid," I told him—and myself. "Remember, it can hold the weight of two thousand airplanes, and Sherm."

"You ain't funny," Sherm shot over his shoulder.

"Thanks," Shea said as he gripped my hand tighter.

We didn't stay on the bridge long, but I swear everyone had at least fifty pictures of Shea looking like he'd seen a ghost. By the end of our day trip, we were somewhat at ease.

"Man, I'm proud of you for conquering your fears," Sherm said, pulling Shea into a big bear hug.

"Thanks, but I can't wait to get back to solid ground," he said semi-confidently.

Our tour guide took several group photos of us. My favorite was one of everyone jumping, except Shea.

"Let me get one of the two of you," Stacy said to Shea and me.

He scooped me up and tossed me. When he set me down, I gut checked him hard.

"Are you crazy? What if the wind blew?" I said, laughing at his antics. But I knew he'd forgotten my panties were in his pocket. He was feeling more at ease. I wrapped my arms around his waist and turned to Stacy, who was taking photos of our entire exchange. She snapped a few more while we mugged for the camera like supermodels.

"You two are too much." She smiled from ear to ear before showing us the photos she took.

"Oh, wow! These came out great!" I gushed. "Well, shit, and shove me in it! Shea, your evil ass was just a little too gleeful when you tossed me into the air."

His ass also forgot I wasn't wearing panties, clearly.

"Yes, and for a change, you have a look of sheer panic on your face!" he teased.

"This was amazing," Tish said, walking over to us.

"I know, right?" Rho seconded.

"Let me get a picture of you all before we leave," Shea said, taking my phone.

We hit a Charlie's Angel pose, a prison pose, and a few hugged up for posterity before we headed off the Skywalk. Sherm, Ellis, and Seamus posed for some photos with their fans, then we all made our way back to the shuttle. Sometimes, I forget they were an NFL star, Olympic gold athlete, and Real Estate Mogul, respectively. Shea was no Donald Bren, but he owned close to a two million square feet of real estate in Chicago, New York, Los Angeles, and abroad.

Chapter Twenty-Nine
DREAMS & REVELATIONS

"This can't be." My voice was barely a whisper as I peered at the two solid lines.

Pregnant.

I heard a loud rap at the suite door. On autopilot, I wandered through the expansive room and answered it.

Seamus. *Why the fuck is he here?* I thought. I opened the door slowly.

"Wha-what are you doing here?" I asked, softly.

"I needed to see you. May I come in?" he asked sweetly.

"Umm." I moved to allow him to pass. He looked like shit. "What happened? Why are you here?"

"To apologize for everything I've said, done, and put you through, Butterfly."

"Seamus, I—" My heart was beating through my chest as I began, "I'm pregnant."

"Pregnant." He looked confused. "Is it…"

"I don't know," I said flatly.

"Wait," he began, "I thought you were on birth control."

"I guess I miscalculated. It's been a little over five years since I got the last one." Tears slipped from my eyes.

"Don't cry." He dropped the test, then knelt before me. "We'll figure it out, Butterfly." He pulled me to him, then kissed my lower abdomen.

I was having a baby, yet I was unsure who fathered it. Adjemi was on one side, and Shea was on the other. When the baby made his appearance, a dejected man dropped my hand and left the delivery room. The baby the spitting image of his father.

Whew…gaht damn!

I awoke with a start, looking around the Sprinter at my friends. All of them were asleep except Shea.

You ok? he mouthed softly.

"Uh." I looked up toward Miss Eveline, who was focused on driving before I answered, "Yeah, just a dream."

Seamus sat staring at me oddly for a moment, then licked his lips seductively. I looked away, feeling heat rush to my face, neck, and chest. He smiled at my reaction to his wanton display of lust. *Fuck! I'm so fucking predictable. Where does Seamus think this is going?* I thought. I heard my phone vibrate from my backpack. I bent down to rummage through the bag, finding my phone quickly. I unlocked it to see I had a missed text from Shea. *Shit!* Shea cheating on Chelsey. She was fucking Zeus. What the fuck were they doing?

Shea: Dreaming of me?

I peeked up at him, then rolled my eyes.

Me: I hate you with a deep-seated passion…
Shea: That's not true. So, tell me about your dream…
Me: You sure you wanna know?

I smiled deviously as I sent the text, never looking up from my device.

Shea: Fuck, yes!

His enthusiasm made my sex pulse momentarily.

Me: I was pregnant, and I didn't know who the fa-
        ther was.
Shea: Did you want it to be me?

I jerked my face up from the screen to look at him. Shea met my gaze unabashed, and something in his eyes told me it was what he wanted.

Me: Idk, Shea. I didn't give it much thought.
Shea: Don't lie to me, Butters.
Me: Don't call me that. Just let it go, Shea.
Shea: I want to be the father of your children, Butter-
        fly.

As I stared at his response, I felt his eyes trained on me. He willed me to look up, but I didn't dare meet his gaze. Being with him that afternoon rekindled the feelings I had begun to let go of in the recent months. I wasn't going back down that dirt road again. Grams always said dirt roads were only good for one thing—getting dirty!

Me: I don't know if that will sit well with your future
        wife, Seamus.
Shea: Why do you always have to fight me?
Me: This is a fact, not a fight. I don't want to allow
        thoughts of what could be when I know it
        won't happen.
Shea: Was it a boy or a girl?

I leaned my head against the seat, rolling my eyes before making eye contact with him. My facial expression bespoke my frustration—sending the unspoken question, *why does it matter?*

Shea: It matters to me...

I looked back at my device. Chuckling, I responded.

Me: I don't know.
Shea: I bet our baby was beautiful.

Tears threatened like an ominous storm cloud as I remembered the tiny little imagined face. Why did he make me feel like this?

Me: Yes, Seamus. Now, can we drop this?
Shea: I hope I get to meet him one day.

"Fuck," I breathed out.

"You ok?" Rho asked sleepily from the seat next to me.

"Yeah, sorry," I whispered, patting her leg. Rho leaned back, falling asleep instantly.

Shea: That was close! LOL
Me: Would you ever cop on to yourself? Feckin' ee-
          jit, I swear you're as thick as a plank!

Seamus's boisterous laughter woke everyone up. Our friends gave him hell for disturbing their rest.

"Really, man?" Ellis asked angrily. "Some of us are trying to sleep!"

"Yeah," Sherm added, "what the fuck is so funny?"

"I'm sorry, guys, for real." Shea tried to appease the natives, but they were too riled up from being roused from their sleep.

"Sorry my ass," J-Boogie imitated Shea. "We wanna know what's so gaht damn funny."

Shea looked to me for help since it was partially my fault. He laughed. I forgot he enjoyed my use of Irish slang. So, I searched through my phone's images quickly to find a funny meme to help the guy out. Shea opened his messages, saw the meme I sent, and guffawed again before sharing the image with the rest of the group.

"Let me find out yo ass had something to do with this," Rho whispered to me. I looked back and shrugged innocently. She eyed me up and down, not buying for a second I was as innocent as I pretended.

> Shea: Nice save!
> Me: I should've let them tear you a new asshole...

Shea cackled again.

"Man, shut yo ass up," Stacy fussed sleepily from her seat.

She was sitting next to Shea and got an earful of his hearty laugh. She had jumped out of her seat and clutched at the air when she woke up. I had to bite my lip to keep from laughing.

"I'm sorry, Stace." Shea pulled her into his embrace to soothe her.

"Man, get yo' goofass off me!" Stacy fought to get out of Shea's embrace, but he was too strong.

"Gotta love me," he giggled while planting kisses on her cheek until she laughed.

"Ok, damn," she said, wiping off the myriad of kisses Shea planted on her. "You play too much."

Their interaction made us all laugh.

"What's on the agenda for tonight?" Tish asked, rubbing her eyes.

"Y'all promised me a show," Ellis blurted out before I spoke.

"Well, damn," I fussed, "a bitch can't get a word in edgewise, huh, El?"

"I'm sorry, Lil Bit," he said apologetically. "Go 'head then."

"Naw, naw...a show it is, big fella. What did you have in mind? Blue Man Group? Jabbawockeez?"

"Barry Manilow," Ellis said.

"Barry Manilow!" we shouted in disbelief.

"Oh hell naw," Tish said as she shook her head.

"Does anyone—besides Ellis' cornball ass—know a Barry Manilow song?" Rho interjected.

"That's what I said when he asked if I'd go," Zeus said, jabbing Ellis.

"Y'all said I could pick the show," Ellis said.

"We didn't think yo' ass would wanna go see Barry-fucking-Manilow," Shea chimed in.

"Shit, I'm not going to see no fuckin' Barry Manilow," Sherm added.

"You muhfuckahs are heartless," I retorted. "Y'all promised to go see whatever show he picked. I wasn't there. So, have fun with that!"

"Wait, what?" Rho asked in disbelief. "Oh no, bitch, if I gotta go see Mr. Copacabana, then you gotta go see him too.

"Wait a minute, Rokurokubi," Ellis said, sliding the jab in so smoothly we almost missed it. "You know Barry?"

"Rokuro-what? What the fuck did you just call her?" Sherm choked on his laughter.

"Gaht damn." Rho laughed so hard she could barely breathe. "A Japanese...a *yokai*."

"Eh! No one knows what the hell that is." Tish stared at Rho in confusion.

"You already know it's some sort of monstrous Godzilla type shit," Stacy said, giggling.

"Oh! Well damn," Tish responded. It was always funny to watch understanding hit Tish. It was like watching *Friends* and seeing the character Joey finally understand the punchline.

"In Japanese horror mythology, Rokurokubi are long-necked humanoid spirits!" Rho finally said when she gathered herself together enough to speak.

"Gaht damn, boy! You really did ya homework on that one!" Sherm said through hearty laughter.

"That's what makes it so damn funny," Rho agreed.

"There were levels to that joke, though. First, Rho's reaction, the fact that he waited for the perfect moment to drop it, and the cherry on top when Tish finally getting it! Whew!" Sherm smirked.

"You good, big fella?" I asked.

"I can't stand their asses," Sherm said finally.

"That was truly the best one you've ever called me," Rho extended her fist to dap Ellis. His smile was so broad you would've thought he won at the Olympics—again!

"Don't think I'm not gonna get your ass back, though," Rho added.

"Oh, it's always on, sis," Ellis volleyed back.

Before we could get back to discussing the evening's events, Miss Eveline had begun blasting "Copacabana." El and Rho began to sing and perform to the music.

"That's the song from *Friends*," Tish squealed in laughter.

"I remember that episode! Hell, I know Barry, too!" Zeus exclaimed.

"What the whole fuck is going on in America?" Shea asked, shaking his head.

After El, Rho, Zeus, and Tish's performance, we all agreed to see Barry Manilow. We got back to the hotel, where I laid down, trying to take a quick nap, when DW's FaceTime call came through.

"My guy," I beamed as Darren's face appeared.

"Sunshine." He smiled broadly. "Are you behaving yourself out there?"

"Umm," I faltered at his question, "see what had happened was…"

Darren laughed. "I knew you was gon' get out there an' show yo' ass! I felt that shit in my spirit!"

"I swear I tried, Darren." I smiled as embarrassment spread across my face.

"I bet you did." His deadpan face sent me into hysterics.

"You are so nasty! You know that's not what I meant, boy," I giggled.

"Yeah, but when you lay the ball out there so easily, I have no choice but to run it." Darren laughed heartily at his own joke. "So, what else are you getting into?"

"I'm trying to be good, I swear," I sang sweetly.

"Mm-hmm," he said knowingly.

"Chile, we're going to see Barry Manilow tonight." I half smiled, waiting to see his response.

"Barry Manilow! Whose idea was that? Tish's?" Darren laughed at his own prejudice.

"Ellis," I said.

"Well, shit, and shove me in it! I didn't see that one coming!" Darren shook his head.

"Chile, Sherm promised him if he didn't gamble away all his money, we'd go see a show. You already know I tried to get out of it. Hell, turns out Zeus, Tish, and Rho all know some Manilow, too," I added.

"I can't," he said, still shaking his head. "Not Boyz II Men, not Santana, but Barry fuckin' Manilow. Just wow!"

"I know, right?" I said sarcastically. "I don't know one song!"

"Even I know 'Mandy', and 'I Write the Songs'! How do you not know one Manilow song? Yo' ass is just uncouth!" Darren laughed at me when I pouted at his comment.

"Forget you, Darren," I fussed.

"I'm just messing with you. Do y'all have tickets?" DW asked.

"Shit! I assumed we could just—" I began.

"Check your email," he said sarcastically. "I got you."

"Darren, what the hell did you do?" I asked after seeing the email. Darren had managed to acquire nine VIP tickets and a meet and greet in the short time we were on the phone.

"You know how I do, baby! Plus, I figured if concierge had seats, they wouldn't be DW caliber." Darren popped his collar and grinned like he'd won a prize.

"See, this is why I love you! You are the shit. I think I'll keep you around for a little while longer." I smiled slyly.

"No worries. You know I got you! Y'all have fun." Darren smiled warmly through the video.

"We will! Seriously, thank you, DW! I truly appreciate this." I placed the phone down after Darren hung up. I was dying to see the expression on everyone's face when they found out we had VIP passes to the concert.

I got off the phone with DW and took a brief nap. While I slept, my mind drifted back to the baby I had dreamed about on the bus. The baby had a spicy personality, which I'm sure we put him through. In my dream, Shea was the perfect father. He changed diapers, fed, bathed, and sang Irish lullabies to the baby. Our son got a healthy dose of his father's Irish blood. He was a green-eyed mirror of Shea.

Chapter Thirty
BARRY MANILOW AND BABY MONKEYS

I woke up refreshed and ready for everything the evening could bring my way. I showered and dressed in a black bodycon dress, black and red Louboutins, and a matching leather jacket. I tucked my Loubisharks in my backpack for later when we'd go clubbing. I had arranged a VIP booth at Shine— one of the hottest new clubs in Las Vegas.

I still couldn't believe we were going to see Barry Manilow. There were a handful of hot contemporary acts in residency in Vegas. The fact that over a third of the crew wanted to go to that show blew my mind. I mentally prepared myself for a boring-ass concert. I knew the club afterward was going to be lit, which would more than make up for the show. Ellis had called up to our room several times to make sure we knew what time to be downstairs and hurry us along.

"El, if you call here one more fucking time, I'm gonna strangle you with my purse strap," I heard Stacy's agitated voice say through my door.

I leaned out the door, laughing. "Not your purse strap!"

"Girl, I'm tired of his ass already! We need to whoop Sherm's ass for agreeing to this shit," she fumed.

"Who knows," I said optimistically, "it may be fun." Stacy rolled her eyes in response.

"I'll be a monkey's auntie if it is," she joked. Stacy turned and headed back to her room to finish putting the final touches on her face. Tish leaned out of her room to beg for more time.

"Girl! That's gon' be yo' ass if you make El miss Manilow," I exclaimed jokingly.

"I need help with my hair! Can you help me?" Tish looked fine, but I obliged. "Can you do some braids in the top?"

"Heifer, fuck I look like Kim Kimble," I fussed. "You gon' get these barrel curls and sitcho ass down!"

Tish's room wasn't as big as mine, but she made it seem even smaller with the amount of makeup, clothing, and shoes she'd brought with her strewn about the room. My expression gave away my repulsion.

"Don't look like that," Tish pleaded. "I tore the room up looking for my contact applicator."

"Bitch, why didn't you use your fingers like a normal human! It looks like a tornado touched down all up in here," I responded.

Tish shrugged, then handed me her curling iron. I finished her hair, hitting it with some hairspray. Rho walked in to ask If I'd hook her up too.

"You hoes need to CashApp me some funds! My services are not free," I fussed while both of them laughed.

Before heading downstairs, we all crowded into my bathroom to snap some photos. On the way to the elevator, I realized I left my backpack in the room. I went back to grab it and noticed a bag of cookies on the couch in the living room. I walked over, picked them up, and sniffed them. They smelled delicious, so I pulled one out and put the rest in my clutch. I ate half a cookie before I made it to the elevator. It stopped on the fourteenth floor to let on some drunken women in their early twenties.

"Omg, I'm famished," the drunken blonde said. "Can I have the rest of your cookie?" Before I could answer, she bit down onto it. I was appalled.

"Have you lost your fucking mind?" I fumed. "You almost bit me!"

"Oh my, I'm so sorry," she half-cried. "I haven't eaten since...I don't know!"

The sober one of the group offered me a Kleenex and some hand sanitizer. "These bitches are driving me crazy. All I want to do is get them to their rooms."

"Bless your heart! I'd hate it if my friends acted like that. Thanks for the sanitizer, and I hope you have a good night!"

We rode down together until we reached the fifth floor, where they got off. I hit the atrium in search of my friends. I saw Tish talking to some guys staying in the hotel. She excused herself from them to join me.

"Girl, did you leave some cookies upstairs? They're fucking delicious," I gushed.

"No, did you bring them with you?" Tish asked as I dug into my bag. I gave her one as Stacy walked up.

"We got snacks and shit," Stacy joked.

"Girl, these cookies are delicious," I mused.

As we each took a cookie, we heard, "Can we have some?" One of Tish's new friends asked for his group.

"Um, these aren't—" I began when Tish interrupted me.

"Sure!" She broke her cookie into pieces and began sharing. Stacy and I looked at one another, then followed suit. Neither of us really wanted to share our treat but we didn't want to be rude. I saw Shea through the group, and waved. We said our goodbyes and joined him and El.

We walked through the expansive lobby filled with all kinds of people—a couple dressed to the nines with an expensive Pram stroller, a large group of college kids with crusty looking beer coolers, and a variety of families. There was also a group checking in for a family reunion—I gathered by their matching attire— and another group for what appeared to be some sort of Comic convention. As we passed the concierge line, I noticed it seemed longer than usual. I wondered if there was an event going on. Once again, I reminded myself to thank DW for his gesture of kindness. Had he not come through in the clutch, we would've had to wait in that long-ass line for our Manilow tickets.

"What do y'all have there?" El asked, snapping me out of my thoughts.

"Oh, you gotta try these," Tish gushed, snatching the bag, handing it to El, who stuck his whole face in it to get a whiff.

"These are good," El said, smacking on the confection. "Imma see if the fellas want some."

"Let me get one," Shea added, following El to the casino floor where the others were getting in some last-minute gambling.

"Where's Rho?" I noticed she wasn't with Stacy or Tish.

"I think she said she left something in the room. She said she'd meet us at the van," Stacy said. I checked my watch quickly to see how much time we had before heading out to the van.

"Tish, who were those guys you were talking to?" I asked.

"Oh, just some fellow *Fanilows*," she said.

"Fani-whats?" Stacy laughed. I seconded her sentiment. I'd heard of the Beyhive and the Barbs—hell, even Mariah Carey's Lambs—but this one blew me.

"Fanilows. Barry Manilow fans—"

"Let me stop you there, sis." Stacy chuckled. "You lost me at Fanilows." Stacy's comment took Tish by surprise.

"You suck!" Tish stamped her foot and stormed off toward the casino.

"Bitch, you did not have to do her like that," I exclaimed.

"What the hell's so funny?" Rho said as she sidled up to us.

"Tish—" Stacy replied.

"Nuff said," Rho quipped. "Hey, did either of you see some cookies upstairs?"

"Yeah, I brought them down." I couldn't get the sentence out fast enough before Rho interrupted.

"You didn't eat them, did you?" She seemed frantic, which was odd.

"Yeah, I had half—no wait—almost a whole one. Tish and Stace had one, then El took the bag. Oh, and we shared with some guys Tish met too. Why?"

"Fuck me," she said, slapping herself on the forehead. "Bitch, those cookies were edibles."

"Well, yeah…that's why I ate it. Cookies are *edible*, duh," I answered, looking at Rho like she was stupid.

"Weed. Marijuana. Drugs…edible drugs, fool." Rho watched as realization spread across our faces.

"Well, I only had half, so I should be fine," Stacy added.

"Half is too much, and your ass ate more than that!" Rho was annoyed. "I'm gonna be babysitting you, morons, all night! Who has the bag now?"

"Are we gonna be ok? Do we need to go to the hospital or something?" I asked frantically.

Rho thought for a moment before responding, "I don't know."

"Shit," Stacy and I said in unison.

Rho left us standing there as she turned to walk away. "Where are the guys?"

"Casino," I responded.

Stacy and I were reviewing Google search results for marijuana overdoses when the rest of the crew strode up a few minutes later, sans Rho.

"Did y'all see Rho?" I asked, being met with a chorus of *no*.

"Shit," I said, glancing at my watch. "Y'all head to the van. I'll go try to find her."

"In those shoes?" El questioned. "Getcho ass on the bus. I'll go get her."

We all headed out the double doors to the van parked in front of our hotel, while El made his way back to the casino, looking for Rho. We told the driver that we were two people short, so he waited. Everyone was chatting when I turned to Stacy to discuss the weed conundrum.

"Let's wait until Rho gets back," she whispered. "No use in getting everyone riled up, and we don't know what we ate or if it's cause for alarm."

"Girl, you right!" I said, smiling at her like she was the smartest person in the world.

Rho and El had been gone for several minutes when we saw them approach the sprinter. We knew it was gonna be some shit when we heard El's loud-mouthed ass fussing and cussing. We all looked at each other, then rushed to get off the bus.

"What the hell is going on?" Shea asked.

"Y'all ain't gon' believe this shit," El was furious. "This muhfucka just asked a woman if her baby was a fuckin' *monkey*!"

"What the hell?" Sherm hollered.

"She had the mother clutching at her chest and shit. I thought the father was gonna beat my ass!" El exclaimed. "I apologized for her rudeness, and snatched her ass up!"

Everyone, including the bus driver, was tickled by the story.

"Y'all, that shit ain't funny," El fussed.

"I swear they diapered a monkey and threw it in a stroller." Rho raised her hand to heaven like her word was gospel.

"Bitch, put yo' fuckin' hand down!" El grabbed at her hand.

"Whew, gaht damn! I done heard it all!" Sherm slapped his leg.

"Rho, all babies are precious!" Tish exclaimed.

"That was not a human baby. *That* was a baby monkey!" Rho tried to raise her hand again, but El shoved her into the van.

J-Boogie and Stacy were holding each other up to keep from falling over. Tish boarded the van shaking her head.

"Oh my damn," I hooted. I laughed so hard my abs were hurting.

"That's y'all's friend," Zeus added.

"A'ight, y'all, let's get on the van. We're gonna be late for the show," I called to everyone. "They had that creature in a four-thousand-dollar Pram stroller," Rho said. I stumbled up the steps.

"Someone shut Rho's ass up! She gon' kill Lil Bit," J-Boogie hollered into the vehicle.

"Was that the couple with the blue and white stroller?" Tish asked. Rho nodded somberly.

"Oh my damn!" I guffawed because I remembered seeing them when we first made it to the lobby.

"Those crazy-ass people had a baby orangutan dipped in a Gucci fit, and yo dumb ass told them *I* was raised by gorillas," Rho snarled to El.

J-Boogie, Sherm, and Zeus exchanged glances and snickers. Once everyone was seated we headed to the venue.

"A baby monkey wearing a designer outfit in a four-thousand-dollar

Pram stroller…that has to be the whitest shit I've ever heard," Tish said, shaking her head.

Tish and Stacy were readjusting their makeup while I made my way to the front to give the driver instructions to drop us at the VIP entrance of the Westgate International Theater. The men chatted about their winnings in the short time they were in the casino. Zeus had won the most—close to four-thousand dollars.

"That's enough to buy a stroller fit for a monkey," El said, side-eyeing Rho, who swiftly pushed his head.

"Don't y'all start that shit," I said, giggling at their exchange.

"Shit, do we have tickets?" Shea asked.

"Yes," I began, "we have the VIP package." El screamed like a lovesick teen when he heard the news.

"Someone's excited," Zeus said, rolling his eyes.

"It's ok, El," Tish said, leaning across the aisle to rub his hand.

"How'd you get those?" Shea asked. I tipped my head to him, looking as if he really had to ask.

"More enjoyment, less curiosity," I said, winking.

The driver pulled around the building and parked. He handed me the bag of cookies before I disembarked.

"The Big Guy gave these to me. I almost forgot I had them," The driver handed me the bag of edibles.

"I hope your ass didn't eat any of these before you drove us here," I laughed.

"I planned to take two home for my kids," the driver responded.

"Sir, Child Protective Services will promptly pick your kids up if you give them those cookies." By my tone, the driver picked up what I was putting down.

"Oh shit, I guess these will be for the wife and me then," he said.

"Shit, you better drop them kids off at someone's house for the weekend," I joked before heading off the bus.

"Good looking out," he said, smiling after me.

I didn't have time to restore the cookies to Rho, as we went straight into the show. We were met by two attendants, given VIP lanyards and glow sticks. They rushed us to our seats in time to see Barry take the stage.

COOKIES AND BULLSHIT

We were high as fuck by the time the show ended, and we were led backstage to meet Barry Manilow. His staff introduced us as friends of DW. Barry looked in our direction and smiled.

"Any friends of DW are friends of mine. I love that guy. Did you all enjoy the show?" he asked sweetly. He was met with a chorus of various affirmative answers.

"Bare...my man, I have a gift for you," I said, hugging him.

He squeezed me back. "And what's that, dear?"

"These are the best cookies—ever! You can have the last one," I gushed and smiled up at him. I hadn't realized he was so tall.

"Are these edibles?" he asked knowingly.

"Shhh," I whispered. "I promise...they are spectaculous!" I slurred over the new word I had just invented.

"I don't normally do this." He bit into the cookie and smiled down at me again. "This is specta..."

"Spectaculous," I helped.

Barry and I discussed DW and how great he was for a few minutes until El butted in. "Are you going to introduce the rest of us to Mr. Manilow?"

"Oops, my bad," I giggled. "Mr. Manilow, these are my friends." I went around the group introducing everyone. Barry shook everyone's hand, greeting them warmly.

"You were in the Olympics, right?" Barry recognized El.

Ellis lit up like a Christmas tree. "Yes, sir, I was."

I stepped away from Barry to let him and El talk for a moment. When I did, Rho snatched me up to ask about her cookies.

"Do you have my fucking cookies?" she asked angrily.

"Yup! But—" I added bashfully.

"But what, MJ?" she whisper-screamed.

"I just gave Barry the last one." Rho stared at me like I was crazy, then shoved me out of the way.

"Excuse me, Mr. Barry Manilow, sir," she said, interrupting him and El. "Do you have my cookies?"

Barry reached into his jacket and gave Rho the empty bag.

"Aww...damn! That's ya ass, Mr. Barry Manilow!" Before she could snatch him up, Zeus grabbed her and took her to the van.

After taking a few pictures with the rest of us, Barry invited us back to his house for drinks, then went to his dressing room to change. His assistant gave us directions to his house and escorted us back to the VIP entrance. The rest of the night was a blur because I'm not sure how I got back to the room.

The next day, I had arranged for all of us to have brunch together. My phone had been ringing non-stop for about fifteen minutes before I had the wherewithal to answer it. I finally picked it up to see DW was trying to FaceTime me. I answered it crankily.

"Hey," his voice boomed through the small iPhone speakers.

"Hey, Big Guy...what's good?" I managed.

"What the fuck happened to y'all last night? Barry Manilow's people were on my phone first thing this morning!" he exclaimed.

"Really? Why?" I perked up with curiosity.

"Apparently, you fools stole his Grammy! Did you give him an edible? His assistant said he was higher than a Georgia pine last night." DW laughed.

"What?" I screamed.

I got out of bed to open the curtains.

"Yeah, his assistant said if y'all don't return it, they're gonna press charges. I can't believe y'all's asses got that old ass man high." DW shook his head like we had embarrassed the entire race.

"Let me talk to the crew and see what happened. Seriously though, ain't no telling. I know I was high as fuck," I added. "I'm so sorry, DW."

"Call me back when you ask everyone. I gotta hear firsthand what the hell happened. I know it's gonna be some shit." DW smiled knowingly.

"Ok," I said before, disconnecting the call.

We weren't forty-eight hours into the trip, and already we'd offended a couple by calling their baby a monkey and stolen a Grammy from a fucking *legend*. I threw on a robe before making my way into the suite. To my surprise, I found everyone sitting in the living room, staring at Rho.

"Bring your Sasquatch hunting ass on over here so I can tell this story," Rho said sarcastically.

"Sasquatch—what the fuck?" I looked at Rho like she was crazy. Zeus was cracking up. Shea scooted to make room for me on the couch. We were in various stages of undress, except J-Boogie's bougie ass, who wore silk pajamas. All of the girls were wearing robes except Tish. She had slept in her clothes and looked like a more disheveled version of the last night.

"First of all, you fuckers owe me some cash to cover all the edibles you ate last night," she stated. We all laughed, but Rho was severe. She raised her eyebrows, staring each of us down. "I accept CashApp, Venmo, and PayPal."

"Ok, can you tell us what the hell happened? Hell, Sherm is still in his room staring at the floor," J-Boogie joked.

"By the end of the concert, you fools were up screaming and hollering like Beyoncé was on the stage. Then, at the meet and greet, Miss James gave my last edible to Barry *fucking* Manilow."

"Are you serious?" I screamed. I was so embarrassed I covered my face.

"Yes, you also called his ass Bare all night, and he fucking loved it."

El was particularly tickled by that.

"Oh, you shutcho ass up, El. You forgot how to speak and started using American Sign Language as a means to communicate," Rho stated.

"Wait, what?" El looked genuinely confused. "I don't know sign language!"

"Well, I do," Zeus chimed in, "and I interpreted for you all night!"

"Did I say why I couldn't speak?" El asked.

"Yup! You said your lips were deflated," Zeus was tickled, relaying the info to El.

"Deflated…what the fuck?"

"Yeah, bro, you said when you looked in the mirror, it looked like someone let the air out of your lips." Tish cracked up at the description.

"No, ma'am." Rho said as she turned to eyeball Tish. "Yo' ass kept putting candy you stole from Barry's candy bowls in people's pockets."

Tish frowned in disbelief. "Why would I do that?"

"Because the candy told you to," Zeus added, "and Seamus thought he was trying to contact himself from the future."

"Check your phone, bro," Rho said.

Shea pulled out his phone, opened his messages, and found thirty-seven texts from himself to himself. He fell over on my lap, laughing.

"This fool was running up to old white men asking them if they were him," Rho finished.

I must've laughed a little too hard because Rho and Zeus began clowning me.

"MJ, yo ass thought everyone with long hair or a fur coat was Big Foot," Zeus hooted. "Hiding behind me talking about Big Foot's gonna get you!"

"Oh hell," I laughed. "I can see myself doing that."

"Please don't think that's all you did," Rho retorted.

"Huh?" I asked.

"You also thought the floor was quicksand. You had Barry Manilow standing on his furniture to avoid it. His assistant was mad as hell at you for standing on his furniture in heels. Shit, we had to go get your other shoes out of your bag," Zeus said, giggling.

"So wait, were you two the only sober ones?" I asked.

Rho and Zeus nodded as they sat opposite us in matching chairs, looking like king and queen holding court with the drunken peasants. The rest of us were either on the couch or floor.

"Ok, what about me?" J-Boogie asked.

"You were mild compared to the others," Zeus responded. "You kept quoting your college lacrosse statistics."

"That's not that bad," he responded.

"Well, at least none of us called a baby a monkey," Stacy said to Rho. Her comment garnered some giggles from the peanut gallery.

"Nope, you don't get to judge today," Rho retorted.

"I am not a novice, so I know I was cool," Stacy replied, pointing to herself.

Zeus laughed at her remark. "Yo' not-a-novice ass might be going to jail for assault."

"Assault?" we all screamed in unison.

"Yeah…so," Rho continued, "you kept bringing me empty bags and round objects, asking if they were my cookies. I tried to get you to stop by telling you not to bring me nan 'nother thing, but when we got back to the hotel, you walked up to a child, slapped the shit out of him, took his cookie, and told him his fat ass didn't deserve it." Stacy's mouth fell wide open, listening to Rho retell the incident.

"Are you serious?" Shea asked.

"Dead ass," Rho responded. "She then told this child to, and I quote, *just say no!*"

Laughter erupted from the group. Stacy hung her head in shame.

"What the hell was in those cookies?" she asked.

"Oh no, baby," Rho laughed, "it doesn't stop there. When asked why you slapped the little boy, you said, and I quote again, *fuck that kid!*"

"Oh my damn," I said, leaning back onto Shea's arm.

Rho continued to our chagrin, "Then, you asked me if the cookie you stole from the little boy was my cookie. Girl, I had to run yo' ass up out the lobby because his parents, and the police, were looking for you."

"Please tell me that's not true," Stacy exclaimed.

"Sis, they are scouring security footage as we speak to find out who slapped that child," Rho responded.

Stacy looked at Rho and Zeus in disbelief for a moment longer. When the realization that they were telling the truth hit her, she laid out on the floor prostrate. We all sat quietly, looking from one another to Stacy.

"Ok, so...maybe not," Zeus said, letting her off the hook.

"What do you mean, Zeus?" I asked.

"Apparently, the kid was in a blind spot. Security was never able to see who hit him, and I saw his family check out this morning on my way down to the tables. So you're safe."

Stacy never sat up, but she cursed Rho and Zeus up one side and down the other in Patois. There were many "suck your mothers" and "blood clots" thrown around by the time she finished.

Stacy ran out of steam and ended her tirade with, "Fuck y'all!"

When we finished laughing, she asked about Sherm.

"Girl, his ass had four of those fucking cookies! He's literally in his room staring at the floor. I don't know if he's slept yet," Zeus added.

I subconsciously began running my fingers through Shea's hair while I thought about all of the other people we had given cookies yesterday. I bet that was some shit! There was no telling how those poor unsuspecting souls behaved. Maybe I'd get a chance to apologize if they were still here.

"Well, damn," Stacy said, finally getting up off the floor to answer a knock at the door.

We all sat quietly, watching the older gentleman wheel in a tray with food from the hallway. He went into the dining room to set the food on the buffet. Our mouths were salivating because we'd had to skip dinner to make the concert on time.

Yeah... we'd gotten high on empty stomachs! I shook my head, too.

Chapter Thirty-Two

THE FUNNY THING ABOUT VEGAS

A
s we ate breakfast, I remembered I needed to find out about Barry Manilow's Grammy. The conversation was flowing like Niagara, but DW's reputation was on the line. I needed to figure it out. I considered waiting until after breakfast, but since Sherm had finally brought his high ass out of his room, there wouldn't be a better time to broach the subject. I took a quick bite of my breakfast before proceeding.

"Y'all," I said, in between bites, "DW called this morning."

"And?" Shea said sarcastically.

I turned to look at him to ascertain his mood. He was trying to be funny.

"Don't get yo ass cussed out this morning." I laughed, then continued, "So like I was saying, DW called—wait, he asked me to call him before I spoke to y'all. Hold on!"

I ran to my room to grab my phone to call him. When DW answered his FaceTime, I turned the phone around so everyone could see him. Everyone waved and thanked him for the tickets. Shea was amiable when he thanked DW for the gift.

"No problem, I'm glad you all enjoyed yourselves," DW responded.

"Ok," I started again, "so, DW got a call from Barry Manilow's assistant. I just have one question, which one of you assholes stole the Grammy?"

Laughter erupted from the table, along with a chorus of *not me*. Rho got up from the table, heading toward her room. She returned, placing Barry's Grammy on the table. We all stared at her in disbelief.

"Bitch," Stacy exclaimed, "you were sober! What the fuck?"

"You gaht damn right," Rho responded, smiling.

"Wait, so you stole it?" I asked.

"No, I told him he owed me for my weed, and he gave it to me," Rho said calmly.

"Girl, you knew he was high! Your fucking weed didn't cost that much," El exclaimed loudly.

"Yeah, what the fuck is your problem?" Tish asked.

"Well, someone needed to pay for my weed! Why not Mr. Barry *fucking* Manilow?" Rho said seriously.

Laughter erupted like Mount Vesuvius. "Motherfuck—woman, we could've taken up a collection or something. Hell, we ate most of the cookies anyway. How much were they, Petty Crocker?" I asked sarcastically.

"I knew it was gon' be some shit," DW said, cackling.

"Barry insisted," Rho said defensively.

"The fuck? I don't give a damn! You ain't need to take that man's award!" El fussed.

"You just mad you ain't gon' be able to hang out with Barry again," Zeus responded.

"You gaht damn right," El said, trying to keep a straight face.

"Zeus, you let her take it?" Shea asked in shock. "Rho, you gotta give it back."

"I didn't know she took it," Zeus raised his hands and shook his head as if to absolve himself.

"I know," Rho said, dejectedly.

"Y'all are a mess. I don't think Mr. Manilow will be upset as long as you return it. Oh yeah, and you give him the recipe for the cookies." DW slipped that last part in there.

"The what?" Rho asked in disbelief.

"The recipe," DW said, smiling back. I could tell he was amused. DW had always thought my friends were a handful. Since we were no longer a couple, my friends had warmed up to him. At first, they didn't understand how I could be friends with him, but they saw how sweet he was for helping me when he was given a chance. I had felt in my heart that one day DW would be a part of the crew. Now, that would be some shit!

"I didn't make them," Rho exclaimed as she began pacing the floor.

"Well, that's what they told me when they called. So—" DW began when he noticed Sherm staring at his plate. "What the hell is the matter with Sherm?

"Oh, him," J-Boogie responded, "he still high."

DW's mouth dropped open in disbelief. "Still what now?"

"He ate four cookies," I said, turning the phone to face me. "We don't know how he made it down here."

"He smelled food," Shea joked.

"Damn! Remind me to never eat cookies Rho brings to the function! Shit," DW grimaced.

"Shut up, DW," Rho half-laughed and half-shouted. DW's laugh, in response, was infectious.

"A'ight DW, we'll get the Grammy, and the recipe, over to Barry. I wouldn't want to tarnish your reputation," I added.

"No worries! Try to be good," DW said.

"No promises," I remarked before hanging up.

I placed the phone down and glanced around the table at my friends, who were still fussing at Rho.

"Did you think you could keep it?" Zeus asked.

"Well," Rho responded, indicating she thought she could.

Shaking his head, El responded, "You can't be this damn dumb." He threw up his hand, then pushed away from the table to make himself another plate.

"Grab me some more of that smoked trout." Tish gestured in the direction of the fish.

"That trout is fire," I added. "Me too!"

"Who do I look like—Geoffrey?" El retorted, referencing his favorite TV show.

"I don't know, but if you don't put that fish on my plate, I'm gonna toss your ass up out of here like Uncle Phil tosses Jazz," Tish responded without missing a beat.

All eyes, except Sherm's, swiveled toward Tish as we guffawed at her comment.

"She told yo ass, Geoffrey," Sherm responded, clapping and laughing.

"Welcome back," I said, winking at Sherm. Zeus was laughing a little too hard when El shot him a dirty look.

"Ok, Dionísio, it wasn't that damn funny," El said, placing the smoked trout on Tish's plate then mine.

"The hell it wasn't," Stacy said as she and Zeus bumped fists. Tish giggled as she cut into her smoked trout. I laughed at El's use of Zeus' real name, causing everyone to look at me like I was crazy when I snorted.

"It was funny to me," I remarked.

"You ok, Big Guy?" Shea asked Sherm.

"Man, what the hell kinda weed was in those cookies?" Sherm rubbed his head as he responded. He looked tired from staring at the floor all night.

"We've been trying to figure that all morning." I rose to grab an empty breadbasket from the buffet. "Alright, you cookie monsters, pay up!"

The men reached to retrieve their wallets as the girls went to their respective rooms to collect funds to reimburse Rho. In total, we coughed up two hundred dollars. Sherm donated twice because he ate so many of the devil's cookies. Rho was content with our collection and agreed to call her provider to get the cookie recipe. After breakfast, we stacked all of our dishes and cutlery neatly for the butler.

"What's on the agenda today?" Shea asked me.

"Shopping and dinner with Chef Martín," I responded. "He agreed to move it from yesterday to accommodate the Barry Manilow concert."

"Cool," Shea said. "So who's going to take the Grammy back?"

"Aww, hell," Rho exclaimed, throwing her napkin at Shea. We responded in kind.

"I'll take it back since I'm the link between DW and Barry," I responded.

"I'll go with you," Shea stated.

"Oh hell no!" El exclaimed. "Make this stealin' ass heifer take it back!"

I shook my head at the recommendation. "They might have the cops waiting on her!"

"I'd beat Barry's ass if he tried to have me arrested. He practically shoved that damn thing in my hand," Rho commented.

"And that's why I'm taking it back!" I took the Grammy from the table and headed to my room to get dressed. I hoped Mr. Manilow wasn't too put out or offended by our behavior. I remembered bits and pieces, so hopefully, he'd had the same experience.

I dressed and met Shea downstairs to take the award back. Shea had a car take us to the address I'd been given the night before. When we arrived, we were greeted by Angelica, Barry Manilow's assistant. Her greeting was warm and friendly as she led us into a quaint sitting room. I handed her the Grammy and the envelope containing the recipe for the cookies.

"Thank you! Mr. Manilow will be with you in a moment," Angelica spoke softly. "Is there anything I can get you? Water or tea?"

"You're welcome, and we're so sorry," I began. "You don't have to trouble Mr. Manilow. We just wanted to return the Grammy and give him the recipe for the...um...well—"

"Cookies," Angelica finished my sentence. "He enjoyed your company last night. Please sit. He'll be here in a moment."

"Um, sure," I responded nervously.

When Angelica left the room, I turned to Shea. "Let's make a run for it!"

Shea laughed, slapping his knee. "Let's see what he wants first... come on. Don't be rude."

Shea and I took seats in two snakeskin wingback chairs. I remembered the room from the night before. I saw the couch Barry and I had jumped on and cringed. I hoped I hadn't ruined the material or the construction.

"You don't weigh enough to damage that sofa," Barry declared as he entered the room, startling me out of my thoughts.

"Oh, God, you remember!" I turned beet red as I rose to greet him. Barry laughed and pulled me in for a hug.

"I watched the security footage this morning," he disclosed. "We were a handful for Angelica. Do you know I had to give her a week off?"

"Oh no," I grimaced, "that bad, huh?"

Barry released me to shake Shea's hand. "You two are something else."

Shea and I turned to look at one another in confusion. *What the hell did we do?* I wondered.

"What do you mean?" I asked. At that moment, Angelica appeared with a tablet and handed it to Barry.

"See for yourselves." Barry seemed amused with himself. He handed me the tablet and pressed play. Shea leaned in to watch the security footage with me. To our horror, it was a video of us sneaking off to another room. Panic set in. *Fuck! Did we have sex in Barry's house?*

The video showed Shea leading me out of the room by the hand. We rounded the corner and went into the living room. Shea pressed me against the wall and kissed me passionately. The kiss seemed to last forever—even though only twenty seconds ticked off the video time. Just when I thought the worst was over, Shea dropped to one knee and appeared to be proposing. *What the entire fuck!* Trixie screamed. I seemed to be the happiest woman in the world when I accepted his proposal.

"What the hell?" Shea and I spoke in unison.

"That's what I said when I watched it," Barry added. "That's not all, though." Barry swiped the video from the screen to pull up another one. It was a video of all of us toasting our engagement.

"Oh my…damn," Shea muttered.

"Everyone wants you to be together. So why are you marrying someone else?" Barry asked Shea.

"It's complicated," Shea remarked, taken aback at how much Barry knew.

"Is there anything I can do to uncomplicate it?" Barry asked genuinely. I clutched my metaphorical pearls at the suggestion. Barry reached into his pocket, retrieved a handkerchief, and handed it to me. Who the fuck still had those in their pocket? Barry *fucking* Manilow, that's who!

"Have you tried contacting the FBI?" Barry responded after hearing the quandary Shea and I were in.

"I can't risk my father going to jail," Shea answered.

"I understand," Barry said softly. "Scandal and celebrity go hand in hand. Sometimes, these issues have a way of working out, though, you know?"

Did Barry recognize Shea as a celebrity, too? Shea was no fucking Barry Manilow! Hell, I thought he was a B-list celeb, at best. Angelica had to have Googled Shea.

I looked to Shea, then back to Barry. "If this could be resolved, I definitely don't see a way out."

Barry patted my hand. "Give it time. I'm sure it'll work out."

We thanked Barry, preparing to leave when Angelica stopped us. "Mr. Manilow, you forgot to show them…"

"Oh, yes," Barry laughed. "One more video if you have time."

"Sure," Shea stated.

Barry pressed play, and there was Rho physically tussling with Barry over the statue. He finally relented, allowing Rho to take the Grammy. She sat with it, cradling it like a newborn. *That bitch is crazy…certifiably crazy*, I thought.

"That girl is a menace," I retorted.

"I didn't want to break it, you know. I assumed Rho wanted to hold it, but I never imagined she wanted it as repayment for the cookie. It was good, don't get me wrong… but not Grammy good. When I noticed it missing this morning, we contacted DW. He vouched for you and said he'd have it returned." Barry looked amused.

"I am so sorry," I said, embarrassed.

"Don't worry about it. I had a great time. The Grammy is in its rightful place, and all is forgiven." Barry's smile lit up the whole room.

Chapter Thirty-Three
SOMETHING ABOUT A GRAMMY

After returning the Grammy, we spent the next couple days trying to lay low. That didn't last long though. The night before the wedding we all decided to go to the strip club. The fellas went to a strip club while girls and I went to see Aussie Heat. When they say, "thunder from down under," they mean that shit. Those men put on one hell of a show. Afterward, the ladies and I were settling down in the room, when we heard loud knocking. We all looked at one another as if to ask if the other was expecting someone. I shrugged, then headed to answer the door. It was Shea, and by the looks of him, he'd been fighting.

"What the hell happened to you?" I said as he pushed his way into the room.

"Fight. I need to talk to you," Shea looked around the room before finishing, "alone."

"Oh, hell no," the ladies squealed in unison.

"We need all of the details about this fight," Rho quipped.

"Yeah!" Tish exclaimed.

I raised my eyebrows and pointed to the empty space on the couch. Shea rolled his eyes. "Can't this wait? I really need to speak with you."

"You heard the ladies. Besides, they aren't going to leave until they get the details, so…" I stared at him, waiting for him to begin.

"Fuck me," he sighed. "So, at the last minute we decided to go to the club. We were all chopping it up, but Zeus was preoccupied with his phone. He got a text...picture, really. I happened to looked over his shoulder and saw Chelsey lying across her bed wearing those fucking red shoes."

"The same merlot Louboutins she plans on getting married in to-morrow?" I asked incredulously.

"Yes, MJ, which means—"

"I was right," I said softly.

Shit! That bitch was bold!

"You were right," Shea acknowledged. "Anger overwhelmed me, and before I knew it...my fists took over. It was worse than the night we fought. How could one of my best friends betray me like that?"

"Don't dwell on it, Shea," I added softly.

"Damn," Stacy said in shock. "Where are the fellas now?"

"We got split up when the cops were called." Shea grabbed his head, revealing bloody knuckles.

"Shit!" Tish screamed, rushing out of the room to get wet towels to clean up his hands.

Rho reached for the phone, calling our butler to request a first-aid kit and bandages. Stacy grabbed the plastic bag out of the ice bucket and ran to the refrigerator to get ice. I knelt in front of Shea, pulling his hands from his head to examine them. They were scraped severely, but none of the knuckles looked out of place. *Not broken, thank God!*

"Seamus," I whispered, looking up at him. "Why?"

Our eyes met momentarily before our friends descended upon him in a frenzy, cleaning, bandaging, and icing his hands. I was pushed to the floor as the girls fussed over Shea.

"What the hell?" I mumbled under my breath.

"Ladies, I appreciate all of the help. I really need to speak MJ alone, though," Shea said sweetly.

The ladies agreed reluctantly as they left the room muttering. I pre-sumed they'd go down to the casino, or perhaps find the fellas. Shea's hands were bandaged with the ice wrapped neatly around his knuckles. It was sweet to see the ladies tending to him. They saw to his injuries like mother hens brooding over a biddy—for all of their talk about how shady Seamus was. Shea patted the seat next to where he was sitting. I took his direction and waited.

"Marry me," he said, looking into my eyes. I could tell he was sincere.

"You've got to be shitting me," I said, laughing in his face. Then I said incredulously, "That ship sailed the moment you refused to believe me." I rose, walking to my room.

Shea stared after me, not believing the words he'd just heard. Did he really think I would date him after all of the shenanigans we'd been through over the past week, month, year? What the hell was Shea thinking?

He followed me to my room, watching me place my clutch and jacket on the seat of the white leather barrel chair in my room.

"You know I was bound by a contract, MJ. There was nothing I could've done to get out of marrying Chelsey. Nothing." He raised hands in resignation.

"It's of no consequence to me now. Our situation-ship is entirely too toxic for marriage, Shea. Did you really think I'd say yes to you on the eve of your would-be nuptials to Chelsey?" I turned to face him, shaking my head while raising my eyebrows trivially.

"I can't find Chelsey...she isn't answering her phone. She isn't in her room, and the concierge said she and her father checked out. If they left before the wedding, that means I'm free," Shea answered.

"Yes, free from the contract. I'm happy for you. Just not happy enough to be with you after all that's taken place," I responded.

"You still love me. I know you do!" Shea rounded the bed, stopping short of where I was standing.

"As Tina Turner said, what's love got to do with it? You didn't trust me, and that cut me deeply, Shea. Now, you want to get married. Am I supposed to wear Chelsey's gown, use her bouquet, wear her Louboutins at our wedding, too?" I knew that cut him. "You must still be high." I laughed at my last remark. Shit, I was genuinely tickled. "Won't you at least think about it?" Shea asked. "Just one chance." "Think about what?" The question bit harder than I intended.

"Let me redeem myself," Shea scrambled for ideas. "Counseling! We can go to counseling," he added optimistically.

I laughed at the thought at first, allowing it to sink in. Perhaps we could see a therapist. Many couples attended therapy before they got married. Did ex-friends turn fuck buddies even stand a chance after all we'd done to each other? The thought gave me severe anxiety. How the fuck did you unpack all of that? Who wanted to unload all of those shenanigans? Did I want to do that? Even Trixie took a seat to ruminate as the memories whirled around in my head.

I stepped closer to the window, trying to gain a view of the mountains veiled by the night sky. The light pollution from the Strip obscured the view. My eyes drifted to the water show at the Bellagio before resting on the traffic below. Las Vegas Boulevard was dotted with mobile billboards advertising a variety of adult shows. People moved along the sidewalk, oblivious to the heaviness in my room. I was instantly jealous of them. I wished I were one of them, enjoying Vegas. Why couldn't I have a carefree, drama free, wild week in Las Vegas? *Fucking Shea!* Anger welled in me and continued to grow as I spoke.

"You act as *thick as a fecking plank, daft! Will you ever cop on to yourself?* All I wanted to fucking do was have fun with my friends this week. All I wanted was to drink, see naked men, and forget my troubles! Instead, I had to endure the emotional roller coaster that has become us." I paused for a moment, realizing my voice was shrill and full of raw, unchecked rage. "I'm tired, Shea. No, drained—fucking drained. Forgive me if I no longer wanna ride this tiresome, toxic-ass train."

My shoulders sagged from relief as Shea sank down onto the bed, looking defeated. And for the first time, I didn't care.

"Are you saying you no longer want to marry me?" Shea stared down at the floor.

"I'm saying...I need time to think, Shea. This isn't a fairytale where things end happily ever after. This is real life where you can't just re-place the bride and go on with the wedding. We've both done and said some shit that requires time to heal," I said more softly.

Shea took a calming breath before he spoke. "I understand. I will give you all of the time and space you—we," he corrected, "need to heal."

Shea stood up, straightened his shoulders, and smiled weakly. He gestured for a hug, and I stepped willingly into his embrace. Warmth spread throughout my body as he squeezed me tightly to him, as though trying to imprint me onto him—mind, body, and soul. I breathed in his familiar scent, taking note of where our hands and limbs fit each other's bodies. I looked up at Shea, and an electric spark passed between our eyes. There was no doubt we shared a strong connection. I lowered my gaze to Shea's mouth as he licked his lips slowly. Shea dipped his head as if to kiss me, halting for a moment before our mouths melded. His kiss washed all of my vitriol away.

As if sensing my yielding, though not bothering to pull back, Shea spoke, "Don't worry, *Féileacán.*" His voice was a low growl. "I'm not going to let you go. I promise I will be everything you've ever wanted in a husband. Marry me."

Shea took my hand and lead me out of my room. The ladies had returned and were sitting in the living room quietly waiting for us to emerge.

"Call up the boys. There's going to be a wedding tonight," Shea shouted joyously.

Yup! I was letting him put a ring on it!

"What the hell," Stacy exclaimed. Her mouth hung open in confu-sion, shock, and awe.

"On it," Tish grabbed her phone and sent out a group text.

Rho was the first to hug us, then Stacy and Tish. They squealed with delight at the news, then began to bombard us with questions. Shea and I answered the barrage of questions as quickly as they were volleyed.

Once placated, Tish called the concierge to have the sprinter waiting for us. All of the fellas, except Zeus, had all made it back to the hotel and were meeting us in the lobby.

We all piled into the van and headed to the first twenty-four hour chapel we could find. The Lil Hunk a' Burning Love was it. On the way to the chapel, the ladies scrounged through their purses to find something old, new, borrowed and blue. Rho loaned me the jade necklace her grandfather had given her. That took care of the old and borrowed. Tish gave me the sapphire studs she'd been wearing that night. They took care of the blue. Stacy gave me the rhinestone "Love" hair pin she'd been using to pull her hair back.

"Take this," Stacy said as she fished it out of her hair, "it's brand new."

Our ceremony, and our vows, were short and sweet. We promised to ask for what we wanted and vowed to not keep secrets. Since I wasn't about to use Chelsey's gown or décor. For an impromptu wedding it was everything. The next day, we all received the shock of our lives.

Chapter Thirty-Four
HELL FROZE OVER

I woke up in the Honeymoon suite he'd booked for him and Chelsey. It was the only thing I wanted to use from the wedding. Shea's phone rang shortly after I woke up.

"Shea," I nudged him, "wake up."

Shea rolled over groggily acknowledging his phone, then laid back down, "I'm on my honeymoon."

The phone began to ring again soon after.

"Yeah," he mumbled into the phone.

I could hear a man's voice, but I couldn't make out what was being said. I knew it was serious when Shea sat up with his mouth agape. Fear took hold for a moment until Shea's laughter boomed throughout the room. My phone began vibrating from multiple incoming messages. I leaned over to pick it up as I heard Shea ending his call.

"Don't," he grabbed my arm, "you are never gonna believe this shit."

"What? What's going on?" I asked him intently.

"That was El. He wanted to know if he and Rho could use the wedding venue. He proposed to Rho last night and she said yes."

"Shut the fuck up," I stared at him in disbelief, "She didn't!"

"I'm sure that's why your phone is going crazy. We have to get up because there's gonna be another wedding," Shea replied.

"Well, shit." I responded before grabbing my phone.

I called the ladies on Google Duo and Rho confirmed the insanity. Hell, we'd come to Las Vegas for a wedding and we were getting two. El said he wouldn't have been a good friend if he'd let Shea's money go to waste. A few of their family members were able to make it at the last minute, too. We all dressed in the attire we'd planned on wearing to Shea's wedding. I looked too good in that tux not to wear it. We had to all but fight Rho to get Chelsey's abandoned gown from her.

"Fuck that bitch!" Rho exclaimed as she ran into the bathroom of the bridal suite.

"What the hell, Rho," Stacy chuckled.

We stood outside of the bathroom trying to persuade her not to wear the dress. It took an act of God, and Rho's mom showing up with another dress to get her out of it. Rho looked good as hell in Chelsey's dress, but the dress her mother brought took everyone's breath away.

"Don't you even think about these fucking shoes." I eyed her with intensity before boxing up the Louboutins that had broken up a friendship. These shoes were my salvation, but best believe I got rid of them. Somewhere in Vegas there's a bum wearing those shoes.

The wedding planner worked out the logistics after we'd explained last night's events.

"The only thing that's throwing me," Celina's face scrunched, "is who's walking the bride down the aisle." Rho's father was in Tokyo on business so he couldn't do it.

"Why don't you do it," Rho's mom suggested gesturing towards Shea.

"I thought you'd want the honor," Shea replied.

"I'm three different types of Asian," Rho chuckled, "If you think this is the last time I'm doing this, you are sadly mistaken." Rho and Ellis ended up doing two more ceremonies for her grandparents in Korea and Japan. The wedding was magical, but the crew got the best wedding gift of all. El and Rho finally shut their asses up.

After all of the hoopla of Las Vegas, Shea stayed true to his word. We started marriage counselling once we got settled into a normal routine. Shea was already seated when I entered our therapist's office. "I apologize for my lateness," I began. "I had a hectic day."

"No need to apologize. Technically, you're not late," Maureen said, gesturing for me to have a seat. "Before we begin, do you mind if I call you by your first names? Also, are there any limits to what we discuss?"

Shea responded with a simple yes and no. My big mouth ass hopped right into the fire.

"Sure, and no, we were both there for all of the shenanigans," I laughed nervously.

"Shenanigans. Is that how you see your relationship?" Maureen began.

"It's a figure of speech...I mean...well," I sputtered.

"I think what Maeve means is misbehavior. You see, I was engaged when the sexual portion of our relationship began," Shea attempted to save me.

"I see." Maureen wrote down notes. "Do you agree, Maeve?"

"No, not really," I said softly. "Shea and I have always had an unusual relationship. I think the misbehavior began when Shea began sharing his sexual exploits with me." I looked over to meet Shea's confused look.

"I take it you're confused, Seamus," Maureen stated.

"A bit. Friends—best friends share all sorts of things. Why didn't you tell me to stop?" Shea asked.

I looked from him to Maureen, suddenly feeling like the couch caught fire. I rubbed my neck, then my forehead, before asking for some water. Maureen walked over to her desk and called for her assistant to bring in two bottles of water. She took her seat, crossing her legs and placing her notepad on her lap. The door opened, and her assistant brought in the water. I opened the bottle and swallowed half of it in three large gulps.

"I...um...I got off on them," I said softly. I felt my face, neck, and chest heat in a deep blush.

"Did you know that, Seamus?" Maureen asked.

Shea paused, looking away. "I wasn't sure, but I thought one night she had masturbated as I relayed a story. The thought of her masturbating..."

"What about the thought, Seamus?" Maureen asked.

"It aroused me," Shea responded, staring down at his hands.

I sat there staring at Shea in utter shock at his words. He was aroused at the thought of me rubbing one out to his stories. We were depraved.

"Did you masturbate, too?" I asked Shea pointedly.

Silence.

"Did you hear the question, Seamus?" Maureen asked.

Silence.

"Maeve, can you give us a min—"

"Yes, I did," Shea interrupted Maureen quietly.

Maureen wrote down some notes before turning to me. "How does that make you feel, Maeve?"

"Relieved," I replied. "May I ask another question?"

"Go ahead," she answered. Maureen glanced between Shea and me, down to her notes, then back to me.

"Why?" I asked, looking at Shea.

"That's a question for another time." Shea was shutting me out.

"Let's switch gears for a moment. Seamus, you wrote in the questionnaire you wanted to apologize to MJ…"

As Maureen spoke with Shea, my mind drifted to the night in question. Shea had masturbated with me. *Trixie* squealed with delight! I assumed because his speech was slurred, he wouldn't remember the events of the night. I was deluded into believing a drunken Shea wasn't perceptive. He couldn't remember kissing me on the couch, but he remembered this shit! I would never understand Shea.

Shame spread across my face as I imagined him stroking himself—as I ground my fingers into my swollen clit as he spoke. Shea had sent pictures of the women he'd been fucking in this particular story. If my memory served me correctly, there was even a picture with his cock buried, to the hilt, in her red-rimmed mouth. *Fuck, it just got hot!* I grabbed the bottle of water off the table, downing the remaining liquid in a few gulps—the plastic crinkled as I drained it, drawing attention.

"You good?" Shea eyed me suspiciously.

I smiled smugly.

"Maeve, what did you think of Seamus' apology?" Maureen asked.

"Apology?" I scrunched my face in confusion.

"Care to share what drew your attention away from the session, then?" Maureen asked.

I choked on my own spittle as I drew in a sharp breath. *Hell no, I don't care to share, Maureen!* I shouted at her in my head. Shea patted my back, shaking his head and eyeing me sideways. He knew me too fucking well.

"A project...at work," I sputtered. "Just...thinking about details for tomorrow."

"Maeve, Seamus and I cleared our schedules for the remainder of the day to do this work. I respectfully ask that you remain present with us," Maureen scolded.

"Of course, I apologize," I said.

"Seamus, do you mind repeating yourself?" Maureen said, returning to her usual chipper tone.

Shea's eyes twinkled when he was holding in laughter. It was killing him that I'd been caught and chastised for not paying attention. He knew I was thinking lewd thoughts about that night. He looked away momentarily as if to quell emotions, but I knew it was the laughter.

Maureen attempted to soothe him. "It's ok, let it out. Thank you for contributing today, Seamus." Maureen turned her disapproving eye on me as if to say *get your shit together and pay attention!*

"Thank you, Maureen," Shea said, finally. "It's been a tough eight months."

I side-eyed him mercilessly. *Faker!*

Maureen handed Shea a few tissues, which he took and dabbed at the tears falling from his eyes. This fucker was laughing! His body shook, but Maureen mistook it as sobbing. *Fuck my life!*

"I apologize for not devoting my full attention to you, Shea. I promise I'll do better," I fudged sincerity.

I didn't dare look Shea directly in his eyes. I knew his composure was hanging on by a thread. I stared at his forehead instead. We each took turns apologizing for the toxicity we contributed to the relationship.

"I accept your apology," Shea whispered.

"Ditto," I whispered in return.

"Do we think another session is in order?" Maureen asked us.

"Yes," we responded in unison.

Shea and I saw Maureen weekly for the next four months. We did trust exercises, worked on our communication skills, read relationship books assigned to us, and put in the work necessary to rebuild our friendship. We unpacked everything from day one. In the end, it was all worth it. We finally learned to love and appreciate one another.

We developed a true friendship that wasn't a crush masquerading as friendship. We set boundaries and respected them. Look at us being mature! Wasn't that what marriage was about?

Chapter Thirty-Five
IT AIN'T OVER

Shea and I celebrated our one year anniversary by having the wedding of our dreams. We went back to Vegas. Barry Manilow walked me partway down the aisle before handing me off to my father. My dad had so many questions when I asked if he'd mind. I thought he was gonna bend me over his knee when he found out we'd stolen Barry's Grammy.

For our anniversary, in lieu of a gift, Rho told the story of how Chelsey and her father were run out of town by a Chinese Triad boss—her grandfather. Who knew Rho's family had connections to Chinese warlords! The night we got high, I had violated the nondisclosure agreement and blabbed about Chelsey, the contract, and Shea being blackmailed. Rho's grandfather put in some calls to a Russian-Chinese connection, and they took care of business.

No gift. Just that fucking story. I couldn't make that shit up! Fucking Rho and her clutch performances!

Rho and Ellis were expecting their first child in a few months. Seemed like we'd be sharing a lot of firsts with our friends. Then, just when I thought wonders had ceased, Tish and Sherm hooked up and were in a relationship too. Stacy and J-Boogie swore nothing happened between them. Each was in new, promising relationships with other people, so we believed them.

I sat in the hospital pondering how the culmination of Rho's gift and Shea's persistence. I looked around at all of my family and friends feeling blessed beyond measure. The day before, Shea and I had been chasing Deci down for a bath and now here we sat. I'm sure Desi was giving the dog sitter fits because he wanted to come with us when we'd left the house.

Our son was born two weeks before his due date, on February fourteenth at eight am on the dot. His sister was born three minutes later. Aidan Rhys and Addison Rose McGhee entered the world, stealing hearts. Both babies were tiny green-eyed replicas of their father. Aidan had sandy blonde hair, while Addison was a ruddy little redhead.

Isn't it scary when you have dreams that feel like you've visited the future?

"I think I was just an incubator." I laughed.

"My mom says I drove you crazy. That's why they look like me," Shea replied.

"Grams said the same thing! Let's just hope they don't have your smartass mouth," I responded.

"Shit," Shea said, running his hand through his hair. "I don't even want to think about that!"

Our attention shifted back to the babies as they fussed.

They were met with lots of love from our families and friends. During the first visit, a nurse came to tell us to keep it down. She said we were a hoot to the nursing staff, but the other moms were complaining.

"I'm still mad that Barry *fucking* Manilow is the twins' godfather." Sherm whined.

"Are y'all ever gonna tell us what really happened at his house?" J asked.

Shea responded, "what happens in Vegas…"

"Stays in Vegas." I finished.

"You two selfish assholes have heard about how everyone else hooked up. Come on, share." Tish chimed in. Shea and I exchange glances before telling them about the security footage, Barry's advice, and their promise to make Barry the babies' godfather.

"Well, I got dibs on the next baby," El joked.

"El, shutcho ass up. You already got dibs on this baby." Stacy patted Rho's belly as she spoke.

Our friends left shortly after the warning, but we had to send our parents home just to get some rest. They had been at the hospital all night with us.

"I am so thankful we have so much help, but I'm looking forward to going home soon," I mused.

"Me too!" he said absently. "They're so beautiful." Seamus looked down at the two bundles he held.

For a brief moment, my thoughts drifted to Chelsey. She must have been a touch envious right now. She'd lost Shea and Zeus.

Life is so crazy, I thought, before responding to Shea's comment. One minute we were destroying one another, and the next, we were welcoming our children into the world.

"Yes, they are," I agreed with his assessment of our children.

"Well," he said, looking at me like the cat who ate the canary.

"I will never question your hunches again," I said, laughing at him.

He leaned down and kissed me on the forehead. Then placed both fussy babies, one at a time, in my arms to nurse. He sat at my feet, smiling while taking in the scene.

"To think," he mused, "we almost missed out on this."

The twins nursed so loudly they made us laugh. Poor little things were hungry and tired of being passed around from person to person.

"Yeah...to think!" I giggled at them.

"I love you, Maeve Alena McGhee," Shea said sweetly.

"I love you, too," I responded softly.

Each baby was nursed for a little while. I couldn't seem to take more than a few minutes each session before my abdomen began to cramp. I knew it was just my uterus settling back into the appropriate position, but someone should have warned me. The nurse on duty had offered pain medication, but I didn't want to miss a single moment.

Shea walked over to take Addison, since she seemed to be done. He perceived it before it dawned on me. Meanwhile, her greedy brother, Aidan, continued to nurse. Shea helped me cover my breast, then swaddled Addison. He kissed her gently before placing her down. Watching him warmed my heart. He was just as tender with her as he'd been with me during my pregnancy. He cooked, cleaned, gave foot rubs, and spoiled me rotten.

Zeus' mom passed shortly after the Vegas trip, as well. We all went to the funeral, offered our condolences. Shea and Zeus made up, and their friendship was getting back on track. Zeus couldn't be in Chicago for the birth because he was home in Ponce, helping repair Puerto Rico's infrastructure after a recent hurricane. It was hard to believe Puerto Rico still hadn't recovered fully after the storm. I sent him a picture of the babies, letting him know he had a new niece and nephew. He said they were beautiful and expressed his regret for missing their birth. Zeus texted saying he was gonna bring them each back a Coquí.

Me:	Don't you dare! I still remember those noisy ass frogs from our trip to Hawaii! 🐸 🙄
Bing!	
Zeus:	Not live ones, silly! The toy version! LOL
Me:	Oh, damn...mommy brain! LOL That would be nice. 💚
Zeus:	I'm bringing Coquito for you! 😊
Me:	This is why you're my favorite! LMAO. We can have it at Christmas. I'm still nursing.
Zeus:	Yes, ma'am! I gotta get back to work. Kiss those babies for me.
Me:	I will! Thanks!! 😊

I was on the phone with my mom the next day when our friends came to visit with the babies. I set the phone down to chat with them.

"Aww, Rho," I said to my pregnant friend. "You are so cute!"

"Thanks. I don't feel cute, though. You know, we can have play dates in about seven months," she said happily.

"Our babies will probably have taken over the world by then," Shea replied proudly.

"I agree!" Sherm laughed. "You two jokers probably made some evil geniuses!" Everyone agreed.

"Aww, be nice to my babies, Sherm!" I fussed gently.

"Our baby will probably talk too much and spill the beans on their evil plans!" Ellis added. Rho hit him, but agreed.

Aidan whimpered loudly, garnering the attention of his new aunt, Stacy. She picked him up, cooing to calm him down. Addison, hearing her brother's noises, voiced her discontent. Tish picked her up, bringing her near her brother. Amazingly, they calmed down.

"Hey," Tish suggested, "let's put them in the same bed." They did, and they drifted right back to sleep.

"They're just like their parents!" J-Boogie whispered.

"Happiest together," Shea murmured, then planted a sweet kiss on my forehead.

"That's because they know a closed mouth doesn't get fed," I replied

Dear Reader, you've reached the end. I'm sorry it's over too. Thanks for reading *A Closed Mouth*. I hope you loved it!

As an independent author, I count on readers like you to spread the word and support future work. If you enjoy this book, please join the ranks of my readers who make it all possible.

NEXT STEPS

1. JOIN THE COMMUNITY

Join the community and get early access to upcoming books. Visit my website and follow me on social media for additional resources –articles, videos and events to support my journey.

WEBSITE
www.laurynpoussaint.com

FACEBOOK
www.facebook.com/lauryn.poussaint

INSTAGRAM
@laurynpoussaint

HASHTAG
#aclosedmouth

2. SHARE THIS BOOK

Please connect with me, I'd love to stay in touch.

Thanks again,
Lauryn